OF THE
LOST
LEVIATHAN

The Unanswered Questions Series

The Unanswered Questions
Of the Curatrix Code
Of the Shadow Soul
Of the Lost Leviathan

THE UNANSWERED QUESTIONS
BOOK FOUR

OF THE LOST LEVIATHAN

LAUREN D. FULTER

Paperback: 978-1736114681
Ebook: 978-1736114698

First Paperback Edition June 2024

Edited by Michaela Bush & **Rachel Scheller**
Cover Art by Jade Lew
Cover Layout by Susan L. Markloff
Formatting by Benita Thompson

laurendfulter.com

To St. Catherine of Siena,
patron saint of strong-willed women

PART ONE

THE CHILD

PROLOGUE

After dark was the only time he was free.

As long as the sun was down and the sky was dark, the Oquelite prince could be alone and think his own thoughts.

He could recall every painful detail of the day as his body was forced to obey every word of that witch with violet eyes. Those eyes had sent him to this dark, windowless cell to endure the pain burning at every inch of his body.

He dipped hand back into the lukewarm water bucket, wringing the knotted rag. He took a deep breath, savoring the moment.

He tried to keep himself from shaking, water dripping to the floor as he dabbed at his chest. He bit back a pained groan as the stiffened blood scraped away from his skin.

It was so much easier during the day.

It was so much easier when she made sure he couldn't feel the pain in his body. His mind was blank, but at least his feelings were numb and all under her control.... He shook himself. What was he thinking?

Being under her control was a waking nightmare he

couldn't figure out how to escape. A year ago, the agreement didn't seem terrible. She would protect the woman he loved, as long as she could give him her mind.

A year of torture he'd done to himself.

He dropped the rag back into the bucket, searching in the dark along the dirt floor. Finally, his fingers caught against the familiar worn fabric of his cape.

He hesitated, holding it gently in his hands for a moment. *It's just a stupid cape*, he tried to remind himself. He'd never been fond of the Oquelite uniform when he'd been required to wear it, and yet here he was missing it.

He tore a strip from the hem and wrapped it tightly around his wound. He bit back a pained groan.

She didn't like the cape, and he wished he could say it was because she didn't like the style. He knew that wasn't true.

She couldn't have cared less about him. To her, he was just a silly little pawn in her game.

The cape reminded her of their father.

He reminded her of their father.

When he was younger, he would've been proud to be told he resembled his father Lord Orion Idicous, but when she said it, he suddenly wished he never resembled the man at all.

He would much rather have her tell him he looked like the lowly servant that had been his mother, like the Oquelite guards used to tease.

But he had no control. *Silas Idicous. Silas Idicous. Silas—*

Silas shook himself. But she'd broken the deal. She promised she wouldn't hurt the only person in the world he cared to protect.

Felicity hated him, and he couldn't blame her.

His hands were raw, hurting to flex them and push the bucket aside.

He picked the cape back up, the last familiar thing to him. He hugged it around his bare shoulders, staring at the light spilling out from the crack under the door.

He could run.

The thought surprised him. Where to? There was nowhere in this world she couldn't find him. She would make him and the others work until they succeeded in bringing that creature out from the ocean…until the storms grew worse.

She was the only one who could protect him from the floods. She might be cold and distant, but she was powerful. She was his sister.

His family was just like that.

They were all awful, and seemed all too comfortable with killing each other.

It was better this way, he tried to tell himself. But the burning in the pit of his stomach refused to leave.

He'd already rebelled against her once. He'd helped those pathetic Council Members and gotten himself a blast to the chest.

But she'd tried to hurt Felicity.

Silas wouldn't let that stand.

No one took advantage of him.

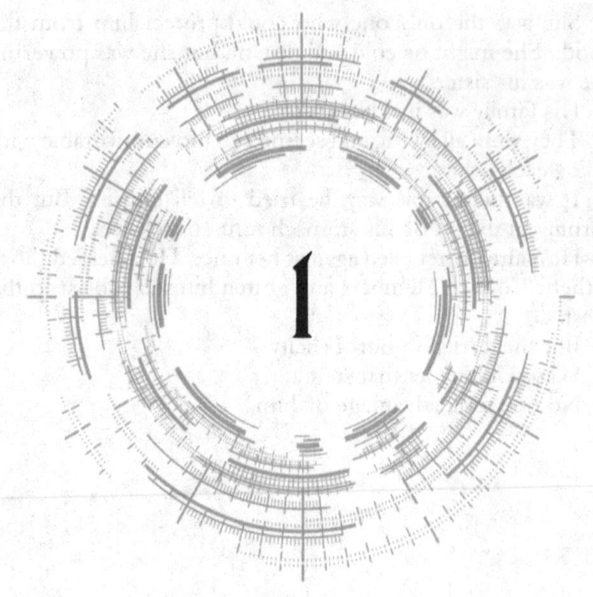

1

MERCY REMEMBRANCE DIDN'T know how to make friends.

Ever since she was a child, her grandmother reminded her of the dangers of letting people in…but then again, the same grandmother had murdered Mercy's mom, so her advice probably wasn't the best.

Bang!

Mercy jumped, her concentration broken. What the heck was that sound? It sounded like something had fallen out of a window—

Fire Wolf jumped, slamming her down to the ground, licking her face. Mercy tried to push him off, smothering her laughter bubbling her chest. "No! Off! Go!"

Fire Wolf finally obeyed, sitting beside her and excitedly wagging his tail.

Mercy sat up, trying to catch her breath, and wiped her face clean of wolf slobber.

"Another failed attempt," she sighed. She stood up, kicking a pebble. Her sandal flew off her foot, smacking the tree trunk. She'd spent the entire afternoon in the front lawn, as

4

she did most days.

It was easier to think…and much quieter. Six months, she'd been trying to remember how to glow.

"How in the world did I do it last time?" she groaned. The one cool thing she had to her name: her glowing marks that gave her the power to enhance things around her. She could finally show The Council she was worth it.

Fire Wolf tried to pull off her other sandal. Mercy squeaked, scrambling back. She glared at him, but the wolf seemed very proud of himself.

She sighed. It wasn't Williams's wolf's fault she couldn't remember how to glow— Wait. Not Williams. *Lawrence.*

Grandmere always said first names were too personal.

It was a struggle for her to even call Mathews "Ray." Most of the time she stuck to Rapheal, which annoyed Ray out of his mind, but she secretly liked the name. It was the first name she'd ever had the courage to speak.

She got to her feet, dusting herself off and storming to grab her sandals when the humming of an auto rumbling down the road caught her attention. Her heart leaped in her chest.

The red auto stopped at the end of the long driveway. Mercy quickly tried to wipe the sweat from her face as Bents— nope, *Felicity* stepped out of the passenger side, waving to the driver.

Mercy quickly put on her shoe, frowning when saw the busted sandal strap. She silently scolded herself. Third time this week!

Fire Wolf yipped, racing around her excitedly.

"Whoa! Calm down! Calm—"

"Mercy!"

Mercy cringed at her name. She was also not used to *that.*

Felicity Bentsworth trekked up the driveway, her long red hair braided back. A large brown bag was tucked under her arm, printed with the logo of the general store on it that matched the logo on her jacket. Even with her flyaways and flushed face, visually tired from walking on her feet, Mercy considered her one of the most naturally beautiful people she'd ever met.

But, of course, Mercy would never say that. It would totally come out stupid, and she'd somehow insult Felicity.

Felicity actually didn't have to work. She was the heiress to the Bentsworth shipping port, which meant her family had more money than most people could even dream of.

But from what Mercy understood, as the Council was *supposed* to be a secret Defender operation, they couldn't ask her family for money. Felicity had refused to stay put when the rest of her friends were working to help pay off their living expenses.

She secretly admired that. Mercy was the only one without a job. The Sergeant had insisted Mercy practice more on training, and "getting used to the Council."

"How was...uh...clothes?" Mercy asked, blushing. *Clothes? Really?* "Uh—I mean, working! Like an employee. At a place. Like you do."

She forced a smile, hiding her broken sandal behind her back. Could she melt away now?

Felicity simply smiled. "It was good. I actually got you more of our overstock."

She handed Mercy the brown bag. Mercy didn't have time to think of the words, scrambling to keep the oversized bag from falling out of her arms. "For— for me?"

Over the past six months since Mercy had moved in, Felicity had gotten her a bed frame so her mattress didn't sit straight on the floor, complete with new sheets. Then Felicity had given her overstock for more shirts than Mercy had ever owned in her life, and then even her old tele. She'd even offered to take Mercy shopping for makeup, but Mercy had declined after making a painfully awkward comment on Felicity's eyeliner being the same color as black.

Same color as black? Good one.

"I noticed you only had one pair of—" Felicity stopped, her gaze falling to Mercy's broken sandal. "Well, no pairs of shoes now."

"You didn't have to do this," Mercy said in a small voice.

"I want to," Felicity shrugged. "Besides, it's not fair that you have to move here and live with nothing. Taryn's used to the boys who could live on hot corn chips and Styrofoam cups."

Mercy stared, stunned at the bag in her arms. That was so incredibly thoughtful. "Well...er...thank you...again."

"I hope you find something in there you like," Felicity

said. "I'll leave you to whatever you were doing."

Mercy cleared her throat. "Uh, I finished."

"Oh! Well then, we can walk up together!" Felicity said. "I had something to tell Taryn anyway."

Taryn. That's what they all called the Sergeant, despite her real name being Jessica. Names were confusing.

Mercy nodded, trying to match her enthusiasm. She followed Felicity up the path. Felicity wasn't a fast walker. In fact, the only reason she was walking at all was thanks to a device Lincoln had invented. Felicity usually preferred her wheelchair, which folded up to fit in her bag around her shoulder.

Despite the warmer summer months, Felicity still wore cargo pants to hide the machinery, rather than wearing her braces to work. Ray had told Mercy they still didn't completely know why Felicity had become suddenly paralyzed.

They only knew it was related to the Shadow Soul—an elusive, powerful woman they'd never met: Kathryn.

Start conversation! Come on, Remembrance!

"I-is there something in particular you have to tell her?" Mercy said, clearing her throat.

"I saw some Defenders in town," Felicity said, adjusting the bag on her shoulder.

"Defenders aren't bad."

"No, but they aren't our Defenders," Felicity said, looking back over her shoulder. "Why would they be here...in North Cordell?"

North Cordell was a bit of a boring region. Felicity had a point there.

"Though it's probably nothing to fret about. Don't worry," Felicity assured her, smiling. "Is everyone back yet?"

"Rapheal's not there," Mercy said too quickly. "I mean...I— I don't know about the rest."

The two went around the back of the Inn, where there was only a pad instead of a doorknob. Felicity pressed her hand against it.

"Member Felicity Bentsworth. Entrance Authorized."

Mercy tried to remain unbothered as she pressed her own hand against the pad. "Member Mercy Remembrance. Entrance Authorized."

The door opened, shutting quickly as they stepped inside

the bustling Inn kitchen. Employees had just started up for the evening dinner rush, ignoring the teenagers they'd grown used to passing through.

Felicity opened the closet door, the holographic steps glowing to life up the hall. The two shut the door behind them and raced up the stairs to the Council's floor.

"Wait! It doesn't work like that!"

"How would you know?"

"Well, if you don't know how it works, we're all screwed?"

"Oh my gosh! Shut up!"

Mercy and Felicity exchanged glances.

"I guess that answers my question," Felicity sighed.

As they reached the top of the stairs, they entered the main room of the floor: An open kitchen and living room with an absurd amount of bean bags.

Currently, however, the dishwasher was overflowing, the floor covered with suds, and the smell of something burning wafted through the air. The tall, dusty-haired, black-eyed Council Member, Lincoln, was soaked, and Mercy couldn't figure out why.

A short blonde-haired girl was digging through the machine, and another boy stood barefoot in the mess, holding a broken plate, his glasses pushed to the bridge of his nose.

"What the heck—"

"Nothing!" Tabitha Delorous said, her head popping out of the dishwasher, shooing them away with her foot.

Mercy quickly leaped out of the way. Tabitha was both her roommate and someone Mercy did *not* want to look stupid in front of. She was everything Mercy was not: confident, not-awkwardly-tall, and every Council Member *usually* loved her.

This was not one of those moments.

"Tabitha got creative doing dishes," Lawrence sighed, tossing the broken plate into the shredder, which Mercy was certain wasn't made to process that short of trash as it scraped and clattered.

"Lincoln screwed it up worse!" Tabitha shouted.

Lincoln gaped. "I did not!"

"You made the top rack of the dishwasher go out the window!"

"So? That was the electro driver's fault, not mine."

So that's what the bang was. Felicity sighed, dropping her bags and edging around the water to the counter. She climbed on top, pulling towels out the cabinet and tossing them to Lawrence.

Mercy wasn't sure if this was a good time to disappear into her room or not. "Why is the tile…burned?" Mercy frowned at the black splotch on the ground.

"Scorched," Lawrence corrected, unphased.

"Lawrence helped blow up the door," Tabitha said, panicking more by the moment.

"Terrible idea really," Matteo Lopez snorted.

Mercy caught sight of the Wingor Member sitting on the arm of the sofa across the room, his headphones around his neck, entirely amused by the whole affair. Matteo, despite being more on the reserved side, had still managed to grow closer to the Council Members than Mercy had.

She stood awkwardly on the edge of the massive puddle. She'd dealt with dishwasher problems before at the motel, and none had ended in a mess like this. Of course, she'd had her bot, B0bbl3, back then.

She dropped the bag, shaking off her one sandal, and rushed into the wet kitchen. Maybe if she helped them with the dishwasher, things would be less awkward!

"Why isn't the water stopping?" she said.

"That's the problem!" Tabitha said. "And I blame Lincoln."

"Well fine—" Lincoln glanced at Lawrence. "Maybe blowing up the door wasn't the best idea I've ever had, gosh."

"You're just blaming the victim of your mess," Lawrence said, tossing another plate into the shredder. "'Teo, stop filming!"

A bang came from the window. They all spun around.

A tall blond boy pushed himself up onto the window sill, holding a bent wire dish basket under his arm. Cole Johnson opened the window and tossed it to the floor. "This is why I moved out."

"Rude." Tabitha caught the busted basket.

Mercy blinked at the twisted, melted basket. "There's no way you're going to fit that back in."

"The water isn't stopping!"

"This is pointless!"

"Lawrence, don't step on the glass!"

"Lincoln, do not—"

"Go home, Johnson!"

"EVERYONE QUIET!"

The entire room dropped silent, as well as Mercy's heart, as they turned to see a bewildered Sergeant Taryn Hunter, a tall, broad-shouldered woman, looking down on them.

"What is going on?"

Lincoln pointed at Tabitha. "She broke it."

"It's not my—"

"Quiet," Taryn said. "Johnson, get down from the window."

Cole did as instructed. Everyone stood on the flooded kitchen tile.

Mercy's face burned under the Defending Sergeant's gaze. Great. When she actually went out of her way to help the Council, she ended up getting in trouble.

The door creaked open.

"Hey guys—!"

"Mathews, get in line."

"What?" Ray dropped his bag with a pout. "I wasn't even here!"

He didn't rebel for much longer, giving a dramatic sigh and dragging himself into the kitchen beside Mercy. She was relieved to see him. He opened his mouth to ask, but she elbowed him, gesturing to the busted dishwasher.

"What the—"

"None of you speak," the Sergeant said, taking a moment to massage her forehead. "I don't need an explanation for…that mess. Just please figure out how to fix it. I'm here about the yelling."

Lincoln elbowed Tabitha. *I warned you all this would happen.*

Tabitha glared at Lawrence. *He's the one who exploded stuff!*

Lawrence ignored both of them.

Mercy cringed. Another thing she was *totally* not used to: The Council Members' weird telepathy link. It worked the same as abilities: as long as their emotions were somewhat stable and they weren't too tired or stressed or too far away, they could talk to each other mentally.

Mercy hadn't figured out how to talk to them yet, so she was just stuck listening to their super-special Council conversations in her head, and she couldn't say anything.

Cole stepped forward. "I'm sorry. I should have—"

"Johnson, I said don't talk." Though the Sergeant's speech wasn't harsh, Mercy still flinched. "A few days ago, it was arguing over training rankings."

"There's absolutely no way Matteo outranked me," Ray said.

Matteo muttered something Mercy didn't understand.

"Matteo," Taryn warned.

Matteo shrugged.

"What did he say?" Ray said, looking from Taryn to Matteo.

"I am not encouraging this fight." Taryn sighed. "And yesterday, it was accusations of robbery."

"Proven true," Lincoln whispered loudly.

"The point is," Taryn started, giving Lincoln a stern look, "I've heard this enough, and I'm not going to get any more complaints about the noise upstairs. I get that you're anxious, but there's no need to rip each other apart for it."

"Anxious?" Tabitha grumbled. "More like useless."

Mercy thought anxious was a good word for her current feelings.

"You are not useless, but you will be if you kill each other first. This is starting to get unbearable."

No one spoke, but from all the glancing around from all the Council Members, Mercy knew they disagreed. For the past six months, she hadn't seen a single glimpse of action. She was relieved, but she could understand what everyone else felt.

This ticking clock in the back of her mind…something was going to go wrong. It was inevitable.

The Sergeant made frequent visits outside the region, but for them, their instructions were to "train and wait."

And now it was simple "get along."

She glanced at Ray, but his eyes were focused on the water trickling from the kitchen into the living room.

"So, I've decided to do something about it," Taryn said, crossing her arms.

"We're going to go track down Kathryn?"

"No, Delorous."

"Dang it."

"You all want to get up and move so bad?" Taryn said. "When I was younger—"

I bet that was like 100 years ago.

Lincoln, she's only 37.

"—I was forced to do a trip for training and to get along with my assistant officer. It could be a short trip. Camping in the woods."

"A camping trip?" Cole frowned. "Now?"

Taryn tapped her foot in thought. "Yes! If you all complain about being useless and restless, don't you think getting out and working *together* on something would be good for you?"

Immediately, the room swarmed with opinions.

Mercy drowned them all out. She didn't want to leave the Inn…especially not to spend more time with the Council! She couldn't even glow, and they were already such so close to eachother!

They don't care that much about you, she told herself, biting the inside of her lip. She looked to Ray for reassurance, but he was too busy talking with Cole.

"Quiet! I think I'm getting a headache." Taryn sank down into a stool at the kitchen island, despite the puddle around her.

"I can make you tea," Matteo offered in a tiny voice.

"That would be fantastic, Lopez." Taryn sat up straighter as Lopez happily scurried through the flooded kitchen to the kettle. "We've been doing plenty of training on your individual abilities and skills, but you're the *Council.* The whole point of that is you being able to work together. And gosh, for a bunch of kids, you sure have no idea how to relax. One night. How hard would that be?"

"There's an immortal, supernatural killer lady out for our blood," Ray said. "That's not very relaxing."

Mercy had to agree…and she'd never seen this "Kathryn" face to face yet. She had seen the destruction her loyal Exerticus, the supernatural warriors Kathryn had created, could do.

And Mercy couldn't even remember how to glow! How would the Council react?

"And our best defense is the Council, which is pointless if they're fighting each other nonstop!"

Matteo pushed his way through with a steaming cup. He pushed it toward the Sergeant. She thanked him.

"Our defenses are secure, and it's been six months of peace," Taryn sighed. "I can arrange any security measures needed. I could even go with you."

"Doesn't that worry you?" Lincoln said. "That she's been so quiet?"

It didn't worry Mercy at all.

She'd like it to stay that way.

Taryn took a small sip. "A little. But it does mean her current priorities have shifted from you...for now. Which means..."

"A bonding trip," Lawrence sighed, with unenthusiastic jazz hands.

Taryn smirked, getting to her feet. "Exactly, Williams. You all better start planning. I expect to hear all about your great trip idea by the end of the week. Nothing too outrageous."

"We all go to the charge station, get slushies, and come home," Ray suggested.

"Vetoed."

"Dang it."

Taryn began to walk to the door. "So clean up this mess. Fix the dishwasher...if that's possible, and report to the basement afterward for your training assessment."

The Sergeant turned to leave and began to count the heads.

She paused, frowning.

"Wait. Where's Nikki?"

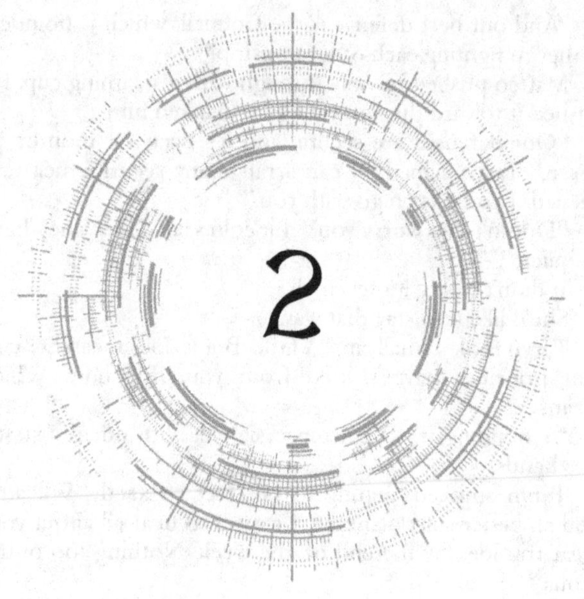

2

NIKKI AGUIRRE STOOD on the back doorstep of the bakery, a brown package under her arm. She knocked a few times and heard something crash inside.

The door swung open, revealing a man with curly brown hair, his apron and beard powdered with a white flour.

"Package for Rosh Tuppik?"

The man's eyes lit up, setting down the sack in his hands. "I wasn't expecting this until tomorrow," he said, excitedly taking the package with a mumbled "thank you." He barely gave Nikki a second glance before rushing inside.

Nikki nodded with a smile, heading down the steps. She checked the package delivery as *complete* on her route tablet.

She was only thirty minutes over.

The package had shown up on the delivery chute right as she was helping close up the office. She'd insisted it wouldn't be a problem to deliver it before she headed home. In fact, she quite enjoyed her delivery runs. It didn't require much conversation, just a lot of walking, something she enjoyed.

She could see and hear more than she ever had in her life,

and she loved it.

Almost as much as her nights training with Taryn.

Speaking of night...it was approaching fast. She hurried down the sidewalk, quickly skirting around the passersby, clutching the strap of her messenger bag.

The blacksmith, E, has been right about one thing: North Cordell summers were the best season of the region.

Rains were less frequent, though the storm clouds seemed eternally brewing in the sky, which E had told her was in fact *not* normal. Ray's mother, Dr. Mathews, seemed concerned about it, but Nikki didn't mind it.

It wasn't snow, so therefore, she liked it.

The weather was comfortable enough for short sleeves and cuffed jeans...or Tabitha's favorite invention: shorts, which Nikki decided to avoid at all costs.

She hit the dirt road that went off toward the Inn. No autos in sight. No looming supernatural threat waiting to pounce, making her stomach twist.

It didn't stop her from touching the crystal shard hanging around her neck.

I thought you told yourself you'd get back early today? Avalon, the soul trapped in the Stone, sighed, bored.

"It didn't work out."

The way you can run on four hours of sleep makes me a little concerned.

Nikki smiled. "I've done worse."

Avalon scoffed.

The camp glittered in the distance, mostly disbanded except for the new security and hospital that had begun construction there. The warmer months had lessened the fever's grip on the poorer population of the region.

Everything was...calm.

And that's how it had been. Nikki wasn't complaining. She pushed herself to a jog as the long driveway of the Inn approached. Autos of residents parked up the road, without much knowledge about how the Inn doubled as a base for eight superpowered teenagers...well, technically seven now.

Cole had moved out two months ago, claiming it was so he could be closer to his job being a farmhand at E's father's farm, but the general unspoken but known reason was that Cole had enough of the chaos. Though that didn't stop his younger brother, Ray, from teleporting for unannounced visits at Cole's camper trailer.

She reached the door, a bell ringing as she pushed it open. A tablet on the front desk glowed with a self check-in sign. Nikki walked through the lounge room occupied by a few late-night guests and a group of professors deep in discussion over coffee. She went through the door into the empty kitchen.

"You're late."

Nikki's heart leaped as she turned to find the Sergeant sitting at the counter, her feet propped up on a stool, with a tablet in hand.

"Outown and Giles are already asleep, and Sallow has his 'babysitting' duties for the night, which before you correct me, is a very accurate way of describing watching over your friends."

Shoot. Had Nikki being late put her in this mood? "I'm sorry for not being on time," she said, slipping the bag off her shoulder and clasping her hands behind her back.

Taryn laughed, getting to her feet to stretch. "No need for an apology, though it is nice to hear one."

Nikki smiled with relief.

The Sergeant's hair had grown lighter over the past year. She'd stopped caring for her roots, her natural blonde now fully showing through.

Her eyes still held the unbroken pain Nikki wished she could fix. But Taryn wore pain well. Nikki had no idea how, absentmindedly rubbing the lemon pin on the strap of her bag.

"How do you feel about a session tonight?" Taryn met Nikki's eyes.

Nikki's face brightened. "Of course!" She quickly threw off her jacket, rushing after Taryn through the closet door.

Nikki excitedly dropped down, pressing her hand on the floor as Taryn closed the door behind them. The ground began to glow around Nikki's hand, the light growing into a square. Nikki jumped up as the ground began to lower into the basement.

"Was the Council...disasterous this afternoon?" Nikki dared ask Taryn as they reached the ground, the training room becoming brighter and the holograms along the walls glowing to life.

One wall was full of statistics and a desk that was hardly used, with their live 24/7 news updates, stats, and the map from the Curatrix Machine, three dots indicating the supposed location of the three remaining Council Members. Lockers took another side of the room with benches. Someone had left their boots.

The center of the room rose to a training platform.

Another wall was full of holographic drawing boards *meant* for serious planning but instead they were full of doodles, like a terribly drawn Kathryn with pointy teeth and hair on fire. And another white board was entirely taken up by stick figure doodles of Lincoln being eaten by a lizard monster, the artist most likely being Ray.

Taryn laughed. "Hardly. Broken dishwasher, and once again, the...low morale."

Nikki dropped her bag on the bench, the speaker announcing "Council authorization only. Sergeant Jessica Taryn Hunter detected. Nikki Aguirre, Ewyon member detected." She flinched at the name.

"Perhaps your morale as well?" Taryn raised a brow as the holographic walls sorted themselves around the mat.

Nikki untied her tennis shoes. "No," she said a little too quickly. "I'm ready."

"Do you know what morale means?" Taryn chuckled.

Nikki pinched her lips together before admitting she didn't know exactly what the word meant.

"Morale," Taryn said, tapping her foot subconsciously in thought. "I guess it's the level of...enthusiasm of people at a given time. Maybe that's the wrong word. You all seem to not be getting along."

"I don't think they lack enthusiasm," Nikki said, proud of herself for managing to say the word. She jumped up onto the mat, sliding into a starting stance. "We always argue, but it's never been...big argue. I think they're just tired of being useless."

Taryn did the same. "You know you're not useless. It's only a down time. We can't let our senses dull."

Almost as if to prove her point, Taryn threw a kick. Nikki knew Taryn's rhythm by heart and was quick to leap back from the attack, ducking a second blow, her hand slicing for the Sergeant's shoulder.

Taryn ducked, twisting her foot around Nikki's ankle. Nikki turned, sending both of them hitting the floor.

Nikki smirked at Taryn's startled face. "You were saying?"

"Your tongue is starting to become as quick as your instincts." Taryn snorted, jumping back to her feet, lunging again. "I understand the Council had…mixed feelings on Orion's death, but I don't think that's any reason to feel useless."

"Mixed" felt like the wrong word.

Nikki was sure the Council all felt the same way: helpless. Their number one known enemy had just been killed…by someone else.

And all they could do was hear about it over the news in shock.

She avoided Taryn's next strike with a spin, landing the back of her hand against Taryn's side.

Taryn must have been distracted today. Nikki never won a match twice in a row. Sure, she'd been slowly re-learning how to fight since her dying accident, but Taryn would never let her win that easily.

"Why couldn't we at least investigate?" Nikki already knew the answer, but every time she hoped that maybe, just maybe, it would be different.

"We're not sending you all on a blind chase after this supernatural murderer. Especially with the Defenders keeping such a close eye on us now. They're just waiting for another slip up…and I don't think the excuse of 'immortal revenge lady' is going to cut it. Besides, I don't feel confident sending a bunch of kids who can hardly keep from fighting each other after them."

This time Taryn caught Nikki's arm, sending a gentle, yet stern tap to the back of her head. "That's why I've decided I'm forcing you all to be somewhat normal and do a small trip."

One for Taryn, still two for Nikki.

"A…trip?" Nikki frowned. There seemed to constantly be things she didn't understand.

"Yes, a trip you all do together…for fun. You won't go

far, and with security of course. The Council's bond is the only thing between the world and oblivion."

"We've done that before," Nikki said. "We went to Imperial together."

"That hardly counts. You were all separated for one thing, and were *very* unsupervised, which was a terrible choice on my part." Taryn turned, sending Nikki's strike stumbling. "Besides, a lot has changed in a year. And you have three new Members since then."

That was true. The journey to Imperial had been very stressful. If they weren't on a SpeedRail, they were walking and sleeping in the woods.

Nikki's palm struck Taryn's back.

Taryn sighed again, slipping back into a starting stance. "Besides, it's best not to engage Kathryn. Every time you fight, regardless of how skilled you are, you bleed. These Exerticus win either way…it's a wonder they haven't gotten all of you yet."

Ah yes. Kathryn's creepy plan to try and collect the blood of each of the Council Members to harness their power for herself. Rather creepy.

"Not Matteo and Tabitha." The odds were still grim. Two out of nine?

They'd come to the definite conclusion that Nikki's blood had been taken after her thought-to-be-fatal fight with the Oquelite prince, and younger half-brother of Kathryn, Silas Idicous.

For two weeks Nikki's mind was Kathryn's, her life protected by the Stone. Nikki also blamed Kathryn for the fact it took two weeks for Lincoln to find her.

In those weeks, Nikki relived every torturous detail of Kathryn's past…or at least the details Kathryn wanted her to.

"And wherever the three remaining members are," Taryn continued. "Unless she's already gotten to them. We can only hope otherwise."

"Lincoln's working to get the Cube working with a larger sensor," Nikki said, excitedly, nearly tripping up.

"Ah yes, the infamous tech used to find you," Taryn said, her eyes suddenly lighting up. "No, that's actually genius. He thinks he can use it to find another Member?"

Nikki nodded, smiling, proud of her friend. "Using the information from the Curatrix Machine, we have good chances. He thinks he can use the artifacts of the remaining Members."

Six months earlier, the Curatrix Machine had actually given them the locations of the final three members, but it had been entirely unhelpful:

One member dot kept moving around and never seemed to settle anywhere.

One was in the middle of the ocean.

And the last was said to be in North Cordell, unmoving the entire time. The map didn't give a specific location, and Lincoln was becoming convinced it was glitchy as no matter how far they searched, the alleged North Cordell member was nowhere to be found.

That's where the Cube would come in handy, to see if the Curatrix Machine was accurate at all.

"That would be incredible," Taryn said.

"Lincoln always is."

"You think of him as incredible?" Taryn raised a brow, throwing out an arm.

"Do you not?" Nikki frowned, confused, ducking. "He even helped repair your outdated projectors for this room."

"True. I don't deny his skill...though the dishwasher might not be his thing."

Nikki laughed. "I guess not."

Nikki's foot caught Taryn's and the Sergeant stumbled back.

Taryn caught herself, with a deep breath. "I must be out of it today," she said, with a shuddery laugh. "We can call it a night. You win, four to two."

The thrill of victory only lasted a moment, seeing Taryn's lips pinch together as she jumped off the lowering mat. "Are you okay, Taryn?"

"I'm fine," Taryn said, grabbing her jacket. "It'll all work out."

Nikki jumped down to follow her. "Are we stressing you out?"

"It's fine. It isn't...entirely their behavior either." Taryn sat back on the bench, unscrewing her water bottle.

Nikki sat tentatively beside her.

Taryn took a long drink before giving a long sigh. "Commander Dean."

Nikki's blood went cold. The name registered an odd, distant shudder that made her squirm. She'd never even met the acting Commander, but she knew that Dean was the one who heavily enforced the illegal full-bloods law.

"It's nothing you should be worried about," Taryn said. "It's mostly boring election things, which of course Council drama gets tied into. And it doesn't help that she wants me dead."

Commander Dean had been one of the biggest public haters of the Curatrix Team. The other Members had told her it was because they had publicly humiliated her when they exposed her political fraud. It sounded boring to Nikki, but to Dean, it apparently meant lifelong enemies.

Taryn tried to play it off with a laugh, but it landed stiff. "I… it doesn't have to do with me…right?"

"No…I hope not. As long as Dean doesn't realize there's any illegal full-blood here, we should be safe," Taryn said, squeezing Nikki's shoulder. "So don't worry about it. You're good at hiding."

But all Nikki could do was worry. She didn't want anyone getting hurt because of her cursed last name. It only seemed to bring problems. Sometimes, she almost longed for the time when she didn't know who she was or where she came from.

Back to being nameless.

Taryn's soft laugh broke her focus. "You look like Lyell when you make that face," Taryn said, with a small smile.

Nikki's heart skipped at the rare mention of her father…especially by name. Her face felt warm. "Really? Even with this scar?" she tried to joke, pointing to the obvious scar on the right side of her face.

"It's a sign you survived." Taryn shook her head dismissively, ruffling Nikki's hair. "Keeping that alive, all of you alive…that's worth stressing over."

Nikki opened her mouth, but nothing came. Taryn looked so serious as she held Nikki's eyes for several long seconds until she broke the silence with an exaggerated yawn.

"Well, you better get some rest before your deliveries tomorrow…and let's hope your friend didn't break anything else."

Nikki couldn't help but laugh. "I better go make sure."

TODAY WAS NOT Tabitha Delorous's day…or week, at that.

"So you're telling me our ancient dishwasher couldn't handle plastic?"

Cole turned the flashlight from the broken machine to Tabitha. "Well it was something plastic. But it's a little too…burnt in there to be sure."

Tabitha groaned. How stupid was she? "You have to be kidding me."

"Pretty dead serious."

"Don't you dare tell anyone."

"No promises, Tabs."

Tabitha glared at him as he epically failed to hide a smile. Tabitha sighed, defeated, turning to the blown dishwasher. The upper level was dark, except for the light shining from Cole's Comm.

"It'll be fine," Cole said, tapping the light off. "Ray said Mercy wanted to go get a new washer first thing tomorrow. There goes everyone's savings."

That was exactly what Cole would say when something

was worth stressing over. They didn't exactly have the funds for mishaps like these, unless Tabitha begged Felicity to borrow from her father…to buy a new dishwasher.

"Mercy?" Tabitha's new roommate avoided her like the plague and basically only talked to Ray.

"And we're going to need them if Taryn insists in this camping trip idea of hers," Cole sighed, picking up the bucket of dirty water.

Tabitha took it from him, dumping it into the sink. "It might not be the worst thing she's ever suggested," Tabitha shrugged. "She once had an idea to tell us she was going to kill us all if we didn't make it to Imperial in time."

To think, times had been *simpler* then.

And yet, even as a Defender hostage with no knowledge of the Council, Tabitha had felt useful. She washed the slime from her hands.

"I have…mixed feelings, and Taryn would use all of them to justify her idea."

Tabitha cracked a smile. "You think it would be hard, wouldn't you? You agree with her. It would be hard to shove us all in an auto."

"Oh. Might as well say impossible," Cole chuckled.

Tabitha wrung her hands. She didn't hate Taryn's idea. Anything to get her back on her feet was good enough. She missed the thrill of the Council versus the world. The adventure that was once exciting had now turned into laundry Tuesdays.

She sighed, hoisting herself up on the counter to sit beside Cole.

"So," Cole said, turning to look at her. "I got a call from Mr. Owenshawn this morning."

Tabitha's blood went cold. "What? H-how? It's not what you think! He's totally over exaggerating!"

"You put me as your emergency contact."

Oh, right.

Tabitha's shoulders slumped. "So you know…uh…know I got fired?"

Cole winced. "Yeah. I got a feeling. Apparently, you broke a bunch of bikes?"

Tabitha shushed him. "Look! I can't have anyone hearing about this. And it was only six hover bikes. He should've known I'm a terrible driver!"

Cole pinched the bridge of his nose, groaning. "Oh my goodness, Tabs. You *ran them over?*"

"Maybe…and also the wall?"

"What?"

"Shush!"

Cole blinked, shaking his head. "Tabitha!"

"I'll get another job real quick, pay off the debt, and Taryn won't even have to know," she said, trying to brush it off and ignore the concern creasing in Cole's brow. "Hey! Maybe I can go to E's dad's farm with you!"

It wasn't surprising—but still disappointing—when Cole laughed and shook his head. "No way, Tabs. It's not an insult to you, but you'd get squished out there."

"I'm not that small." She jumped off the counter, crossing her arms.

Cole raised a brow before standing up straighter, which forced her to have to turn her head up to meet his eyes. She scowled, jumping back up onto the counter.

She buried her face in her hands. "I— I can't sit here doing nothing anymore."

"You're just frustrated."

"Who's not?" She was sick of sitting still and breaking stuff and being lectured and waiting. So much waiting. "Really, you can't tell me you're content with your little camper trailer on the Hernandez farm."

Cole shrugged. "Yeah, it's not ideal, but there's nowhere I'd rather be. Here with you, the Mathews, and the Council. There's something out there for you, Tabs."

She found it hard to believe him.

Tabitha Delorous was good at cracking jokes and maybe a last-minute throwing of traffic cones…but besides that, she felt completely and utterly useless sitting here at the Inn.

And Cole didn't even live here.

Tabitha knew she couldn't be bitter about it. The farm was a forty-five minute walk on a good day, and Tabitha's driving was out of the question.

Felicity and Nikki worked most of the time, and as much as Tabitha loved the boys, they weren't exactly great company. And Mercy avoided anyone who wasn't Ray like the Fever.

Cole was lucky his family lived here, even if he hadn't grown up with them.

Not that Tabitha's family was great.

Cole placed a hand over hers. Her thoughts stopped spinning, and her words caught in her throat as she tried to look into his eyes and force out something positive. "I'll figure it out."

"We can figure it out together?"

"It's okay, Johnson. Nothing to worry over. Just a few bills to pay." And lonely hours to fill.

"You don't sound okay."

She rolled her eyes, giving him a teasing smile. "Maybe stop listening then."

He returned the smile. "Well, unfortunately I don't think—"

"Okay, fine, fine. Why don't you rant to me about your problems and we can call it equal?"

Cole rolled his eyes. "How about you come over tomorrow and we can research places hiring nearby? Sound better?"

Tabitha's heart leaped. Her smile was genuine. "That sounds great."

Cole sighed, taking back his hand and tucking his Comm into his back pocket. "Well, I better get going before your babysitter Defender arrives."

Tabitha laughed, rolling her eyes. "They're not."

Taryn had initiated a rotation system between Miriam and Jack to make sure everything was in order at night.

Most would have assumed it was to prevent them from going into each other's halls or sneaking out.

But no.

It was to prevent late night coffee binges and stopping any loud debacles that would disturb the poor guests on the floor below.

"You're just too grown up and independent to understand," Tabitha sighed dramatically.

"Your local adult man," Cole said, with fake pride.

"I don't know," Tabitha teased, tossing her arms up in an exaggerated shrug. "Lawrence might be replacing you."

Cole sighed. "He's only been eighteen for like two months! Doesn't count."

"Well then, you better stop by more often to reclaim your title."

"Just as long as you don't destroy any more dishwashers."

Tabitha laughed. "I'll try."

She tried to hold her smile, but the longer she held Cole's eyes, the more she could still see the worry hadn't faded from his brow, and the knot in her stomach was still there.

He was going to leave, and she'd be alone to deal with it again.

"Just try to sleep," he said, planting a gentle kiss on her forehead. "And also maybe try and call me before you come up with some insane idea to rob a bank or something to pay Taryn back."

She smirked. "No promises."

He rolled his eyes with a smile, and with another good-bye, he left quietly through the door, leaving Tabitha stranded alone in the kitchen. The warmth in her chest began to chill.

She sighed, jumping down from the counter.

Maybe she could ask Felicity to put a good word in for her at the general store?

The door to the stairs creaked open. Tabitha spun around, quickly scrambling to remember her starting fight stance.

Nikki's confused glance met hers as she stopped to catch her breath at the top of the stairs. "You want to spar too?"

Tabitha blinked, quickly standing back upright. "It's just you," she sighed with relief. "Another late shift?" "And training with Taryn," Nikki nodded, wiping the sweat out from under her bangs.

Nikki's job required most of the day hours that the rest of the Council typically trained, so Taryn offered to train her one on one. Tabitha couldn't be jealous. Nikki would hand it over in a heartbeat if she knew that would make Tabitha happy.

She was sweet that way, and still looked so young, despite the scar slashed across her face.

"I hope it went well," Tabitha said, walking to the girls' hall door, ruffling Nikki's hair.

"It was good. I heard about this trip idea." Nikki smoothed out her bangs.

Tabitha pinched her lips. "Yeah, that. It's happening for sure."

Nikki tilted her head, narrowing her eyes. "You don't look excited."

Tabitha couldn't help but smile at Nikki's confused face. "No, no. I guess it's just…complicated. What about you? Are you excited?"

Nikki shrugged. "I'll let you know when I figure out what it is."

Tabitha laughed. "Knowing you, you'd *love* something like this."

"Are lemons involved?"

"I don't understand how that relates."

"I should probably take a shower," Nikki said, biting back a yawn. "See you later?"

"You know it. Tell the lady in the rock *hello* for me."

Nikki rolled her eyes, opening the door and walking down the girls' hall.

Tabitha let her shoulders slip, watching Nikki disappear into the darkness until the light from the bathroom at the end of the hall switched on and the door closed.

She sat on the counter again, back in the dark silence of the night. The top floor of the Inn was sectioned off for the Council, and it had become a second home. The main common room consisted of the kitchen, which was clean *most* of the time, and the living room that was never clean. There was a framed photo of Fire Wolf over the film projector, and footprints on the ceiling from Ray.

Two doors were on the opposite wall. Each led to two identical halls, each consisting of three bedrooms and a bathroom. The boys' hall was to the left. While Cole no longer lived there, his room was left untouched. Lincoln and Ray being roommates was the cause of many practical jokes, including one that had Lincoln's eyebrows blue for a week. Lawrence and Matteo, their next door neighbors, often had noise complaints.

Tabitha heaved a sigh, jumping down from the counter and heading through the right door into the girls' hall. The first door led to Felicity's room, which smelled of perfume and paints.

The next door was Tabitha and Mercy's room. She

pressed her thumb on the pad on the door. It clicked open. Tabitha held her breath as she stepped inside and slowly closed the door behind her.

Tabitha had been excited about the idea of a new girl Member, but so far, Mercy had avoided Tabitha like the plague. Tabitha at first tried to offer to take Mercy to the river, or a trip to the charging station, but she'd been rejected.

Tabitha didn't dislike Mercy at all, but she certainly didn't understand her.

Mercy's back was turned to her and she was curled up tightly, sleeping soundlessly on the bed on the left side of the room.

Buzz!

Tabitha's tele went off in her pocket. Her heart skipped a beat. Shoot. Shoot. Was Cole calling her? Right now?

She scrambled to pull it out of her pocket, pounding on the screen to silence it.

Her sweat went cold seeing the notification.

New message from #ID-32910-29102*

Lucas.

Tabitha groaned internally as she flopped on her bed. Tonight, of all nights, her older brother was trying to get her attention again. Ever since he'd found out where she was staying thanks to Ray and Mercy, he'd been messaging her frequently, and she'd made it her mission to keep him satisfied with as dry responses as she could conjure.

Lucas was her oldest brother.

A valid child in her mother's eyes.

She clicked on the message.

Hey Tabby! Hope you're doing well. Let me know if you have a chance to catch up soon.

Tabitha swiped the message away, a new notification taking its place in bold red.

PAYMENT DUE.

Tabitha frowned. Payment? She clicked on the notification, unable to hold back a groan as Owenshawn's shop logo appeared.

Damages: Six (6) Model 601 Electro Cycles, Wall Damage (drywall, electrical unit...

Tabitha's eyes rushed to the end of the message, her

hand slowly moving to cover her mouth.

4,000 POUNDS DUE.

Tabitha's heart sank into her stomach. Four thousand pounds? That was practically all her savings.

She tore her sweaty hands slowly through her hair, her heartbeat thundering against her skull.

Don't freak out. The Council always helps you out.

But she didn't want to always rely on them. She always asked for help. She was always stuck. She had nowhere else to run.

She grabbed her pillow, buried her face into it, and screamed. She fell backward again, lying flat on her bed staring up into the dark ceiling.

Her phone buzzed again.

Goodnight, Tabby. Please respond soon.

Tabitha kicked her tele off her bed.

She took a deep breath, trying to not think of Lucas or money.

Or the strong scent of peppermint.

The smell of her family's home.

Her room smelled like the rain of a brewing storm. Not the stuffy, over saturated peppermint smell of the luxury penthouse back in Liberty…with that enormous glass wall that overlooked the docks and the ocean until it reached the border of the Dome.

She would sit awake, curled up in a blanket and face pressed up against the glass, watching the rain, listening to the distant hum of her brother's music box playing upstairs.

Tabitha shook herself. Was she insane?

There was nothing good about Liberty. There was nothing to miss. She should just forget it, like Lucas's text messages.

Tabitha held her pillow over her ears.

She squeezed her eyes shut and prayed that the night would be quick and dreamless.

"Your sleep is never dreamless, child."

The world was cold, and everything felt numb and static, suffocating slowly but never dying.

Tabitha had lived in nightmares long enough to know you couldn't breathe in them.

The sooner you accepted that fact, the easier it became.

But what threw Tabitha off was the overwhelming smell. The strong scent of peppermint almost suffocated her as she shot up, her heart pounding, the light adjusting around her.

She was in a room, the wall made of windows, the pristine white leather couches hovering above the ground. The air was still except for a little maroon bot pouring a teal kettle of tea.

Tabitha turned to the windows, her sweat going cold as the realization came upon her. It crept in slowly as the enormous skyscrapers begin to light up against the all too familiar Dome. It stormed outside, rain pelting against the glass. She could see the docks from here, the waves raging like she'd never seen before. She stepped closer, her eyes widening as an enormous wave rose up, crashing down onto the docks below.

This wasn't the first time she'd had nightmares about home, but that voice…

"Ryynar?" Tabitha whispered, slowly turning and bracing herself for the strange, powerful, sunglasses-wearing man that had a habit of lurking.

"Now that's a funny name."

Tabitha froze, her eyes widening. She begged herself to move. To hide. Run. Wake up!

"Why don't you address me as I am?" The door to the living room beeped open.

The door creaked open, a pair of deep green eyes staring straight into Tabitha's soul, an unusual pristine smile on her painted red lips. Her blonde hair was gelled into place, her bright pink pantsuit looking identical to the last time Tabitha saw her…the image that was plastered forever in her mind as a kid.

"The storms will only grow worse, child."

This isn't real. Tabitha backed up to the window. It wasn't real. It was just a—

Thunder shook the sky. The window behind Tabitha flew open, throwing her to the floor. Rain poured inside.

Tabitha's heart seized in her chest.

The waves were rising; they'd drown. They'd—

The woman rushed to the window, quickly shutting it

with a click. Tabitha lay frozen on the floor, gasping for air. It was okay. The storm was outside; she was safe.

The woman crouched down.

"I just saved you, child. Don't just stand there gaping like an animal. Be a good child and embrace me."

Tabitha swallowed, bowing her head.

She couldn't disobey.

It had been three years.

The woman opened her arms, and Tabitha fell into them. They felt so inviting as they held her tightly. "It's been too long, hasn't it, Tabitha?"

Tabitha let the peppermint aroma fill her senses. It felt so familiar. It felt so real.

"Yes. It has, mother."

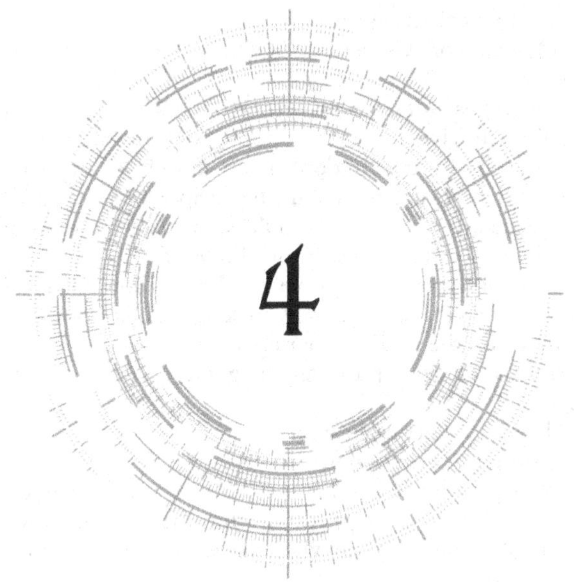

4

THE ONLY TIME Mercy felt like herself was before six in the morning and with Ray to tease.

"Why in the world did you have to wake up this early?" Ray groaned, dragging himself down the sidewalk. The two pulled the heavy box on its floating platform behind them.

"You want to have a dishwasher, don't you?"

Would the Council notice her then? *Wow! Thank you, Mercy, for getting us a dishwasher! You're so awesome! Let's be besties now!*

"When were you ever concerned with dishwashers?" Ray yawned.

"Well, I don't think your friends want dirty dishes," Mercy said with a shrug. "And me and B0bbl3 used to fix dishwashers all the time."

Ray raised a brow at her. "They're your friends too."

Mercy swallowed, feeling a hard lump in her throat. "I guess."

Ray quickened his pace to meet hers, but she took a harsh turn, the heavy dishwasher nearly running into his feet and tripping him off the sidewalk.

"Oh come on, Glow Girl," Ray said. "Don't get down on yourself."

Sometimes, Mercy was tired of Ray's persistence. He wasn't one to give up…ever. A good, yet annoying trait.

"You all are just…I don't know. So close, and so talented," Mercy said, tightening her grip on the cord. "I-I just…I'm sure the Council would appreciate me more if I helped fix something. I can prove I'm useful."

"You don't have to prove anything, Glow Girl." Ray rolled his eyes. "That's not how making friends works."

Mercy bit the inside of her lip.

"Did you have to prove anything to me when we became friends?"

"That's more complicated."

"I promise you, it's not."

"You're naturally good at this!" Mercy said with an exasperated sigh as they stepped out onto the dirt road toward the Inn. "Literally anyone who talks to you for two minutes is your friend."

"Not Lincoln."

"I don't understand you two." The two claimed they were rivals, which would've made sense since Mercy knew that at one point in time, a mind-controlled Ray *had* attempted to kill Lincoln. But in reality, the two seemed to do every mischievous act together. They shared a room, which they claimed they hated, but when Taryn suggested they change it, the two protested.

"Fine. Lincoln and I are a special case," Ray admitted. "But still, I've had an entire lifetime to practice friend making. You've had…what? Six months?"

"Six months is plenty of time. I haven't proved myself yet." Mercy pulled tighter on the rope, wishing she could walk quicker. She hadn't prepared to be confronted today.

"Look, Glow Girl, I know it's hard for you to understand, but you don't have to prove anything to them. Maybe all it takes is…actually talking to them?"

"I talk to them." *Sort of.*

"Asking where the milk is doesn't count."

"How much coffee creamer do we use in a week?"

Ray laughed. "A lot. Haven't you noticed?"

They reached the back of the Inn, where Mercy was surprised to see Matteo and Lawrence already awake.

Matteo sat with his legs crossed on top of a stack of crates, his headphones around his neck and a tablet in hand.

Lawrence perked up on seeing them. "There you are! We've been looking for you everywhere. Lincoln wants everyone upstairs."

"I thought we told you we were leaving."

"You can't tell him anything before he's had his coffee." Matteo smirked, jumping down from his little tower. "Do you like the idea of crossing the ocean?"

"What?" Mercy and Ray shouted in unison.

"Matteo insists that for the trip, we should visit Manifest," Lawrence sighed.

"That's a long roadtrip," Ray said. "There's no way Taryn would approve of that, and traveling through the Tube, no less."

And no way Grandmere would approve of that. Mercy shook it off. Grandmere didn't have a say anymore. Besides…

"The Tube?" Mercy frowned.

"It's the underwater SpeedRail tunnel system that connects the continents," Lawrence explained.

Traveling underwater?

Water crashing against the locked top of the casket—

Mercy shook herself. She wasn't going to think of that either.

"Need some help with that?" Lawrence offered a hand to Mercy.

Not even thinking, Mercy jerked back. "It's alright. I— I've got it."

"Okay. If you insist," Lawrence shrugged.

Ten minutes later, and Mercy regretted it.

Lifting a heavy dishwasher—even on a floating platform—up the stairs was not a two person job. Her palms were sweaty, the box nearly slipping and pushing her down.

As they reached the top level with a heavy thud, Lincoln perked up from where he was sitting on the counter. Taryn often joked that the Council didn't even need stools, since they always insisted on sitting on the kitchen counter anyway.

"Hey! You guys made it!"

"Dishwasher and all," Ray said, still catching his breath as he patted the box.

"I can help set it up!" Mercy butted in, stepping on the back of her busted sandal. She lost balance, crashing down on the kitchen floor.

"Mercy! You okay?"

Mercy's face burned as Ray helped her to her feet. She internally groaned as she saw the entire Council gathered in the room.

Looking at her.

"Okay. Just let me know if you need any help," Lincoln said. "Technology is kinda my thing."

"I got it," Mercy choked out, wanting to hide in her hair.

She tapped the side of the box, the packaging quickly dissolving.

"The reason I've gathered you all here this morning is for a very important meeting." Lincoln cleared his throat. "Since we're all being forced to endure an upcoming bonding activity, I've decided now is a good time to debut my current work in progress."

"You mean those inventions that interrupt my beauty sleep every night?" Ray groaned.

"If you don't want one, that's fine."

"Wait, no!"

"We're the Council, and we're prone to disaster, so this time I think we should be more prepared," Lincoln said, pushing the sheet off the counter to reveal an array of gadgets lying out.

Mercy heard Ray snort, whispering, "He's so extra."

Once again, this supported her complicated Ray-Lincoln friendship thing.

But she had to admit that her curiosity was piqued. She actually hadn't seen many of Lincoln's infamous inventions in her time with the Council.

"First off, I made Lawrence goggles."

"What?"

Lincoln picked up a pair of circular goggles with thick tinted lenses, a large metal rim, and a coated elastic band. "Let's be honest, Williams. Glasses are your greatest weakness in combat."

"Yeah, but goggles?" Lawrence narrowed his eyes at the invention.

Lincoln shrugged. "Taryn even helped me match them to your prescription. So you'll be able to see, and they're fire proof. But if you hate the aesthetic, I'll just—"

"I'll take them. Thank you," Lawrence said.

"And that's not all. I also made you bracelets!"

Lawrence blinked as Lincoln held up two metal bands, one silver and one gold.

"I call them Flint and Steel, even though they're a little more complicated than that. When scraped together, they create a spark. I know without Fire Wolf, it's hard to find a fire source."

"That's actually…kind of genius," Lawrence admitted, taking the bracelets from Lincoln and staring at them before clamping one over his wrist.

"Okay, this next one is a bit more boring." Lincoln picked up a leather strap, the end with a half-cut, oval-shaped metal frame with magnetic clips. "This is for Fidelis, Nik."

Nikki's eyes lit up as she stepped forward, taking it from him. "Really? Thank you! This is so cool! It's like my bag."

"Yeah, but weapons instead."

"A weapons bag."

Another friendship that confused Mercy. Lincoln and Nikki felt like the two most opposite people on the planet. Nikki was often optimistic, and she was never anything but kind to Mercy. Lincoln was always planning for some sort of depressing doom.

And yet, every time she was around, his face seemed softer, and his touch more gentle.

It was weird.

Lincoln cleared his throat, picking up a short metal pole. "Next thing, Felicity, I've been working on a retractable spear. I know it's not super convenient to carry around your current spear, so maybe this could help."

Lincoln tapped a button on the side, and immediately the pole shot out longer, a spear head creating itself and scraping against the ceiling. Lincoln quickly pulled it back, nearly hitting Lawrence in the head.

"Watch out!"

"Sorry!"

"That's amazing, Linc…but maybe you should let me handle the spear things," Felicity said with a nervous laugh as she rolled forward.

Lincoln tossed her the spear, and Felicity caught it effortlessly. She tapped the button, and it closed back to the small pole.

"It's much more portable," she said, admiring it as she turned it in her hands.

"Exactly." Lincoln turned back to the remaining gadgets. "The others aren't super complete yet. I'm working on making us all trackers, in case we get lost again. But I've only completed one."

He picked up a chain necklace with a little blinking blue fish on it.

"Why the fish?" Tabitha asked, peeking out from under her hat.

"It was the only scrap the right size in E's pile." Lincoln shrugged, setting it aside. "And I was also trying to come up with a flight suit for Matteo so his shirt doesn't burn up every time he flies, but I'm having a hard time manufacturing a fireproof green material."

Matteo nodded, approvingly.

"What about me? Do I get anything cool?" Ray said with pleading eyes.

"Ray, you can teleport and shoot blasts from your hands. What more could I enhance?"

"I would like some noise canceling headphones like Matteo's so I don't have to listen to you make stuff all night."

Lincoln rolled his eyes. "How about some platform shoes to make you a little taller?"

Ray crossed his arms. "Now you're just rubbing it in."

Lincoln smirked, pleased with himself as he collected his unfinished inventions in his arms. "Don't worry. I'll think of something you can't do."

"I'm sure you will," Ray said.

"As much as I'd love to watch you two continue insulting each other, I have a shift to get to, and I'm sure some of you do as well," Felicity said, rolling through the crowded room to the door. She tapped the edge of her headband, which began to glow to life, and with Lawrence's help, she pulled herself up. She turned the handles on the wheelchair, and it began to collapse in on itself until it became small enough for her to slip into her bag.

She met Mercy's eyes, despite Mercy's best efforts to hide behind the dishwasher. "Best of luck on the dishwasher, Mercy."

"Thank you," Mercy said quietly.

At least Felicity had noticed.

She let out a sigh as she unfolded her tools. She *would* prove herself worthy to the Council.

Ray had no idea what he was talking about.

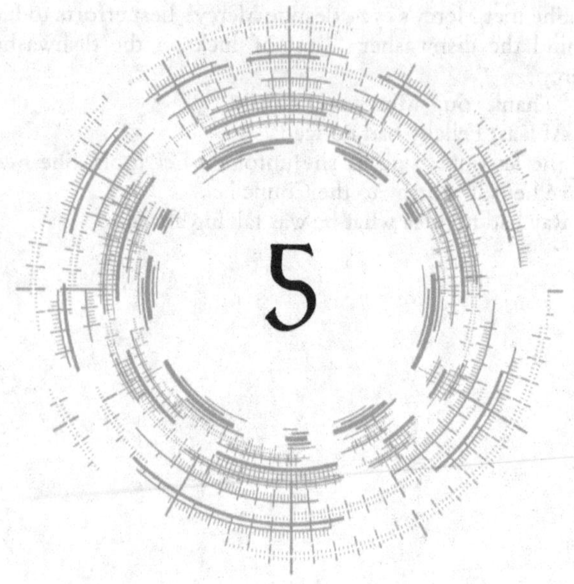

5

Felicity's morning stroll down the driveway made her feel human.

Working on the Nathaniel Street store made her feel part of something insignificant, and she liked that. Just once.

It let her breathe and not feel like, at any moment, she might be going crazy realizing the fact that she was indeed not actually human.

But could a mammal shapeshifter work at a retail store? Make herself lemon tea at sunrise, and braid her hair into two braids to compliment her glowing metal headband?

Felicity tried not to think too hard about it.

She tried to focus on breathing in the crisp morning air and studying the storm clouds rolling in. The storm had been looming for weeks, and it was eerily similar to the ones they'd seen the likes of back in Algery six months ago.

Hopefully it wouldn't come to that.

She was enjoying the peace. She was enjoying, for what felt like the first time in her life, being normal.

Or as normal as life could be when you were paralyzed

from thigh down on both legs and could only walk with high tech devices made by an ingenious teenage boy and a leader of the rebel Marketeer group.

Felicity hurried, seeing her co-worker Nayeli's hover waiting at the end of the driveway. The girl sat waving in the window, adjusting her topaz earrings that matched her bright lipstick.

"You're a bit late today, Hunter!"

Felicity's heart skipped a beat, the name always throwing her off. Liz Hunter. It was Taryn's suggestion. Not everyone in the world needed to know her true identity. They already had enough curiosity around them as it was.

The door to the auto opened automatically, and Felicity held her breath as she jumped into her seat, clutching her bag. Thanks to Lincoln's midnight boredom, he'd made her wheelchair collapsible and easy to carry wherever she needed. And now she had a spear to match.

Knowing she at least had that under control made her feel a little less uneasy about riding in an auto every morning.

"Acting Commander of the Defending Department Cadissa Dean now announcing supernatural supervision squads as part of the investigation action plan after the Capitol North prison break in…"

Great. The news blasting through the radio was a great way to ruin a perfectly good morning. The break-in to the elite icy prison in the region at the top of the world seemed to be the MEDIA's new favorite topic, paired with Commander election drama that always seemed to relate back to the Curatrix team.

All of it felt a little too close to home now.

Felicity knew it wasn't their fault for not stopping the break in, but it felt so…wrong to have their public enemy number one, Orion Idicous, killed just like that.

And all they had was a glitchy Curatrix Machine and a vague idea about some immortal woman and her associates with powers relating to trying to steal all the Council Members' blood.

This was not what Felicity had imagined life at nineteen to be.

"You seem a bit down," Nayeli said, switching the news over to bubbly music blaring through the speakers.

"Down? I-I'm fine," Felicity said. It wasn't a lie. She was fine. This whole roadtrip debacle had been her only thing on her mind. She'd gotten up in the middle of the night in a burst of nervous energy to begin painting a map.

Nayeli's dark brown eyes studied Felicity before her eyebrows shot up with a little gasp. "It was your legs again, wasn't it?"

"Oh no, Nay—"

"You ever considered, like, a natural treatment? I got a cousin all the way from Manifest. He has the best healing oils. Let me tell you, those things fix my headaches like a charm!"

Felicity laughed nervously. "I-I don't think that would help."

Nayeli didn't seem to hear her, rattling on excitedly about oils as they drove down the hill.

Felicity sighed with defeat, a small smile creeping on her lips as she focused on her coworker's voice rather than the movement of the auto. At least Nayeli cared enough to try to help. Felicity enjoyed being out with normal people…people who had no idea how much worse the issue at hand actually was.

Even if Giles didn't. The pesky teenage Defender had been very unsure about letting Felicity work, and he questioned her daily on any potential stalkers or Exerticus.

"And it worked to get me over a breakup. Like the one last week, not last month. That keeping you up too?"

Felicity laughed. "No. Not really a priority."

"Good. Seriously, the worst kind of nightmares are about dumb guys."

Felicity could agree with that.

The worst dreams were watching Silas kill every one of her friends in front of her as she laid trapped in a destroyed auto, utterly helpless—

Felicity shook off the thought, her breathing growing tight.

Not now.

Don't think about him.

They pulled up to the store, its hologram sign blinking in the morning light.

Nayeli stepped out, and Felicity followed suit.

"Need help with the chair, Liz?"

"Nope! I got it!" Felicity said, her gaze still stuck on the sunrise. "I'll meet you in the back."

"Cool, cool!" Nyeli walked through the automatic doors of the shop.

Felicity took a deep breath of the cool morning air, unzipping the bag, and with a click, the wheelchair set itself up automatically.

And now was her least favorite part.

She sat down in the chair, tapping on her headband, bracing herself as the numbing sensation sparked through her body as her braces powered off. The one downside to the brilliant invention was that they quickly lost power and needed to be recharged frequently.

She clutched the arms of the chair, taking in a deep breath, double-checking to make sure she remembered how to move, even though she used the chair every day.

She spun around, facing the sunrise again, the sun now higher in the sky. The day had begun, and she'd better get a move on. Nayeli would be worried if—

A shiver ran through Felicity, pulling her to a halt.

Her breath was stolen from her as she sat frozen for a moment. Her sweat went cold as the sensation passed.

What was that? Was it her legs? Was her condition worsening?

A hum of energy beat through her, making her stomach twist.

No. She'd felt this before.

She was feeling new essence.

Another wave hit her, and she quickly moved into the store. She had to get away from it. It was powerful. Her stomach flipped as she reared to a stop, catching her breath, the doors closing behind her.

Don't panic.

It had been months since she'd felt new essence like that. It couldn't have been one of her friends. Her body was around their strong essence daily, so it didn't affect her.

This?

This was nothing like she'd felt before.

Her vision threatened to blur.

The Shadow Soul? Exerticus? Had Giles been right?

Felicity tried not to bump into anything as she made her way for the back, trying to tug her tele out of her pocket. She flew through the door. She ignored her confused coworkers as she sped past, struggling to catch her breath, typing with her shaking hands:

"Felt something near the shop on Nathaniel Street.
Something big."

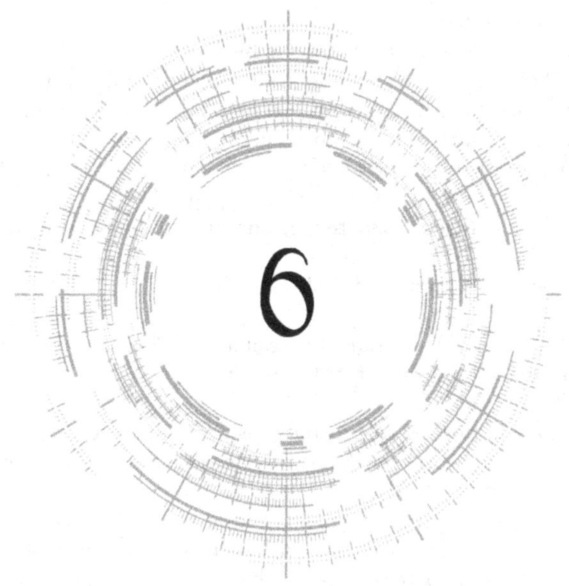

6

"THIS IS IT, Nik! Finally a chance to test it!"

"To test Super?" Nikki couldn't help but smile as she removed the undelivered package from her bag and into its appropriate cubby.

Lincoln rolled his eyes at the name Nikki and Ray insisted on calling his Cube. *Cube* was a very boring name in Nikki's opinion. *Super* fit much better.

"Felicity's felt a strong energy surge! This is the perfect opportunity!"

"I'll go with you," Nikki said with a small shrug. "That's what you're here to ask, right? You don't get off early all the time."

Lincoln laughed awkwardly, looking down at his uniform he hadn't even bothered to change out of. He helped fix tech at the North Cordell border with the Defenders. "Didn't mean to make it *that* obvious. Come on! Hurry!"

He took the last package from her bag, shoving it into its place. He was practically bouncing, grabbing her arm.

Nikki couldn't help but laugh, pulling the door shut as

they raced outside.

Lincoln dug the Cube out of his bag.

"This was worth leaving your Defender job early for?" "Nik, that job is hardly exciting. I fix laggy message servers and sign papers, not hack into enemy files or anything." Lincoln clicked the Cube to life. "They have me, the guy who can barely write his own name, sign papers!"

Nikki laughed. "You're working on it though? Spell your name!"

"Seriously, right now, Nik—"

"Spell!"

"L-I-N-C-O—" Lincoln hesitated. "Wait no, don't remind me. Uhh. Oh! L-I-N-C-O-L-N!"

Nikki beamed. "You did it!"

Lincoln flushed red, turning his focus to the Cube. "Still. Just because I can spell my name doesn't mean I'm becoming a Defender."

"You've never thought it's a little bit cool?" Nikki had wanted to apply for an internship herself, but even if her medical history wasn't an issue, she'd have to reveal her identity, and that was a risk they couldn't take.

Lincoln shrugged. "Sure. But realistically, I can't see myself being under the command of Cadissa Dean…too much politics mixed in, Nik. Defenders shouldn't be celebrities, they should be protectors."

Nikki flinched. He had a point. "You think that's why Taryn is trying so hard to keep us out of the news?"

Lincoln's brow raised.

Nikki's hands twisted over the strap of her bag, meeting his eyes and lowering her voice. "She doesn't want us to end up like the Curatrix team?"

"We're not going to end up like the Curatrix team," Lincoln said quickly.

How did he know that?

Lincoln was rarely wrong, but she didn't fully trust the forced smile on his lips. "Besides…after what happened, I doubt they'd let me."

"What happened with Kathryn?"

Lincoln didn't respond, but he didn't need to. It was one of the few things he never talked about with her. He'd been questioned by Taryn, but he couldn't remember whether he'd told Kathryn his name or not.

If Kathryn knew his name, she could control him at any time. So far, nothing had happened.

She nodded as she took a deep breath, deciding to change the subject. "Okay. What does your Cube say?"

Lincoln's mood instantly brightened, his smile becoming genuine as he hurried to show her the small screen on the top of the Cube, tapping on a blinking red dot. "See that energy signature? That thing is insane. It's even brighter than yours was."

"What about those dots?" Nikki said, pointing to two red red dots moving slowly in the corner of the screen.

"That's us," Lincoln explained excitedly. "If we could make this work long distance, whatever Council Member is hiding in North Cordell will be found in seconds."

"What if that is the Council Member?" Nikki said, her heart leaping.

"Right here? In the city? Don't you think we would've run into them?" Lincoln said, raising a brow.

"Maybe they're a runaway, like you. Hiding in the alleys and stuff."

Lincoln laughed. "Then I totally would've run into them. Trust me, Nik. There's nowhere these streets could hide from me."

A glimmer passed in Lincoln's eye, and Nikki couldn't read his expression as he pressed his lips firmly together to look back at the Cube. He didn't talk much about the few years of his life he'd lived alone on the streets.

He'd broken down to her about it a few months ago, but she'd been too sick to remember all the details. It was one of the few times she'd ever seen Lincoln cry.

"How far is Felicity's shop?" Lincoln asked.

"A few blocks down west. It's that fancy Nathaniel Street," Nikki said. She'd been there a few times, when the night shift was especially late and she needed a ride back. She would usually wait for Felicity in the back, and they'd somehow convinced Felicity's co-workers she was Felicity's adopted younger sister.

Nikki liked being called that.

"Huh. The energy presence is a street away now," Lincoln frowned. "Do you think it moved?"

Nikki tensed. "Or was the energy just that strong?"

"Maybe it's an Oquelite?"

If it was an Oquelite, Nikki could take them. She tightened her fists. "Most likely not."

"There's probably a few refugees still around," Lincoln said. "It's not like they have many places to go. They're either taken in by the law, or mind controlled by Kathryn."

"And what would we do if we found one?"

Lincoln shrugged. "We're good at coming up with plans on the spot."

He had a point. Impulse was their specialty.

An Oquelite wouldn't be very new, but it would certainly be something different from the usual routine of the past few months. Nikki hated to admit she felt thrilled, her steps lighter.

"I wish I had time to grab the bow," Lincoln sighed. "Did you bring Fidelis?"

Nikki shook her head. "Too big."

She hadn't touched the shield in weeks. It mostly sat proudly on the windowsill in her room now.

Lincoln began to hurry into a jog. Nikki raced to keep up. "Honestly, what the Defending Department is missing out on is the true power of tech modified shields and bow and arrows. Yeah, they have honorary swords, but those are useless."

Nikki knew Miriam and Jack both had been gifted swords by Taryn, but when it came to practicality, they didn't have much value. She was still confused by formalities. "And you say you don't want to become a Defender," she laughed. "That's a good idea."

As soon as they turned the corner, Nikki felt like she was hit with a gust of wind, nearly stumbling. It passed quickly, leaving her shivering.

Lincoln must have felt it too, the mischief in his face draining quickly. They exchanged a quick glance. "Felicity wasn't kidding."

The two broke back into a run. The streets had mostly been abandoned for the evening, and the few stragglers didn't pay the two much notice.

Nikki weaved around a traffic bot, meeting up at Lincoln's side, glancing at the screen. The red dot was glowing brighter now, her and Lincoln's dots growing closer.

Thunder rumbled above.

Nikki pushed faster. "Maybe it's not an Oquelite?" she said. "A Lyntox?"

"From the woods?" Lincoln paused, struggling to catch up. "You could have a point. But if it's from the woods…it could be something far more dangerous than a Lyntox."

"Creatures with stronger essence." Nikki had heard stories about the creatures Lincoln and Lawrence had encountered, and she herself had faced bloodthirsty wolves.

If one of them managed to make their way into town, it could be disastrous.

"Maybe we should contact Taryn," Lincoln said as they grew closer and closer. "It could be another trap."

Nikki felt her sweat grow cold against her will, the hair on her neck pricking up.

Dusk was falling quickly, and a truck's headlights flicked on as it passed. Nikki wasn't turning back now. The adrenaline was too tempting. They turned the final block, a glowing blue sign printed out clearly: *NATHANIEL ST.*

Nikki slowed to a stop, Lincoln scrambling to her side.

A cool breeze swept through the abandoned street.

A shiver crawled through her skin, forcing her to cringe, her heart beating into her ears.

"You felt that too." Lincoln's voice was hardly a whisper.

He tapped the Cube off. There was no need for it now. The essence pulse was too strong.

It was an energy like Nikki had never felt before.

Powerful and new. Exhilarating and terrifying.

Lincoln and Nikki crept quickly down the sidewalk, not breathing a word.

The essence pounded like a pulse on her senses, her body scrambling to adapt to the new power flowing through. She moved quicker, pulling ahead of Lincoln.

The lull commanded her to turn. The next alleyway.

Nikki braced herself. She would be ready. She ran her drills over and over in her head, preparing for a lizard monster or a caped madman as she held her breath and burst into the alleyway.

It was empty.

Completely empty except for a few cardboard boxes.

She let out a loose breath.

The feeling didn't go away. It swelled inside her, beckoning her.

She took a slow step forward. She heard Lincoln, out of breath, catch up behind her.

Maybe it was a creature. A shifter…perhaps it was invisible?

A shiver ran down Nikki's spine. She froze, turning her head slowly to one of the discarded boxes against the wall.

She frowned.

"Nik?"

Lincoln's voice echoed a few feet back. She ignored him, crouching forward.

She knelt down in front of the large box, damp from the humid air.

She held her breath, timidly peeling back the loosely-shut cardboard flap.

Her heart jumped to her throat. Her sweat went cold.

Panic. Run. Scream.

Dead.

No. It breathed.

It was alive.

Hardly.

Lincoln's knelt beside her, a gasp escaping his lips. "A… baby?"

7

NIKKI'S MIND REFUSED to function. Whispers stirred her mind to a panic, threatening to drag her to the past.

"Nik! Outside! Let's go outside! Nik, Nik!"

She pulled away from the thoughts. *What's going on?*

She watched Lincoln bravely reach his hand out, brushing away the child's auburn curls from his sweaty forehead.

The child was so small, curled up tightly and clutching a worn green stuffed animal Nikki didn't recognize. The child had a shade of light brown skin, similar to Nikki's, thick with sweat. The child looked at least older than a year old, but it looked so underfed Nikki couldn't tell.

His breathing was heavy. He didn't stir as Lincoln touched him.

Lincoln's eyes widened. "Fever."

"F-fever?"

Lincoln spun on her. "The Fever, Nik. The kid has the fever." He scrambled to pull the Cube from his pocket, scanning it over the child. "102."

Nikki's heart leaped back to life. "We don't have time!"

she said, her hands shaking.

Before she could even think, Lincoln scooped up the little toddler into his arms. "I'll lead. I can see in the dark. We need to run!"

Nikki didn't argue. She just leaped to her feet and ran beside Lincoln with all her might.

There was no way they could catch an auto this late. How long would it take to run?

Nik. Are you coming? Faster, faster!

She shook off the little voices in her head.

"Who would leave a child in a box?" Nikki said, a burning in her chest as she grew tense.

"I have no idea," Lincoln said, his voice quiet and his face blank. He was just as confused as she was. "Maybe they feared the Fever that much. Maybe they had it too? I-I have no idea. He's so young."

"So they left him to die?" No one would have found the baby alive if they hadn't felt— Her eyes widened. "The energy…it— it was coming from him, wasn't it?"

Lincoln met her eyes for a quick second. "It would make sense. But— but essence doesn't manifest so young. It's not possible…or at least, we thought it wasn't."

They burst past the rows of empty shops barreling down the dirt road.

Had the child been abandoned for his Fever? He couldn't have been there long. In this condition, he would die in— Nikki tried not to think of it.

He wouldn't die.

Taryn was going to make sure of it.

Nikki would make sure of it. She'd seen the face of death before.

Had the child been lying in that box in the dull heat all day? Ten hours, at least, since Felicity felt his energy.

"Nik! Send a message!"

"Doing it now!" *Someone get Dr. Mathews! Or Ray! Any Medic! It's important!*

"Are you not going to explain?" Lincoln shouted to her.

"How do I explain this?"

Lincoln paused for a moment. "Okay, fair."

"Maybe you can use your abilities?"

She could almost feel Lincoln cringe. The topic was sore.

Lincoln had successfully been able to use his Aviduous abilities with the guidance of Kathryn *once*. Aviduous had a connection to the earth, and Lincoln had been able to control the growth of a plant. Once he rejected the Shadow Soul's help, he hadn't been able to do it since.

What use is a stupid Aviduous without his abilities? Avalon grumbled from the Stone around Nikki's neck.

Do you have anything useful to say?

Your Council is a mess.

Nikki shouldn't even have been surprised. They reached the driveway to the Inn. The front porch light burst on as they raced up.

Taryn burst through the front door.

"It's a kid! A— a toddler!" Lincoln shouted. "With the Fever!"

As they reached the porch, Lincoln quickly handed off the child to Nikki, taking her bag. He burst up the steps, rushing past Taryn. "I'll go find the slowest Mathews in the world."

Taryn rushed to Nikki, ushering her inside. Nikki held the little boy close. She could feel the life in her arms, so alive. So fragile. His little eyes were now open to small slits. A bright sea green reflected in the light of the Inn.

Taryn closed the door behind them.

Nikki opened her mouth when she felt a dozen eyes burning into the back of her head. She slowly turned to see the entire lounge room staring at them.

Taryn wrapped an arm around Nikki and they raced down the left hall. They reached the end, and Taryn pushed open the thick glass door. The lights of the Med Bay burst on as Taryn raced through it, tapping all the hologram screens to life.

The Med Bay was small, all just made of one room except for two cots sectioned off by curtains. One wall was covered in shelves stocked with anything anyone could possibly need for various injuries, organized by Dr. Mathews herself.

"Oh my mortals."

Nikki jumped, spinning around to see Lincoln and Ray in the doorway. Ray's jaw was hanging as he stepped closer. "He really is a little guy."

"Do we need the P9F file?" Lincoln said, following Ray as he moved the blanket from the child's face, his hazy little eyes turning to the new movement.

"I— I don't know," Ray said, quickly clipping a band onto his wrist, double tapping it to bring up a holographic screen. "Do we know how long he's been sick? Is my mom coming? She might know better. I think all we can do is give him medication for the Fever and check his oxygen levels."

Nikki met Lincoln's worried gaze.

"Nikki." Taryn's voice was stern, a hand rested firmly on her shoulder. "Fill up this basin with warm water. Our Med basins are too big for him. Lincoln and Ray can help me with that. Upstairs, there should be some extra blankets and pillows in the hall closet. He needs hydration. Food. Something."

Nikki knew Taryn was just trying to get Nikki to feel useful and out of the way. Nikki didn't argue, handing the child quickly over to Lincoln and taking the basin from Taryn.

She'd do whatever she could to help.

Something in her burned. Her stomach twisted to see the child survive. A feeling that felt oddly familiar…yet so far away.

"You said you'd play! Come on!"

She ran the basin over to the spout behind the curtain in the MedBay, letting the water run, trying to calm the unfamiliar voices beckoning her in her head.

She quickly switched the water off and heaved the bucket up, rushing back to Taryn, the water splashing over her. Ray rushed to take the basin from her.

Taryn didn't look up from her work, trying to measure a dosage of medication. "Blankets! Now!"

Nikki didn't hesitate, rushing out the doors, ignoring all the glances as she tore through the lobby, kitchen, and then up the stairs to the Council's level.

She slammed the door open, out of breath.

"Whoa! Nik!" Lawrence jumped up from his seat at the counter.

Matteo rushed to steady her. "Are you okay?"

She started to shake her head, correcting herself with a nod, pulling back as Matteo tried to lead her to a seat.

"There's a little boy. Me and Lincoln, we-we found him."

Screw trying to remember words. "Big Fever. Big essence. Blankets. Food. What do you feed toddlers?"

"You need blankets?" Matteo asked. "We can do that."

"Where are they?" Lawrence said, placing a warm hand on her shoulder.

She held her cousin's eyes. "The MedBay."

Lawrence nodded. "We can take it. Get cleaned up. You said it was a little boy? Like Charles?"

Nikki shook her head. "Very small. Maybe two?"

Lawrence's brows raised. "Get Isabel. She might be able to help."

Nikki paused. She wanted to help Taryn, but finding Isabel would be equally as helpful. She nodded. Lawrence's older sister, and Nikki's cousin, thankfully lived in the Inn in a room downstairs.

Lawrence gave her a reassuring squeeze before rushing after Matteo down the boys' hall. Nikki could hear the echoes of Lawrence's surprise.

"Only two years old? What is going on?"

Nikki wanted an answer to that question too. She wanted to know what was going on with her head, spinning around, trying to pull her back to the voices chanting her name excitedly in the back of her mind. Haunting her. Threatening to overtake her vision—

She shook it off, running into the opposite hall.

Felicity's room was dark, meaning she was most likely asleep; Mercy no doubt didn't want a part in this; and Tabitha was most likely still on her way back from visiting Cole.

Nikki rushed into her room, locking the door behind her, trying to multitask changing and messaging Isabel at the same time.

She didn't bother putting her hair up. It now reached a good three inches below her shoulders. She quickly shoved her Comm into her back pocket, racing out of her room, only stopping to scrub the grime from her face in the kitchen sink.

She started for the door when a familiar green jacket hanging on an armchair caught the corner of her eye.

She grabbed it without thinking much of it and ran down the steps.

She found Isabel's room easily, as it was somewhere she visited frequently, but never in a rush like this.

"One moment, Nik!" Isabel called from behind the door.

Nikki shifted anxiously.

Isabel unlocked the door, ushering Nikki inside.

To Nikki, her cousin was beautiful in every way.

She had long blonde hair, with two perfect curls by her ears and glittering green eyes that held an eternal youthful joy that differed from her brother's. She was only about Nikki's height, despite being twenty-one. Her pregnant belly was well rounded now.

Nikki could tell by the enormous smile on Isabel's face that she was thrilled to be needed.

"I got your message," Isabel said, quickly turning to her dresser. "I don't have too much that I feel like would be useful. Perhaps a bottle if he's too sick to feed himself."

She opened the bottom drawer of the dresser. "Jack's anticipating a newborn when he brings these things, not a child his size, otherwise I'd offer clothes. Poor boy."

Jack Sallow's past six months was an interesting subject, and Nikki felt like no one noticed. Jack had been put on leave from his Officer duties to recover from being tortured by both the Exerticus and Oquelite, then used to force Miriam Outown to give over information. While he'd physically recovered, Nikki had seen the Officer pacing throughout the night at the MedTent in front of her room when she'd been confined there.

Isabel and Jack knew each other from spending time together at the camp across the mountain. Nikki remembered when Jack had approached her, asking if she knew what Isabel might need as a gift after learning about the Williams' financial situation. Nikki was thrilled for a distraction other than staring at the ceiling and feeling the numb pain in her side.

She knew nothing about what newborns needed, but it led Jack down a rabbit hole, and it was a perfect distraction.

Isabel picked out a few things, placing them into Lincoln's jacket, then tied the arms up like a bundle and handed it back to Nikki.

"Thank you, Isabel." Nikki took the bundle gently, holding it close to her chest.

Isabel smiled. "Anytime, Nik."

Nikki helped Isabel to her feet. Isabel groaned. "A month couldn't pass any faster," she said with a pinched laugh.

"It will," Nikki assured her. "And then there will be a whole other...human."

The fact was still entirely mind boggling.

Isabel ruffled her hair. "It will be crazy, Nik. No doubt you'll be the best cousin this kid could ask for."

"I'll be their only cousin."

"Point proven," Isabel laughed. "Now you better hurry. They're going to need that."

Right. Nikki had gotten distracted. "I'll be back soon!" she said, racing for the door.

"Looking forward to it."

Nikki ran down the hall to the propped-open MedBay door and burst in.

"Ah. Another Aguirre-Williams arrives." Dr. Mathews stood beside Taryn over a hologram, her focus to turned to Nikki and the bundle in her arms.

"Isabel gave me some things she thought might be useful," Nikki said, offering over the bundle.

Taryn rushed to take it from her, unwrapping it. "Bottle. Smart idea."

"I have no idea what the toddler can handle. It's best to play it safe and just get something in him." Ray's mother took the bottle, beginning to create a mixture, before handing it off to Nikki with the instructions to take it to Lincoln.

Nikki did as she was told, taking the bottle and Lincoln's jacket into her arms and walking quickly to the closed curtain. She pushed quickly through the curtain to find Ray standing in front of the same holographic screens as his mother, looking at her with a sharp "shush" and a very threatening glare.

"If you wake the kid up, I will do something violent," Ray said in a harsh whisper.

Nikki blinked, turning to see Lincoln in the cot, the little boy asleep on his chest, wearing an oversized shirt. Lincoln perked up, seeing her enter.

"I brought this for him...and thought you might need this," Nikki whispered, holding out the bottle before extending the jacket.

"Thanks Nik—"

"Linc, don't wake the kid up," Ray snapped, taking the bottle and jacket from Nikki himself.

Lincoln sighed, slumping back in defeat. "Well, how am I supposed to do this?"

Ray blinked, looking first to Nikki and then back to Lincoln. "Wait, are you joking?"

"What would I be joking about?" Lincoln glared.

Ray smothered a smirk. "The Ingenious Black Eyes Archer Man doesn't know how to feed a toddler a bottle?"

Lincoln's face was slowly growing more red. "When would that have ever been useful to me?"

Ray smiled, lavishing in his 'older-brother-of-three' status, shutting off the Scroll.

Ray sat down on the stool beside Lincoln, shaking the bottle.

Nikki crept closer, curious at how this mechanism was used for such a small human.

He forcefully took Lincoln's hand, firmly guiding him on how to turn the child over in his arm without waking him.

The child's face scrunched, and everyone held their breath.

His face relaxed, back to his peaceful sleep.

Ray gave a relieved sigh, then showed Lincoln how to place the rubber end of the bottle to the child's mouth.

"Now you can't move," Ray said proudly, giving Lincoln's head a pat.

All Lincoln could do was deadpan Ray, both of his arms trapped.

"Why can't he move?" Nikki asked in a whisper.

Ray looked back and forth from Lincoln to Nikki. "Do neither of you have any experience with little kids?"

Silence.

"We're both amnesiacs. What exactly are you expecting?"

Lincoln had a point. Even with the familiarity that the child gave Nikki, she couldn't remember it…not that she wanted to. The youthful voices chanting 'Nik' in the back of her mind sent chills through her, and she couldn't pin down why.

"Well, two things: If you move, he'll wake up, and then

we'll probably have to deal with crying——"

"Crying?" Nikki frowned. "Why would he cry?"

"Because that's what little kids do?"

"Why?"

"I don't know. Just because." Ray was less patient with her questions than Lincoln was, and unfortunately for Nikki, Lincoln was just as lost. "And, second reason is that it would stop him from feeding. At this stage, getting him nutrients is the most important part to getting him to defeat the Fever."

"Like war?"

"Sure, like war."

That made sense.

Ray got up from the stool, taking the Scroll from the desk. "I'll report back to my mom and the Sergeant. Don't mess with him, Black Eyes. Nikki, don't let Lincoln move. Permission to slap granted."

"Who gave you that authority?" Lincoln huffed.

Ray ignored him, leaving through the curtain. Lincoln sighed, turning to attempt to pick up his jacket with his knee.

Nikki picked it up for him, draping it over the child.

She sat on the stool beside the cot, leaning her head against his shoulder, studying the small boy's face as he drowsily clung to the bottle in his sleep. His face was so perfectly round. She very gently reached her finger out to brush her hand against his small feverish cheek, seeing how similar their skin tones were. His copper hair contrasted against his light brown skin in an unusual, yet beautiful way. Nikki wished she could see his brilliant sea green eyes again.

A shiver of the powerful essence ran through her.

How could he hold such power and be so…small? So pure and innocent.

She didn't even know his name, yet she ached to protect him.

"Ray decided I had to be the one to hold him because I'm the one who got thrown up on. We have a 'shared experience,'" Lincoln mocked Ray's voice to a high-pitched crack. "We all know he was just trying to get out of it."

"Do you want me to hold him?"

Almost too quickly, Lincoln said, "Nah. It's okay."

The two sat in the dim light. It seemed both of them were equally entranced by the little boy.

Nikki finally looked back to her best friend, his sand-brown hair with a choppy uneven cut, his fair, sun-beaten skin, and his deep black eyes struggling to stay open.

She rarely saw him like this.

Even before her incident, he always seemed to resist vulnerability. That he was somehow under the notion he had to be strong for her because of the things he'd done in the past.

She appreciated his efforts to protect her, but deep down, a lie ate away at her. She knew it was a lie. She knew Lincoln didn't care about her past, and yet she…

You're an Aguirre.

Lincoln's breath slowed to sleep, his head leaning against her shoulder. Nikki smiled softly as she gently guided him to lay down, the toddler snuggled to his chest. She brushed a loose hair from Lincoln's face before sneaking away.

"They're both asleep," Nikki said as Ray, Dr. Mathews, and Taryn all turned to look at her.

"Surprising," Taryn snorted. "I didn't think Lincoln was capable of that."

"It was bound to happen, considering his numerous all-nighters this week."

Now everyone turned on Ray.

Ray shrugged. "What? Taryn was the one who assigned me to share a room with him."

Dr. Mathews sighed, shutting off her screen to look longingly at her son. "You know the offer to stay with us is always open."

Nikki watched as Ray gave a hoarse laugh, looking away firmly at the chart in front of him.

After the Mathews' residence in Glorgory had for the most part been destroyed, they had taken up a small house in North Cordell for the meantime.

Nikki broke the silence, leaning against the table beside Taryn. "Any new updates?"

"His fever has gone down," Dr. Mathews sighed. "The bath and food appears to be helpful. We're keeping an eye on his pulse."

"I'll be here all night to keep an eye on them," Taryn said, stretching. "We're processing the DNA sample as we speak, but it might take all night to find a match with his File in the Department's system. It's best you get some sleep. It'll be ready by morning."

"I can stay up with you!" Nikki said excitedly.

"You have work tomorrow."

Oh, right.

Nikki nodded, but it didn't mean she wasn't getting up early to check on him.

"You can say no, Raphael. It's alright." Dr. Mathews' head tilted with gentle concern.

Ray still avoided her eyes. "Maybe next week."

She didn't push him further, though. "Alright. Maybe next week then." She folded her Scroll shut, tucking it under her arm. She turned to Taryn. "I'll be back in the morning to check up on the child, and I might bring Jenna by. She might be excited about this. Contact me if anything irregular happens tonight."

Taryn nodded. "Will do, Doctor."

Dr. Mathews pulled Ray into a side hug, kissing his hair before leaving the room without a word.

Ray's eyes were still on the floor.

Taryn's face quickly snapped to a frown, shaking her head with a scowl as she turned back on her screen. "I can't believe you can ignore her like that."

Ray's face went red as he quickly looked up. "I-I'm not ignoring her," he said, defensively. "It's just safer if I'm here. I can't risk putting them in danger."

"It was *their* choice," Taryn reminded him. "They wanted to be closer to you and Cole. I think your mother is well aware of the dangers Oquelite can bring."

"So that's why she married one," Ray grumbled.

"Ray," Taryn said sternly.

Ray just grumbled a form of goodnight, leaving the room.

Taryn sighed. "That kid doesn't realize what an amazing mother he has…"

Taryn's voice faded out. *Nik! Nik! Nik!*

The voices were back.

"Not now. I'm busy."

With what, Nik? The mudpies will get all cracked without you. Pleaseeee.

"I'm busy. I have to finish this."

You can finish it with Da. Da makes it beautiful-er.

"Hey! Fine. What flavor of mudpie?"

Uh…pinecone?

"My favorite pie is pinecone."

"Nikki Aguirre!"

The world flew back into focus. Nikki gasped for air, nearly tripping over her own foot as Taryn grabbed her shoulders, leading her to sit on the floor.

"Whoa there. Don't cry," Taryn said softly. "Are you okay?"

Cry? Nikki didn't realize her eyes were glassy till she felt Taryn brush away a wet tear. She shook her head, listening to her heartbeat, holding her legs to her chest. "I'm okay," she whispered.

"Don't lie to me when you almost passed out like that," Taryn said, holding her shoulders. "Nikki. You can tell me. It's okay."

Nikki met Taryn's eyes.

She loved Taryn's eyes. They were a mix of color, and they made her feel safe. Taryn knew what to do. Taryn always knew what to do.

"Tonight just felt like a…remembering thing."

"Reminder," Taryn said. "Of what?"

Nikki felt her cheeks warm. "What I am."

"Nikki, you are a lot of things. And all of them are very good."

Nikki shook her head. Were they all good? She could hardly remember. The voices terrified her as they swarmed without her permission in her mind. She didn't want them there. She didn't want a reminder that she was more than just Nikki.

She had a past.

A responsibility. A reputation. A history.

"Nikki?"

"I… I don't know." She couldn't describe how it felt. So stuck and twisted and limited in vocabulary she wanted to kick something. "I don't know what I am. I only know what I feel. And I feel a *lot* of stuff around the little boy. And around Ray and his mom…. It feels—"

"Empty?"

"No." Nikki rubbed the knot in her chest. "Something is there."

Taryn looked at her for a long moment. "I think I know how you feel."

Nikki's eyes fell. "Maybe."

"The best is to not let it consume you. You're Nikki Aguirre on your own…and while you might not have what you think is required…"

"But what if I don't want that?"

Taryn blinked. "Want what?"

Nikki opened her mouth, but no words came out. *I don't want these memories, Taryn. I don't want to remember.*

"Losing people is hard, Nikki. Losing your mother was also one of the hardest things that's ever happened to me. I can only imagine what that's like for you," Taryn said. "Coming to terms with the past is hard. I've been trying to accept it for over a decade. I…I don't know what you need, but I'm here."

Nikki forced a small smile. "Thank you."

Taryn smiled back, ruffling Nikki's bangs. "Anytime."

Nikki left the MedBay, walking back to the upstairs through the sleeping Inn without much of a second thought. The walk had become a habit.

She took a quick shower, focusing on the warmth of the water rather than the echoes of her own mind. She wouldn't black out like that again.

Closing the door behind her, Nikki paused, staring out the window where light rain began to pelt the window. The familiar voices tried to echo back. She shook them away, creeping for her bed.

Those voices knew her. She knew them.

Their names clung to her.

She glanced at the disc on the bedside table, swallowing hard.

It didn't matter if the voices of her younger siblings haunted her, because that's all they could do: Haunt. They were gone.

Nikki's hand twitched to touch the disc, but she pulled her hand back. Lincoln had extracted the NMA file, the file her mother Reyna had fought so hard to keep safe, onto the disc for Nikki.

And yet, she hadn't touched it.

Something about it made her unable to breathe.

She buried herself under her covers, hugging herself, wishing she could smother out the thoughts and everything could just be normal.

Whatever normal was.

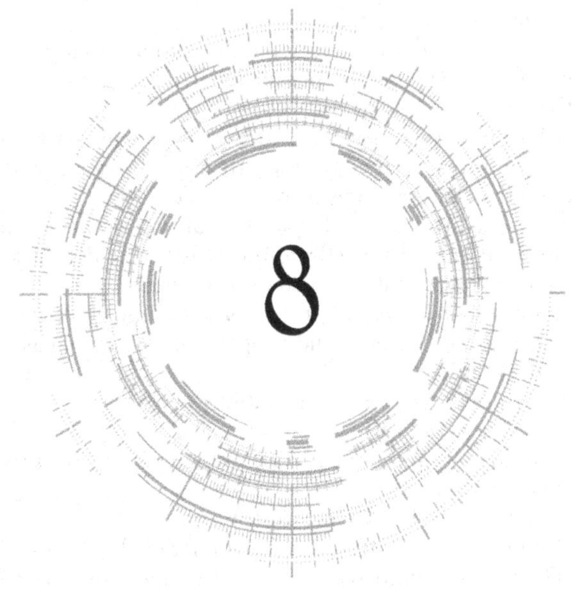

8

TABITHA WOKE UP gasping for air.

She was alive. It wasn't the sound of bomb sirens like in the nightmare. It was just the usual sound of her alarm going off like crazy.

"Are you okay?"

Tabitha spun around, tangled in the blankets, hitting the floor. Mercy stared at her from the corner of the room, applying lotion to her arm.

"I'm fine," Tabitha said, clearing her throat. "Totally fine."

Mercy raised a suspicious brow.

"Do you need—"

"I don't need anything," Tabitha snapped, laughing nervously. "I'm totally fine."

She instantly scolded herself as she saw Mercy's face fall.

This is what she got for staying up till three in the morning.

She totally lied to Cole about having a ride back to the Inn, making the walk alone in the dark and nearly getting lost after taking the wrong turn.

Cole would've totally lectured her about walking home alone in the dark, but she felt terrible having him drive her so late.

Her hair was a mess, and to her dismay, the dark lines under her eyes seemed deeper than yesterday. She dug through the cluttered drawer for concealer.

Mercy didn't say another word, turning to her corner where there was a dissected pre-EarthShaker model clock. It was a weird clock that strapped on your wrist.

Tabitha hadn't seen it before. "Where'd you get that?"

"Bentsworth," Mercy said simply, not elaborating as she twisted the little knob.

She was definitely avoiding Tabitha's eyes now.

Great going, Delorous.

According to Ray, the only friend Mercy had was a server bot back in Kennedy.

And Lucas, Tabitha's mechanic brother.

Tabitha shook it off. It didn't matter. She didn't care.

Their door slammed open. Tabitha almost dropped the bottle of concealer, jumping to her feet.

In the door stood Nikki.

"Holy freaking cow, Nikki. What's—"

"MedBay."

Since Nikki didn't stop to comment on the word 'cow,' there had to be something going on.

Her eyes widened.

Something was going on.

She raced after Nikki, keeping pace as they moved quickly down the stairs. "What happened? Was there an at- tack? A crash?" Her excitement went cold for a split second. "The farms?"

"No." They broke out into the kitchen. "A baby."

"Isabel?"

"No."

They ran into the lobby, and Tabitha didn't care whose breakfast they disturbed as they wove around the table to the hall. "Nikki, you gotta be more straightforward," Tabitha groaned.

"We found a little boy," Nikki said, spinning around and walking backwards, trying to find the right words, flapping her hands with frustration. "Very small. He has the Fever. Power. Essence."

Tabitha's relief was quickly replaced with a cold sweat sweeping through her body. Echoes pulled her back months. The Fever. The slowing heart rate. The utter failure. The cries.

Another child with the Fever.

Tabitha shook herself. "How bad is it?" she said, clearing her throat.

"He was doing better last night."

That was good at least. He was alive…whoever "he" was.

Tabitha ran with Nikki down the dark hall, the Inn's Med-Bay door propped open. The two girls ran through the door to find Taryn sitting at the table.

From the steaming cup of coffee and her falling-out ponytail, Tabitha guessed the Sergeant hadn't slept at all.

Taryn glanced up. "Good morning, Delorous…or at least, I hope it was good." She raised a brow, which made Tabitha subconsciously want to tear her fingers through her uncared-for bob.

"I heard you were out late last night."

Tabitha froze, glancing to Nikki. Nikki shrugged.

Tabitha turned back to Taryn, laughing nervously. "Really?"

"Really." Taryn narrowed her eyes. "It's starting to happen more and more."

You're not my mom. Tabitha held it back. Her real mom couldn't have cared less about how late Tabitha stayed out-…or Tabitha's wellbeing in general.

"How would you know that…if it was true?"

One word: "Johnson."

Tabitha shouldn't have been surprised.

"He called to make sure you'd been picked up."

The blood drained from Tabitha's face.

"Don't worry," Taryn laughed. "I told him there was nothing to worry about. But I'm surprised you'd *lie* to him, Delorous."

Tabitha swallowed hard. That made her feel sick. "I won't do it again. And we didn't do anything illegal or break rules—"

"Johnson wouldn't let you. I know," Taryn said. "I'm not

worried about you two. I'm more worried about you. Specifically. Alone."

"I'm fine, Sergeant." Tabitha tried to crack a smirk and a small bow. She hated losing arguments, and even worse, she hated admitting her feelings to the literal Sergeant of North Cordell.

Nikki popped out of the curtain before Tabitha had to do either. "Still asleep," she said, her voice quiet.

"The kid?"

"And Lincoln." Ray followed Nikki out.

Tabitha blinked. Ray was never up early.

He saw Tabitha and rushed excitedly to the table. "You guys wanna know something we found about our little friend?"

He was practically bouncing.

"Did you sleep at all?"

"A full two hours."

"I'd prefer if we had *everyone* present before making that announcement," Taryn said, placing a sturdy hand on Ray's shoulder with a weighted sigh. "If true…this is going to make things complicated."

Tabitha almost felt bad for being excited. Complicated. Finally. Something was going wrong.

"I guess you'll have to wait," Ray said, tossing his Scroll to the table. "In the meantime, I'm going to wake up Black Eyes."

Nikki gasped. "What? Ray!"

"You can't stop me!" He proved his point by disappearing in an instant, Taryn nearly stumbling over.

Tabitha and Nikki glanced at each other before running to the curtained-off room to find a startled Lincoln sitting straight up, grasping a bundle like his life depended on it, and Ray standing proudly.

Lincoln looked like he was about to slap Ray back. "You little—"

"Watch your language around a child."

"You're all children!" Taryn snapped from outside, shutting the curtain as if it helped.

Lincoln's hair was a disaster, sticking to his face from sleep.

Tabitha held her breath as she tore her eyes from her

friend's familiar rageful face to the tiny child wrapped in Lincoln's jacket, cradled in his arms. Despite the chaos, he was asleep, his copper hair swept up against Lincoln's chest.

"How was your beauty sleep, princess?" Ray said, unrolling his Scroll device, not even bothering to smother a smirk.

Lincoln ignored Ray, looking down to check on the infant in his arms.

Tabitha felt her throat tighten as she kneeled down beside Lincoln. She let herself breathe, seeing the rise and fall of the little boy's chest. Sweat glistened on his round cheek, his hand clutching the fabric of Lincoln's shirt. "He's so…small."

"Taryn says he's probably only two," Nikki said quietly beside her.

Ray scanned his Scroll over the boy. "The fever has gone down drastically from last night," he said. "The treatment seems to help calm the adrenaline rates…but the essence. It's still insanely high."

So that was the weird feeling in Tabitha's gut.

She couldn't tear her eyes away. She gently touched the child. It was like the soothing song of the ocean that she heard from her open window back in Liberty. It rushed over her.

"You didn't need a machine to tell us that," Lincoln snorted. "I don't think anyone's essence has ever affected us like this before."

Tabitha was a Humanic, so she didn't even feel Impure essence like Nikki, Lincoln, or Ray did. The fact this was affecting her…. It was literal supernatural logic bending itself—

The child whimpered.

Tabitha's heart leaped. "I can take him."

Lincoln didn't hesitate to pass the child to her. Almost immediately, the little boy's green eyes opened, landed on Tabitha, and he began to cry. She looked up for help, but Ray, Lincoln, and Nikki looked as horrified as her.

"What's wrong?"

"What did you do?" Ray tried to take him, but it only got worse.

"Ha! See, it wasn't me!"

"Are you guys hurting him?" Nikki asked frantically.

"You *hurt* him?" The Sergeant burst through the curtain.

"No!"

"He just started!"

The poor kid wriggled against Ray's arms before freezing, his watery eyes going wide with terror, seeing the adult.

Taryn stepped back. "Well…figure something out!"

"Figure out what?"

"I don't know!"

"Shh! Don't yell, you're probably scaring him."

In the rush, Nikki took the child quickly from Ray, holding the jacket tighter around him, gently trying to rock him in her shaking arms.

Almost instantly, the child's cries dropped to a sniffling whimper as he looked up to Nikki with a dazed confusion.

Everyone held their breath as he turned to look at the rest of them. At any moment he could…

Reach his arms out?

He stretched out for Lincoln, who looked around as if it was some sort of mistake before swallowing hard and taking the child back.

The child stared up at Lincoln, unblinking. "Mama?" came the tiniest voice.

Ray burst out into hysterical laughter, tripping over himself and hitting the floor with a thud.

"Well, I guess we know who he prefers now," Taryn whispered. "Solves that—"

The room went dark.

Lincoln cursed.

Taryn scolded him.

The glowing Scroll on the bedside desk went dark.

Tabitha's heart skipped a beat. First crying toddlers, and now no power? What was going on?

"You have got to be kidding me," Taryn scowled, pushing out of the room.

The Cube lit in Lincoln's hand as he quickly passed it off to Tabitha. "I can see in the dark. You guys are going to need it more than me."

He rushed out after Taryn, baby and all.

Tabitha stared at the glowing Cube in her hand. What was going on? Was the Inn okay?

Maybe it wasn't okay.

Maybe there was an attack.

Darn it, Tabitha Delorous. Why are smiling about the possibility of an attack? Are you insane?

They all rushed out of the MedBay.

Emergency glow sticks were beginning to light the halls. Whispers of panic followed.

"Sergeant!" came a man's voice. Tabitha caught sight of Officer Jack Sallow holding up a glowing blue stick, Isabel Williams clutched to his side.

"Jack!"

They rushed out into the lobby. No wonder it was so dark. The sun wasn't out.

"It's raining," came Nikki's tiny voice.

The storm clouds had broken.

"I don't know what's going on! It was just a drizzle twenty minutes ago, and now we're at…this!"

"Is it worse than last time?" Taryn rushed to the window.

"There was a last time?" Tabitha frowned. She'd never seen anything like this…or heard anything like it. It sounded like rain was pelting against the windows, and at any moment it would shatter. The Inn creaked, everyone holding their breath.

It wasn't true. It was just a coincidence. It was just a dream.

"When you were in Court Illegia…it stormed pretty bad when the Oquelite escaped," Lincoln said, his brows furrowing in thought. "But I thought that was just…their power."

At this point, they knew better than to just assume Oquelite.

Lightning flashed across the sky.

The building shook.

Tabitha fell back. A window flew open. Water sprayed. A group of Inn residents screamed. A blur rushed to push it closed.

Tabitha sat on the floor trying to breathe.

Her mother.

Mother's not here.

The dream.

No.

"Delorous, are you alright?" Mercy's voice.

She tried to breathe, pushing herself to her feet.
The dream had been right.
Ryynar had been right.
Her *mother* had been right.

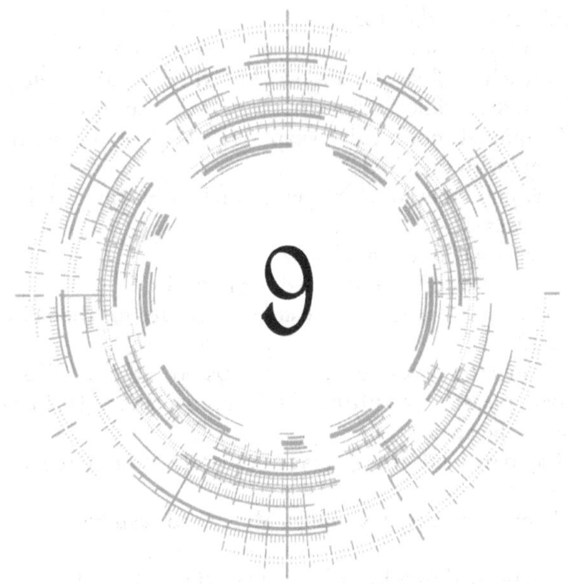

9

"My mom is out there!" Ray shouted in almost perfect unison with Tabitha shouting about Cole.

Mercy stood frozen, pressing herself against the wall as she watched lightning strike down from the sky. Only an hour ago, it had been a lazy weekday morning…and now it was this nightmare storm.

Her heart hammered.

It wasn't natural, the way the rain fought through the sky.

"I'm sure Dr. Mathews is reasonable enough not to go out in a storm like this," Taryn tried to say, but Ray was already running for the door.

"She said she was coming back this morning! She was on her way *here*. She has Jenna with her!"

Mercy's heart flipped in her throat. Wasn't Jenna just fourteen?

Ray grabbed the handle. "Don't open the door!" she shouted at him, running to stop him.

"You're not going without me!" Tabitha said.

Were they stupid? They could get hurt in the storm. They

could get *lost* in the storm.

"I'm going too!" Lincoln stepped out, blocking Mercy from reaching Ray. She almost shoved him before catching sight of the toddler in his arms. Her eyes went wide.

"Definitely not," Taryn snapped. "Of all of you, we need you here with the child."

The child met Mercy's eyes and raised his tiny hand with a small wave.

She frowned, waving back.

"It's not safe." Taryn drove the point in.

"My mom, brother, and little sister are out there!" Ray shouted.

"You'll be safest in your rooms. If any supplies are needed, please let an Officer know immediately." Jack began to shoo the crowd.

Ray remained firm, his face dead cold as he stared at the Sergeant.

There were very few things Mercy had seen him so upset about.

She pushed past Lincoln, taking her eyes from the child's. "Ray can teleport," Mercy piped up.

"Exactly!" Ray said. "If you're going to send anyone out in that storm, it's going to be me!"

"And the Council Members have a telepathy link. No Comms needed." This was the most helpful Mercy had felt in ages…even if she had no idea how the telepathy thing worked.

"We're running out of time as we speak!" Tabitha shouted.

Taryn pursed her lip before letting out a heavy sigh. "Sallow!"

"Sergeant?"

"Call Outown and Giles. Contact Dow." She then turned to the five teenagers standing in anticipation. "Only Remembrance, Mathews, and Delorous are permitted. I trust you will stay in constant contact and come back here immediately at any sign of any direct danger. Have I made myself clear?"

Mercy nodded, trying to hide her shaking hands. Ray exchanged a determined smirk with her. *This* was it! She was going to help save the Mathews!

"Got it, Sergeant. Thank you," Tabitha said before turning to Ray and Mercy.

"Delorous. You're the most defenseless." Taryn quickly unbuckled her knife from her thigh. She tossed it over to Tabtiha. "You'll need this."

Tabitha's eyes widened. "Seriously? Your epic Curatrix knife? I'm pretty sure I read an article about this in secondary school."

"You're *borrowing* it."

"I'll take care of this thing like it's my own child, Sergeant." Tabitha quickly strapped the knife to her thigh.

Tabitha was even confident with no powers. Mercy's stomach twisted, but her heart leapt in surprise as Ray grabbed her hand. "Ready?"

Ray actually didn't wait for either of them to be ready. Without warning, he jumped, and the world was torn from around them. Mercy was thankful no one could hear her scream in the blip of the Void as she felt every particle of her being torn apart before being thrown back together as they came flying to the ground, collapsing in the mud.

Mercy lay on her back for a second, trying to catch her breath.

Everything was so dark.

Were they still teleporting? No. She could feel the rain. She could feel the mud soaking into clothes. She sat up.

Don't panic. You're not scared. Don't show them you're scared. You're here to be helpful.

Being scared is not *helpful.*

At least no one could see her shake as she pushed herself to her feet. "Raphael!" she screamed over the rain.

"Mercy!" A cold hand touched her shoulder. She nearly screamed, and slapped it before it held up a glowstick to reveal Ray's face. "You okay?"

She managed a nod.

The storm totally feels supernatural, Ray's voice echoed in her head.

The Lady of the Universe. Though Mercy didn't dare say it. It seemed to already be implied.

Ray was drenched, but his hair wasn't flying wildly in his face like Tabitha's, who was struggling to hold it back. "Well, this is fun!" Tabitha shouted over the storm.

Mercy had to agree with the sarcastic sentiment. She

turned, feeling the soft earth cling to her sandals, seeping between her toes. She shaded her eyes from the rain, straining her eyes to see the glowing lights in the distance…dozens of autos stuck in the storm.

"Hey, Mer, you think you can go all Glow Girl on us?" Ray shouted.

Mercy went rigid. Of all times, this would be it. She couldn't disappoint Rapheal. She clenched her fists, trying to feel the warmth under her skin. *Come on. Come on! Just DO IT.*

She wasn't even surprised to feel her skin still cold and numb. "It must be the storm."

More than that.

"Well, on foot we go, then!" Tabitha didn't hesitate to trudge against the storm.

Mercy couldn't help but be relieved they didn't question it further as she followed Tabitha through the storm. The rain fought against her and Tabitha, who struggled to keep up with Ray. Her feet were heavy as she trudged along.

If she fell over, she was done for. The mud and wind would have her.

Ray reached the road first, offering his hand out to Tabitha, helping her up onto the sanctuary of asphalt.

Mercy rejected his hand, grabbing the road railing, pulling herself with a gasp. Her legs ached.

None of Taryn's workouts compared to this.

She held herself together, trying to stay upright and focus on Ray, who stared down the long line of autos backed up down the road.

"Searching the autos will be our best bet," Tabitha said. "Ray, search for your mom and Cole. We'll follow behind and warn people to stay put."

Ray didn't argue, blipping out of view in and out. He scowled. *It's hard to teleport in these conditions.*

Just search the cars like a normal person! Tabitha snapped. She looked to Mercy with a smirk. "Oquelite, am I right?"

Mercy forced a laugh.

"Check every other auto. Instruct the people to *stay put* until this blows over. Any emergencies, call the Sergeant. Got it?"

"Got it." Maybe if she was impressed, Tabitha would report back to the Council about how awesome Mercy was and they should totally all be friends.

Is that how friends worked?

She shook herself. Not the time.

She followed Tabitha into the street, and headlights flashed in her vision.

"Left side, Mercy!"

Mercy ran to the first auto, knocking on the glass window. The driver didn't dare lower the window. "Stay put till the storm calms down! Contact Sergeant Hunter if you need to!" Mercy said, repeating what she heard Tabitha say.

Auto after auto, Mercy tried to convince herself she was being helpful.

Mercy could see the end, the void of darkness ahead of her. She finished the last two autos. No Mathews in sight.

Now what?

"Did you find them?" she heard Tabitha call out.

"No."

Mercy frowned, looking around into the darkness of the storm, her hair beginning to stick to her face. "Raphael?" Her voice barely forced out his name.

Her heart leaped.

Was she too late? Had he gotten lost in the storm? She couldn't glow. She couldn't save him this time—

"Took you guys long enough!"

Mercy screamed, spinning around to see Ray behind her.

"Where were you?" Mercy snapped. "You shouldn't wander off. Especially with weather like this—"

"Chill, Glow Girl. It was just a second."

A second was long enough for everything to go out of control.

"Did you find anything?" Tabitha said, walking up with much more calmness than Mercy.

Ray let out a heavy sigh, his face hardening. "Nope. Nothing."

"So where does that lead us next?" Mercy asked. She secretly hoped it meant back to the Inn, where there was no imminent threat of death.

But she should've known better when Tabitha and Ray turned to the eternal stretch of darkness ahead of them.

"We're going out there."

Mercy swallowed. Her grandmother would for sure call

this a stupid idea.

But if Mercy was going to do this Council Member thing, she'd have to get over that.

They trekked out into the darkness, against the wind and the rain, the light of the autos growing further and further behind them.

Of all times, Mercy wished she could ignite now. She tried to remember the feeling. The warmth growing under her fingertips. Her heart beating into her ears. Her skin tingling—

Crack!

Mercy froze. Lightning flashed through the sky, reflecting off of an auto on the side of the road. Mercy gasped.

"An auto!" she cried out.

"What?"

"I saw an auto!" Mercy couldn't breathe. "On the side of the road! Right ahead!"

She broke out into a run.

Tabitha and Ray followed with the glowing light of the Cube. "I think I see it!"

Mercy strained her eyes.

Another bolt of lightning.

"Yes!" Ray cried, his voice ragged. "That's it! That's her auto!"

Ray teleported away, appearing at the door of the van wedged in the mud.

"Rapheal!" Mercy shouted. Mercy and Tabitha ran to him. He tried to pull on the handle, but the sensor glitched.

He unsheathed the Shadow Blade. "Break!"

Mercy would never get used to shadows collecting in the blade as he sent the sword crashing down.

The shadows exploded the door, window and all.

Tabitha and Mercy jumped back.

"Ray! The entire door?" Tabitha gaped.

Ray didn't listen. He sheathed his sword and climbed into the van. Tabitha and Mercy climbed in after him.

"Back here!" came a familiar male voice from the rear of the auto.

Mercy breathed a sigh of relief. They were alive. Ray tore into the car, scrambling over the seat. "Cole?"

The Cube glowed brighter over the inside of the auto.

The left side windows were ajar, rain pouring in and dampening the seats.

Dr. Mathews sat crouched, her face calm and calculated as she looked up from her dead tele. She clutched the shaking figure of a young teenage girl, her hands buried in her curly hair, holding her head. Her stepson stood beside her, looking far more panicked. The two were as drenched as they were.

His face quickly relaxed on seeing them. "I knew you'd come…I mean, you weren't the three I expected, but it works nonetheless."

"Aw, are you disappointed?" Tabitha teased.

Mercy swallowed, looking to Jenna. "Is… is she okay?"

"No!" Jenna shouted, crying out in pain and holding her head. "Mama, she's back! I can hear her! She's—"

Dr. Mathews held her tighter. "We need to get out of here."

Ray paled. "Jen—"

"Rapheal," Dr. Mathews looked at her son sternly. "She'll be fine as soon as we get somewhere safe."

"The Inn will be safe," Mercy suggested.

"What about the other Mathews kids?" Tabitha said, frowning.

Mercy's face heated. She'd almost completely forgotten about Ray's other younger siblings.

Dr. Mathews nodded in agreement. "Besides, the Inn is too far. I doubt Ray will be able to teleport very far in this storm."

"Mom, I've teleported four people across a continent once."

"*Once*. This is five people! And not during a supernatural storm like this. You are not taking that risk, Raphael Mathews."

Ray flinched at his full name, bowing his head in defeat. "Alright."

The group awkwardly huddled over to place a hand on Ray. Mercy squeezed his shoulder. He met her gaze. Her heart flipped at the sight of his shimmering gold eyes.

There was no usual mischievous shine in his eyes as he jumped into teleportation.

The next second, Mercy thought she was drowning.

That wasn't normal—

The world was wet. The rain poured down. The ground was thick, enveloping around her.

"We're in the storm drain!" came Tabitha's ragged voice. "Under the bridge!"

Mercy was too busy trying to not choke to imagine the usually murky storm drain flooding.

This wasn't supposed to happen.

Her head dipped under the muddy, churning water, which went up her nose and mouth. She couldn't breathe. She hit something concrete. She clung to it, pulling herself over the water.

"RAPHEAL!"

"MERCY!"

Tabitha.

"MERCY, CAN YOU GLOW?"

"What's going on?" She clung to the cold, solid concrete slab with her life. She pushed herself up. Maybe she could climb out—

Her hands sunk into the mud-slathered wall.

"Who else is here?" Tabitha cried over the storm. It was too dark to see.

Glow! Try to glow!

Nothing.

Not even a spark.

"Jenna?" Dr. Mathews gasped. "Where is Jenna!"

Mercy kicked the muddy wall. She bounced back, slipping back into the muddy water. The rush dragged Mercy down with a scream, her fingers scraping against the wall. Her head would go under. She would die. Everything was dark.

GLOW. JUST REMEMBER HOW TO—

A strong arm pulled her above the water. "Girls, do not let go!" Dr. Mathews commanded.

Mercy didn't dare disobey, clinging to the doctor with everything she had as the muddy water rose to her waist, threatening to pull her away with it.

She could feel Tabitha's warm, panicked breath on her neck, also clinging to the doctor.

Maybe it would be better if you drowned. It seems like the only time you can ever figure out how to glow.

She squeezed her eyes shut.

"Mom!"

A voice above them.

"Ray! Where's your sister?"

The furious desperation in Dr. Mathews' voice made Mercy's blood go cold.

"I have her! Don't worry! I'm coming down there!"

"Don't you dare—"

Flames burst to life above them, light shining down over the edge of the wall and into the storm drain.

Mercy almost let go of Dr. Mathews before she shook herself back to reality.

Mercy could see clearly now. Cole's sword was ignited, buried into the ground. He held onto the hilt, holding Ray with his other arm. Ray reached down for his mother.

"If I let go, we fall!" Dr. Mathews shouted, holding onto the pipe wedged into the muddy wall.

Mercy could do it. Mercy was tall enough. Mercy could reach out. But her entire body was frozen. *Do it!*

Instead, Tabitha jumped out, grabbing Ray's hand "You're not going to be able to pull us up!"

"I'm not going to! We're all touching right? I'm going to teleport!"

"Last time, it didn't go so well," Tabitha said. "You dropped us in a storm drain!"

Ray flinched. "I— I know. But we don't have another choice."

If you could just glow. Maybe I could enhance Ray's abilities—

"Rapheal." Dr. Mathews' eyebrows furrowed.

"I won't fail this time," Ray's voice cracked. "Please trust me."

Ray held his mother's stern eyes for a moment before she gave the tiniest nod. Mercy's heart flipped. Ray's face hardened, and in a split second, he pushed himself off into a jump.

The next moment Mercy knew, she was hitting solid ground.

Her head whipped up as she gasped for air, still clinging to Dr. Mathews.

"We're alive," she choked out, the words running over and over in her mind.

"Mercy!"

Tabitha's voice shot a cold shock through Mercy's spine, and she whipped her head to Tabitha, who still crouched over, gasping for air. "Why didn't you glow?"

Her voice sounded ragged, desperate…confused.

Her eyes met Mercy's in the dim light. They weren't angry, they looked…*betrayed* as her brow deepened.

Tabitha was disappointed in her? Did Tabitha hate her? Of course she does. She can do literally everything better than you!

Mercy went rigid. "I-I can," she said, fumbling to defend herself. "I-I just—"

"It's alright. You were nervous." Dr. Mathews' strong arm wrapped around Mercy's shoulders, helping her to her feet. "Tonight had many supernatural mishaps."

Ray bowed his head. "I'm sorry."

"It's not your fault," Dr. Mathews sighed. "It's no one's fault, so let's not go pointing fingers. We need to get inside and cleaned up. Jenna, are you alright?"

Jenna was leaning against Cole, as slicked in mud as the others. She gave a small nod.

Mercy swallowed, feeling the dirt scratch at her throat. Everyone around her was covered in mud head to toe. She didn't even want to know what she looked like.

She could still feel Tabitha's cold stare.

Dr. Mathews took a step forward. She let out a pained breath through gritted teeth. Mercy rushed to support her, her body going colder than she thought possible now.

"Mom?" Ray's voice was suddenly quaking.

"I'm alright," Dr. Mathews said, taking a deep breath, holding on tightly to Mercy's shoulder. "Let's just get inside."

Mercy helped Dr. Mathews up the stone steps. She tried to keep herself from shaking. This was partially *her* fault.

If she could just glow for once, maybe Dr. Mathews wouldn't be hurt.

Dr. Mathews, the woman Ray looked up to most in this world…Mercy had let get hurt.

The door pushed open. All six had to rush in quickly, taking both Cole and Ray to push it closed against the wind.

The Mathews's home was small but cozy. An open space held a kitchen and a well-surfaced living room of quilts and patched sofas. A doorway led off to what Mercy could only assume was the bedrooms. It smelled of pine wood and disinfectant.

"Mom! Jenna!" Fifteen-year-old Noah Mathews jumped from the sofa, a lantern in hand glowing through the cutout of a star. Noah's eyes widened. "M-Mom?"

"She's okay, Noah," Cole said, quickly rushing in, quick to try and smear the mud from his face. "Don't worry."

Noah looked unsure. "Did— did they attack you?" His voice was hardly a whisper.

"No. Not yet," Jenna whispered.

"No, Jen," Dr. Mathews said with a sigh. "It's alright. You're safe. We just need to rest."

Noah nodded, handing off the lantern to his younger brother, Adam, who was standing beside him. "I'll get the MedKit."

"Adam, go find more lanterns," Ray said, rushing into the living room. "Maybe we find that stash of wood and the lighter."

"Maybe showers are in order too?" Noah scoffed.

Mercy's face heated. They looked like monsters caked in mud.

"Go get the MedKit." Ray rolled his eyes.

Dr. Mathews leaned away from Mercy, supporting herself against the kitchen counter. She turned the sink on, splashing water on her face and scrubbing it clean. "I hope you all don't mind cold water," she said, her laugh cracking.

Jenna rushed into the kitchen, nearly slipping on a puddle before crashing beside her mother, flinging open the box. "Mom, what do you need?"

"Help the others first. I can wait."

"Ray, what did you want with this wood?"

Mercy turned to see Ray throwing the plastic decorative wood out of the fireplace, not even responding to his brother as he took the wood from him and threw it in.

A lighter wasn't needed. Cole's sword was good enough.

"Anything I can do to help?" Mercy said, raising her voice.

"Oh child, don't worry. You've done enough this evening."

Mercy knew Dr. Mathews words were meant to be comforting, but it only felt like the knife twisted deeper. *But I want to help. What am I if I'm not helpful?*

Dr. Mathews must have noticed the fall in Mercy's face. "Perhaps Jenna can help you fill up the tub and get that mud cleaned off. The boys can take the guest restroom…I'm not sure what to do about changes of clothing, though."

"I'm sure Tabitha and Mercy could use some of mine," Jenna said excitedly.

Mercy was relieved to see that life was beginning to return to her eyes.

"But what about Ray and Cole?" Mercy said. The closest boy their age was…Noah.

"We'll make it work."

"As long as you take the bathroom first," Mercy insisted.

Dr. Mathews opened her mouth to insist otherwise.

"Please. I-I would feel a lot better if you did," she said in a small voice, hoping no one but Dr. Mathews would hear.

She felt some of the weight leave her chest, seeing a slight smile on Dr. Mathews's lips and a small nod. "Alright then. If you insist."

"Hey, Glow Girl! Wanna run to the basement with Adam to get some food?"

"Ray's just scared because he's never been down there!" The youngest Mathews shouted back.

"Ray's *never* been here at all," Noah scoffed, throwing another log that looked suspiciously like the leg of a chair into the fire.

"Sure," Mercy said, peeling a flake of mud from her cheek. At least Ray wasn't disappointed in her.

Tabitha was still studying her, and when Mercy met her eyes, a brow lifted.

Mercy looked away, quickly following Adam Mathews along the hallway and down into the darkness.

This was it.

What was she more scared of? Looking weak in front of Tabitha, or her grandmother?

She took a deep breath, stepping down the stairs into the damp darkness of the basement.

She wanted Tabitha to be impressed by her. She would show her she was a real Council Member…but how?

She helped the youngest Mathews carry up a crate to the first floor, and after a cold shower, Mercy joined the circle by the fire, offered a can of lukewarm beans by Ray. He offered her the other half of his blanket.

Dr. Mathews was kneeling beside Jenna, dabbing at the scratch above her brow. Jenna held the blanket tightly around her, her eyes beginning to slip away.

Mercy glanced back to Ray, who seemed to notice the same thing.

"Jen? Are you okay?"

Jenna jumped, quickly looking to the ground. "Y-yeah. Why do you ask?"

"You were screaming about hearing things," Tabitha said bluntly.

Mercy cringed.

Dr. Mathews paused. "You don't have to talk if you don't want to."

Jenna looked up to her mother. "She doesn't want me to talk," she whispered, her voice hoarse. "She tried to make me forget."

"Who? Kathryn?" Ray leaned forward.

Jenna had been kidnapped by Oquelite six months ago, but they had wiped her memory when she was rescued by Matteo.

"Ray—"

"It's okay, Mama," Jenna said, lifting her chin.

"I remember. She wanted me to forget the storms."

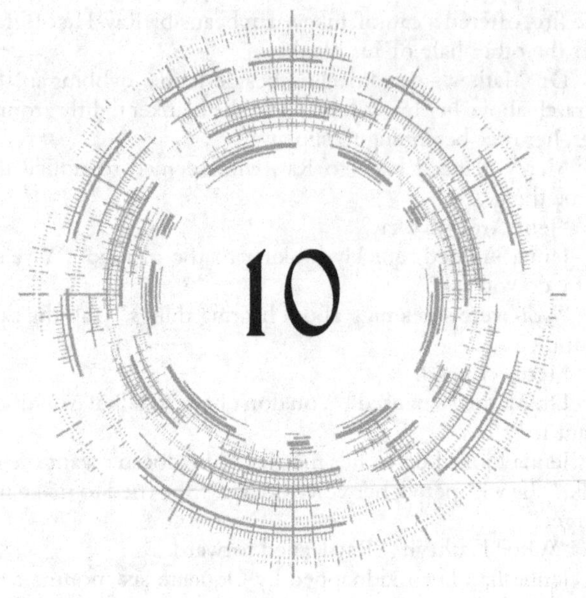

10

THE ONLY POWER left in the Inn was apparently in the Council's super powered Basement.

It was the same Basement Cole and Tabitha had fallen into over a year ago, and it was all that remained of the old Defending base besides a few empty catacombs underground. With a mix of Defender tech and Lincoln flair, Felicity shouldn't have been surprised.

And due to Felicity's condition and Lincoln's new sidekick, the two were banished there. Well, banished might be too strong of a word, but it felt right to Felicity.

She pulled her blankets tighter, bundled up in her wheelchair with a mug of tea in hand.

Lincoln was slouched on the bench beside her, with the tiny child swaddled and asleep on his chest.

"I hate this," he grumbled. "Do you know how long it took for him to sleep? He's still sick and he insisted on just calling me 'mama' and pulling my hair."

Felicity bit back a laugh. "You're not honored such a kid took a liking to you?"

It definitely wasn't something Felicity expected. She took a sip of her mug to hide a growing smirk.

"It's inconvenient."

"I think it's sweet."

"I wish he liked you, then."

Felicity still couldn't believe that little breathing bundle in Lincoln's hoodie was the intense energy she'd felt the day before. She could still feel the faint pulse if she focused hard enough. "It must be very confusing for a child so young. You're doing a good thing."

"I guess so," Lincoln grumbled.

The two sat in silence. Felicity rubbed her thumb on the arm of her chair.

"So when does this debriefing session start?" she asked abruptly. Sitting in the silence was really testing her patience and anxiety.

"Whenever Taryn decides." Felicity jumped at the new voice.

"Ywondie Member Lawrence Williams. Entrance authorized."

Lawrence descended the holographic steps, wiping his glasses on his sleeves, his curls damp. "She said she'd be on her way. She was trying to reboot connection with the Mathews residence."

"I could do that easy," Lincoln snorted.

'Wingor Member Matteo Lopez. Entrance Authorized.'

Lawrence and Matteo seemed to travel in a pair, or a quartet if you included the occasional tagalongs of the supernatural Fire Wolf and Lawrence's five-year-old brother, Charles.

Felicity rolled forward. "How is it outside?"

"Bad." Matteo shook his head.

Felicity shuddered. "Really? Did you get to use your abilities?"

"There was too much going on," Lawrence sighed. "It was crazy. I could stand out there no problem. It was like I could feel the strength of the storm...but it didn't affect me."

"That's just like what happened with me, Ray, and Nikki like a year ago!" Lincoln said, his eyes growing wide. "It's the sign of a supernaturally created storm...like Ray said."

"Yeah. But it didn't stop the rain," Lawrence snorted.

"Fire doesn't exactly do much good in a storm."

"I would've probably blown up the Inn if I tried," Matteo said, slumping down on the bench opposite of them.

Felicity had only heard of Matteo's wings. Only Lawrence had seen them, but from what she heard, they were enormous, and on fire, like a Phoenix. That's where they'd derived their Council name from.

Though no one seemed to call them the Phoenix Council.

Council kids, or "those-darn-teenagers" was more common.

"The lightning was already insane," Lawrence said. "It's unbelievable."

Felicity had seen it strike down from the sky as she looked out from the window in her room. She hadn't panicked like that in months...

"It was pretty believable. We all saw it with our eyes."

"Ewyon Council Member Nikki Aguirre. Entrance Authorized."

Nikki stood on the last step of the holographic stairs, more soaked than Lawrence and Matteo. She was barefoot, and unlike the other two, she hadn't bothered to change out of her dripping clothes, just held a towel around her shoulders for warmth.

"It's just a weird word," Lincoln said. "About how it goes against what we technically believe to be true, even though it's happening."

Nikki blinked.

"Why did people make words so complicated?" she sighed.

Felicity sat back in her chair. At least nothing interesting happened without them. Everyone was alright for now.

Not that she'd ever be in an exciting situation again at this rate.

Not even if you break your essence?

No. She refused to do that. The idea of shapeshifting into a mammal? No thanks.

"Nik, you want to take over?" Lincoln said, sitting up quickly with hope in his eyes.

"She's soaked, and he's already sick. Not a good idea." Felicity looked sternly at Lincoln, and he sat back with an exaggerated sigh.

She wished the little guy would let *her* take him. She was always sitting. At least she would be able to put it to good use.

"You're stuck with him," Lawrence smirked. "Beware. He'll grow on you."

Lincoln rolled his eyes, opening his mouth to give a smart comment back, but the speaker interrupted them.

"Sergeant Jessica 'Taryn' Hunter. Entrance Authorized."

Everyone went quiet.

The Sergeant hurried down the stairs without so much as a wave, her eyes glued on the Scroll device in hand. She stopped in the middle of the room, stomping her foot, a holographic table rising around her. She swiped up from her Scroll, the screen displaying up against the wall.

Felicity's chest loosened, seeing Dr. Mathews's face on the screen. Even with her wet hair braided and a thick blanket around her shoulders, she looked in control. The youngest Mathews, Adam, leaned against her shoulder with wide eyes.

"It works," Dr. Mathews confirmed in a calm voice. "We can see you and the others behind."

Everyone quickly exchanged glances before rushing to the screen.

Felicity had the advantage of wheels, pulling up beside Taryn. She'd learned her lesson too many times already. She already had to stretch to see in her chair, but when a tall teenage boy stood in front of you, it was impossible.

"I think it's very safe to say it was a supernatural cause."

"What makes you say that?" Taryn frowned.

The camera shifted over the side to Jenna, her black curls dripping and her face unusually pale in their screen light. "I heard her talking about it," she said, quietly.

"I knew it," Nikki said. "Kathryn."

Lawrence nudged her.

Jenna wrung her blanket in her hands. "It's all blurry. I-I remember being in a room. I remember a woman…she was really tall, long blonde hair, pointy ears…she actually was very pretty."

Kathryn. It had to be.

The woman who had created an intricate plan to almost

murder Nikki simply to taunt her with her own memories, tortured the rest of the Council's minds for the past year, and had the power to control people with simply their name seemed like a very likely suspect.

It had to be her.

It was too perfectly timed. These big storms always happened when Kathryn was up to something.

"But when she looked at me, her eyes were…purple. There was nothing there. It felt like my bones were burning and growing tighter and tighter and…" Jenna held her legs to her chest. Dr. Mathews rubbed her back gently. "She was talking about a storm.…. That she was going to drown 'them' out."

So poetic, Lawrence scoffed.

"Is there anything else?" Taryn asked.

Jenna looked up, her amber eyes meeting the camera. "She called it the Leviathan."

"And that's where her memories cut off," Dr. Mathews finished for her. Her face was cold, hardened, trying to fight the anger Nikki could see burning in her eyes.

"You seem conflicted, Doctor," Taryn said.

Dr. Mathews sighed. "I am," she said. "I've heard of the term Leviathan before. You see, I was part of a group."

She tugged on a string around her neck, a wooden cross falling out.

"Hey, Lawrence has one of those," Matteo said.

Lawrence's eyes went wide. "I-It's my uncle's. I have no idea what group she's talking about."

"You stole Lyell Aguirre's necklace?" Lincoln frowned.

"Just focus."

Dr. Mathews ignored the interruption. "It's a small organization who call themselves The Founder Association. They claimed to be Believers, but in reality, it was more of a twisted version of playing god. They had questionable methods of trying to ensure the Council would be brought together." She was quiet for a moment. "Obviously, they failed. Sergeant Hunter managed to bring together more Members than they ever could, but they were desperate, and would do anything for information."

"Did they…ever succeed?" Matteo piped up.

"Once," Dr. Mathews said, swallowing hard. "Luckily,

once their association dissolved, the Council Member was able to escape."

"What? You know of another one?" Ray said excitedly. "Who is it? Where can we find them?"

"It's not important for you to know," Dr. Mathews said. "Don't worry. They're very safe. The association itself was very small and obscure, but they were connected with many others across the world. Believers are known for restoring and protecting old pre-EarthShaker documents."

"And…how does that relate to now?"

"They also knew about something codenamed Leviathan," Dr. Mathews said. "I knew nothing more than that."

"These are some of the worst I've ever seen," Taryn sighed. "The flooding is already worse than the winter by far."

"Floods," Lincoln perked up. "There were floods in the EarthShaker."

"Uh, yeah. Like 340 years ago, genius," Lawrence said.

Lincoln shook his head. "No. That's not what I mean. *Supernatural* floods. That's why full-blooded Aguarious are illegal!"

It all clicked together.

"Because of their power of the water," Felicity breathed in realization.

"A tall tale has it that they even beckoned a creature of the sea made of bone to help them," Dr. Mathews said. "Hence, the codename Leviathan."

"A sea monster causing floods? Why?"

"That…I don't know," Dr. Mathews said. "There's a connection to the Shadow Soul for sure, but Kathryn can't control the creature…if it's even real…without an Aguarious."

Taryn cursed.

The entire Council scolded her.

"The timing is just perfect," Taryn grumbled.

She tapped her Scroll, a file opening up on the screen.

Felicity frowned. Taryn clicked open a mostly empty citizen file.

"This is our new small friend's File," Taryn explained, zooming in.

"No name," Felicity noticed.

"That isn't the important part," Taryn said. "We ran the tests last night…. Look at why his essence rates were so powerful."

The room went quiet.

Felicity narrowed her eyes, her heart seizing in her chest. All in a moment, the point of the meeting made sense.

Everyone froze. No one even dared to breathe.

This wasn't about the storm.

This was suddenly so much bigger than that.

"The kid," she choked out, looking around to the stunned faces around her before her eyes settled on the blissfully ignorant face of the tiny child asleep in Lincoln's arms.

"He's a full-blooded Aguarious."

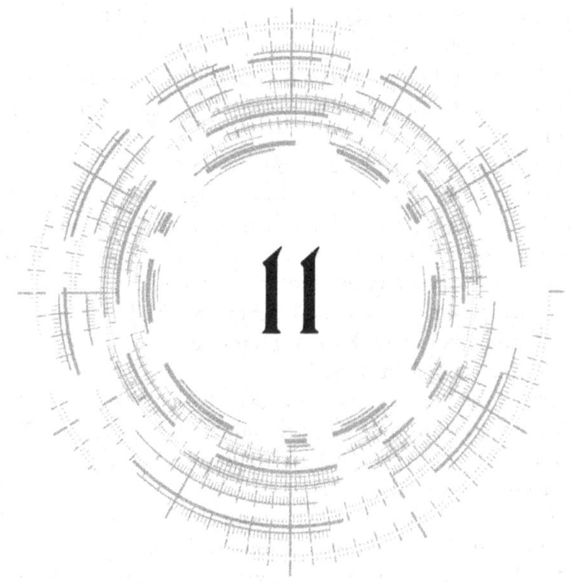

11

"AN AGUARIOUS?" TABITHA'S jaw fell. The same little kid she'd seen crying for Lincoln this morning? There was no possible way.

It couldn't be right.

Could it?

Ray sighed. "Yeah, sure. That might as well be."

Mercy just looked confused, huddled closer to Dr. Mathews with an eyebrow raised. Cole's expression hadn't changed much, his lips parting slightly as his eyes sunk deeper into thought.

"But *how* can that be?" Tabitha said, rushing behind Dr. Mathews to get a closer view at the screen, yet clear before her the results on the test read: *100.00% AGUARIOUS*.

"He's hardly two!"

"That's what makes it more pressing," Taryn sighed. "The fact his essence is already so prominent means he's very powerful."

"How is he even here?" Cole said, looking up. "I thought the Defending Department was set on making sure the illegal races didn't even make it to birth…I mean, like what they tried to do with Nikki."

Tabitha shuddered. Taryn had told them that her parents were put on trial as soon as it was discovered Nikki was a full-blood.

But Nikki was still here…somehow.

"Seeing as he doesn't even have a name in his File, whoever his parents were didn't officially register him," Dr. Mathews said. "This is a very poor region. People not registering their babies isn't uncommon, which makes it easy for him to fly under the radar. The Aguirres had the disadvantage of being very well-known Defenders."

"Where are his parents?"

"DNA matches led me nowhere. If they're still alive, they don't seem to want him," Taryn said, his face twisting. "They left a toddler with the Fever suffocating in a box."

Tabitha felt sick.

"If the Defenders find out about this," Cole said, letting out a nervous breath, "they'll come for him."

"And Kathryn!" Lawrence said. "She's already looking for Council blood, and if she's trying to make this flood with some Aguarious sea monster, she's going to need him!"

"We're already assuming he's a Council Member?" Tabitha said, biting her lip.

"It matches the marker on the Curatrix Machine that says a Council Member is in North Cordell," Lawrence said.

"A two-year-old Council Member? And we all thought teenagers were too young?" Ray laughed.

Jenna elbowed him, Ray choked.

Taryn groaned.

"If the Defenders found out about—uh—Water Kid… and Nikki." Tabitha met Cole's eyes. "That would be disastrous."

"We have the fact they *don't* know about us to our advantage," Nikki said.

For all Tabitha knew, Taryn hadn't even told the Defenders Nikki survived her fight with Silas, and much less her true identity besides a few trusted friends.

"If they don't know, then we still have time to get him to safety, right?" Cole said. "If we can hide him in a safe enough place, we can have an advantage over Kathryn."

"Where even is a safe place?" Felicity said.

"I can start making a list," Matteo offered. "We're already going on a trip, right?"

"I can help," Nikki said, turning quickly to him. "I've been studying the map on Lincoln's tablet."

"Whoa, whoa!" Taryn said. "You are *not* leaving North Cordell. This is way too dangerous."

"When did you start expecting us to be safe?" Tabitha asked. "Wasn't the first order you gave us a death threat?"

"Those were different circumstances." Taryn cleared her throat. "I'll *consider* it. Once this storm passes, we'll pick this up again."

"So, we *can* once the storm is over?" Matteo said, with a mischievous smile. "Esto es perfecto!"

The two turned to run off before Taryn called after Matteo in his first language. Matteo simply gave her a quick remark back in the same language that caused Lawrence to snort before he ran up the stairs.

"Williams! This is not what I meant by trip!"

"Sorry, Sergeant." Lawrence had no apology in his eyes.

Taryn grumbled something about teenagers under her breath before turning back to Dr. Mathews.

"This ends the briefing," Taryn said. "Do you need anything over there, Doctor?"

"I believe we're all good," Dr. Mathews. "I've been through my fair share of disasters."

Taryn nodded. "Till the storm passes, then."

"Stay alive!" Lincoln shouted before the call shut off.

The room was quiet all except for the crack of the fireplace. Tabitha felt like her whole head was spinning.

Yeah, life had been boring recently, but she wasn't expecting all *that*. And all on top of her unspoken debt?

She looked up to Cole, but his eyes were fixed on the flames of the fireplace.

Dr. Mathews got to her feet, clapping her hands and taking a deep painful breath. "Well, that's the end of that. I think it's time to get some sleep after today."

"I don't think I'll sleep ever again," Jenna grumbled.

Noah sighed, poking her with his foot. "We can play Blue Check in my room if you're quiet."

"I get the remote."

Noah groaned. "Alright, fine."

The two got to their feet, taking up a lantern and running to the back hall.

"Jenna, please don't forget to take your dosage tonight!" Dr. Mathews called after them.

Jenna froze, her face going red. She nodded silently before rushing back after Noah.

"Is that for her nightmares?" Cole asked, quietly.

Dr. Mathews nodded. "It only takes the edge off it. Sleep has been very difficult for her since the…incident, even though she won't admit it. I know tonight's revelation won't be easy."

Tabitha's heart ached. She understood Jenna's pain, though she knew she'd never understand the trauma Jenna no doubt hid after being kidnapped and having her head messed with.

Another reason her blood burned to do *something*.

Kathryn was causing too many problems.

Dr. Mathews offered Adam her hand. He took it, helping his mother walk to the back hall. "Can we call Dad?"

Tabitha swore the room went colder. Ray went pale, and Cole turned away.

Dr. Mathews must have sensed it too. "Maybe soon."

Adam followed his mother down the hall until finally the footsteps stopped.

"You had a chance to speak to your father and you rejected it?" Mercy said, her mouth hanging open in horror at Ray.

"I didn't even say anything!" Ray sat down by the fire.

"Exactly!" Mercy said.

Ray ignored her and wrapped his arms around himself, hiding his head.

Tabitha glanced at Cole. Cole met her eyes this time, pursing his lips before heading for the fireplace, sitting beside Ray.

Tabitha crawled over the couch. "Cut him a break," she grumbled to Mercy.

Mercy didn't respond. She looked away, pulling the blanket tighter around her.

What the heck was going on in the Glow Girl's head? Tabitha knew that Mercy's father was missing, and it was one of the only things she knew about the girl's past. Taryn had even suggested sending out an official search, but Mercy doubted it would work.

And of course, she never talked to Tabitha directly about it.

No doubt there was a hint of disbelief or even envy that Ray wouldn't even want to talk to his father when Mercy wasn't sure she'd see hers again. Tabitha could relate. She'd only really known Dr. Mathews for the past six months, yet her gut still twisted at seeing a mother who genuinely cared about her children.

What had gone wrong with hers?

She fiddled with Taryn's knife, pretending to inspect its intricate blade, scorched from Taryn's time in her prime.

"Are you scared of him?" Mercy asked quietly, breaking once again into the silence.

Tabitha opened her mouth to scold her, but she found herself curious, her eyes drifting to Ray.

"No," Ray said defensively. "I'm *not* afraid of him. How could I be afraid of someone who I haven't seen in ten years? Someone who *left* ten years ago? Left behind four kids, and one of them happens to be screwed up with his monstrous abilities."

"Ray, you're not screwed up," Cole said.

Is that how your brothers view you? Do Clarence and Lucas think you're a screw up?

"No? Well then, I'm some sort of monster. Out of all of us, I'm the one who inherited his abilities. I'm the most like him." He tore his fingers through his hair. "And I don't want to be like him! I don't want to leave because I put everyone in danger like he did!"

Tabitha's heart leapt. *I don't want to be like him.*

You don't want to be like *her.*

"You-you aren't, Ray," was all she could manage to stammer, trying to pull herself away from her own thoughts.

"I am his son."

You're her *daughter. Her third child.*

STOP. THINKING.

But unlike Ray's father, you left *her. How does that make you better than her?*

"Ray!" Cole's shout pulled Tabitha back to reality.

He grabbed Ray's shoulders with a jerk. "I'm his son too! I'm the reason he left you. So he could protect *me*. I don't know why they had to do it the way they did, but *I'm* the reason he left you alone. If there's anyone you should be angry at, it's me!"

Cole was out of breath. He squeezed his younger brother's shoulders. "Ray, I'm the monster who took your father."

Cole's words shattered the voice in her mind, and Tabitha clung to the drop of silence.

She held onto every word of Cole's strong, controlled voice as he held Ray's trembling shoulders.

Ray squeezed his eyes shut, shaking his head, leaning into Cole. "No," his voice cracked. "No, it's not you."

Cole wrapped his arms tightly around Ray.

The room was quiet, the fire crackling as the storm raged outside. Tabitha pulled her knees to her chest, feeling that twist in her gut grow tighter.

"Mercy's right," Ray said softly. "I'm terrified."

They all sat in the silence of the storm, Ray and Cole side by side by the fire. Mercy didn't say another word, her eyes fixed to the floor with only a few occasional glances.

Tabitha turned away, trying to force herself to sleep.

She loved Cole, but Ray needed him right now. Another way she needed to figure her own things out. That's what she loved about him. He had an ability to take care of others like no other.

He was a good brother. He and Ray had a good relationship. They wouldn't ghost each other for months on end and abandon each other once things got tense.

Why on earth did she miss her brothers now?

No matter how much she tried to force it from her mind, her nightmares would always remind her that she could never outrun the hatred in her own blood.

She was her own monster.

Felicity watched the clouds slowly lighten with anticipation.

The hours had been eventful. She had spread out the paper at her desk under the window, setting out the paint holder device her younger sister had sent her months prior on the window sill.

Her skill, she thought, had been improving since her shaky paint job attempt on her spear. In University, it had all been in a digital format, and the chaos of the Oquelite and Shadow Soul hadn't given her much time to continue her practice.

Slowly, she'd been working on painting her wheelchair when the pain made it too hard to sleep.

But right now, it was more than cute doodles of flowers. She had a mission. A purpose.

No one had assigned it to her, but once Nikki and Matteo began submitting locations to the group chat, she knew she could make herself useful. They needed a map.

The Northwestern regions were large and easy to paint for the most part. North Cordell, Algery, Midventern, Elery, Isledowle, Imperial, Glorgory, Sulfur, Liberty, Norris, Kennedy, Court Illegia.

She had finished the yellow frame of Algery, glancing over at the rough sketch at the Eastern Regions across the sea.

She knew it would've been more reasonable to paint those first. Matteo had a point when he said the Exerticus wouldn't suspect them to go there. So far, the Council hadn't traveled past the cluster of regions on their Continent.

Felicity herself had only visited Boli when she was ten on a family vacation that turned out to be, in reality, a business trip to get her father tighter relations to the land transport central there. Regardless, that was the only region Felicity knew of the Eastern regions.

And the thought of crossing the ocean…being so far away from anywhere she called home…it felt intimidating. Matteo had booked the tickets a few days ago with Taryn's approval for the road trip, and now they might a serve a much more important purpose—

"Are those blobs supposed to be something?"

Felicity cried out, whirling around, her brush flying from her hand and smacking Officer Armstance Giles right in the face.

"Ah! Jeez, Bentsworth!" Giles stumbled back, scrubbing the paint from his face, only making it worse.

"Serves you right," Felicity said, trying hard not to smile. "What gave you the idea to sneak up on me?"

"I knocked."

"Oh really?"

"Yes," Giles huffed, crossing his arms, though his scowl lost nearly all intimidation from the yellow smudge across his face. "I was sent by the—"

"Let me guess, Taryn?" Felicity glanced at the paintbrush on the floor. "Can you grab that for me?"

Giles sighed, scooping it up and handing it over. "Your friend, Lopez, actually."

Felicity turned back and dipped her brush into her glass. "When did you start taking orders from Matteo?" she teased.

"Look, he can be very demanding when he wants to be."

Felicity raised a suspicious brow. "Or you did it voluntarily, perhaps?"

Giles was quiet a moment, but the rare blush in his face gave him away.

Felicity's frown deepened. "Do you *want* us to do this? You're team pro-road trip?"

Giles opened his mouth, trying to defend himself before he gave up with a sigh. "Look, 'road trip' aside, I don't think that Aguarious kid is safe in any region here."

Giles sank into a seat beside her at the desk.

She watched his dark Aviduous eyes as they examined her maps. "Not just from the Exerticus…"

Felicity blinked, her heart stammering. "Defenders?"

Giles turned to meet her face. "Look, Bentsworth. There are people I've gotten involved with who'd be happy, no…- more than happy, *exhilarated* to see that little boy and Aguirre dead in an execution room."

Execution room? Felicity's heart plummeted.

She should've known. She knew there were a fair number of political figures who had mixed feelings on them.

"What does Nikki have to do with this?"

"What do our new tiny Aguarious and our Aguirre have in common?" Giles said, as if it was plain as day.

Felicity frowned. "They both appear to be from the South West regions…Uh, their eyes are kinda different? I don't know. They—" Then it struck her.

"They're both illegal full-bloods."

"Took you long enough," Giles snorted.

"But Taryn…the Council. I thought…"

"It's not going to matter. People in high places believe full-bloods are dangerous and against human nature. And some will go to great lengths to see to that."

"Such as…murder?" The thought was horrible. Felicity knew it was right. "Because they've tried doing it before," she said, softly.

"I would do anything to know how our little Aguirre survived," Giles said. "If someone knew they'd failed to kill the Aguirre, your friend would be done for. They'd be sending all their personal Agents for Nikki and that toddler too. There is someone in the Department who's made it their personal mission to kill all full-bloods."

"Who are you insisting we should be so afraid of?" Felicity said. She wished Giles would quit being cryptic. She could tell by the look in his eyes he was begging to tell her something. This was so unlike him. He was always brash and direct.

"I legally can't tell you," he spat out. "Or I'll be in an Execution room with a bloody snapped neck or a needle in my wrist before you know it."

Felicity couldn't breathe, trying to force away the taunting images that quickly rose into her mind.

She stared at him in silence.

Giles' eyes widened, before his face softened. "I-I'm sorry, Bentsworth. I shouldn't have said that," he said, quietly. His hand flinched near hers.

"You can touch my hand."

"That wouldn't be right." Giles pulled back. "I'm your protector."

She grabbed his hand back from it, squeezing it. "And my friend, stupid."

He rolled his eyes, ignoring her as she refused to let go of his hand, flapping it around playfully. He removed a chip from his pocket, sliding it to her. "Trial 270. You'll get an answer there…and you drew Manifest wrong."

She dropped his hands, glaring at her outline of Giles' home region. "Look, borders of islands are hard. You think you can do better?"

She was almost disappointed when Giles got to his feet. "Nah, you're the artist here, and you better get to Lopez. I'm sending you my aunt's Manifest address just in case."

"You can't stay longer?"

"I've got border patrol with—" His voice dropped to a grumble. "—Outown."

"Oh, Miriam isn't that bad."

"She's got one eye and an ego to replace it."

"I bet that hurts *your* ego real bad."

He glared at her.

Felicity laughed back. "You know I'm your favorite."

He scoffed, crossing his arms. "Whatever you want to believe, Bentsworth."

She took a clean brush and threw it at him as he left the door. "Hey!" His smirk escaped his scowl. He picked up the brush. "You're never getting this back."

Felicity simply laughed as he left the room. She only felt at ease for a moment before the loneliness dawned on her, and Giles' warning echoed back.

They had other enemies to worry about.

She washed off her brush, setting it on the window sill and then wiping her hand off on her pant leg. She picked up her tele and rolled out of the room.

The Inn wasn't the most wheelchair-friendly place, and finding the kitchen and living room empty wasn't a good sign.

It meant they were *downstairs*.

Felicity groaned, tapping her headband to power it on.

She plugged in the chip, tapping *Trial 270*.

To her surprise, a Defender document was tucked under the third result. Of course, that was probably in part thanks to Lincoln helping hack a few private Department sites into their net feed.

"*Department V. Aguirre'* titled the page neatly. Felicity scrolled down further.

Charge: Conception of an illegal full-blood in deliberate, known attempt to break the established post-EarthShaker laws.

A harsh claim to say that Reyna and Lyell had intentionally had a full-blood, something they had no control over. Who would even go as far to claim that?

Proposal: Termination of full-blood, and higher-blooded fathering component.

Felicity's stomach felt sick. She knew Nikki's life had been on the line, but Lyell's? Nikki's father? The beloved Defending Agent? Who would've ever suggested such a thing? Something so sick and lowly?

    Plantiff: Executive Cadissa Dean.

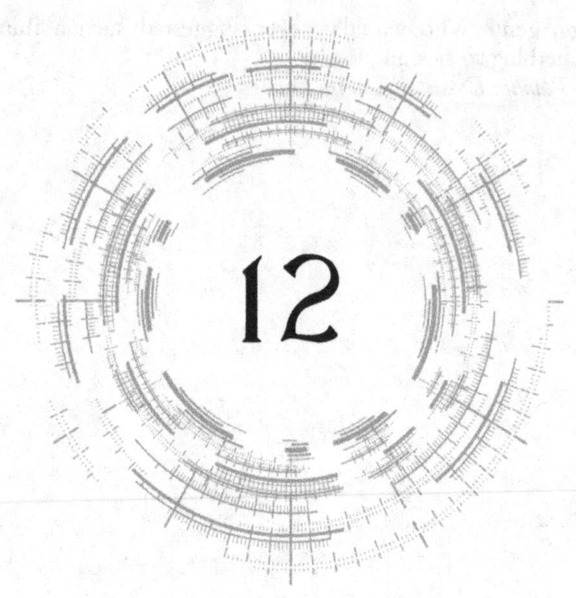

12

"¿Qué nombre le vas a poner?" Matteo looked up from his tablet to Nikki.

Their road trip planning session that morning had been surprisingly productive...with only a few arguments and mishaps. Taryn had allowed them to keep the little boy on the steps of the back porch, wrapped up in blankets as he slept.

"Nombre?" Nikki repeated the word under her breath.

"Name," Matteo clarified.

In the past few months, Matteo had been attempting to teach the Council to speak a little of his first language. Some were picking it up better than others. Ray was confident, but couldn't actually say words to save his life. Lawrence's pronunciation was horrendous, but he tried. Felicity acted as if she was awful, but she was probably the best of all of them, having taken classes in her school years.

Nikki's father spoke the language fluently...but she couldn't even remember his face most days.

She repeated the word under her breath. Nikki watched

the little boy, feeling the strange memories try to creep back. "He sleeps an awful lot."

"That's because he's getting over a Fever," Ray said, scooting by on a tool cart, his grocery store uniform soaked. "And Cole better be grateful. I cleaned that truck *and* myself."

Nikki glanced to Cole's truck parked behind the Inn. After the old one had been destroyed, the vehicle had been his pride and joy…and despite being in the muddy, rural terrain, was still in near perfect condition.

"Do you think we could ask him his name?" Nikki said, circling around the basket.

"I don't think that's how it works," Ray said, getting up to join her. "I wonder if he ever had one…."

"Well, maybe we can name him," Matteo said, tucking his tablet under his arm.

"Hey!" Lincoln scoffed, rolling out from under the truck, oil smeared on his cheek. "You're naming him without me?"

"Oh right, we can't forget his 'mama.'" Ray teased.

Lincoln jumped to his feet, wiping the oil from his hands to his jeans and rushing over. He shoved Ray.

"How do you name people?" Nikki asked, crouching down to examine him.

"I've never had children," Ray shrugged.

"Whoa. Hold up. Who's having children?" Lawrence walked out the back door of the Inn and down the steps, already dressed in his Defender gear for his shift, a box under his arm.

"We're naming the kid."

"That…that makes a lot more sense." Lawrence moved down the steps. "I named Charles."

"You did?" Nikki spun around.

Lawrence nodded, clearing his throat uncomfortably under the stares. He tossed the box into the back of the truck. "That's my stuff. No one touch it."

"So, how'd you do it?"

Lawrence pursed his lips, quiet for a moment. "Well, after Miz had him, he was basically left in my and Isabel's care. He didn't have a name for a while, but we went for Charles because of the meaning."

"The meaning?"

"It meant 'free.'"

"I'm named after my mom's brother," Ray shrugged. "So, that's not that cool."

Nikki perked up. Taryn had told her back when they'd made the whole Aguirre revelation that Nikki had most likely been named after her father Lyell's stepfather: Nikolas.

"Who would we name him after?"

"Tabitha Jr."

Ray groaned as Tabitha popped out the back door. She'd left for a moment to refill her bucket. "Aw, what? You don't like that name?"

"Disgusting."

"Okay, so naming him after someone probably isn't an option," Lincoln sighed.

"How about you?" Nikki said.

"Uh…naming him Lincoln? No thanks."

"No. I mean, how did you get *your* name?"

"That's a good question," Lawrence frowned. "Did you pull a Nikki and forget everything but your name?"

Lincoln rubbed the back of his neck. "I-um…I named myself after a street."

"Wait, you mean you had all the names in the world to choose from for *yourself* and you chose a street?" Ray frowned. "Not something cool like Your Royal Majesty of Arrows?"

Lincoln rolled his eyes. "Look. It was simple, and it was right there. Names weren't like my number one priority."

Streets. Nikki tilted her head, studying the little boy's face. "Nathaniel," she whispered.

"Neil? That's kinda a weird name for a little kid," Ray said.

Lincoln knelt down beside her. "Nathaniel," he repeated. "I like it."

"I thought you didn't like the kid," Lawrence scoffed.

"Doesn't mean I want him to have a lame name!" Lincoln said, quickly scrambling to his feet, his face flushing.

"Nathaniel's…alright." Tabitha shrugged. "It doesn't really roll off the tongue, but I guess it works."

"What if we called him Greg?"

"How is that better?"

"I don't know. He kinda looks like a Greg!"

"How in the world does he look like a Greg to you?"

The back door burst open, Felicity barreled down the steps, nearly knocking Lawrence over. Her face was flushed red, her eyes darting every which way, and paint still stained her fingers.

Nikki's heart leaped, as she dropped her mail bag and rushed to support her, everyone else running to her a heartbeat later.

The toddler, Nathaniel, woke up with a small cry, instantly trying to free himself from his blanket prison. Lincoln scooped him up.

"What's wrong?" Lincoln said, pushing through.

"Wrong," came the little boy's voice, his little hand popping out of the blanket.

Nikki helped Felicity sit down on the concrete step. Felicity stopped to catch her breath, massaging where her leg braces met her knees.

"Are you okay?" she asked quietly.

Felicity paused, touching Nikki's arm gently, staring at her for a long moment before turning to the rest of them. "The Defenders. The kid."

"Yeah? Didn't we already talk about how the Defenders would be mad if they found out about a full-blood?"

"No, no," Felicity shook her head, out of breath. "It's worse. Giles…Giles warned me about exactly who." Felicity ran her fingers through her hair. "Someone who will stop at nothing to kill the illegal full-bloods…." Her eyes locked on Nikki again. "…Someone who'd almost succeeded before."

Everyone was quiet.

Felicity handed Nikki the tablet.

Nikki's eyes widened. "Commander Dean…tried to kill me," she said quietly.

Even the wind seemed to have gone still.

Nikki tried to keep her thoughts from spinning out. It shouldn't have been shocking. It was obvious. Dean hated fullbloods. Dean hated Taryn, which in turn meant she probably hated the Curatrix Team.

The woman leading the Defenders hated *her.*

"D-does she know?" Nikki asked. What would she do? Would they try to kill her again if they knew? Could she prove them wrong?

"Giles seemed to think she doesn't…but something's changed." Felicity grasped Nikki's hand.

Nathaniel changed.

"But even if she knew about Nikki, the only record of the Aguirre's eldest child is that they're *dead*," Ray said. "There's no way she could."

Nikki looked around, her sweat growing colder at her friends' unconvinced faces.

"Right?"

"The best we can do is hope so," Lawrence said. "Only more reason to continue the plan."

Everyone could agree on that.

Nikki nodded, pushing a smile onto her face. Why, of all times, would Giles hint at this?

"Meet you all tonight then," Lawrence said, with a small dramatic salute before rushing back inside. Nikki could see the coldness in her cousin's face. As much as he tried to hide it, she could tell he was worried.

And if Lawrence was worried…then it was serious.

While the others dispersed, Lincoln stayed behind, not saying a word. Just watching.

"Do you need help getting to your ride?" Nikki asked, turning to Felicity.

Felicity shook her head with a shaky breath. "I'll be fine."

Nikki and Lincoln exchanged glances, but Felicity pushed herself up by Nikki's shoulder. She adjusted her headband, tightening a brace around her knee. She looked back at the two of them. "And if anyone asks…don't say Giles was involved. He said he wasn't supposed to tell anyone."

"Since when did Giles do what other people told him?" Lincoln said.

"Since they threatened to kill him, apparently," Felicity said in a small voice.

Nikki's eyes widened. "What?"

"I don't know, and I don't want to know." She took another deep breath, tucking a tuft of hair behind her ear. "Stay safe."

"Stay alive," Lincoln said, offering to help her again, but she rejected it.

Felicity walked off, with a small glance over her shoulder to Nikki before disappearing around the corner.

"Do you want me to walk you to the post office?" Lincoln said, turning on his heel to Nikki.

"Don't you have to be at the camp soon?"

"Taryn called me out for 'other duties,'" Lincoln sighed, glancing down to the boy who had now freed himself from the bonds of his blanket and was chewing on the tail of his green stuffed animal.

Nikki still hadn't figured out what creature it was.

"I guess there's no harm in it. He's already looking better."

"And fresh air might do him some good, right Nat?" Lincoln said, looking down to the toddler at his hip.

The little boy tilted his head. "Nat?" He reached out his slobbery hand for Lincoln's face.

"No, no, no." Lincoln swatted his hand away. "You're Nat, I'm Lincoln."

"Mama?"

"Linc-oln."

"Linc!"

"Yeah! There you go!"

Nathaniel beamed at himself.

"We have to keep Nathaniel safe," Nikki said, turning to Lincoln and beginning to walk around the Inn toward the driveway. "From Cadissa Dean."

"I'm hoping we have time before she finds that out," Lincoln said with a hoarse laugh. "What's that lady's problem with fullbloods anyway?"

Nikki shrugged. "No idea."

"She's probably jealous of your epic abilities," Lincoln said with a nudge and a smile.

"I don't have any abilities."

"Not *yet*." Lincoln tapped his temple. "In due time."

Matteo and Lawrence were the only Impure Council Members with broken essence and functional abilities so far. Something about the idea of having her own powers felt childishly exciting, but also terrifying.

She'd always relied on her fists and her shield.

She felt content with that. And she certainly didn't want abilities if it meant that some Commander would be after her.

"You too, right?" Nikki said.

Lincoln paled. "I-I guess…maybe."

"Was it 'epic?'" she asked. She knew it was a sensitive topic in the way Lincoln winced. He'd only told her briefly that Kathryn had offered him his abilities early in exchange for his name.

"I guess it was," he said quietly, his eyes on his feet. "But the timing wasn't right. Power should be earned, not given."

That made sense enough.

"You'll earn it," she said, placing a hand on Lincoln's shoulder.

He looked up. "*We'll* earn it."

Nikki smiled, and it felt real.

Together. That's all she wanted.

"Linc?"

Nathaniel reached over and tugged on Nikki's sleeve. His big, sea green eyes looked up to her with a small frown.

"Nah, that's Nikki," Lincoln said, shifting Nathaniel to his other arm.

Nikki couldn't tear her eyes from the little guy as he watched her from behind his little stuffed animal.

She gave a shy wave and he buried his face into the toy.

"Nik, be careful," Lincoln said. "It looks like there might be construction coming up."

Lincoln grabbed Nikki's bag strap, jerking to the side.

"Ah!" Nathaniel cried out, clinging to Lincoln's jacket and looking up to him with betrayed eyes.

"They're actually working on the road?" Nikki's heart jumped with excitement as she craned her head to see the orange holographic lights in the distance.

"It's nice to see the regions being put back together," Lincoln sighed. "Especially after all the chaos that's gone down."

Nikki could relate. Six months had been a good time to put the pieces back together.

They turned the corner, and suddenly Nathaniel began to squirm in Lincoln's arms. "No, no!"

"Hey, what are you doing?"

Lincoln switched sides, hoping to satisfy the little boy, but Nathaniel remained unpleased. "No," he said bitterly, looking up into Lincoln's eyes.

"You're not hurting my feelings if that's what you're try-ing to do." Lincoln gave Nathaniel the same look back at him. "Your cuteness doesn't apply to me."

"So you admit he's adorable?" Nikki smirked.

"No," Lincoln said quickly. "I'm not inflating his ego."

"He's two."

They turned over into the next street, which was bustling with the early weekend crowds.

"No, no, no," Nathaniel said, trying to squirm away again.

"Dang, Nat. What's wrong? I don't understand children!" Lincoln held out Nathaniel, his eyes narrow as they studied the squirming toddler.

"Don't panic," Nikki said. What could be wrong? Nathaniel had been fine just a moment ago.

A woman suddenly screamed behind them, her grocery slipping from her hand. Nikki spun around, skidding on the ground, the bag landing safely in her arms.

Underneath her, the concrete trembled. It was subtle, but ominous.

She slowly got back up to her feet, looking down to the sidewalk, where a crack was slowly growing.

She looked up, eyes wide to the woman. "Here you go," she said, faking a smile.

The woman grabbed her bag and ran off.

"Lincoln, the sidewalk!"

"One second! I'm dealing with an angry baby!"

The crowd began to slowly panic. Someone whipped out their tele. The ground continued to shake, the concrete slabs beginning to slide apart and…

…water shot up from the ground.

The crowd screamed, someone cheered, but Nikki was too shocked to move as dirty water soaked her.

Another pipe burst through the sidewalk a few feet away.

A lid to the sewer exploded open, an auto swerving out of the way and crashing into the traffic bot on the side of the road.

It was chaos like Nikki had never seen before.

"A Purizie!" someone screamed.

"An Oquelite?" Nikki panicked, dropping into a stance and bracing her fists. She didn't have a weapon on her. That was fine. She was training with Taryn. She could take down an—

Her jaw dropped as her eyes settled on a stream of water dancing in the air, weaving over the roof of the store.

That wasn't the weirdest part.

Inside a bubble, floating happily, was Nathaniel's green stuffed animal.

Nikki was unable to blink as she slowly turned around to see Nathaniel, face now lit up, his hands now reaching out as the bubble slowly made its way to him.

It popped, the stuffed animal dropping into Nathaniel's arms. He hugged it tightly with a small squeal.

Nikki's jaw dropped, looking to Lincoln, hoping he'd seen the same thing.

His face was pale, frozen as he stared at Nathaniel. "Did-did he just…?"

"Look!" Nathaniel slapped Lincoln in the face with the stuffed animal excitedly, beaming proudly at himself.

Lincoln shook himself out of his shock, holding Nathaniel tighter. He took a nervous step back.

Nikki turned around, swallowing hard, looking back over the split-open sidewalk, crashed auto, and broken pipeline waterfalling out of the road.

The world felt too eerily quiet.

The chaos of the street was all too knowing. Glances flickered in their direction.

Lincoln pulled up his hood, cursing.

"We have to get out of here."

Nikki didn't argue, following Lincoln back down the alleyway.

The two didn't exchange a word the entire way to the Inn. They broke off the dirt road, running through the fields till they met the dirt lot in the back of the Inn.

All the Council Members were gone. The truck lay abandoned.

Nikki pushed ahead of Lincoln, running up the steps and swinging open the back door.

Her heart dropped.

In the empty kitchen stood the Defenders, Dr. Mathews, and worst of all, Taryn watching over a Scroll laid out on the counter.

Taryn looked up, her eyes like daggers as her unreadable

gaze pierced them while they shut the door behind them.

They stood in silence.

What was there to say? How in the world did Nikki even begin to explain? They were Council Members. They were training to avoid disaster.

She stepped forward, forming a puddle on the door, still soaked from the burst pipe.

"Nath— the toddler," she started, clearing her throat. "He can control water. He-his essence…it's already broken."

Taryn heaved a sigh, standing up.

She picked up the Scroll, turning it around to play a shaky video. Nikki's sweat went cold as she saw herself scramble back as the water shot out from the split sidewalk and the bubble formed over the tiny toddler.

"We know."

13

"TABITHA, DO WE really need fireworks?"

"You guys are so boring! Fireworks would be such a cool distraction!" Tabitha said, holding up her two proudly-purchased purple fireworks in the kitchen. "Apparently, since something terrible is probably going to happen."

"Look. Nothing bad's going to happen," Felicity said, as she rolled back and forth in her chair, her fingers tearing through her long red hair. She didn't want anything bad to happen. "Oh gosh. This is exactly what Giles was warning me about!"

It had been over two days since the incident and so far, Felicity had been right.

Nothing bad had happened. The video quickly disappeared from the Net, and Taryn had basically banned Lincoln from taking Nathaniel outside.

"The video footage was cruddy quality anyway," Cole said, refilling his coffee cup. He'd stopped by that afternoon to drop off the final supplies for the road trip, which Taryn was finally becoming more weary about.

The door to the girls' hall creaked open. Mercy slipped out for a moment, only catching Nikki's eye for a second before rushing to the steps.

"Mercy?" Felicity quickly turned around, but the girl was already gone.

Felicity sighed. "I've hardly seen her the past few days."

Mercy had hardly been involved in the road trip preparations. Anytime she *did* see her, it was a mandatory Taryn meeting or the other night when they'd accidentally run into each other leaving and entering the shower room.

Felicity had tried so hard to be welcoming to her.

"Are you sure you can get the package of echo bits today?" Cole asked Nikki. "I don't want you to work later than you already do."

Nikki shrugged. "I should be fine."

The coffee in Cole's cup slowly began to rise, forming into a bubble.

"Uh, Cole…"

Cole groaned, trying to trap the bubble in his mug before it exploded in his face. "Where's the toddler?"

"Right here!"

Lincoln stumbled through the door, alongside Matteo and Ray. All three were soaked.

"You'd think he'd be better about baths," Matteo said, shaking the water from his hair.

"Taryn says he might be getting restless," Lawrence sighed, walking out behind them. "So much energy and so little space. Can't be good for the little guy."

"Don't worry. She's given me clearance to go the fields." Lincoln said like it was his saving grace as he hoisted the copper-haired toddler up onto his shoulders. Nathaniel struggled to find his hand in the oversized shirt. "No magical woods. No rivers. Just the fields."

"And what if you lose him?" Felicity lifted a brow. "He seems very capable of getting lost."

Ray snorted. "He literally hates being touched by anyone *other* than Lincoln. I doubt that will be a problem."

"Already thought of that." Lincoln swept Nathaniel down from his shoulders. The little boy squirmed as he got too close to Cole. Cole stepped back.

Lincoln untucked the fish tracker from around

Nathaniel's neck. "I found good use for it. And I can track it straight from the Cube."

Nathaniel picked up the fish pendant and stuck it in his mouth.

"I-it's also waterproof."

"And slobber-proof?" Felicity teased.

"I better get going," Nikki said, picking up her delivery bag from the ground. She headed for the door. "I'll see you all tonight. And I won't forget your package, Cole!"

"Yer okay with making the farm rounds yerself, girlie?" the mail truck driver called as Nikki hopped from the passenger side out onto the dirt road, her messenger bag heavy from the next few deliveries.

"I'll be fine," Nikki insisted. She'd done the farm rounds on her own a few times before, and she requested this round for a reason. The Hernandez farm was one of the last stops, but it would give her time to deliver her own package to Cole.

"Just radio in if it starts storming again," the driver said, looking out the window nervously, scratching his ragged beard. "If it's anything like last time, get yerself inside."

She nodded, thanking him as he drove off. She started down the road, her eyes focused on the stirring clouds above.

So many new words swirled in their own storm in her mind.

Leviathan. Aguarious. Nathaniel.

But what was causing it?

It felt like they had so many strings but nothing to tie them together with.

A Leviathan storm attack. A little boy with bright green eyes and powerful essence, who also happened to be a full-blooded Aguarious.

Everything seemed to point to Kathryn.

Nikki *wanted* it to point to Kathryn.

If she could just figure out why, it would make this all so much easier.

But no matter the cause of the storm, Defender or Exerticus, someone would be after Nathaniel sooner or later. The thought made Nikki shudder.

Nathaniel was still so young…so small. There was something so eerily familiar about the touch of his tiny hand. He even had a complexion like hers, and he was an illegal full-blood too. She wouldn't let his life end up like hers.

She tightened her grip on the strap of her bag.

Nikki would protect him from those people who wanted them dead. She would never understand people who were so eager to kill.

But she knew deep down, she could fight them.

She'd done it before, and she'd won.

She shook it off. She didn't want to think like that. She just wanted peace. Nothing required violence, right?

She broke out into a jog. She only had a few hours to beat the storm.

The usual rounds on the east side farms took an hour, with only light rain. Compared to the poorer, much more corrupt farming systems of the west side, the east side was quieter, and the lavish growing farmland brought a sense of peace as she walked.

She went up the steps of a whitewashed farmhouse, tapping on the door alert pad.

A few moments later, an older woman opened the door, wiping her wet hands off on her jeans. "My goodness," the woman said, heaving a sigh. "It's raining again?"

She looked back down at Nikki. "A package today?"

Nikki nodded, removing a heavy package wrapped in a sturdy brown plastic wrapping and handed it to the woman. The woman took it. "Thank y—"

She stopped, her eyes stuck on Nikki for a moment.

Nikki raised a brow. This didn't usually happen, except for the one time a farmer had insisted on questioning her scar.

Was the woman staring at her scar too?

Nikki suddenly itched to push her bangs down.

"Be safe out there," the woman said, clearing her throat and quickly backing up into the house, shutting the door.

Nikki blinked.

She tried not to think of it, heaving back out down the long dirt road. Had she seen the video?

She could just ask Cole for a ride back to the Inn if it got too dark, but she had to hurry. She removed her stylus from her pocket as she stepped out from the driveway, turning to walk alongside the road.

She crossed the address off on her tablet.

A slow grumbling sound vibrated through the air. Nikki frowned, looking up toward the sky. She'd never heard thunder like that before...maybe it was a new kind of storm?

She continued down her path, her brows deepening as pebbles began to quake on the road. She kneeled down, picking up one of the small stones.

A loud, harsh horn tore through the peaceful quiet of the countryside afternoon.

Nikki's heart dropped, and she dared to look over her shoulder.

There she saw enormous trucks. That was the only thing she could even compare them to. Their enormous boxy figures with clear white stripes and an all-too-familiar emblem engraved in the side.

Machines she'd only seen once before when Dow had visited eight months ago.

But these were bigger.

Louder.

More important.

Nikki's sweat went cold.

Now, the thunder did really shake the sky.

The rain began to fall again. Nikki's body finally caught up with her mind, and she dashed across the road, rolling into the low dip beside the road in the long wet grass. She pulled her Comm out of her pocket. She wasn't sure if it was the ground shaking or her hands.

She typed as quickly as she could with her hands slipping on the wet surface.

"DEFENDERS"

"ARE"

"HERE"

Her Comm slipped from her hand, landing in a puddle beneath her.

For a moment, everything was still. And then a large mechanical roar tore through the air. It was right there. Right next to her.

Nikki ducked, covering her head with her arms, pressing her face into her legs. The earth shook beneath her. She grit her teeth as the machine continued to cry destruction as it moved along.

Her Comm vibrated against the puddle.

Nikki dared to look up.

One word.

One message.

"Run."

Nikki knew she was running the wrong direction.

She was running right where that terrifying Defender machine was heading, but she didn't have time. She tore through the fields.

Who knew how long she had before they arrived and the storm picked up?

Why were they here? These looked like high-up Defenders. No ordinary Officers.

Her heart sank.

Had Giles *known*? Had he been trying to warn them of *today?*

Had they found out about Nathaniel?

She broke out of the corn field, rolling under the fence out into the wild grass field. The uncared-for grass cut at her bare ankles. She left behind her jacket, feeling her T-shirt and jeans, now soaked, clinging to her frame.

She jumped over a fallen log, nearly tumbling down the steep hill before reclaiming her balance. She could see the back of the Inn now.

Her heart seized in her chest.

The getaway auto was gone.

What if they left without her? *Guys! Anyone?*

What was the point of telepathic powers if no one responded?

It didn't matter now.

She reached the back concrete steps, pushing through the door with all her might. The door banged open, the kitchen employees jumping with a start.

"The Sergeant," Nikki gasped between breaths. "I-I need to see the Sergeant."

She didn't even see who said "Med-Bay." She just took off, not caring about her trail of mud or the stunned expressions of the residents as she burst down the hall.

She needed to get to Taryn.

She tripped over the MedBay step, quickly rolling back to her feet, coughing as she nearly collided into the Sergeant's arm.

Taryn grasped Nikki's shoulders, her eyes wide in surprise. "Nikki! Are you okay? What's going on?"

The word was frozen on her tongue. "D-Defenders," Nikki finally spat out, tears burning at her eyes and anger in her chest. "Defenders are coming."

Taryn froze, but only the slightest hint of surprise came in a raised brow.

Nikki's heart sank even further. So the rest of the Council really hadn't told Taryn they'd left.

"This can't be good," Taryn breathed. "I was sure all the files were kept on an incognito filter. You have to go, *now.*"

"But-but I can't go without you," Nikki said, stubbornly looking up into Taryn's eyes, and for once she could see them as clear as day. She could see, at least for a split second, at the right angle, the pale blue she'd always believed the infamous Jess in her mother's stories to have. "You have to come too."

Taryn pinched her lips together firmly. "Nikki, I can't."

Nikki felt the blood rush from her face. "You have to! If they find you here, they can—"

"They won't," Taryn squeezed Nikki's shoulders tighter. "They have no proof any of us have done anything wrong."

You don't know that.

Taryn's eyes glinted, and she placed a gentle hand against Nikki's face. "Nikki, if they find you, and what you really are…it's all over."

Nikki knew it was true. She wished she could just lean into the warmth of Taryn's hand, but she knew every moment she stood here was in vain. Every moment she stayed here, she put her friends in danger, everything her parents fought to preserve at risk, and Taryn in trouble, but all she could stammer was a frustrated "No."

"You don't have much time. Get Lincoln and leave."

They'd left without *Lincoln?* It was getting harder and harder not to be tempted to question the stupidity of the Council. That meant Nathaniel was still here. The whole point of all this!

He must've seen her massage too late when he was in the fields.

This made the situation levels more urgent.

Nikki held onto Taryn's eyes. "I don't want to say good-bye this time."

"Then don't." Taryn pulled Nikki into a hug. Nikki's heart leapt, only for a moment before melting into Taryn's embrace and squeezing her tight. "This isn't goodbye."

Taryn finally let go of Nikki, her gaze lingering for a little moment longer. "They'd be very proud of who you're becoming."

Nikki's face warmed. Would they really be proud of their daughter who'd been imprisoned and used as an experiment for nearly a decade, and couldn't even remember a thing about it? And the only way she'd escaped was with the help of an ancient talking rock? And was in a coma nearly for a month when her friends needed her most?

Nikki forced herself to speak up. "I think they'd be proud of Jessica too."

Taryn was still for a moment, her face unreadable at the use of her real name. She swallowed hard with a small nod.

"Now, go! You need to find somewhere safe for Nathaniel to stay. Somewhere he won't be in danger. Do you understand?" she ordered, straightening herself, heading for the door. "I'll deal with the Defenders."

Nikki obeyed, running from the MedBay, Taryn behind her. She couldn't waste a moment as she raced up the steps to the Council Quarters. "Lincoln!" she shouted up the steps.

"Nikki?" His voice echoed back.

She reached the top of the steps, Lincoln zipping up a backpack stuffed to the brim, Nathaniel sitting beside him on the couch, clinging onto a blanket wrapped around him.

"Where are the others?"

"We were all in different places when we got the warning," Lincoln said. "So everyone decided to meet by the river, on the road that's a straight getaway through the border of the region."

So they didn't abandon him. Good. Otherwise, Nikki had a word for the Council.

"Why didn't you go with the others?" Nikki said, trying

to keep herself from shouting. "You and Nathaniel are in the greatest danger."

Lincoln looked away, hoisting his bag up. He glanced back at her for only a split second before running for the stairs. "I couldn't leave without you. I don't know if we'll make it in this storm…especially if it gets as bad as last time."

She stared straight forward, her face hardening. "We'll make it. I just need to grab something."

She raced down the girls' hall, throwing the door open to her room. Her precious window had been blown open by the wind, rain pouring in. Nikki's heart twisted, but she didn't have time to waste. She grabbed the NMU file disc from off the nightstand, shoved it into her backpack, and ran back out to Lincoln. He was waiting impatiently on the steps, heaving bags weighing him down and Nathaniel practically tucked under an arm.

"Let me take him," Nikki said, holding out her arms.

Lincoln looked down at Nathaniel, but the toddler didn't look back, mesmerized on the rain banging against the window panes. Lincoln handed the little boy off, and to Nikki's surprise, Nathaniel didn't cry. His eyes were fixed on the storm behind him.

"Rain," he whispered, so gently that Nikki almost thought it was another memory. "Bad rain."

They tore through the kitchen, giving the crew their second heart attack of the evening before breaking through the back door into the storm.

Lincoln's Comm lit up as they ran. "They're moving further down the road for us!" he shouted over the wind. "By the mountain base!"

Nikki's stomach twisted. The goal was to get *away*, and they'd just drawn their friends closer to the danger.

She knew the route well. It was the exact route she'd taken running to the woods when this had all started a little over a year ago.

To her surprise, Nathaniel remained calm. No squirming, no crying. His eyes were simply wide, almost entertained by the chaos of the water falling from the sky.

They broke into a nearby aspen grove, a flash of lighting revealing the truck and trailer waiting near the bridge by the lazy brook.

Lincoln's Comm went off again.

"The Defenders are at the Inn!" Lincoln shouted.

Nikki hoped so.

Through the grass, she saw the small rickety bridge approaching. The sound of rushing water caused her heart to seize in her chest. She broke into the clear.

The lazy brook was no longer lazy.

It was deep, flooded from the storms, thrashing at the wind.

But she couldn't stop. She had to keep moving. She ran to the old bridge.

Before she could process what was happening, her foot slipped. She tried to catch herself, but her one free hand wasn't enough. The next she knew, she hit the ice-cold water.

And she couldn't feel Nathaniel.

She tried reaching for him. She opened her mouth, instantly regretting it. She needed to get to the surface. She needed to breathe. She needed to find him.

But she couldn't move.

Her body refused.

She couldn't breathe.

She was sinking.

Her mind was scrambling, coming to a horrifying conclusion as she thrashed at her watery captor:

She couldn't remember how to swim.

PART TWO

THE FUGITIVE

14

THE HORROR ONLY lasted a second before an arm wrapped around her. Her head was pulled above water, and she was dragged up the bank. She gasped, choking and coughing, her fingers clawing into the mud.

"Nik! Are you okay?"

Nikki's eyes widened, pushing herself to her feet and nearly stumbling over. "Nathaniel!" she screamed, rushing for the water.

"Nikki!"

"He's still there! He's still down there!"

Lincoln grabbed her, but Nikki struggled against him, sending an elbow to his face.

Lincoln cried out. "Nik! Calm down! Nik, he's alright!"

Nikki froze. Lincoln gently turned her around to see the little boy sitting in the mud, splashing at the puddle below him.

"H-how? He-he fell in!"

She fell in.

"I don't know," Lincoln gave a shuddering breath. "I

found him perfectly fine under the water. He didn't cry or anything."

He looked back to Nikki. "What about you? Are you okay?"

Was she okay? She felt her face warm as she turned to Lincoln. "I-I couldn't remember."

Lincoln frowned. "Remember?"

Nikki tangled her fingers through her hair. "I couldn't remember how to swim," she whispered, almost as if she didn't believe it.

She didn't want to believe it. She'd had difficulty regaining her ability to fight after the incident, and while Kathryn had messed with her memories during the two weeks she was out, she couldn't have imagined this.

Why swimming?

Lincoln wrapped a warm arm around her shoulder. "It's alright, Nik. I'm sure it was just the panic. We need to hurry. Come on."

It wasn't just the panic.

Nikki was certain of that. Her instincts always took over…but in that moment, it was like there was no instinct to begin with.

Lincoln picked up Nathaniel, Nikki still clinging to his arm as they ran toward the trailer. The door clicked open, multiple arms rushing to pull them inside.

The door was slammed shut after them, and everyone was sent tumbling to the ground as the vehicle lurched forward at full speed.

"Uh...who let our baby friend play mud monster?"

"Mud!" Nathaniel exclaimed gleefully, slapping his dirty hands.

Nikki looked to Lincoln, drenched from the storm and blood trickling from his nose.

Her heart lurched, reaching for his face. "Oh. I'm so sorry—"

Lincoln gave a tired, lifeless laugh. "It's alright, Nik."

Nikki's vision was blurred, and she didn't want to get up from the floor. What had come over her? She'd never hurt Lincoln like that.

She just wanted to curl up into a ball and clutch to the Stone hanging around her neck.

They were safe.

They were all safe.

Everyone except Taryn.

Taryn was alone to face a problem Nikki feared she had a part in creating. Just like that they had been thrust from their home, out to fend for themselves in a storm.

In less than an hour, everything had changed.

"So, our mission is to find the baby a safe home?"

Mercy instantly regretted speaking, realizing nearly every Council Member was now staring at her. All Members except for Lawrence, Tabitha, and Cole, who were thankfully in the truck that was pulling the trailer…but it didn't make it any better.

She instantly dropped to the floor with the rest of the Council Members. She scooted up beside Ray.

"Taryn makes a good point," Felicity said, giving Mercy an encouraging smile. "He isn't safe in North Cordell…and definitely not with us."

"I don't know. He might be more of a threat to those around him," Lincoln said. "I think he can breathe underwater."

"He is a full-blooded Aguarious," Felicity said, looking up from her Scroll device. "It would make sense."

That ability would've been useful when Mercy and Ray had been trapped in the lake that winter.

"He sure scared the living daylights out of Nikki," Mercy said.

Nikki hadn't said a word since they arrived. She'd simply washed herself, curled up in a blanket on the couch toward the back of the trailer, and fell asleep.

"Do you want to test this theory, Mercy?" Ray said, nudging her. "Sounds like a fun experiment with no potential moral consequences whatsoever. Dunk-the-baby-and-see-if-he-doesn't-drown-challenge!"

Mercy punched him the shoulder. Ray simply smirked.

"What if we dunk you?" Matteo piped up from the corner from under his quilt. Mercy could hear the grin in his voice.

"He's been hanging out with Lawrence too much." Ray sighed.

"Keep it up, 'Teo," Lincoln said.

"That might have to wait for another day," Felicity sighed, closing her paper pad. "If we're going to cross the ocean, we're going to need to be well rested."

Cross the *ocean*? No one had told her this was part of the escape plan.

Matteo got to his feet, his quilt secured around his shoulders. "I think we also need to be educated before we rest."

"Educated?" Lincoln frowned. "I thought we'd already learned enough words."

Matteo sighed. "*¡No interrumpas!*"

"What?"

"He said don't interrupt," Felicity whispered loudly. "You apparently haven't learned enough."

Mercy smiled, seeing Felicity's smirk. She wished she had Felicity's natural snark and confidence. She seemed to practically radiate with an effortlessly feminine fierceness Mercy couldn't explain, except for the spark in her eyes that glimmered occasionally.

Apparently, if Mercy was anywhere but the motel back home, she was a floundering awkward mess. But she was a Council Member now, and soon…somehow, she'd prove it to them.

"This is our new home, correct?" Matteo said, getting up onto the table, gesturing to the trailer.

It was a rather impressive size, considering Cole had bought it off a shady guy trying to sell it before leaving the region. It connected to the back of his truck. On the far side of the trailer were couches and a table that, when folded down, made a bigger bed. Currently, it was a mess full of bags, wet coats, and blankets. It passed the door and moved into the kitchenette and two booths, and a small door that broke off into a tiny bathroom. There was a small bedroom through the door, but no one had dared claim it as it was technically still Cole's. A loft also was tucked into the ceiling.

"I wouldn't start calling it home. What's your plan?" Ray said, raising a brow.

Matteo set his tablet down on the table, tapping it with two fingers and jumping down.

A hologram exploded from the screen, displaying a painting of a map.

"Felicity painted that," Ray whispered to Mercy.

How much cooler could she be?

"Our new goal is no longer vacation. It's finding Lincoln's baby a safe place to stay."

"He's not my baby," Lincoln grumbled, cradling Nathaniel closer.

"We're going to use the Tube to go to Manifest," Matteo said, swiping his hand across the hologram. "From there, we'll investigate the Manifest OHS—"

Lincoln gagged. "The Orphan Housing System? Really?"

"It's one of the most secure places on the planet," Felicity said. "And maybe being around normal kids will help his…water outbursts."

Mercy tightened the blanket around her shoulders, looking to Ray beside her, who was completely transfixed in the display. Putting him in an orphanage just felt *too* easy.

"If that doesn't work, we'll be heading to the Eastern Market," Matteo suggested. "Cole thinks it's a good idea to see if Cecileo and Echo Rueder are interested in taking him."

"I'm like 99% sure that Cole is an official Marketeer, which makes him a criminal," Ray whispered to Mercy.

She rolled her eyes.

"And then?"

"Well, I actually haven't figured that out yet." Matteo bit his lip. "I had more ideas before we realized he had literal supernatural powers."

"Fair point."

He clicked off the tablet. "I've contacted some safe houses with Lawrence and Cole's help too."

"Sounds like the beginning of a plan," Mercy said, trying to be encouraging as the pit in her stomach grew deeper.

Maybe this would go super well, and she wouldn't be forced to use her abilities.

The faster this was over, the sooner she could go back to hiding.

She was surprised they'd remembered her in the first place. The Council would've functioned just fine without her.

"Now it's really time for sleep," Felicity sighed.

Felicity snapped her fingers and the lights turned off.

In the relative quiet that followed, Mercy curled up on

one of the booths, hugging a quilt around her shoulders.

She didn't *want* to be insignificant. She'd grown up her entire life with her grandmother telling her she was too special to even go outside most days…and now she lived with nine others who were all best friends, and *also* part of this special group.

Her grandmother wanted to keep Mercy for her own legacy…and she apparently left out the whole "Council" part.

She had to figure out *where* her grandmother had even gotten that information about Felicity—

"Whatcha angry about, Remembrance?"

Mercy's heart leaped into her throat, and she turned around to see Ray staring at her from under the table, lying on the opposite booth seat. "What are you doing here?" she hissed.

"Uhh, we're in the same trailer? Not a lot of space."

She raised a brow at him, though she couldn't help but feel a tiny twinge of relief at having Ray close by. He felt like the only person she didn't have to worry about being disappointed in her. "Just don't be creepy and stare at me."

"Funny of you to assume you're worth staring at."

"Can you two be quieter?" Lincoln groaned.

Mercy smothered a laugh, her face burning.

Ray put a teasing finger to signal her to be quiet, which made her wish she had a pillow to throw. Instead, she lay on her back, taking in a deep breath.

"Were you thinking of him?" Ray whispered.

"Him?"

"Your-your dad?"

A knot formed in Mercy's throat, the brief moment of relief fading fast at the sharp reminder. Her father had been missing for over a year. Her grandmother insisted he left, but Ray and Mercy had reason to believe *she* had something to do with it. The Sergeant had even offered to look for him, which surprised Mercy, but the thought of her grandmother finding them scared her more.

"I always think about him," she said softly.

I always think about how I lost him. Maybe it was my fault…- somehow.

"Hey, maybe we'll come across something to help you

find him along the way."

Mercy let out a breath. "If she hasn't gotten to him already."

"Mercy, don't think like that. There's no way. You saw how easy it was to escape her once you activated Glow Girl mode. We could squish her like a grape, no problem."

She rolled her eyes. How did he have such a talent for making her want to smile? "Why are you so willing to help me with my father but not your own?"

Ray's face faltered. "That's different."

"It's not really."

"I know where my father is," Ray said, his voice growing even quieter. "And at least you *like* your dad."

"You haven't seen your dad since you were five."

"My point proven," Ray huffed.

From the crease between Ray's frustrated brows, Mercy knew there was more. It had nothing to do with this. They both knew full well that Ray's father had left to protect Cole.

"Look. At least you have a chance to save your dad," Ray said. "I think mine is too far gone."

"You don't know that. Cole doesn't think so."

"That's because Cole's not…me." Ray pursed his lips. "He doesn't have abilities that make him steal the power of people he kills."

Mercy's eyes widened in horror. "Rapheal…you think your father left because of *you*?"

She couldn't see his eyes, but she could hear the strain in his voice. "What other reason would he leave behind a wife and four children to fend for themselves? Why didn't he try and fight for us? Fight harder? Why didn't he even say goodbye?"

Ray squeezed his eyes shut, clinging his legs to his chest.

Mercy never felt so tempted to hug someone before, but she kept herself still.

"But this isn't about me," Ray said, hoarsely. "If I can help someone with their dad, I'm gonna do it, you know? So I want to help you."

He looked up. She could see his glassy eyes.

"Okay," she whispered. "You can help, but only if you promise me something."

"Oh, no."

"Hear me out."

"Mercy, I don't have any cheese crisps left."

"What? No. This has nothing to do with…whatever. Promise me you'll have one conversation with your dad. Just one. And if it sucks, I'll quit annoying you about it."

"Sounds more like a dare."

"Fine, I *dare* you."

"If you get to dare me, I should get to dare you." Ray narrowed his eyes at her. "I dare you to try and talk to more than three Council Members a day."

Mercy's heart dropped. "I— That's easy," she said, clearing her throat.

"Pfftt. We all know you avoid them like the Fever."

"I do not."

"You do too."

"Rapheal," Mercy scowled.

"Look. It's a mutual dare." He smirked.

As much as she wanted to hate him for that wicked smile, she still had to hold back a laugh. "Fine. I get to make short jokes if you lose though."

"Deal," Ray said.

"Stop flirting and go to sleep," Lincoln groaned from the floor.

"Oh, wow. Sorry, Mom."

"Ray I'm going to—"

"Quit it," Mercy sighed, feeling the tiniest pang in her chest…like she was a part of something, even if it was just a quarrel. "Just sleep."

Ray threw his sock at Lincoln. "Sounds like a good plan."

She closed her eyes, trying to focus on the sound of the road speeding below them and the whir of the air conditioner.

"Mercy?" Ray whispered quietly.

"What?"

"About my comment earlier. I don't actually think you're bad-looking."

Mercy felt a hopeful warmth in her chest as she rolled over, pulling the quilt over her shoulders. It was an unusual feeling. It made her happy, but it felt so wrong…so vulnerable.

Mercy didn't respond, her entire face feeling like it was on fire. Maybe if she could use this trip to find out more about her grandmother…maybe she could find more about her dad, and *then* impress the Council!

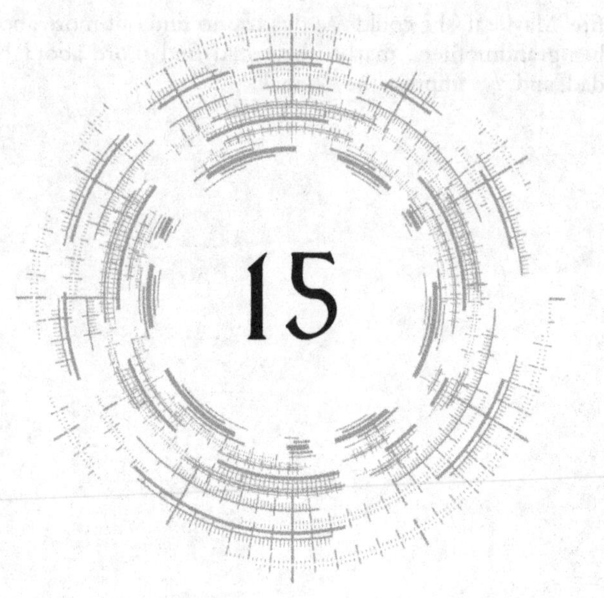

15

Mercy sat on the edge of her seat, for once her height seeming to be an advantage.

The Council, or what Members were left in the trailer, were crammed around Lawrence and Felicity's tele.

"Can you all take, like, a full step back?" Lawrence said to the bodies crammed around him. "We're going to freak her out if she has seven people staring as soon as I open the call."

Everyone reluctantly obeyed.

"So we finally get to meet this person you've talked about?" Lincoln said.

"Yes, and don't make a fool of us," Lawrence said.

"That's difficult," Tabitha snorted.

She'd even left the truck for this, leaving Cole to drive alone. Mercy had considered joining him, but the intrigue was too great…and being stuck with Cole alone just felt awkward.

Lawrence took a deep breath and pressed the *accept* button glowing on the screen.

The call loaded for a moment before the face of a woman appeared on the tele. She wore a beige veil that covered her hair and the same necklace Mercy had seen before.

So this was one of those Believers Sader and Trinity back in Kennedy had been talking about.

"Quite the crowd you have there," the woman laughed with a small wave. "I'm Sister Lillian, and you must be the Council that's been causing quite the stir."

Lincoln groaned. "What has Lawrence told you?"

"Oh no. It's not just Lawrence. Word gets around quickly. You must be Lincoln, the Aviduous, but I'm…less familiar with the little guy there."

Lincoln's face reddened. Nathaniel sat on his lap, more interested in chewing on his little stuffed monkey's ear than the tele.

"This is Nathaniel," Lawrence said. "He's actually the reason we're calling."

"Sadly, I'm not really an expert on children…"

"He's not just a child," Felicity said. "He's the Aguarious Council Member."

The woman's eyes opened wider. "I'm sorry. That child…is a Council Member?"

"We have quite a lot of reason to believe so," Lawrence sighed. "He practically ripped a waterline through the street, all for a stuffed monkey."

"Heaven help you," the Sister sighed. "That was not what I was expecting. I thought when Zita died, it would surely be a long time before another Aguarious full-blood was born…yet here we are."

"Zita?" Nikki perked up. "Zita Klirkpatrick? The Curatrix Team member?"

Sister Lillian nodded fondly. "I never met her, but Father Cruz always said the Aguirres spoke very kindly of her. She was apparently a very gentle soul, especially for children, and was very involved in trying to reform the Orphan Housing System."

Mercy caught a small smile on Nikki's lips, as if even the smallest mention of the Curatrix Team comforted her. Mercy didn't know much about Lawrence's friendship with the nun from Algery, but she did know Taryn had given him strict instructions not to mention the fact Lawrence and

Nikki were related to the Curatrix Team.

Mercy wanted to slink away from the tight group, but Ray was watching her. She scowled, remembering the dare. Be social.

"Right," Lawrence said. "Okay, so basically, we're trying to find a place Nathaniel will be safe until we can handle our…problems on our own. And we also have reason to believe he's related to something called the Leviathan, an Aguarious sea monster…a codename from possibly a Believer group?"

The Sister's face paled. "The Founder Association?"

"You've heard of it?"

"I've been warned of it," Sister Lillian said, clasping her hands and pressing her lips together firmly in thought. "It's a bad representation of what we set out to do, though I do think they have the best of intentions. I think they began to fall apart a few years back after they leaked information to a sketchy woman from Kennedy."

Mercy's blood went cold. A woman from Kennedy? Leaked information? "Do you happen to know her name?"

The woman looked up, seeming surprised to see Mercy peeking through. "Well, I can't really recall it. It was a very…unique name. In fact, I don't believe I thought it was a name on first hearing it."

"Oh, that's definitely your evil grandma," Ray whispered.

Virtue Faithful, Mercy's grandmother, had a very unusual name. Not that Mercy Remembrance was much better.

Of course her grandmother was part of some creepy organization using sketchy methods to find out information about the Council.

That's probably where she learned about Felicity!

"So you think the Shadow Soul is using the…sea monster to create a storm?"

Now that Mercy said it out loud, it did sound a little strange.

"Yes. And that she'll need an Aguarious to control them," Lawrence said. "And we still have the upper hand. Kathryn, for as much as we know, has no idea Nathaniel exists."

"I would say keep it that way," Sister Lillian said. "An Aguarious could only make the storms worse. In fact,

Lawrence, I could send you some coordinates to a fellow Believer research facility in Boli if you're interested. I'm sure they'd be able to help you further, and they might even provide shelter for your little friend."

"That would be amazing," Lawrence said.

"How would someone find the Association?" Mercy perked up.

The whole Council went quiet.

Her face flamed. *Congrats, Mercy. You just asked how to find this creepy, evil group. How awesome!* "Just curious. Maybe...- maybe it would be helpful."

"Well, since the Association allegedly disbanded, I'm not sure it's even possible. But it was always said that if you brought them something of the Council's and turned your Comm signal on and inverted, they'd find you eventually."

Something of the Council's? Like her sandal?

"They were collecting Impure artifacts?" Lincoln said, his eyes widening.

Mercy didn't really understand the whole artifact thing. Apparently, they were ancient materials created by the various Impure races, like Cole's medallion or Ray's sword.

"Most definitely. The Impure artifacts contain incredible power. And it would explain their ability to know things no one should."

"Thank you for your help," Lawrence said. "This is a lot of good information."

"Always and whenever, Lawrence." The Sister smiled kindly. "Just let us know if there's anything I can do."

"Of course. We'll be in touch."

With that, Lawrence ended the call. "So basically we just learned what we already know," he groaned. "I hate this."

"Hopefully that location she sends you will help," Felicity said, setting a gentle hand on Lawrence's shoulder. "We do need more places for Nathaniel to stay."

Mercy tuned them out, slinking toward the booth near the window.

Ray practically pounced on the seat beside her. "Why were you asking about how to contact the Association?"

Mercy's heart nearly leaped out of her chest as she shushed him. "It's for the plan? Maybe they know more about Keypers!"

And maybe she could finally figure out how to really use her powers!

Ray raised a suspicious brow. "Look, Glow Girl. I don't know if contacting them is a good idea. My mom said they were bad news."

"And so is Grandmere," Mercy said. "Don't you think the Council will be happy to know?"

"Know what? There's nothing we need to know from them."

But *Mercy* needed to know. She needed to find out how to glow.

"Mercy?"

She turned to meet Ray's eyes.

"Please don't try and contact them. It's not worth getting hurt for. It's crazy."

Even Ray thought her idea was ridiculous? She bit the inside of her lip. "You're right."

"You're *agreeing* with me?" he frowned. "Are you sure you're the same Mercy?"

"Don't worry about it, Rapheal," she said, shooting him a forced smile. She scanned the room.

Her eyes settled on the glowing green stone hanging around Nikki's neck.

"I've got this figured out."

16

"Welcome to the Tube, humanity's *strangest* accomplishment."

Tabitha blinked awake at Lawrence's voice. Her neck was sore, and her body felt heavy, wanting to do anything but wake up and process her surroundings. Her head leaned against the window, her eyes half-focused at the view beyond the glass.

It took her a second to register that they *weren't* moving.

In fact, they were inside an enormous building.

Tabitha shot up.

They were in line behind a series of other autos all coming out of enormous thick tinted transparent tunnels and into a colossal station, half submerged underwater. Dozens of lines of autos were being hooked up to carts and shipped through even more tunnels as lines of people crowded desks and security queues. Walls were covered in holographic projections indicating arrivals and departures.

And then Lawrence's words processed.

The Tube.

The underwater Rail system connecting the major continents. She quickly unbuckled, trying to shake herself as she pushed between Cole and Lawrence in the front of the truck. "It's awfully expensive," Cole grumbled under his breath. "We'll have just enough to get back and charge the truck a few times. I've worked enough hours in the last week to help top it off."

Tabitha's face burned. *And that was a problem she couldn't even help with.* Cole's supposed-to-be life savings going down the drain for this?

And here she was with a ticking time bomb of death.

"Why don't you just ask your filthy rich patrons for some money?" Lawrence asked.

"I can't just ask the Outowns for anything whenever I feel like it."

"Then what's the point?" Lawrence rolled his eyes, turning his attention back to his Comm.

"Are we sure this is a good idea?" Tabitha said. "What if the Defenders are looking for us?"

"Good thing Matteo is the master of fake names."

"Oh dear. Should I even ask?"

"We're all siblings under the last name."

"Don't tell me that means what it sounds like?" Cole sighed.

Tabitha frowned. What *did* that mean?

"Oh, it totally does," Lawrence chuckled.

"We only have a few face disfigurers, and I think we should only give those to the Council Members with the most publicity…like Felicity," Cole said.

"And you," Tabitha said, recalling the media spotlight Cole had received six months ago.

Cole swallowed hard. "Right."

They finally pulled up to the gateway to a woman in a bright blue suit in a booth, a little bell-shaped hat on her head. "Please exit the vehicle and head through security." She peered back at the trailer. "How many is your party?"

"Ten."

The woman blinked. "Ten?"

"We're a pretty big family," Lawrence said with a dramatic sigh. "And we've been sitting in this auto for over ten hours, and so it would be in your best interest to—"

Cole cut Lawrence off, offering the woman his Comm. She scanned his device. "Yep. Ten. Does that hinder anything?"

The woman blinked. "Nope. Not at all. Big family." She cleared her throat, looking back at her tablet. "But you only have nine registered tickets."

Tabitha's heart dropped, cursing under her breath. "We forgot to register Nathaniel!" she hissed under her breath.

"He's just a toddler," Cole said, laughing nervously.

"He still needs to be registered. You can enter the line to the left. The rest of your…family can head through security to the right."

A plastic ticket printed out the end of her tablet. She slipped it into the window of Cole's truck. "Your vehicle will be in pod #3106. You can head there once you've completed the registration and security."

Cole sighed, hopping out of the truck. "Thank you. Tabs, you're coming to get tickets!"

"Ah, yes!" Tabitha was happy to be able to leap out the truck door and stretch her legs. It felt almost weird not to have the ground moving below her.

"Lawrence, get the others out. We'll meet up with you," Cole said, closing his own door.

"Why is this always my job?" Lawrence said, though he got out the opposite door without a hesitation. "Alright, captain."

Tabitha had to run to catch up with Cole as he moved into the mass of people.

"General admission to the left!" a security guard shouted.

They stepped in behind a family that was obviously also tired from a long trip, a young child falling asleep in her father's arms, and her brother complaining as his mother tried to take away his tele.

"So have you ever been in the Tube?" Tabitha asked.

"Never had a reason to cross the ocean." And he couldn't afford it, but he didn't need to say that. Cole turned to her. "And you?"

"My brother, Clarence, used to have an agent in Elizon, so I got a free ride a few times. Upper class in the private car. I've never driven in an auto in a pod," Tabitha said.

That's why the Tube was such a convenient use of transportation. While you booked your ticket and went through security, your vehicle was placed in a pod. Each pod was attached to the other and pulled through the airtight tunnel under the ocean for your twelve-hour trip to your destination.

They would be in Manifest by the next evening.

"Welcome to the average citizen life," Cole said with a teasing smile.

"It's quite thrilling, Goldfish. Truly an experience."

Cole only shook his head, holding back a laugh. Even now, with dark circles under his eyes and his clothes mussed from being stuck in the driver's seat all night, she thought his features suited him, especially over the past year. He was no longer the skinny boy who avoided attention in the back of a history lecture.

He was alert, standing tall with a hand resting on the buckle where the hilt of his sword usually was. She felt stupid to admit she'd always liked his eyes, especially when they were focused like right now.

His security was contagious. It felt safe near him, despite the hundreds of others crowded around them.

If anyone would know what to do about Lucas, it would be Cole.

"Next!"

Though that conversation would have to wait. Cole nudged Tabitha to go first, which she did so confidently and without problem as the holographic red wave ran over her.

"Next!"

Cole looked up to the frame, a crease forming between his brows.

"It's completely safe," Tabitha said, though Cole seemed unsure as he stepped in.

He held his breath until the hologram flashed green. He ran up to Tabitha. "Alright, let's go," he said. "This place gives me a weird feel."

"It's basically just a big SpeedRail station."

"But way more people," Cole said, his eyes scanning the crowd as they were enveloped into the mass of people pushing forward to the ticket station.

Tabitha didn't *feel* anything, but that didn't mean anything. Her feely power things weren't exactly the world's most reliable, since she wasn't Impure. She was used to crowds and their harsh nature.

"Name for the tab?"

"Er…Estúpida."

The clerk began to type out her name before he looked up out of the edge of his shades. He looked at Cole. "You look familiar."

"Oh, that's funny." Cole cleared his throat, clasping his hands behind his back.

Why was he being so weird? Where would the clerk—

Then it hit Tabitha.

Cole hadn't had time to put on his face disfigurer. The guy couldn't recognize him? Could he?

The public opinion about him was mixed to say the least.

"We have a party of ten," Cole said, quickly changing the topic. "One's below the age of three."

"Oh *you're* the one they were talking about over the channel," the clerk scoffed, adjusting his shades to the bridge of his nose. "Look *kids*, we have a full train this morning, and I don't know how much time we have to screen and approve ten new tickets—"

"We already have tickets. We just need one. He's only two."

"Are you his father?" The man frowned, rolling his eyes.

"No…but it's really important."

"That's what they always say," the guy sighed. "We can do some additional screening." His face lit up as he swiped his screen to show a poorly designed brochure. "Or perhaps you kids would be willing to pay for a quicker route…"

"What's taking so long?"

Tabitha's heart leapt, seeing her fiery redheaded friend push through the crowd, obviously growing uncomfortably on her feet and fidgeting with her headband. Felicity *was* wearing her face disfigurer, but when you'd known Felicity since you were seven, it was impossible not to recognize her.

Tabitha smothered a smile.

Cole darted a look to Tabitha. His face twisted, like he was fighting between asking for help and shooting down the mischief forming in Tabitha's mind.

She spun around. "Felicity!" She hooked her arm with her friend's. "It turns out we actually can't catch the Tube today."

Felicity's widened, out of breath. "We can't?"

"They say we have to wait because Nathaniel is too hard to screen," Tabitha said with a dramatic sigh.

Felicity's brows furrowed.

Tabitha, are you playing with me? Felicity's voice slipped into Tabitha's mind.

Yes. A little. But we need to get on that Tube. If the Defenders catch up...

I'm too tired for this.

Felicity's face hardened into a scowl as she straightened herself. She tightened her grip on Tabitha's arm, dragging her forward toward the clerk.

"Excuse me, *sir*. I request we be cleared to board at this time. Bentsworth orders."

The man's eyes widened. "Bentsworth?"

Tabitha sighed dramatically. "Does she have to explain herself further?"

Felicity blushed, struggling to keep her frown. She leaned on Tabitha, tapping on the face disfiguring device on her jawline. The disfigure dropped, her real face showing through. "You can verify if you like, but I'm requesting passage."

"Or she'll tell her father," Tabitha whispered loudly.

The clerk paled. "I-I'm sorry. I-I just thought you-you, I mean...Yes. I'll have someone sent to assist you right away." He began quickly typing away at his pad. "Should I reserve an express car?"

"No need," Felicity said, rubbing her forehead. "I just would like to be able to sit down and get in that pod."

Her discomfort was evident as she darted a look at Tabitha that screamed "you-owe-me."

Tabitha could hear the whispers beginning to grow behind them.

"A Bentsworth?"

"Felicity Bentsworth? All the way out here?"

"Is that the crazy one?"

It only took a moment before two employees ran to unhook the chain divider open, nearly tripping on their heels as they ushered Felicity forward, nervously greeting her.

Felicity didn't respond.

Cole followed them quickly.

"Can we get you anything, Miss Bentsworth?" one chirped. "A glass of water? Or—"

"I would like to go back to my pod," Felicity said with an annoyed sigh.

"Oh." The two employees looked at each other. "Of course, Miss Bentsworth."

"We have a party of ten," Cole reminded them. "Could you make sure they all get to pod #3106 after security?"

The employees didn't respond to Cole, their eyes still glued on Felicity.

"Just listen to him," Felicity said, tightening her grip on Tabitha's arm.

"Oh! Yes, miss. We'll go direct the rest of your party immediately."

One ran off, having to tear her eyes from Felicity.

The other led them through a back door into a room crowded with desks and glowing maps lining the walls.

A few others peered up from their desks.

One even snapped a photo.

Cole quickly stepped in front of her.

Tabitha almost felt like they'd been transported back to their school days, just this time there was much more on the line than Felicity's discomfort.

The employee finally reached the door on the far end, which opened automatically from the wall to the main Tube entrance.

Tabitha held her breath as she stepped inside. She could see the blue reflection down the tunnel. Only a hundred feet away lay the ocean that they would be riding through.

Hundreds of autos were inside pods, their walls being raised and secured shut.

It wasn't hard to find the Council with their trailer and truck, having to be crammed onto an oversized pod. With the pull of a lever, a human-sized hole disintegrated in the pod wall, holographic steps descending to the group. Felicity rushed up the steps.

She pulled the door to the trailer open, nearly collapsing to the floor. Tabitha grabbed her, easing her to the ground. "Thanks Liz," Tabitha said.

"Glad being a Bentsworth could be useful for something," Felicity half-laughed, lying on the floor and taking in a deep breath.

"I'll get your chair," Cole said, rushing to grab Felicity's neatly packed bag sitting on the counter.

"Thank you, Cole." Felicity closed her eyes.

"Are you okay?" Tabitha dared to ask. "Are you pani—"

"No, Tabs. I'm fine. It just hurts to walk with these machines." Felicity opened her eyes, patting Tabitha's knee. "No need to worry."

But that's all Tabitha did.

That's the only reason she'd come to North Cordell. Because she'd been worried about Felicity being on her own and descending into panic about her food being poisoned or an auto being too loud.

But Felicity had grown, and what about Tabitha? Was she still that same loud, impulsive teenager with mommy issues?

"Okay! The chair's ready."

Tabitha offered her hand to Felicity. "Still need a little help?"

Felicity flashed her a smile. "I'll take it, Tabs."

General admission started only a few minutes later. Crowds began to flood through from security, employees rushing to try and drive passengers to their respective vehicles. Tabitha sat on the step of the trailer, watching the people go by.

For some reason, it felt more helpful than just sitting inside.

It wasn't hard to spot the rest of the Council, especially with Lawrence being the tallest and not afraid to push his way through.

"You guys made it!" she said, rushing to help them up the steps.

"Hardly. Lawrence almost fought some lady before some dude came and told us that a Bentsworth had cleared us," Ray said. "It was a very dangerous journey."

"I did *not* almost fight some lady," Lawrence scoffed.

"That's the nice way of putting it," Matteo added.

Before they could squabble for a second more, a broadcast blasted through the tunnel.

"Please be seated as soon as possible. Launch begins in 5 minutes."

Everyone exchanged glances.

"Beat you guys to the trailer!" Ray shouted.

The race was a bit rigged, seeing as Ray disappeared in a split second, reappearing in the window.

"Someone needs to talk to him about teleporting in public," Lincoln said, rushing after him, Nathaniel in his arms.

Tabitha started to follow before she stopped herself. She was about to go into the *Tube*, a pinnacle of human accomplishment, and she was about to pass up a chance to have a front seat as they launched into a glass tunnel underwater?

She ran for the truck, jumping into the shotgun seat.

"Same idea?"

Tabitha jumped, crashing into the window at Cole's voice. He sat in the driver's seat, trying not to laugh. "You good?"

"I was definitely not caught off guard," Tabitha said, straightening herself. "Whatever you saw was a figment of your imagination."

"Whatever you say, Tabs." The humor was in his voice, but his face was cold and his lips pinched, constantly darting toward the fluorescent light at the end of the tunnel, where they would be submerged into the transparent tube under the ocean.

"PLEASE REMAIN IN YOUR VEHICLE UNTIL LAUNCH. PLEASE REMAIN—"

Tabitha met Cole's eyes. "Are you ready?" she whispered.

Cole gave a nervous laugh. "No going back now."

Tabitha grabbed his hand, weaving her fingers through his.

"PLEASE BE SEATED, BUCKLED, OR LYING DOWN. ROUND WILL COMMENCE MOMENTARILY."

Cole took a deep breath, squeezing her hand. She squeezed it back.

Without a warning, the lights shut off and the pods shot forward. Tabitha's body flooded with a sudden nausea, her sweat instantly going cold.

She couldn't tell if it was her or Cole who cried out.

The panic lasted for no longer than a second before they were spit back into the light, speeding through the tunnel through the water.

Tabitha didn't even know how she'd ended up clinging to Cole, and him to her. He was squeezing her so tightly she could hear his heart thundering in his chest.

She slowly sat up, gently easing out of his arms, watching the water speed by.

Tabitha opened the door.

"Tabitha, what are you—"

Tabitha stumbled out the door out onto the platform, rushing to the railing. She laughed. "It's fine, Goldfish! Look at this! It's incredible!"

It's nothing like she remembered.

As a child, she'd been cooped up in one of the express cars. She'd never seen the ocean like this. The colors and the light were like nothing she'd ever seen as they went deeper and deeper.

She felt a smile on her lips, goosebumps rising on her skin.

Tabitha could feel it.

And it felt so good.

She closed her eyes just to feel for a moment the speed around her as she left all her problems behind on land…just for a moment.

17

"GOOD MORNING, DAUGHTER."

Tabitha's eyes burst open. The light was muted, and the dusky maroon walls were so tall she couldn't see how far they reached. The mattress felt soft and the covers heavy. Far more soothing than the backseat of the truck.

She sprang up, feeling her face.

No, no, no.

Not again.

She didn't want to dream. Not now. She wanted to go back to the truck.

"Ryynar! Let me go!" Tabitha cried out. It was pointless. The creepy Oquelite in sunglasses wouldn't save her. He was the one causing this torment.

She threw her covers off, scrambling off the bed.

"Where are you going in such a hurry?"

Tabitha scrambled back, nearly colliding with the all-too-familiar figure of her mother with her strong scent of peppermint perfume, bleached hair, and crisp smiling red lips.

Her *dream* mother.

This wasn't real. *This isn't real.*

"You're not real," Tabitha stammered out. She'd meant for it to sound a bit more intimidating and less like a whimper from a scared child. "You don't exist."

She tightened her fists.

The woman pouted. "Oh honestly, Tabitha Alyssa. I thought you would have been more considerate. What about that embrace? I know you truly don't feel this way."

Tabitha's face burned. "Last time wasn't real either," she said, clenching her jaw. She turned, storming to the window. "Go away."

"You still don't understand, do you? I'm trying to protect you."

A burning sensation overcame her. It took everything in her not to punch the window in front of her and run out into the storm. "The last time we spoke, you said you'd disown me if I set foot in your house again!"

"You really think I'd disown my own daughter?"

Tabitha's heart fluttered. She'd called her daughter. She'd never called her that. She shook it off. "I know my worth."

The woman gave an irritated huff. "Has anyone ever told you how arrogant you are?" She snorted. "A very unattractive quality, though I guess losing a few pounds would help you out too."

Tabitha's face flushed, suddenly feeling the need to hide. "A-arrogant is better than abusive."

"Harsh claim," the woman sighed, walking up beside Tabitha. "We didn't have many choices, but your father thought it would be cruel to get rid of you." She spoke the words as if they were just a simple fact, a minor inconvenience. "We kept you under our roof when we had no obligation to. You've seen the filthy streets and the states of some of the poorer farms. Homeless children are rampant. It could've been you."

Tabitha tore herself away from the storming window, pressing her hands over her ears, trying to ignore the voice that still rang perfectly clear.

"Of course, we still treated you different. You *are* different. We had no obligation to love you. You were a much happier child before you grew jealous of your brothers. You knew your brothers would always be the priority."

"Stop! Don't bring them into this!" Tabitha cried out, her fingers tearing up into her hair. She squeezed her eyes shut.

"Arrogance, Tabitha. *Arrogance.*"

Hot tears boiled. Arrogant. Jealous. Unattractive. "Wake up! Someone wake me up!" she screamed. "Someone! Cole! Cole! Please!"

"That seems to be our only roadblock. That…boy." Her mother spat. "We'll have to do something about him."

"COLE! Wake up!"

"Or are you simply using him? Just like you use jokes? You always relied so heavily on your sense of humor. Everything is a joke to you. When I provided you with all the luxuries of Liberty, you still chose that bastard-born lowlife from a mining region. Perhaps his own shame makes you feel more deserving."

"I don't care! Leave him out of this!"

"No daughter of mine should be seen with someone such as this. You won't survive. You can hardly stay out of debt."

She collapsed against the door. The knob wouldn't turn. She flattened herself against the door, refusing to turn her head toward the voice that strode toward her. "I don't care what you think."

A harsh laugh. The smell of peppermint was overpowering as a cold finger dragged across Tabitha's cheek.

"Oh daughter. That is where your mistake lies." The woman clicked her tongue. "You care very much what I think."

Tabitha couldn't breathe, and for a moment, she thought she was still in the nightmare until she realized she was lying face down in her pillow.

She pushed herself up, taking in a deep breath of sweet air.

She sat up fully, quickly trying to scrub her face of tears. To her relief, the trailer appeared empty. Everyone was probably enjoying the view from the outside platform.

Good.

No one had heard her cries.

Her eyes were sore and her breathing heavy. She was tempted to sink back down into the couch and fall asleep, but there was no way she was returning back to those night-mares.

She couldn't give in.

She wrapped her arms around her legs, rocking slowly. Was she really what her dream mother said? Arrogant?

Everything is just a joke to you.

What was she without Cole? Without the Council? Without her sense of humor?

What did her mother want from her?

Ryynar is the one torturing you with these dreams, she reminded herself. *Not your mother.*

And yet, she wanted to feel her mother's arms around her again. Even if it was just Dream Mom. It seemed like that was the only thing that could fix that.

But Mom hates you.

Tabitha couldn't take it anymore. She buried her face between her legs and cried.

Then I'll make her love me.

18

"Where's Tabitha?"

Felicity rolled to where Mercy sat dangerously on the edge of the cart that the truck and trailer sat on. Her foot almost scraped against the pod as she looked up the tunnel.

"I haven't seen her," Mercy said, not taking her eyes from the sight. "I think she fell asleep inside or something."

"I don't blame her." Felicity wasn't overly fond of the Tube. Especially riding with her truck and trailer strapped down to a cart like this. It felt...unsafe. Would the Tube break and they'd all float away and get eaten by a whale? And Giles wasn't here to laugh and tell her otherwise.

But Tabitha didn't share Felicity's anxieties...

Tabitha didn't just fall asleep too often.

"She's been asleep for a while." Felicity's eyes widened, and she spun around.

Mercy frowned, hurrying after her. "What's wrong?"

Felicity didn't stop, activating her headband quickly, pushing herself out of her chair and up onto the steps, the wheelchair deconstructing into a bag behind her as she ran into the trailer.

It was dark and eerily quiet. Too quiet.

The pile of blankets lay still, unmoving.

Felicity's throat tightened, taking a cautious step forward. "Tabitha?"

The bathroom door swung open. Tabitha stood in the doorway, pushing her wet hair out of her face.

"What?" The crack in her voice gave it away.

Felicity's heart swelled. "Are you okay?"

"I'm fine."

Tabitha shut the light off.

Felicity rushed to grab her arm. "What was it this time?"

Tabitha paused, looking into Felicity's eyes for a long moment before quickly looking to Mercy standing behind her.

She pulled away. "Nothing."

Mercy began to back away toward the door. "If-if I'm making it awkward, I can go."

"There's nothing to even be awkward about," Tabitha said. "Everything's totally cool. Totally fine. Very normal."

Felicity was never the comforting friend. Usually, she was the one in need of comforting. She sat awkwardly beside Tabitha. Did she hug her? Did she give her a firm shake? "Well, if you need anything, me and Mercy are here for you."

Mercy coughed, looking more interested in a loose thread on the sleeve of her hoodie.

Tabitha just chuckled half-heartedly. "Thanks."

They only had a couple seconds of silence before the door flew open, echoing with the sound of a toddler's tears.

"It wasn't my fault!" Ray shouted. "He just got upset for no reason!"

"You *looked* at him weird," Lincoln snapped, pushing past Ray inside, desperately trying to bounce the clearly unpleased Nathaniel. "And now I have to deal with it!"

Mercy moved out of the way, and Felicity got to her feet.

"Lincoln, calm down," Felicity said. "I doubt Ray looking at him did anything."

That was weird. She was never the voice of reason.

"Yeah! He's probably tired or hungry," Ray said.

Mercy moved out of the way of the door.

"Hey guys. What's—" Matteo and Nikki stopped dead in their tracks.

"Toddler crisis!" Lincoln shouted, looking down at the teary-eyed child. "Please don't be tired."

"He's probably tired of you talking!"

"That's stupid!"

"Hey!"

"Guys, don't insult each other!" Nikki tried to step in.

"Yeah, Black Eyes."

Felicity was starting to feel like Giles. No one was communicating, and everyone was a mess. And all Felicity could do was shout while no one listened. Being a Bentsworth had no effect on her friends. "You're going to traumatize the poor child! I almost hope we find a better home for him!"

Everyone dropped quiet, even Tabitha looked up.

Even Nathaniel went quiet for a moment.

Oh shoot. Now everyone was looking at *her*. As if she knew what to do.

Felicity rubbed her temples. "I-I'm sorry. I shouldn't yell."

No one responded.

Felicity swallowed. Now she'd made things tense. "This was supposed to be a relaxing, bonding trip before it turned into toddler rescue…so maybe we can-uh-play a game? That's a road trip thing people do."

No one made a quippy comment or jab. Instead, everyone slowly settled into place as Lincoln rummaged through the fridge as Nathaniel stubbornly decided on a perfect snack.

"What game?" Nikki asked quietly.

Felicity bit her lip. What game? She'd never road tripped before. "Well, my friend in primary school, Tuesday's father used to travel all around the regions. She told me about this cow game."

"Cows?" Nikki's eyes lit up.

"Basically, every time you pass a pasture, you get one cow. If you see a government building, you get double the cows if you point it out. You pass an Earthshaker memorial and point it out, everyone loses a cow for respect. If you pass a cemetery and point it out, all other team members' cows die."

"Poor cows."

"We're underwater," Ray pointed out.

"There's no underwater cows?" Nikki said, disappointed.

"How about dare or truth?"

"Boring," Ray yawned.

"What's that?"

"You give someone the choice between a dare or telling the truth," Ray explained.

Tabitha chuckled, rubbing her swollen eyes. "Sounds like this could end badly. I'm in. Matteo, dare or truth?"

"Er, truth?"

"Who do you think would die first in a horror net film?" Tabitha smiled mischievously.

"Me," Matteo said bluntly.

"That is not true!"

Matteo shrugged.

Felicity sighed with relief as she stepped back, quietly slipping out. She set down her wheelchair, and it folded out. She powered her leg braces off, relief rushing over her as she sat back. If she could ignore the occasional echoing whispers of the other passengers from their carts, she could live in the illusion that she was alone.

Over the past six months, she'd grown more and more comfortable with other people. But being *seen* by other people? That still made her shudder.

She was Felicity Bentsworth.

She wasn't human.

Felicity shook it off, forcing herself to close her eyes, trying to simply focus on the fact she was flying through a giant glass tube and less on the fact that any moment, a single mishap could very easily kill them.

The silence became poignantly clear.

And then a roar shattered through.

Felicity's eyes flew open, pushing back in her chair. She spun around, her heart thundering in her chest.

The couple on the next cart over didn't seem phased, continuing to sit on their blanket, sipping on their coffee.

She must have just been hearing things. There was no creature she'd ever heard that could make that sound.

The low growl returned. Felicity's entire body went rigid, and the hair on the back of her neck stood up as it slipped into a low wail.

It was low, deep, and…in pain, echoing over and over as

it went.

Felicity looked back over to the couple. They were laughing over something on the man's tele.

Her eyes widened. "What's going on?" she whispered. "Am I so stressed out I'm hearing stuff? This has never happened before."

The next wail was high pitched and short, almost as if it had a voice. *Help…me…*

Felicity flinched, slowly turning toward the water. She swallowed hard. "What are you?" she shuddered.

She'd had a creepy woman speak in her head before, and she'd been able to understand a Lyntox shapeshifter before.

But this?

She'd never heard anything like this.

"Are you Kathryn?" she asked.

The wail returned, lower and drawn out, causing the pain in Felicity's legs to rise. She doubled over, gasping for air. "I'll take that as a no," she said, struggling to breathe.

Another low moan. *Very…sorry…*

Was she seriously considering this?

She pushed herself up. "Look. I don't know what you want, but I've seen a lot of weird stuff in the past year. How am I supposed to know I'm not crazy?"

"Hey! You good?"

Felicity jerked back, turning to see the man and woman now staring at her from the neighboring pod. She cleared her throat. *Oh my gosh, you look INSANE.*

"I-I'm fine!" she shouted back, with a forced smile, before turning away and hiding her face in her hands. She was simply being anxious. That's all. There was nothing more to it.

But the hum in her mind still echoed, slowly moving further and further away down into the depths below until it left her alone, the only one able to hear them and the distant cries for help.

19

THEY ENTERED THE waters of Manifest at midnight, and no fights had broken out.

It was much to Nikki's surprise that everyone behaved themselves throughout the day, but it wasn't like anyone really interacted. The darkness of the Tube, only lit by flashing florescent light, gave off a weird atmosphere as they went deeper.

She was watching Nathaniel as he fixed himself comfortably on top of Lincoln's chest, watching the dark waters roll by with wide eyes, occasionally using his tiny hands to push his dark red curls out of his face. He was entirely fixated by the water.

Lincoln, on the other hand, was not so entertained. He lay on the floor of the outside platform, nearly dozing off out of boredom.

Everyone else *was* asleep, except for Nikki, who'd snuck silently to the steps of the trailer. Nathaniel would have no such a thing.

The ocean captivated him.

Watching him was a nice distraction from her own mind, and so far, it hadn't triggered a weird relapse into her memories like last time.

Nikki shuddered just thinking of it.

Didn't she want to remember? She had no doubt they were echoes from the past. But something about them made her stomach twist and her throat tighten, unable to breathe.

She could hear Kathryn's mocking voice echo *Little Aguirre* over and over in her mind.

Little Aguirre.

Little Aguirre.

Little—

"Excited for the East regions, Nik?"

Lincoln's voice caused Nikki to jump from her corner. He turned to look at her, his eyes twitching with boredom. How did he know she was awake?

"I suppose so," she said. She had never really thought about crossing the ocean before…well, twenty-four hours ago. North Cordell had the post office, her room, and her friends. What else was there to want?

A creak from the neighboring pod caught Nikki's attention. Nikki frowned, seeing the couple peering out of their van at them. The woman held a Comm in hand.

Lincoln noticed too, exchanging a look with Nikki.

He sat up, much to Nathaniel's disappointment, holding him close and turning him away from the prying eyes. "Hello?"

The couple slammed the door shut.

Nikki had the perfect word: "Weird."

There was no way average civilians would know about Nathaniel…could they? The video had been removed.

"It's probably nothing to worry about, Nik," Lincoln sighed, getting to his feet. "They were most likely curious why a bunch of teenagers are traveling alone with a toddler."

A ring of red light passed them.

Nikki blinked in surprise.

There were no sirens going off. It was just…another red light…and another.

They were part of the tunnel. She looked up, noticing glowing red arrows floating on the ceiling.

"We're getting close," she said, her stomach flipping with

excitement. She got to see what the world across the ocean looked like. If nothing else, that was going to be amazing.

Lincoln got to his feet, groaning as he held out Nathaniel in front of him. "My arms have other uses," he said.

Nathaniel didn't seem to care, more interested in chewing on Lincoln's jacket string.

"Maybe we can come up with a sort of system," Nikki said, moving to Lincoln's side. She gave Nathaniel a small wave. He stopped to give her a disturbed look.

"Yeah, maybe. Where's our first stop—"

"*APPROACHING EXIT TUNNEL. PLEASE RE-MAIN SEATED IN YOUR VEHICLES.*"

"Oh shoot. Let's go, Nik!"

Nikki didn't need to told twice. She raced up the steps and into the trailer, holding the door open for Lincoln to barrel in, locking it behind them seconds before the tunnel was plunged into darkness.

Nikki stumbled to the ground, colliding with Lincoln, who was perched against the door.

"Almost lost you there."

Not Lincoln. Lawrence.

"You're awake?" she said, feeling her cousin's arm tighten around her shoulders as the rail car shuddered.

"They're all awake," Lincoln said.

"Well, it's not exactly super easy to sleep here, Mr. Did-You-Know-I-Can-See-In-The-Dark?"

"Ray is definitely awake, unfortunately."

"Lincoln, I dare you to come up with a more clever insult."

"We're not playing this again!"

"We technically never stopped."

"Fine. Ray is unfortunately awake and despite being an Oquelite, can't even see in the dark."

"That was terrible."

"I dare you to lick Ray's elbow as an apology."

"No! I'm not doing that."

Nikki could feel Lawrence's warmth beside her, more noticeable due to the fact he was a Ywondie and, as Giles put it, "had fire in his veins." Her nerves settled a bit.

"Nik! You gotta hurry up or we're not gonna have any time to see if the fishing pole works!"

"I'm not as fast as you. Wait! Wait up!"

An exasperated sigh. "Grab my hand."

"Your hand is very warm. Did you know that?"

Nikki jumped up, gasping for air and feeling for the floor below her.

The lights were flashing.

The air conditioning was cold.

The ground was hard below.

"Nikki!" Lawrence hurried around to face her.

The lights of the trailer burst on. Lawrence's green eyes studied her through the thick lenses of his glasses. "You okay?"

She nodded. "Your hands. They're very warm," she stammered out.

He took his hand off her shoulder. "Oh. I'm sorry. I didn't—"

"No, no. It's okay," Nikki assured him. "Just nervous."

She was *not* nervous. Had she just heard a young Lawrence's voice in her head? Why now, of all times, were memories trying to resurface?

"Nik, can you grab Nathaniel?" Lincoln whispered, gesturing to where he left Nathaniel, pushing himself to feet. "If I sneak away now, I can grab my stuff."

She nodded. This was a simple enough mission.

Lincoln scurried off, and Nikki quickly ran and scooped Nathaniel up from behind. He instantly squeaked, looking up to see his captor. His face scrunched up. "Ew! No!" he protested, trying to squirm away. "Linc! Help!"

It seemed like he was gaining new words every hour.

She felt the pod begin to slow. And luckily, so did everyone else. Felicity rolled to the window and her eyes widened. "We made it," she said, her voice soft.

"The easy part is over," Lawrence sighed, pushing himself up to his feet. "It starts here."

Nikki was ready to get started.

If they could get Nathaniel to safety and life back to somewhat normal, she'd be satisfied. She quickly left the trailer.

"Nikki! Don't get lost!"

The Tube station was much different than the one they'd left in. The exit halls were huge, and instead of human em-

ployees, bots stood in their place, directing offboarding passengers.

"Big," Nathaniel whispered, echoing her thoughts. He
reached his hand out toward the water tunnel.

The gate of their rail car had been unlocked, and Nikki
raced down the steps and into the anxious river of travelers.
She felt almost invisible among the hundreds. She liked it.

The crowd filed out into the main station. Nikki's eyes
widened, but not wide enough to be able to take it all in.

The floor was see-through, making it look as though they
were walking on water, and the ceiling stretched high above.
Hovering carts transported people from floor to floor. Holograms were sprouted about with different politicians, or ME-
DIA stars Nikki didn't recognize.

"Linc! Bad m-uh-ster!" Nathaniel pointed toward the
crowd.

Monster? There was so much light. So much metal. So
many holograms. So many people.

"ID, please."

Nikki turned to see a bot behind her, a mechanical claw
outstretched. Peculiar. The little machine demanded something from her.

She didn't exactly have an ID, but she did have the ticket
Cole had given her. She kneeled down, setting Nathaniel
down beside her. He reached out a little finger before the
bot's head spun around and caused him to stumble back.
Nikki handed the little sentient object the paper and it
handed it back to her, its little claw transforming into a rec-
tangular block, a holographic bar shooting out of it and
scanning over her.

She blinked. That was unexpected.

The thin screen loaded, the circle turning eternally. And
then it beeped—

A hand clamped over her mouth.

Nathaniel cried out.

Nikki's instinct took over her senses, thrusting her elbow
into the gut holding her. She twisted back the hand and
whirled around, her attacker buckling over in a pained groan.

Nikki's heart leapt. It was the woman from the neighboring car.

She scooped Nathaniel up, holding him tightly.

"Come quietly. We're going home now." The man of the couple stepped out of the crowd.

"What's going on here?" A passerby stepped out, a man dressed in a suit with a burgundy bag around his shoulder.

The woman pulled herself up, grabbing Nikki's shoulders hardly. "I'm sorry. My children are just being difficult."

Nikki wrenched from her grip. "I don't know you!"

"Hey! What are you doing?" A familiar voice called through the crowd.

"Ray!" Nikki's shoulders relaxed as her friend pushed through the crowd. She ran to him, shooting dagger eyes at the woman, who paled.

"That-that's my daughter."

Nikki was tempted to scream: "My mother is dead!"

"Okay, miss. Maybe you're mistaken?" the man with the bag said, trying to step between them, but the man pushed past him.

But before he could do anything, the bot finally finished loading with one long loud and prominent *BEEP!*

"FUGITIVE DETECTED."

Ray turned to look at Nikki, his mouth hanging open. "You mean we leave you alone for three minutes and you're wanted—?"

"No hurt!" Nathaniel shouted.

Before Nikki processed what was happening, she spun around to see the enormous glass fish case come falling to the ground.

She didn't have a moment to scold. She ran like her life depended on it. The glass shattered to the ground, water splashing all across the floor.

The crowd erupted into chaos. Nikki couldn't see Ray.

She just needed to get to the doors.

Every bot's glow had turned red. It was good for her that she didn't feel the slightest bit of guilt in drop kicking them.

She just needed to get to the door.

Avalon began to vibrate. *What a situation you've gotten your-self into.*

Says the woman who got herself trapped in a Stone!
Low blow, kid. Low.

Nikki slowed herself, taking a harsh turn. There was an unguarded door right past the holographic barrier. Unfortunately, a bot pulled up right in front of the barrier.

But Nikki didn't slow.

"Bad!" A spinning gust of water hit the bot with a thud, throwing it through the barrier.

"Good job, Nat," Nikki breathed. She jumped over the barrier, landing on her feet.

She tore for the door. *Lincoln!*

Nik! Are you alright? Do you have Nathaniel?

She broke through the doors, racing down the steps. "Stop there!"

Nikki froze. Not because of the demand, but because it was human voices guarding the exit, not bots.

Two armored Defenders.

"It's her," one of them breathed. The other raced for her.

"Wait!" Nikki set Nathaniel down. Her heart hammered against her chest. She couldn't take this on with one hand. She looked at him firmly. He seemed to get the message, clasping his hands together.

Nikki clenched her fists, letting the Officer have only a moment of victory in grabbing her for a split second, as she unbuckled the weapon from their waist, whipping it out and smashing it into their face.

They cried out. Nikki twisted out of their grip, turning with the unfamiliar weapon to the other officer.

"Drop the gun. Your charges aren't lethal."

Gun. Right. That's what Taryn called it. Nikki had no idea how to use it, and she didn't want to know. But it scared the guards, and she needed to get out of here.

She needed to get *Nathaniel* out of there.

The Defender pulled out his weapon. Nikki stood her ground for a second, shifting the weapon in her hand. She had one chance at this.

She took a subtle breath and threw the weapon.

The Defender panicked.

She didn't even turn to see if it made impact. She spun around.

Nathaniel's eyes lit up, knowing this was the moment. Water rushed out the doors of the station, sweeping Nathaniel off his feet, and to Nikki's horror, tossing him up in the air. He laughed, pleased with himself as he landed in her arms.

Nikki ran.

Fugitive.

Nikki didn't even know what that word meant. But it meant *something* bad, and it made people want to grab her. She needed to get away. What other people would try to grab her?

There were no alleys to escape into. Every building was a pristine steel and reached high into the gray sky.

Out of the corner of her eye, Nikki caught a flash of color.

In the window of the lowest level of a building, colorful holographic displays were shown in the window. Long flowy dresses and suits, nothing like Nikki had even seen before. But the door was propped open.

She rushed inside, slowing her pace, quickly reminding herself to act casual before she slid herself between two clothing racks. The city was definitely different from North Cordell.

She thought she'd seen all a Golden Region had to offer on her visit to Imperial…but this city screamed technological advancement, and everything smelled like the cleaning chemical closet in E's workshop. She peeked out from her hiding spot to see the women in the shop all wearing fitted outfits with bright pastel colors and lips to match, their hair pinned up in a tight fashion. *That* was similar to Imperial.

No one looked like her. No one even remotely sounded like her.

She thought they'd at least all sound like Giles, but their accents were more gentle than his. Or was that just a Giles thing?

The adrenaline was wearing off. She could hear her heart beating into her ears. She held Nathaniel close to her, settling her chin in his curls.

You attacked a Defender, great going. Avalon sighed, her voice dry.

Nikki, where are you? Lawrence's voice. *Do you have Nathaniel?*

Stuck. I have him.

Do you need help?

She glared at the colorful little shop. *No, I'm okay.*

Thanks to this new situation, we're taking a detour to a safe house.

Felicity found the address. She'll meet you at the bakery with a giant neon sign of a...muffin south of the station.

Is Nat okay? Came Lincoln's worried voice.

He's fine.

Good. Lawrence sounded so done, he might as well have sent a mental sigh. *Please stay safe. Stay alive, no dying.*

She wasn't planning on it. She'd already almost done that once, and it wasn't very fun. She eased herself into a crouch, balancing against her hand on the ground. She focused on the propped-open door. She could do this.

She leaped from her hiding position, preparing to launch into—

"Can I help you?"

Nikki froze, looking at the woman with tightly-coiled blonde hair and a blue striped jumper at the checkout counter. She stood beside a bot stuffing a bag for another woman, whose eyes were wide.

"Doesn't she look like Reyna Aguirre?" the woman said excitedly, her two high buns bouncing. "Aw, and he's adorable."

Nathaniel stuck out his tongue.

Nikki's heart seized in her chest, and she backed up. "I'm not an Aguirre," she said quickly. "I-I don't know what a Reyna is. Never heard of...that."

"You can't just tell everyone that comes from the Southwest regions that they look like the Aguirre Agents," the woman beside her with short, bright green hair said, shaking her head at her friend.

What did she do now? Run?

"You look lost," the blonde cashier said, going up to meet her.

Nikki flinched back, her eyes darting toward the door.

"She looks like the fugitive from the Defender announcement," the green haired woman whispered.

"What?" the blonde said.

This was it. Nikki was going to do it—

"She's just a kid," the cashier said, slamming down a hanger. "There's no way. How old are you?"

Nikki's body screamed to run, but something in her told her to stay, to hold her own. "Sixteen."

"Is that your brother?"

Nikki swallowed, unsure how to answer.

"Help!" Nathaniel babbled, swinging his legs. "Scar-ee! Help! Bad man. Fight!"

"Are you being chased?"

Nikki gave a tiny nod.

The cashier ran down from her table, grabbing a jacket and a knit hat. "Quick, tuck away your hair."

"Emily! What are you doing?"

Nikki took them quickly, doing as the woman instructed, not stopping to question her kindness. The jacket was big, but worked to cover her form. She tucked away her hair and bangs into the hat. She dropped the Ewyon Stone necklace down her shirt.

Another found a light pink beanie, able to cover Nathaniel's red curls.

One look in the mirror and she knew it wouldn't work.

"Her scar."

The long, jagged scar down her face was now on full display.

The woman with the buns in her hair rushed to shift through a wall full of little colored bottles. Nikki had seen one like it on Felicity's desk before.

The woman pulled out a light brown bottle, handing it to the Emily woman. "This should be close enough."

They rushed her to a stool as Emily dabbed the paint out onto a little sponge. "Do you mind?"

Nikki didn't even know *what* she was supposed to be minding. Were they painting her?

"Paint Nik," Nathaniel gasped.

She let Emily dab the sponge on her face, blending it in with her thumb. "That should be good enough."

Another glance in the mirror, and Nikki had to do a double take. The scar was gone.

Well, if you looked long enough, you could still see its rigid form on her skin…but its color…it had disappeared.

Emily handed Nikki the bottle. "Keep it. You might need it," she said with a smile.

She stared speechless, the little bottle wrapped in her hand.

She was going to have a lot of questions for Felicity the next time she saw her.

And then she frowned, looking up to the excited faces of the women around her as they waited for her. "W-why are you helping me?"

"I have no idea," the woman with the buns squealed. "But it's really fun!"

"That so-called Executive Cadissa Dean ought to give more clarification before calling for a girl's arrest with no explanation," Emily said, crossing her arms. "The Defenders haven't even elected her as Executive yet!"

Nikki's sweat went cold. "Cadissa Dean?"

"Oh, pish posh. Some old lady with a bad haircut, and a red shade of lipstick that *totally* doesn't go with her complexion," the green-haired woman said.

She had to get back to the Council.

"Thank you," she said, genuinely wishing she could give each woman a hug...though she'd learned that it wasn't always an accepted way of gratitude.

"Tank you," Nathaniel repeated.

She got off the stool, racing to the door, only pausing to glance back at the women waving to her. "Don't get caught!"

She didn't intend on it.

Nikki broke out into the crowded streets, trying to resist the temptation to run, weaving between people while repeating Lawrence's directions over and over in her mind.

She slipped around the corner to an even busier street.

How many people knew?

Did Cadissa Dean know? Did she know what Nikki was?

Did she know *who* Nikki was?

Finally, she caught sight of a giant floating neon muffin. It was hard to miss. She dashed across the street. She pushed through the crowd and inside the door.

A small bell dinged.

Nikki! Felicity's mental voice filled her mind.

Nikki turned to see Felicity sitting in her wheelchair, nervously tapping on the armrests, her eyes begging her to come.

Nikki shifted over to her, trying to keep it casual. She clenched her jaw, keeping herself from bursting out.

You got a makeover?

A what?

Never mind. I just hope you didn't rob *anyone too.*

Nikki looked down at her ensemble. *Oh. No. They gave this to me.*

Felicity tilted her head, raising a brow. Her confusion only lasted for a second before a bell rang, the door opening.

We need to go. I have a lot to tell you.

Felicity nodded, rolling for the second exit out the side. *I think we might have more to tell* you.

Nikki followed Felicity out, trying to keep close to her chair as they rolled down the wet Manifest streets. Unlike North Cordell, the sidewalks were impeccably clean. Not a sign of overgrown grass, or plants of any kind now that Nikki thought of it. No trash. No dirt.

The buildings began to stretch higher and higher, scraping into the clouds.

Traffic bots buzzed by. Nikki quickly pulled the collar of her jacket up to hide her face.

Felicity rolled up to a side door of one of the enormous buildings, looking to her Comm. "This should be it."

She knocked on the door. It took only a moment before the door swung open.

A woman with red, frizzy hair and a firm face ushered them inside. "Is this the last of you?" she said, her voice gruff.

"All of us," Felicity nodded, following the woman as she rushed to the elevator.

Something about her was familiar. But Nikki didn't dare make a sound as she stepped into the elevator beside Felicity.

The door shut, and the woman's eyes went straight to Nikki. "So this is your newly wanted friend?"

"That's one way to put it," Felicity said.

"Leave it to Armstance to befriend fugitives," the woman grumbled.

Nikki blinked.

"Nikki, this is Giles' aunt, Josephine," Felicity explained.

The resemblance made sense now. It was like looking at the older, female version of Giles, with the same sharp features, hair color, and broad shoulders…which Nikki didn't even know was possible.

Was Giles okay?

If he gave Felicity this address and contact, maybe that meant he was fine.

She didn't have anything to worry about.

Giles was fine. Nikki's shoulders relaxed.

The elevator door opened. Josephine led them down the longest hallway Nikki had ever seen, the walls a pristine white and the carpet red all the way down. They stopped at a door, and Josephine swiped her card over the handle.

The door opened, and she ushered them inside.

"You're alive!" Tabitha shouted, tackling Nikki with a hug.

"Nathaniel!" Lincoln pushed past her, taking Nathaniel from his arms.

Nathaniel let out an excited squeal, a bubble of water rising from a pitcher on the counter before it exploded on top of them.

"Nat! Don't!"

Lincoln turned toward a disappointed Josephine. "I'll clean it up."

Nikki looked at the other eight crammed in the tiny apartment living room.

It was cozy, and it had more color than the entirety of the city so far. The air smelled of potatoes, and it was warm from the cold outside.

Josephine locked the door. "So, how was *that* introduction to Manifest?" She laughed dryly, waltzing into the kitchen.

"Thank you for taking us in on such short notice, especially with the legal trouble," Cole said.

"Oh psh, kid. This is nothing." She removed a pot from the oven and slammed it down on the counter. She scanned the room, biting her lip. "Now the only problem is where to put the lot of ya."

"It'll only be a night until we can reach our next safe house. I'm sure this will be fine." Cole rushed to help her with a stack of plates, ushering the other boys to do the same.

Tabitha offered Nikki a wipe from her bag, indicating to her scar.

"And when exactly do you plan to leave?" Josephine asked.

"We need to get out of the city with Nikki undetected," Cole said.

Nikki scrubbed the paint from her scar, pretending not to notice the fact everyone had turned to stare at her.

"Nik, do you know what happened?" Lincoln said, a sleepy, soaked Nathaniel on his hip.

"Yes. I would like to know this too," Josephine chimed in too.

"Want food!" Nathaniel shouted.

"One sec, Nat."

Nathaniel went flimsy in Lincoln's arms in protest.

"Not entirely," Nikki said, answering Lincoln's question. "I-I just know it's Cadissa Dean who sent out the…fugitive thing."

Just like Giles warned.

"You're wanted by the top gun of the Department," Josephine said, far more casual than Nikki expected. "Very lovely company."

"She's technically not wanted. She didn't commit any crimes," Mercy piped up from the floor.

"True. The announcement was weirdly worded." Lawrence frowned as he read over Josephine's shoulder at a Scroll. "Reward granted to anyone who can locate and *deliver* to Department."

"They don't use my name," Nikki said with a breath of relief. It felt like a giant weight had been lifted from her shoulders. She dropped onto the floor beside Mercy.

"Then why do they want her?" Ray said, frowning.

The room was quiet. Nikki could feel the looming uncertainty. She pulled out the Stone, rubbing her thumb over it.

"I don't know," Cole said. "We need to get in contact with the Defenders…I mean, *our* Defenders."

"Already tried that," Tabitha said. "None of them are picking up. Not even Dow."

Nikki's heart skipped a beat. Was Taryn okay? Was Giles okay?

"I-I thought you got this address from Giles," Nikki said.

"He gave it to me before we left," Felicity said, the crease in her forehead deepening as she turned to Nikki. "Why?"

Nikki swallowed hard. "I don't know. I just hope he's okay."

That was the truth. And it hurt Nikki to see Felicity's face twist in pain, quickly pulling out her Comm.

Josephine cleared her throat. "Well, I'll let ya help yourself. Don't be loud. That's my only rule."

"We'll be so quiet, you'll totally forget we're even here," Ray said, already stuffing his plate.

Tabitha snorted. "That'd be a miracle."

Everyone was too hungry and exhausted to argue any further. Nikki felt so heavy, and her mind was spinning so fast, that she could only stare up the ceiling, hoping to calm it.

She didn't like this stress thing. It was very tiring. She just wanted lemon tea and a hug from Isabel.

"Well then," Felicity said. "Where is our next safe house?"

Matteo handed Cole his Scroll.

A small smile formed on Cole's lips as he slowly looked up. "Remember our old friend Sinni?"

20

MERCY HADN'T BEEN in an auto long enough before to learn that she had terrible motion sickness.

It was a cry of freedom when the small recharge station finally appeared on the horizon.

"How are you holding up?" Cole asked, who was the one who'd recommended her to sit in the truck next to the window.

"Great," she groaned.

She was mortified, but she'd taken up his offer anyway because throwing up in front of the rest of the Council would be even worse. To her luck, Tabitha had been switched out for Felicity in the truck, so that was one less person Mercy had to make a fool of herself in front of.

She hadn't been in autos much as a child. She had nowhere to go…nowhere she was allowed to go. Her *pere* would take her to the cabins for a weekend when she was too little to remember much besides the warmth of his smile and the sand under her feet.

She rested her head on the window sill, taking in the fresh

air. She watched the fog roll through the long grasses that flowed like a green ocean and the mountains rising up, untouched by war and time.

Felicity had explained that a majority of the island countries had been decimated by war. The regions made the decision to accept the destruction of their past and rebuild as strong as possible…hence the amount of tech and modern buildings. It lacked the color and culture Mercy had grown used to in her small town in Kennedy. Manifest once served as the world capitol, as it was one of the first of the rebuilt cities.

It left the countryside an empty place, but it was like no countryside Mercy had ever seen. There was no life in the fog.

They finally rolled into the charge station, and as soon as Cole rolled to a stop, Mercy jerked the door open, toppling over into the asphalt. Sweet stable ground. She took in a deep breath of the cold, fresh air, praying her stomach settled down.

"Looking rough, Glow Girl!"

Ray's laugh made her heart leap. She looked up to him as he stood there, offering a hand. She sighed with defeat, taking it. "I'm great."

Ray rolled his eyes. "You missed out on the epic cow games. I absolutely killed Lincoln and Matteo's cows."

Mercy frowned. "What?"

"It's a game," Ray sighed, dusting his hand. "Want to go check out the station with me and Black Eyes? Maybe they'll have that mysterious Founder Society artifact you're looking for."

Ray made an obnoxious whimsical sound that Mercy could help but quirk a smile at as she shook her head. "It's the Founder Association. And I doubt they'll have anything at a dingy countryside recharge station."

"You'd be surprised. My younger brother, Noah, found an authentic shark tooth at one in Glorgory."

Mercy raised her brow. "Really?"

"Okay, it's probably not real," Ray admitted. "But don't tell Noah that."

Mercy had never seen Noah without the necklace, and she almost felt cruel for laughing at his misfortune. "So, what are you looking for?"

"A very special gift for my single teenage mom friend," Ray said.

Almost as if he was summoned, Lincoln shouted, "Hey!"

"What? It's true!"

Lincoln scowled, hoisting the little redheaded toddler onto his shoulders, rushing over to Ray. "He keeps insisting that it's something *very* important."

"It is. Trust me. Our little guy Nat will love it." Ray attempted to give Nathaniel a pat on the head, but Nathaniel leaned away, eyeing Ray suspiciously.

"Well, you guys better get on that, then," Mercy said, secretly hoping Ray would invite her along.

"And you better get on not looking like you're about to vomit." Ray gave her a teasing smile.

Mercy's face warmed, and she punched Ray in the shoulder.

Ray just laughed. "Come on, Black Eyes!"

"You're lucky you're not cooped up in the trailer with him," Lincoln groaned.

Mercy felt like she would go insane if she had to sit at the window of the truck, nauseous, and not talking to anyone. Her boredom was almost as sickening as her motion sickness.

But instead of saying anything, she watched Lincoln chase after Ray. Nathaniel bubbly laughed as they ran. "Dead cows!"

Mercy's heart swelled. They seemed so happy. She wanted to be a part of that so badly…but first, she'd fix whatever damage her grandmother had caused.

Whatever damage she'd caused.

She walked down the road toward the grassy field, taking in deep breaths. She just needed the perfect plan to get Nikki's necklace.

It would only be for as long as she needed to summon the Founder Association, ask a few questions about her grandma, and then she'd give it right back.

And yet, it still made her feel heavy.

How was stealing from Nikki supposed to make the Council like her? Would finding information about the Founder Association even help? Was she just on a blind goose chase…?

"You feeling alright?"

Mercy jumped, whipping around to see Felicity rolling up beside her, her eyes focusing on the rolling storm clouds.

Mercy cleared her throat. "I'm feeling much better."

Felicity nodded. "Good. Another reason I hate autos. I don't blame you."

Mercy rubbed her arm. Her auto sickness didn't even *compare* to Felicity's auto accident. "How much longer do we have left?"

"Only an hour or two. Not too long." Felicity gave a long sigh. The two stood in the silence for a long moment.

Mercy tried not to breathe, scrambling for a word to say to keep Felicity there.

"Giles was lucky to grow up here," Felicity said, looking to Mercy.

"I prefer Kennedy." The words slipped out before Mercy could stop them. *Shoot.*

Felicity raised a brow. "You do?"

"It's beautiful there too," Mercy said, squeezing her hand. "There's lots of trees. And there's fields too, but there's so much color. The sunsets looked like paintings and the storms brought the mountains to life."

The smell of freshly baked bread at Uki and Ahnah's deli, and the sound of Lucas singing off key at the top of his lungs in the mechanic shop.

Mercy's eyes burned. She quickly blinked the tears away.

"Do you want to go back there?" Felicity asked, softly.

Mercy swallowed hard. "Not-not exactly. I can't."

"I understand."

Did she? Felicity didn't have a grandmother with murderous intent…and information that she used to guide the Exerticus to Felicity. A grandmother who'd shot her own daughter with no regret and had no problem chaining up a teenage boy as he was electrocuted for hours and—

"I'm sorry. I realize home is probably a touchy subject."

"No!" Mercy snapped herself out of the daze. "You're all good!"

"If you ever want to talk to someone other than Ray, I'm here." Felicity gave a small smile.

Mercy felt her heart flip. All at the same time, half her

mind was screaming at her "that's against the rules!" while the other half of her mind was positively screaming with joy.

Felicity wanted to…talk to her?

Was this friends? Had she done it? But she hadn't proven anything to Felicity!

"Thanks," was all she could manage.

"Of course," Felicity said. "How's the glowing going?"

All her excitement dissipated in a second. "Great."

Felicity eyed her suspiciously. She rolled out in front of Mercy. "Show me."

A lump formed in Mercy's throat. "Show you?"

"Sure. If it's not intrusive." Felicity clasped her hands together.

"No, not at all."

What was she thinking? If she wanted to be Felicity's friend, she had to prove herself!

She took a deep breath, sliding into her usual solid stance, clenching her fists, holding her arms in front of her. She closed her eyes, trying to recall the times before.

Feel the need.

Feel the heat.

Let the energy flow, rising through her marks—

She cracked an eye open. Felicity tilted her head, confused.

Mercy laughed nervously, her shoulder slumping forward. "I-I can't do it when I'm nervous."

Yeah, that was it.

Would the Founder Association know how to fix her?

"Don't be hard on yourself. It's easy to get nervous when someone's watching," Felicity said, rolling over. "Not everyone has their abilities totally figured out."

But even the Members currently without supernatural abilities, like Nikki, Lincoln, and Tabitha, all seemed to serve a purpose. Nikki was quick on her feet and brilliant at hand-to-hand combat. Lincoln was a genius inventor and deadly with his bow. Tabitha was funny, good at pep talks, and could beat someone up if needed…everything Mercy was not.

"What about your abilities?" Mercy asked.

Felicity went pale. "We'll get to it."

"I'm sure they'll be epic once you do," Mercy said, recalling what Ray had told her about Lyntox. "You'll be able to shift into animals and stuff. That sounds so cool."

"Epic…shifting into animals…yeah. Whatever word works for you." Felicity cleared her throat. "It's not really that important. I do have a tip for you, though."

Mercy perked up. "Yes?"

"Loosen up," Felicity said, relaxing her own shoulders. "You're tense."

Mercy snorted. "I'm always tense."

"Only more of a reason. It might help you be able to glow easier."

"I did it!" Ray's shout overtook Felicity as he triumphantly ran from the charge station door. He spun around, throwing his hands out to the door. "Presenting, Lincoln!"

"Ray, please shut up," Lincoln grumbled as the automatic door opened, Nathaniel happily giggling from the baby carrier buckled around Lincoln's shoulders. "Now I'm *literally* carrying our mission on my back."

"That was pretty good, Black Eyes."

Mercy almost laughed, turning back to Felicity.

"This is going to need some serious modifications," Lincoln said, already beginning to pull at the buckle.

Felicity sighed, shaking her head with a smile at the boys. She met Mercy's eyes, with the words Mercy wished she'd never have to hear again: "Ready to get back in the auto?"

Out of all the Council Members, Felicity had known Sinni Hutson the longest.

When she'd first arrived at the Inn at age sixteen, freshly out of the Liberty hospital and shipped across the continent, she'd had so many questions. How old was Inn? How long had it been since the pipes were checked? Who produced the food for the nearest grocer? What was the likelihood of a gas leak or the heater exploding?

Sinni hadn't seemed to mind, and she'd answered all of Felicity's questions to satisfaction. Felicity had thought it was a sign of friendship then, though now she knew it was much more complicated now. Sinni was imprisoned by the Oquelite by the mark on her arm and forced to operate the Inn and report any potential Impure so the Oquelite could use them for their essence.

And she was Taryn's cousin, another fact Felicity was regularly randomly reminded of and still found bizarre.

They pulled up a long, twisty cobblestone road. Felicity could smell the ocean air. She spotted a small house sitting among a cluster of yellow aspens.

Felicity couldn't help her hair from standing on the back of her neck as they pulled in. She opened the door, throwing down her bag. The chair activated immediately, and she managed to get herself in before Cole could run to help her.

A loud, creaky door swung open. "Holy crud, you made it here in one piece!"

There Sinni stood, dumbstruck, on the steps. Her short blue hair had grown out to show a hint of blonde roots, much like Taryn, swept back into a stub of a ponytail. She still wore a shirt with one long sleeve to cover her marked arm. She snapped out of her stare, racing down the steps, not even batting an eye at Felicity's wheelchair.

"Wow, Liz. It's been an eternity. You look different."

"I-I know—"

"Healthier. Stronger. Looks like you manage yourself in arm wrestle," Sinni winked, clapping Felicity on the shoulder. "Oh, and hi to—"

Mercy stumbled out of the truck, slamming a hand over her mouth, waving Sinni away as she ran to the field.

"That's Mercy. She…uh…has a weak stomach."

"That's all?"

"She has more impressive qualities than that," Felicity laughed.

Sinni nodded. "So, she's new."

"Our newest, actually," Felicity said, with a sigh. "She only arrived six months ago. She's learning."

Mercy stumbled back, defeated, with a tired wave before Sinni offered her instructions to find a bathroom inside. Mercy didn't stay a second longer.

"Oh my gosh! It's you! Inn lady!" Ray barreled out of the trailer, nearly dropping everything in his arms as his jaw dropped. Lawrence and Matteo followed.

Sinni crossed her arms. "I hear you're an Oquelite now."

Ray snorted, tossing the bag over his shoulder. "*Hybrid.*"

"Ah, right, gotcha," Sinni said, playfully tugging on a tuft of Ray's hair. "You haven't grown much, Mathews."

Ray just shook his head. "Well, neither have you."

Sinni glanced at Felicity. "So the attitude stayed."

"Got to make up for height somehow," Ray said with a smirk.

Sinni rolled her eyes, turning her focus to Matteo and Lawrence. "And you must be the Wingor and the Ywondie. Jessica told me you two were inseparable."

"I'm Matteo," Matteo said, before turning to Lawrence, who was studying Sinni through the brim of his glasses. "And this is Lawrence."

"The Williams boy. I'd seen you around town before. I don't think there was another kid with glasses," Sinni said. "Never made the connection that you were *that* Williams."

Lawrence didn't say a word, but his frown softened to something more relaxed. Felicity gave a silent sigh of relief.

"And you're Court Illegian, aren't you?" Sinni said, her eyes brightening.

Matteo flinched. "My-my accent?"

Sinni responded perfectly in Matteo's mother tongue.

His eyes widened in surprise, responding back quickly to her.

Felicity's lips parted. "How?"

"Did you forget your Sergeant and I grew up there?" Sinni said, excitedly.

Felicity *had* forgotten. She'd grown used to the fact that Taryn was bilingual and understood Matteo perfectly. It hadn't exactly crossed her mind.

Sinni took a bag from Ray's overstuffed arms. "Let me help you. We have much to discuss."

Felicity tried not to feel unhelpful as she just followed Sinni, asking anyone if they needed any help. Per usual, it was a wide array of "no's" and "I got this!"

Sinni couldn't seem to stop talking. She didn't even make it to the steps of the house before she caught sight of Cole and began doting over how much he'd grown. Ray proudly told her a summarized version of Cole's recent Marketeer ventures, with Cole turning redder by the second.

Sinni nearly dropped her bags as Lincoln walked out of the trailer.

"Holy cow. You're not the same dirty kid who would steal firewood off my back porch anymore," she said with a breathy laugh. But her eyes quickly left Lincoln to the small boy in his arms. Nathaniel hid his face in Lincoln's jacket, clutching the stuffed monkey tighter.

Her voice grew quieter. "So when Jess said he was young, she wasn't kidding."

"He's almost two," Felicity said.

Sinni's jaw dropped.

"Two!" Nathaniel repeated in a loud whisper. "No touch. Fight."

He growled.

Sinni only laughed.

"He's still practically a baby. That's insane," she said, looking from Nathaniel to Felicity before she rushed toward the house. "Only more of a reason to get you all inside. And settled in—" Sinni stopped dead in her tracks, looking down at the porch steps and back to Felicity. "Oh dear. Sorry about that, Liz."

Felicity was growing used to being disappointed by stairs, though she still didn't like having to be carried up the steps and through the door into Sinni's little hillside home.

It was dimly lit, the walls wooden and crafted to look like logs. The living room had a few mismatched couches and a small dining table, made of the same wood as the trees that grew around the house. A knit blanket was draped over the arm of the couch, and a painting of the waves was fixed above the dying fireplace.

It felt like she was stepping into a history book. Besides the knob to turn the fireplace on, it felt like she'd entered a world where modern tech had never been seen.

"This is amazing," Felicity said as Lawrence helped her back into her chair. She was a bit envious of the beautiful solitude.

"All thanks to my roommates. I don't get paid enough for a cute little place like this," Sinni said, setting down a bag on the dining room table. "They're out this week. So down the hall, room to the right for you girls, and the room on the left for the boys. Try to not destroy anything. Or clog any pipes. It's impossible to get a plumber out here."

She tapped a tablet, a holographic screen bursting up. Various shapes spun slowly, and unanswered purple messages forced their way to the forefront before she pushed them away, picking up an abandoned cup of coffee.

"What are you up to now?" Felicity asked, feeling bad as she realized she had never really checked in on Sinni since she left North Cordell.

"Odd jobs here and there. When I was still working for the Defending Department, I was an information manager. But now it's graphic design and dealing with whatever my cousin begs for on the side. Like taking in her ten children while she faces trial."

Felicity's blood went cold.

"She what?" Nikki's voice cracked. "T-Taryn's on trial?"

The entire room was frozen, all staring at Sinni. Felicity's heart beat heavy against her chest. Taryn? On trial? She hadn't done anything wrong, had she? She would get out of this quickly. Right?

Sinni looked around the room. "I thought you knew. Why do you think Nikki is suddenly being pursued?"

Before Felicity could stop herself, she turned to see Nikki's face fall.

"Is she okay?" Nikki said, stepping in beside Felicity, clutching the arm of her chair.

The rest of the Council slowly began to crowd around. Felicity could see the panic growing in Sinni's eyes as she began to flip through the holographic screen.

"Oh, well she wasn't arrested. Seriously, *nothing* to worry about. Only some guy named Armstance Giles was arrested."

Felicity's blood went cold. "Giles?"

Giles had warned her about this. Her heart sped up against her chest. Had she given him away somehow? What was Cadissa Dean going to do to him?

A shaky "no" escaped her lips.

Nikki squeezed her arm.

"But good news, only *one* of you is wanted," Sinni laughed nervously as the Council stared at her. "There's no public news about *why* Nikki is wanted, if that helps. No one knows she's an Aguirre…but if I were to suspect, our friend Commander Dean now does know."

Wasn't this what Giles had warned her about?

"What about being an Aguirre is illegal?" Cole said. "That's just unjust."

"It's not being an Aguirre, most likely. It's the fact she's a full-blood…and so is your baby Aguarious friend."

Felicity looked up to Nikki. Her face was stone, unwavering, but her grip on Felicity's arm tightened.

"That's what Giles said. Commander Dean hates full-bloods more than anything. She's tried to eradicate them before," Felicity said, her head hurting.

"This means as we speak, your Sergeant is in Imperial trying to keep that Aguarious and Nikki from being discovered and killed. You don't have Defenders on your side this time…well, except for, like, four Defenders." Sinni cleared her throat. "Anyone want tea?"

The Council didn't say a word, but Felicity could feel the mood stiffen. She could sense the shifting and exchange of glances. They didn't even need to speak telepathically to know how serious this was.

A tiny part of her couldn't help but be more worried about Giles. He'd mentioned execution. What a terrible way to die.

He *wouldn't* die. If it came down to it, she'd fight. She'd go straight to her father and beg for him to be bailed.

"I'll take straight black coffee," Cole said, rubbing his temples.

"Great. I'm guessing none of you are really tea drinkers anyway," Sinni said with a forced smile. "I'll brew a pot while you all get settled."

Nikki finally let go of Felicity's arm as they exchanged glances before going down the hall to their room. The room was nice enough, despite one broken window covered in tape. There was a small fireplace, newly installed by the looks of the shiny on switch. There was one big queen bed, made neatly with teal cotton blankets that matched the walls, and a long couch that overlooked the outside.

Mercy claimed it quickly, sitting cross-legged and staring out into the fog. Felicity rolled up beside her. "You know, we're not too far from the ocean. I bet when it's less foggy, you can see the beach from here."

"Really?" Mercy said, her eyes widening.

Felicity nodded, the knot in her stomach loosening as she saw the wonder in Mercy's eyes. Something about making Mercy more comfortable helped Felicity feel the same. It was something she hadn't been able to do for Nikki…in fact, she'd absolutely despised Nikki when they'd first met.

The circumstances weren't great.

And yet, even that couldn't get her mind off Giles.

"Where do you want to sleep, Liz?" Tabitha said.

"Uh, you choose for me," Felicity said as she quickly rolled out of the room.

She moved down the hall and peeked into through the small door that led to the pristine white kitchen, where Sinni was scrolling on her tele as she stirred a large pot of coffee.

She glanced up at the creak of the door, her face softening. "You look worried, Liz."

"Somewhat. I'm always worried," Felicity laughed nervously. "It's odd to have you back."

"Trust me. You're not the only one feeling weird about it," Sinni said, shutting off her Comm. "Hungry for pot pie leftovers, or are you still vegetarian?"

"I'll pass." Felicity watched as Sinni took out a few mugs and wiped up a pile of spilled coffee beans before she couldn't hold it in anymore. "Why is Giles on trial?"

"Not sure," Sinni said, setting a container out on the counter. "I believe it has to do with some broken oath, but I don't know why Jess—" Sinni stopped, frowning. "You're awfully red, Liz."

But *what?* What could a Defender so young know that painted such a large target on his back? Why was he just arrested now?

"Did you care for him?" Sinni asked gently, snapping Felicity's attention back.

"He's my friend," Felicity said quickly.

"Just your friend? Or like, friend-friend, like that Oquelite prince?"

Felicity's face flamed. "That wasn't ever *anything.*"

Sinni shrugged. "If you say so. I saw the way you looked at each other."

And it was pointless. Even if Felicity loved him then, he'd ruined everything. It hadn't been real. It had all been a trick. *Pointless.*

"He betrayed me…us! He's a murderer and a liar. He was just faking it to bring me to his stupid cult."

She didn't care if Silas had warned them of an Exerticus

attack *twice*. Nothing would forgive him for what he'd done.

Sinni was quiet a moment, staring hard at the counter before looking back to Felicity. "Look, I hold no sympathy for him either, but have you never considered he might actually…love you?"

Felicity's stomach flipped. She never wanted to even consider it. The thought of him genuinely caring for her felt worse than him being fully evil.

She didn't want to consider him human.

"I'm by no means saying you should accept him, but all I'm saying is try to not let your feelings distort what might be reality," Sinni said. "And not just with Silas."

She winked, and Felicity didn't even want to consider what she meant by that. She didn't want to think about her feelings. She wanted to think about making sure Giles didn't die.

And she could care less about what happened to Silas.

But the glimmer in Sinni's new smirk caught her attention. "Besides, if Silas does have a soft spot for you," Sinni said, raising a brow, "that might be something you could use to your advantage."

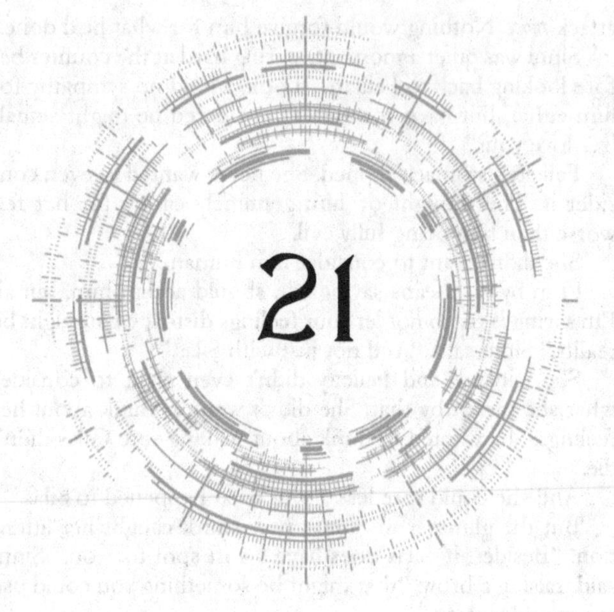

21

MERCY FOUND THAT *sleeping* was the solution to motion sickness.

But it was hard to sleep to all the little noises Tabitha was making on her Scroll.

And the fact Tabitha was awake made it impossible for Mercy to start her plan to get the Ewyon Stone, but she couldn't help but be relieved.

She was woken up before she even knew she'd fallen asleep, and she practically dragged herself through the morning until someone mentioned her name.

"I think Mercy would be discreet enough," Ray said.

It took Mercy a second to realize they were talking about the next mission to relocate Nathaniel.

"Really?" Cole said, raising a brow.

"She's quiet and won't blow any cover. Besides, she hasn't gotten out much," Ray said, flashing a smile to Mercy. "Right, Glow Girl?"

Mercy felt her face heat as all eyes turned to her.

"Uh, sure," she said, standing up a little straighter. *She* was being volunteered for a Super Important Council Mission? This never happened!

And that's how she ended up in the back of the pickup truck, squished against the windowsill with Ray squashed in the middle between her and Lincoln.

She knew the only reason she was going was because Ray felt bad for her, but she was determined to maybe prove her worth a little this time around. She *would* be helpful.

"You're awake, Glow Girl," Ray said, nudging her. "About time. Have a good nap?"

"It was absolutely amazing," she said, and it wasn't a lie. "Are we there yet?"

"Almost," Sinni said from the passenger seat. "So what's your plan for this mission?"

"It's simple. We get in and out to see if the Manifest Orphan Housing System is a good fit," Cole said. "I think it's best if Mercy's the face of this mission. Ray's already been recognized, and we can't risk Lincoln."

Mercy's heart leapt. *Helpful! She could be helpful!*

And Ray was there too. There was no way to mess this up.

"In that case, we're going to need aliases, right?" Mercy said.

"Aliases?" Ray said.

"Yeah, like new names? So they can't use our real names against us?"

"Interesting. Good point," Lincoln said. "Hiding our names from the government just like we do with a rageful, blood-hungry immortal."

"I used to come up with fake names when I had to go grocery shopping for a while," Mercy said. "Maybe you and Ray are brothers."

"Estranged, reluctant brothers," Ray corrected. "And you are—?"

"Your motivated and professional distant cousin, Stella Maris," Mercy said, straightening herself before having to instantly pull her skirt over her knees. It belonged to Felicity and was inches too short.

"Oh, and they're *totally* going to fall for this," Sinni snorted.

"They did accept our forged paperwork, so they stand a

chance," Cole said. "If anyone asks, Nathaniel's last name is Brooks."

"Oh, because he controls water? Har-har. Genius."

"*I* came up with it," Lincoln said, elbowing Ray.

"That explains a lot."

"It sounds cute," Mercy piped up.

"What? You're siding with Lincoln now?" Ray said, blinking.

"At least someone is siding with me," Lincoln grumbled.

Mercy heard Cole give a long sigh. "Look, I know you had a bad experience with OHS in the past, but you can't let that affect what could be a great opportunity for Nathaniel."

Lincoln had a past in the OHS?

She'd thought he'd always just been roaming alone in North Cordell.... Well, it did make more sense.

OHS had constantly been on her father's back, and her grandmother took it as justification of his bad parenting skills.

"I've never met anyone who went through the system," Mercy said, hoping maybe they could have something in common. A conversation...which led to socialization...and then—

Lincoln laughed. "Oh no. I didn't go *through* it. I escaped," he said proudly.

Mercy blinked. "Escaped?"

The auto began to slow. An enormous domed building began to show over the rolling hills.

"Long story. For another time."

The windows were colored, and large divided grass fields circled the building. It had to be multiple stories tall. The biggest Mercy had seen...maybe only second to the Tube station. As they made their way further down the road, she saw bursts of children in the fields, some stopping and staring through the gate as they passed.

It appeared peaceful, but she couldn't ignore Lincoln's glares.

They stopped at the entry gate, and Lincoln, Ray, and Mercy unloaded from the truck.

Mercy stretched, having to pull her skirt down again. She was lucky she had tights, both for the awkward-fitting clothes and to avoid showing the marks. The only mark visible was the one on her neck. She took a deep breath.

It was just a mission. It wasn't even a very illegal one.

She could get through this.

Lincoln buckled the carrier, Nathaniel looking around excitedly at his new environment.

Sinni rolled down the truck window.

"Please *don't* almost die?" Cole said. "It would make life way easier."

"We'll try," Lincoln joked dryly.

They quickly backed out, leaving the three of them to fend for themselves. Ray pushed Mercy into the lead.

"Hey!" she snapped.

"You heard Cole. You should lead this." He winked.

She resisted the urge to elbow him hard.

A loud beep caused them both to jump. The entry window screen loaded, an automated voice going off. "Name and Inquiry."

Mercy looked back at Ray nervously. Lincoln gave her a thumbs-up, which was more encouraging than Ray's smirk. "Stella Maris, second cousin of child Nathaniel Brooks. We're here on an arranged visit."

The screen flashed from green to red, and the gate opened. A ticket printed from below the screen. Ray snatched it. "Enter the main lobby, and be seated until your guide arrives," the voice directed.

Mercy felt her bones freeze. There was no way she would've been allowed to enter a government building.

And yet, here she was.

She had to.

She couldn't let them down. *Breathe.*

Ray thankfully took the lead, giving her a second to shake herself off and rush after him. After a short flight of stairs, the doors slid open to a lobby room.

It smelled like an odorless chemical cleaner, all the seats were made of metal, and a little plant was the only splash of color in the center of the room.

The door slid shut behind them.

The three of them jumped and silently decided to squeeze together on a bench. Lincoln unbuckled Nathaniel from his carrier, placing him on his lap and holding him tightly.

Mercy caught the toddler's eye. She tried to smile, but the little toddler just frowned.

"Weird that even across the ocean, they still look exactly the same," Lincoln grumbled.

His disdain for the place just seemed to be begging for her to ask. But was it rude to ask? It was none of her business. It would probably lead to awkward conversation.

"How long were you in the OHS?" Mercy said quickly before she could think of another excuse.

"Six months. And then I was out of there."

Mercy glanced back to the giant handless door leading out of the waiting room, a DNA pad on the wall, and then back to the gate outside, the bot guards' heads spinning. "You *escaped?*"

"Technical genius," Ray said with a sigh. "He won't let you forget it."

"Yeah, but Nathaniel *isn't* a technical genius." Nathaniel looked up to Lincoln at the mention of his name. "How is *he* supposed to escape?"

"We're here to find a place for him to stay. It kind of defeats the point if he just escapes," Ray huffed.

"Well. He should. It sucks here. If it was up to me, this wouldn't even be a consideration!" Lincoln said.

Nathaniel whimpered.

Lincoln's eyes widened, and he hurridly began to pet down Nathaniel's curls. "No, no. I'm sorry. I wasn't yelling at you. It's okay."

"How do we plan on hiding his…" Mercy tried to wave her hands in the air to imitate Nathaniel's powers, but Lincoln and Ray stared, confused, while Nathaniel thought the display was hilarious.

The door swung open. Mercy's head snapped to see a woman walk through the door, wearing a tight, hot pink pantsuit, her black hair buzzed. She had a clear clipboard tight in her grip.

"A tour was requested?" she said, her voice a little too high-pitched and enthusiastic for Mercy to believe it was trustworthy.

"Thomas Brooks," Ray said, jumping to his feet, offering Mercy a hand. "And my cousin, Stella Maris."

She nodded, feeling her throat go dry. *Pull it together, Re-*

membrance!

"It's our honor to meet you!" Ray said, offering the woman his hand.

She frowned at it before raising her wristband and, with a band, spritzed sanitizer at him. Ray stumbled back, coughing.

"We're dedicated to keep the OHS sanitary, Mr. Brooks." She took a side step. "Now, is that the child?"

Lincoln glared as he rose to his feet, Nathaniel at his hip.

"Yes," Ray said. "This is my brother..."

He glanced at Mercy nervously. "Damien Brooks," Mercy finished quickly. "He's a bit grumpy, I'm afraid."

Ray flashed Mercy a quick smile.

"Understandable. Children can do that to a person." The woman pushed between them. With her long nails, she turned Nathaniel's face to hers. He wrenched away with a similar glare to Lincoln's. "Name?"

"Nathaniel." Lincoln avoided her gaze.

The woman clicked her tongue. "Good, good. There is no shame, Mr. Brooks. You've made a good decision considering our care for your young boy."

"He's not *my* boy."

"Fight please," Nathaniel whispered loudly.

Mercy cringed. The woman blinked.

"Perhaps we could start the tour," Ray said, clearing his throat. "He's a bit uneasy, I'm afraid."

The woman spun on her heel, clasping her hand together. "Excellent suggestion! Let us get a move on, then."

The woman swiftly moved to the tall glass door, placing her hand on the keypad. The doors slid open. Mercy swallowed hard, looking to Ray, who gave her a nod. She wanted to smile back.

She was supposed to be the face of this mission, but it was all falling to Ray.

Once again, she was failing her task.

Tabitha's judging frown echoed back at her.

"Here in Manifest, we are proud to have one of the most efficiently run and sanitary OHS's of all the regions."

As they stepped out into the center, the ceiling of the building was raised high above them. Walkways crisscrossed higher and higher, leading to what could only be dozens of stories. Large planters held trees and plants beside benches. Children of all ages sat at the tables, intent on their tablets or walking to and fro. A few were squatted on the floor over a holographic bot fighter game. They quickly shut it off as the woman passed.

The OHS smelled distinctly like the back of Mercy's Grandmere's auto. It had always been pristine, and one time when Pere had been out of town when she was five, Mercy had made the mistake of crawling in after making mud cakes in the rain.

She forced the memory of her Grandmere's scolding out of mind as a bot rolled by, offering her hand sanitizer. Mercy took it, rubbing her hands, taking a deep breath as she followed the woman and the boys into an elevator.

She couldn't help but look at Nathaniel, whose green eyes were growing wider as they rose higher. He slowly sank into Lincoln's chest.

His anxiety was contagious. She tried to keep her head level, unclenching her fists. With the amount she was sweating, she was totally going to give them away.

She took a deep breath. *You got this. Felicity said the key was not being tense.*

"Manifest OHS is highly secure, as you know from the online briefing," the woman said, proud as she adjusted her collar, having no clue that not one of the teenagers in the elevator with her even *knew* there was an online briefing. "No one leaves unless they're with a hand-selected security team or until they are seventeen and dismissed from the system."

Lincoln grimaced.

Mercy's heart skipped a beat. If he'd never run away from the OHS, he'd still be stuck in a place like this…and for another four months until he turned seventeen.

The elevator stopped, the door shimmering away to reveal a young woman with her hair braided and twisted up into a bun. She gave a small curtsy. "Ms. Petzel."

"Ah! This is Olivia Fields," the woman said, leading them out. "She came to us at only a few days old, and she now works for us as a tutor."

"And there is nowhere I'd rather be," Olivia said with a beaming smile.

Lincoln rolled his eyes.

Ray elbowed him. *See! Some people like it here.*

Yeah. Keyword: SOME.

"Oh! I love your skirt!" Olivia said, throwing Mercy out of the boys' telepathic conversation.

She blinked, looking down to her awkwardly fitting skirt. "Thank you," she stammered with a small smile.

Ms. Petzel beamed, patting Olivia on the shoulder. "Such a great example of OHS manner and culture classes. Why don't you follow me this way?"

What happened to YOUR manner classes? Ray smirked at Lincoln.

Lincoln grumbled something unintelligible.

Mercy shook her head at Ray.

"We have classes for the appropriate age levels, of course. For six hours a day. They're not mandatory at every OHS institute, but I'm very honored to have this opportunity," Olivia Fields said.

See! He wouldn't even have to go to school if he hated it so much. Is this why you don't know how to read? You skipped class?

RAY. I was at OHS for literally six months. And yes. I did skip class. I was too busy trying to get out.

Mercy could see why. Something about the structure was unsettling…and definitely not like Lincoln's typical style. She wanted to ask him how he did it, but she didn't want to reveal she *still* hadn't figured out the whole telepathic conversation thing.

"Boys!"

A group of boys no older than seven came to a harsh halt, their laughter quickly dissipating to horror in their eyes.

"No running in the hallways," Petzel snapped. "And you, young man, did you shove your fellow?"

Lincoln gave Ray a comical shove from behind Petzel's back, and Mercy watched as the boys' fear quickly turned to struggling to hold in giggles at the rare display of a joke.

Petzel, oblivious to the two troublemakers behind her, crossed her arms. "Do you need to spend your weekend in the detention basin?"

The boys quickly shook their heads.

"I'll let you off with a warning." Ms. Petzel flashed a fake smile and laugh over her shoulder before shooing the boys off.

They ran without missing a beat. They rushed past Lincoln and Ray waving, their eyes practically glowing.

Nathaniel watched them curiously pass, raising his tiny hand to wave back.

Mercy felt a small twinge of pride. Something as simple as cheering up the silly little boys made her nerves settle. They could do this.

"Behavioral difficulties are easily squashed. Good habits and behavior are taught and enforced," Ms. Petzel said, her smile glued to her face. Olivia nodded to reassure them.

"What about the newest— er-supernatural resurgence?" Mercy said boldly. Would she even know what she was talking about? Was she shooting herself in the foot?

"Like those strange Purizies who attacked Imperial?" Fields said. "Plenty of children claim to have special powers, and some even have…oddities about them, but it's nothing a few days of detention basin and behavioral therapy can't help."

How much longer? Lincoln groaned mentally.

We have to take the whole tour.

I've already made up my mind. The answer is no.

It's a collective decision, Black Eyes. Not just yours.

Mercy wanted to agree with Lincoln. She couldn't place exactly why she didn't like this place. In theory, it should've been fine. Kids got meals, a place to stay, and an education.

And yet the idea of being behind these walls…it made her shiver.

She knew how that felt.

A teacher passed by, frowning at her. Mercy's heart stammered, quick to smooth out her crumpled collar.

"Are kids ever adopted?" Ray butted in.

"Only infants are put up for adoption. Too many difficulties with trying to integrate an older child."

Whispers seemed to grow louder. Mercy could still feel the teacher's eyes burning into the back of her skull. The chatter of a line of young children seemed to chant, "We know! We know what you're hiding! You're giving it away!"

She tried to force a smile, but she just heard a laugh in response.

A bell rang, and the entire building seemed to erupt into chatter. Mercy stared at her shoes. If she didn't make any direct eye contact, no one could think she was suspicious, right?

Residents pushed around her, not giving her a second glance.

She felt relieved.

Maybe there was too much chaos going on for them to even care. Maybe there wasn't a reason—

"What class are you supposed to be in, young lady?"

Mercy's hair stood up on the back of her neck, and she spun around to see the teacher standing with her arms crossed, her monocle floating above her eye.

"I-I don't have a class. I-I'm on a—" Mercy looked behind her, hoping Ray would step in to explain. Her heart dropped.

Ray was nowhere to be seen.

Just the crowded halls of the OHS.

They were gone.

22

SHE WHIPPED BACK around to the teacher.

"Uh-uh. You're old enough to be in the senior sessions right now. Don't try and make any excuses." The teacher sighed, unclipping a Comm from the pocket of her skirt.

Mercy felt her sweat go cold. Weren't classes optional? *How* optional?

"I guess I'll just call security to come escort—"

Mercy didn't take another second to stand around as the teacher began to ramble on, typing into her Comm. She pushed past a group of girls giggling over a magazine tablet, dashing around the corner. Her heart hammered against her ears.

Where were they?

She was going to get them all caught and ruin any chance Nathaniel had. Nikki was already wanted. It had to be illegal to lie about your identity and break into an OHS facility.

Mercy didn't want to go to prison.

An elevator door opened. An escape! There!

Mercy didn't think twice before leaping between the

doors, flattening herself against the wall as they closed, catching her breath.

A group of kindergarteners stared at her with open mouths. Meanwhile, their chaperone was unfazed, scrolling through his Comm.

She straightened herself, giving an awkward wave.

They blinked.

One waved, and then stuck their fingers in his mouth.

This had to break, like, every single one of Grandmere's rules.

What if they found out they lied their way in?

She'd go to prison…or worse: back to Sulfur and the cabin in the woods.

Back to the watery coffin to die before she could ignite to escape—

Ding!

The elevator doors opened. The children cheered, pouring out and startling their chaperone, who chased after them.

Mercy shook herself. *Snap out of it! You're a Council Member. Act like it!*

The hallway was entirely unfamiliar. Marble floors and blank white walls with a few holographic portraits and plaques.

It was empty of children, besides the group she'd entered with. She watched as the group made their way to two large glass doors into a dark room glittering with holograms, and…glass cases.

Mercy's eyebrow rose. She followed after them. Above the doors in gold print read: *In Remembrance of Curatrix Team Member, Officer Zita Klirkpatrick.*

Mercy frowned. She rarely heard Zita's name alone. She was often meshed together with the other members.

It intrigued her. Why in the OHS? And the room was dark. Perfect place to hide. She stepped forward, the door sensing her and opening.

"Please keep your voice down and respectful, thank you," a little automated voice chirped.

The room was lit by spotlights over cases and holograms, and most notably, a holographic photo of Officer Zita herself.

The Curatrix Member had a dark complexion and long

braided hair that reached to nearly below her hair, most of it dyed a pastel blue.

She wasn't wearing the typical armored top of the Defender uniform, but a simple tank top, and a chain with her identification tags…and a peculiar blue stone.

Mercy felt her nerves settle a bit at seeing the woman's kind, gentle expression. There was an entire timeline written out along the wall.

A tribute to the member.

One of the first displays held a tiny OHS school uniform.

So that's why she has a tribute here. Apparently, Zita had been put into OHS at a young age. Her little ID photo showed the young Defender was tiny, her uniform oversized, but her smile was big.

Part of the Curatrix Team story was that Zita had a "contract with the government" that stated if she didn't pass, she would be in government containment. There were various theories as to why, but Mercy had now learned it was because of Zita's full-blooded Aguarious nature.

Just like Nathaniel.

The next section focused on Zita's involvement in the Bandit and child abduction problem, and therefore, her own personal mission to improve living conditions in the OHS.

"Though Zita didn't have any children like most of the Curatrix Team, she made an impact for hundreds of others," the speaker read.

Her mission had been to keep the children safe. And yet, here were a group of children trying to keep the world safe.

What would she have done?

"A shiny rock!" one of the children gasped, breaking the quiet.

Mercy frowned, turning to see the group swarming around a case a few feet away.

"It's only a replica," the chaperone said. "The original was lost when she died. Rumor has it that it was connected to Zita…" The chaperone jazzed his hands. "…magically."

The children awed in amazement.

Mercy's eyes widened. *Zita* had an artifact too?

An artifact she could use to contact the Founder Association? Who was she kidding? How was she even supposed to *find* a rock that had been missing for over a decade?

She was better off using the Ewyon Stone.

Stealing from Tabitha? Or even Ray? She wouldn't feel so guilty. But stealing from Nikki? That idea made her sick to her stomach.

But if she could find the Aguarious Stone, maybe after she contacted the Founder Association, she could use it to help Nathaniel! Maybe she could use it to prove to the Council she was in fact useful, and not some useless Member with faulty abilities.

She could feel the excitement bubbling as she spun around. This could be it. This might be—

She stopped mid-step, her heart stopping at the words engraved in the plaque before her, bringing her right back to reality with a cold pinch:

Zita Klirkpatrick died at twenty-eight in Sulfur.

A picture was posted beside the plaque of a picturesque house in a field of lilacs, but the details made such a peaceful photo so much more horrifying.

Mercy didn't even want to read the details, but her eyes refused to leave.

Only hours after the successful assassination of Aaron Outown, Sergeant Rayder Dow found Officer Klirkpatrick's body in the fields behind her home—

Mercy's head was spinning, forcing her to take a step back. Dow had been the one to find Zita? She'd met the Sergeant herself on one occasion.

The assassin confessed and detailed their crime. Zita, along with her three other killed Team Members, were honored three days later in Imperial, home of the Defending Department.

All of Zita's assets were left to an OHS child in her care.

"Depressing, isn't it?"

Mercy jumped, turning to see the chaperone standing behind her. The children were over at the next exhibit, playing excitedly with an interactive map.

"V-very," Mercy said, clearing her throat and readjusting her headband. She took a small step to the side, keeping her eyes on the image of the house.

"I'm not a Curatrix Team mega fan like some, but I always had a soft spot for Zita," he said. "She just never seemed to care about the politics. She never wanted the fame that came with it. It makes it a far more interesting tour."

And then she'd paid for it with her life.

Just like Reyna and Lyell Aguirre, Nikki's whole family, had. Just like Aaron Outown, Miriam's beloved older brother. The entire region of Defenders killed in front of Taryn.

Only six months ago, the Curatrix Team had been some media fascination Mercy only heard about on her tele.

And now?

She *was* the Curatrix Team. She was part of a group just like them, and most possibly could have a similar gory end.

Mercy tried not to focus on that. First, she needed to focus on the Stone.

"Where is Zita's magic stone?" she said, trying to sound dumbly curious as she turned to the tour guide.

He shrugged. "No one knows. It was never found when she died." A glimmer of mischief sparkled in his eye. "Maybe it *poof!* disappeared."

Mercy gave a nervous laugh. "Maybe it did."

She cleared her throat again. "Thanks for answering the question. I better be going."

Mercy slipped away quickly before he could ask about what class she was in. The tour had to be nearly over now. Lincoln and Ray wouldn't leave without her, would they?

The chaperone shouted after her. "Wait!"

Mercy froze. Shoot.

"I'm supposed to give visitors a keychain! And I think you'll like this one!"

Mercy slowly turned on her heel. A keychain couldn't hurt, right?

He dug it out of his pocket, tossing it to her. "Thank you for your educational visit to the OHS Officer Klirkpatrick memorial. You can donate to the OHS cause on our web link and uh—well, you know the rest," he said with a shrug, before turning back to his group of children.

That was oddly…nice of him.

Mercy looked down at the keychain. A plastic blue stone.

Her heart leapt. A replica of the Aguarious Stone.

If the last place the Stone was seen was the place Zita had been…that would lead her to Sulfur. Maybe she could double check with Matteo on their route.

Mercy pulled out her Comm to clip on the keychain when a message popped up on the screen:

"*MATHEWS: Where the heck are you?*"

Why hadn't Mercy thought about messaging him? She wanted to slap herself for being so dumb. She was too busy panicking.

"*At some Zita exhibit on the first floor.*"

"*Stay where you are. We'll come find you.*"

His tone felt unusually serious. *Great going, Mercy. Your shot at leading a mission and you got lost.*

She stepped outside and sat on a bench by the door.

Mercy looked down at the Aguarious Stone keychain. Something about Zita intrigued her. Would the Curatrix Member have ideas about Nathaniel?

Mercy shook it off. She was too much of a floundering mess to try to find that out. Maybe she'd be stuck in the background of the Council forever…and maybe she should start getting used to it.

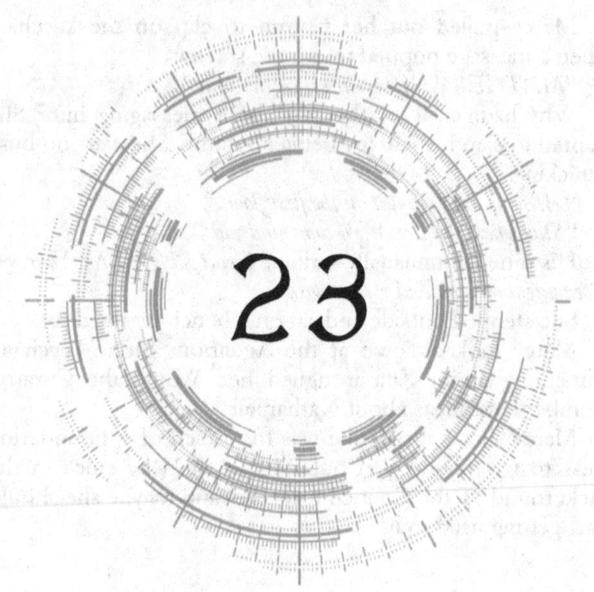

23

"Tʜᴀᴛ ᴡᴀs sᴏ close to being a disaster," Cole sighed, pinching the bridge of his nose.

"But it wasn't," Ray pitched in with an enthusiastic smile.

Cole didn't return the sentiment, and Felicity caught Mercy scooting behind an armchair out of the corner of her eye.

Felicity narrowed her eyes. Mercy had been more quiet and skittish than usual.

Was she embarrassed she'd gotten lost? Felicity had been lost in far worse, and more dangerous places, which resulted in being chased by a literal reptilian Shifter.

"But at least we now know that the OHS is a bad, dumb, absolutely terrible idea, and that's the end of it. Right?" Lincoln said with a hopeful smile.

He sat on the floor by the fireplace, Nathaniel sitting beside him playing with the Super Cube, which Lincoln had now programmed to flash rainbow colors. It was the one thing that distracted him from trying to lick outlets or stick his hand in the fireplace.

"The OHS actually seems like a secure option. While sure, it's not a very fun one, it's safe and that's what matters," Cole said, beginning to pace. "The security would be a real advantage."

"That's the worst part!" Lincoln shouted. "Kids are just another plug in the system to them. When I came in at eleven years old, only with memories about random Impure facts, they put me in a detention center."

The room was quiet.

"Nathaniel will be two. He might even have a chance at being adopted," Felicity said, biting her lip. "He most likely won't be as rebellious."

"He's a Council Member. It kinda runs in our blood," Lincoln scoffed.

"Felicity, do you think there's anything *you* could do to maybe…I dunno, encourage Nathaniel to be adopted?" Cole said.

Felicity shrugged. "I could always try."

It would be an odd request, but surely if someone heard the name Bentsworth it would be easier.

"But what about his abilities?" Lincoln said. "You know, the whole *controlling water* thing?"

"The OHS *did* say they had a system for that," Ray admitted.

"And it sounds like it sucks."

"If he grows up around normal kids, there's also a chance he won't be influenced to use them," Cole said. "He'll blend in better."

Lincoln opened his mouth to argue, but he shut it with a scowl.

Nathaniel stopped chewing on the Cube and crawled up into Lincoln's lap…almost as if he felt the gravity of the situation.

"I know it's not an ideal situation, but getting Nathaniel with a family is probably the best bet we have," Cole said.

Lincoln refused to look at him.

Cole looked to Felicity as if she'd have answers. She shook her head. She wished she could side with Lincoln. Her heart ached to denounce the cold-hearted OHS and comfort Lincoln from his past experiences…but Cole was right. If they could give Nathaniel a family, that was the best possible option.

"Sometimes to protect the people you love, you have to do hard things," Lawrence said, and before Lincoln could open his mouth, Lawrence countered: "And don't you dare say you don't love him."

Lincoln shut up, but he didn't look happy about it, grumbling something under his breath.

"We'll finalize this tomorrow," Cole said. "It's been a long day. Rest is long overdue."

No one argued, but no one seemed particularly restful.

Lincoln started off down the hall.

Cole placed a hand on his shoulder.

Lincoln shrugged him off and walked faster.

"Just give him space," Felicity said. "This is a lot for him…for everyone."

Cole pursed his lips, looking longingly down the hall. "I wish we didn't have to do this." He left up the stairs.

Felicity didn't like the unease that was left in the room. She rolled into the kitchen to see Sinni standing there. "Are all your meetings this depressing?" she said, with a half-hearted chuckle.

Felicity sighed. "Could I just have some tea, please?"

She took her tea to her room, taking her time in the shower in hopes that the rest of the room would be asleep by the time she got out.

Her wish was granted, much to her surprise. Nikki and Tabitha were night owls, through and through, and yet they were sound asleep.

Nikki was curled up in her respective sofa, her back turned to the rest of the room. Something about sleep made her look vulnerable.

Felicity could hear Tabitha's snores from the edge of the bed as she eased herself into it. She rolled over, pulling her tele on the bedside table.

It lit up.

One message from 'Army Giles'*

Felicity pushed herself, smothering a squeal with her hand. She tapped on the notification.

ARMY: I'm fine. Don't worry. Stay safe.

Very short and vague.

YOU: All I do is worry.

She shut off the device. At least she knew he was still alive. That was all that mattered.

Now all Felicity needed to do was sleep, cozying down into the bed, wrapping the blanket around herself. Soon this whole ordeal would be over, and Nathaniel would have a safe new home. She could be back in her own bed. Giles would be alive and well. She could maybe finally finish helping Nikki paint her room yellow.

She drifted off to sleep.

That's when an earth-shattering roar echoed through her skull.

Felicity jumped up with a cry, trying to catch her breath.

The window was open a crack, the thin curtains dancing in the wind.

Again, no one else had heard it.

Maybe she was hallucinating. It couldn't be happening again. It couldn't. She plopped back down.

A whine rang through her mind. Very deep…and very annoying.

Come now!

It didn't stop until Felicity sat up with a gasp. "Fine! Alright. Couldn't you pick a more convenient time?"

Whatever creature this was really thought the middle of the night was a good time to bother her.

It had to be the same creature. It had the same deep, vibrating undertone.

It was *calling* her.

What creatures even had the ability to telepathically communicate with humans?

Guardian. Come now! Hurry.

Felicity swallowed hard. Right. She was the Guardian Member…a Mythical creature.

But how was she supposed to protect them? She was still figuring out how to protect herself. She eased herself into her chair, praying the floorboards didn't squeak as she rolled for the door.

She breathed a heavy sigh of relief as she entered the hallway with no one waking up. She moved slowly to the main room. The kitchen light was on, but Sinni was nowhere to be seen.

It would've been just Felicity's luck for her to walk in.

The creature's moaning echo brought her to the front door. Was she really insane enough to do this?

You've done worse, she reminded herself.

But that's when she could walk and easily run away. She didn't even have her spear.

Whatever she was getting herself into, she was going in headfirst.

The moaning grew louder, as if it was annoyed at her for taking so long.

Felicity slipped out the door, a cold gust of air seeping in. She shivered and cringed as her chair bumped out onto the bench. "Maybe bother someone else who can easily go down stairs!" she said in a harsh, frustrated whisper.

She was now trapped in the howling cold wind, the smell of the salty sea being the only consolation.

She could've sworn the creature's moan echoed throughout the entire plain, but she wouldn't be surprised if, once again, she was the only one who heard.

What if she *was* crazy? Just like her aunt Olivia said.

This was all just a figment of her shattered imagination—

Her brother! Coming! Hurry!

The creature called to her again, its melodic rhythm soothing her doubts.

Now all she had to do was face her greatest enemy: stairs.

She had to lower herself off the chair, sitting down on the wet porch in her sweatpants, and deactivate the chair, tossing it to the ground. She scooted down the steps, activating the chair with her foot, crawling to pull herself up into it.

The whole process was a workout.

The creature became excited, the rhythm of its voice jumping back and forth through her mind.

Felicity moved toward the sound, the wind beating against her. She strained her eyes as she went down the cobblestone path before she hit grass and sand. Another challenge.

She was heading for the ocean.

Hurry! The storms!

The wheelchair slowed as she hit the rocky beach. Felicity rolled to a stop, watching the dawn-approaching sky and the dark waves crashing against the rocks, seeming to dance to the creature's hum.

Felicity moved toward the water.

Last time a voice intruded into her head, she'd lost her ability to walk. Why was she listening to this one now?

It didn't even have a human voice.

She reached the line where the water crashed against the rocks. Felicity sucked in her breath, taking in the strong scent.

But the creature was not satisfied, whimpering. *He's coming!*

Felicity blinked, staring wide-eyed as a wave crashed against the rocks. "There's no way you want me to go in there," Felicity laughed, shakily.

The creature went silent. Was that it? Had it just wanted her here? Or was she really imagining the whole thing?

A pained, piercing whistle shattered through her mind. Felicity cried out in pain, clamping her hands over her ears. The world spun and for a moment of panic, she thought she was back in the Oquelite Labyrinth, right after Silas had betrayed her.

She thought she was dying.

And then…it stopped, Felicity gasping for a sweet relief, her ears feeling as though they were bleeding.

The realization trickled in.

"Something's hurting you," she said, looking out toward the ocean. "Why?"

It didn't respond, but a strange feeling swelled inside her. She knew it was an awful idea. She'd left her leg braces on the nightstand back at the house.

Not like it mattered. The braces weren't great with water.

Felicity pushed up against the arms of the chair, taking a deep breath as she pressed her foot up against the stone. Putting weight down on it sent a horrible pain through her spine, tears pricking at her eyes.

She just tried to ignore it…if she could just balance for just a moment.

Her knees buckled, and for a split second, she thought she'd hit the rocky, shallow water below, unable to get up out of the crashing sea—

But instead, she tumbled into Nikki's arms.

"Good timing," Felicity wheezed.

"Felicity!" Tabitha's voice echoed from behind. "What the heck do you think you're doing?"

Felicity ignored her, clinging to Nikki. "Help me down to the shore."

"Felicity! You're not supposed to be out!" Mercy dashed in front of Nikki and Felicity, catching her breath. "You might catch a cold! Or get captured by bandits! Or fall—"

Felicity was almost caught off guard by the genuine begging of Mercy's eyes.

"Mercy, coming up with all the ways things could go wrong is *my* job," Felicity said. "Give me some help here."

"But—"

"I'll explain later. Hurry! I don't think we have much time."

Mercy's face hardened, biting the inside of her cheeks with clear distaste, but she quickly ran to slip her arm under Felicity's, supporting her from the other side.

"Felicity, you can't swim!" Tabitha nearly tripped over the rocks, stopping to catch her breath, shivering.

"I'm not going for a swim," Felicity said with a frown.

Nikki gave a relieved sigh. Mercy's eyebrows shot up. "So what are you—"

"I just have a feeling!"

"I hope it's a deep feeling of guilt for sneaking out and not even telling me, the master of sneaking!" Tabitha said, crossing her arms.

"You usually always get caught," Nikki pointed out.

Another wail echoed through Felicity's mind, rising to a sharp whistle. She cried out.

Her friends froze.

"What's going—"

Felicity cringed in pain. "Just get to the water!"

Now there was no hesitation.

Instant relief swept over her in a cool wave as the icy water touched her feet. She clung onto Nikki and Mercy for her dear life.

"Okay, what now—"

Felicity didn't hear the rest of what Tabitha said. Her head jerked back, her vision black and her mind blank. The sound of the waves drowned out.

And then she was thrown into a memory she'd never

seen before.

It was a dock, late at night, only dimly lit by lamp posts. A few cargo ships were at dock, crates waiting to be loaded. Felicity felt as though she were peering above the water, watching.

She heard the creature's whistle. This time, more gentle. *Look!*

"It's okay. I'm here," she whispered.

Was she seeing what the creature saw?

A steady set of footsteps sounded on the dock. Felicity's heart leaped. The glow of a lantern approached around the corner. Two people stepped into view.

Felicity immediately wished she could dive below the waves.

The face of the man holding the lantern was all too familiar, obscured by a ragged cloak. The other had a dark, clear complexion and a bright white braid over her shoulder. But what struck Felicity the most was her glowing red eyes.

It struck her.

That was the Exerticus who'd attacked her in Liberty. The creature clicked to agree with Felicity's disdain. *Yes! Bad!*

The Exerticus woman led the way. "Come now."

"Don't tell me what to do," the familiar voice grumbled as he tossed back his hood while he examined the dock. "Night is supposed to be *my* time. I don't need her bossing me around more than needed."

Felicity felt nauseated.

Prince Silas Idicous had changed. He was still striking, but his sharp features had thinned with exhaustion and malnutrition. His hair had grown to his jaw and was in desperate need of a wash. Brown roots were showing through the usually solid white of his hair.

For some reason, Silas having naturally *brown* hair was more shocking than him having white.

Felicity's mind and stomach weren't exactly sure how to feel about this, but the twisted disgust of Silas's face summed it up pretty well.

"The faster you get this done, the faster you can go back to moping in your chamber," the Exerticus woman said with a tired sigh as she adjusted her scarf. "I promise I won't keep you long like Ekerus."

"That's only because she favors you and would never scold you for bending her orders," Silas scoffed.

Kathryn?

"I don't think of it that way," the Exerticus woman said. "I'm here to make sure the storm comes, just as she wants and as all the others do."

Silas rolled her eyes. "Don't deny it. You're the first Exerticus she summoned, and the *only* one she even remotely has any sort of company with."

"You deny your sister any humanity. It's not a crime for her to have a friend."

"Kathryn and *friend* don't belong in the same sentence."

The Exerticus woman sighed, surprisingly unphased by Silas' complaints, her eyes far more focused on the waves. "It can't be more than a couple miles out now. It can see us."

"Those two phrases don't go together," Silas scoffed.

"Don't underestimate it. Its sight and hearing are a millennium old. You Oquelite always seem to boast your age, when you seem to forget, you age *slower*. You're simply a child…hardly older than a human teenager." She looked almost pained as she looked back at Silas, a glimmer of sadness in her eyes. Sympathy.

"I'm not a child," Silas spat. "And I didn't ask for any of your pity."

The woman sighed. "You're so much like your sister."

"Ugh! Nope, not this again! Let's just get this over with!" Silas tossed off his tattered cloak, setting down the lantern. He was already barefoot, walking to the edge of the dock with a deep breath.

He cast a weary glance at the Exercitus over his shoulder. He turned back, looking at the water. The stone-cold expression faltered. Felicity had only seen that expression once before.

Silas was afraid.

And yet, he jumped into the water.

The next moment, Felicity was drowning. The waved crashed. Hands clawed at her, a painful rush of power pulled at her. She couldn't deny it. A horrified roar erupted, suffocated by the waves.

"Felicity!"

She gasped for air, and the world flew back to reality. Her head was pulled up above the water, Mercy and Nikki dragging her back up to the rocks. Her vision was blurred, but she could feel the sand below her as they set her down. "Felicity!"

A sharp pain flashed across her face.

Felicity's vision instantly cleared as she cried out. "Tabitha, you slapped me!"

That's what she meant to say, but instead, it was mostly coughing up salt water. Mercy, Nikki, and Tabitha sat around her, all three of them drenched.

"What-what happened?" Felicity sputtered, pushing herself up.

"The waves started going crazy!" Tabitha said. "I swear it was about to storm, but then you passed out."

"I-I—" Felicity's eyes widened, remembering. "I saw Silas!"

Tabitha's jaw fell.

Nikki frowned. "You what?"

Felicity's mind was spinning too fast to even process the cold. She had seen Silas after six months of happily never seeing his face. "He was at the docks. In Liberty."

Thunder crashed above them.

"In Liberty?" Mercy frowned.

"He and some Exerticus…they were talking about some sort of creature they were trying to summon," Felicity said.

"How the heck are you seeing this?" Tabitha frowned. "What have you been drinking?"

"A creature," Felicity said, cringing as she realized how crazy the words sounded out loud. "There's a creature in my mind. It keeps crying out for help. Kathryn is doing something to it…and she's using Silas for it."

The girls were quiet.

"Wow," Tabitha whistled under her breath. "That's…kinda insane. Do you think that's the Leviathan?"

A lump formed in Felicity's throat. Lightning flashed across the sky. "It has to be."

"We should get inside. We'll talk more about this later," Tabitha said, scurrying to pull Felicity up.

Apparently, there wasn't much time to lug the wheelchair through the water, so Felicity had to endure the humiliation of being carried back to the house on Nikki's back. Despite her size, she was surprisingly strong.

As they approached the house, rain began to pour down. The door swung open, and Lawrence and Cole ran down the steps, dressed and up.

Felicity was relieved that they didn't automatically ask questions. Cole scooped her up into his arms and rushed them inside. He set her down on the couch, and Lawrence slammed the button to start the fire with an unimpressive smolder. He scowled, reaching inside and with a snap, it roared life.

"What were you all thinking, going out by the ocean? In a storm like this?" Cole said, looking more confused than angry as he ran his fingers through his hair. "Are you guys alright? Were you attacked—"

Tabitha was quick to jump in. "The storm started later. And it was *my* idea—"

"Tabitha, it's fine. You don't have to cover for me," Felicity said.

Both Cole and Tabitha turned to look at her with stunned faces.

"It's my fault. I'm the one who left. The others just came to bring me back."

Tabitha had always jumped in to defend her since they were young, often taking the blame in grade school for Felicity's own mishaps. Felicity hadn't appreciated it then, but now she couldn't stand to let Tabitha lie for her sake. Especially not to Cole. Felicity hated to think she could cause them to drift apart.

"Felicity?" Cole said, his brow furrowing.

"I'm sorry," Felicity said, feeling like every eye in the world was burning into her skin. "I heard something in my head. It was calling for me to follow."

"I thought we decided to *not* listen to the voices in our heads?" Lawrence said.

Nikki sat beside her cousin, shaking her head. "It can't be Kathryn," she said quietly. "I would've felt her. This isn't like her."

"It didn't sound human," Felicity said, remembering the rhythmic hum. "It was calling for help, and as soon as I stepped in the water...I saw something. A vision. Silas was there…with a female Exerticus."

"Sergia," Nikki said.

"Kathryn's governess-servant-friend person from your story?" Tabitha said with a frown. "Anyone else think that's kinda creepy?"

"I really don't think Kathryn cares if we think she's creepy."

"Fair."

"What did you see?" Cole said, his voice becoming gentle as he studied Felicity's face.

"I don't know how or why, but they're at the Liberty docks. They're trying to summon a creature…and I think it's the creature who asked for my help." Felicity realized how crazy that sounded as the words left her. "The Leviathan."

Cole paled. "This just makes getting Nathaniel to safety a bigger priority. Are you alright, Felicity? Silas didn't…"

"No," Felicity said, shaking her head. "I'm fine."

Cole's face softened, nodding. "Just…feel free to talk if you have any concerns. The fact that the Leviathan is trying to communicate with you is a big deal."

"Thanks," Felicity said, pushing a wet strand of hair behind her ear.

"It's five in the morning," Cole said. "Maybe it's a good idea to take a shower and try to get more sleep."

"Aw, you don't like the smell of salt water and mud?" Tabitha said, raising a brow.

Cole wiped a smear of dirt from her chin. "It's fantastic."

"Maybe next time you should join us, Goldfish," Tabitha said, a small spark of amusement in her eye.

"Maybe I will."

Felicity was relieved to see the two getting along, not that a small quarrel would tear them apart. It would take a lot more than that at this point.

Tabitha spun around quickly. "By the way, we should call the Leviathan Craig. Leviathan is way too long of a code name."

"You want to call this sea creature who talks to me… Craig?"

Tabitha smirked. "It fits. Admit it."

She disappeared around the corner.

Felicity sighed, shaking her head.

The group slowly left to go about their business, but Felicity was content on the sofa by the fire.

"Are you sure you don't need help?" Cole asked.

Felicity nodded. "I'm fine."

She had her wheelchair folded beside her. But the thoughts in her head were far more suffocating than her lack of mobility.

"If you say so," Cole said, though he didn't look convinced. "I'll try researching about recent activity on the docks if you want."

"That would be great," Felicity said with a small smile. "Thanks."

"Take care of yourself. We'll figure it out." Cole nodded, turning down the hall.

Felicity laughed. "I know."

She didn't know.

She knew nothing. About who she was. About how she could be helpful. About how to keep the people she loved safe.

About what was in her head.

And what Silas was doing to it.

MUCH TO LINCOLN'S disappointment, the decision was made.

And that meant it was time to move on from Sinni's cabin. Nikki admitted she was disappointed, partially because she genuinely loved the place. It felt safe and cut off from the rest of the world. But mostly because she far preferred it to being crowded in a trailer, and the wet outside world.

At least it wasn't *snowing*.

Nikki shivered just thinking about it, tapping her fingers on her shield that lay across her lap.

Sinni had been kind enough to lend them her auto to drop off Nathaniel, as the truck and giant trailer would probably draw some attention and was a much harder getaway vehicle.

Lincoln hesitated before getting in the door. He'd been quiet all morning.

"Are you okay?" Nikki asked, patting the seat beside her.

Lincoln jumped as if he hadn't noticed her. He cleared his throat. "Yeah, I'm fine." He plopped beside her with an exasperated sigh. "I just don't think this is a good idea."

Lincoln's eyes were hard to read. They were big and dark, and often Nikki could only see herself looking back in them.

"You did say you couldn't wait for Nathaniel to be gone and safe," Nikki said. She looked at the little boy. Even if Lincoln would insist otherwise, she'd begun to grow rather fond of him.

Nathaniel reached for her hand. She frowned. He'd never done that before. She offered it to him. To her horror, he pulled her hand to his mouth.

She quickly wrenched it away. "Ah!"

Nathaniel burst out into bubbly laughter.

"He tried to eat me?" Nikki frowned.

"Apparently, toddlers just do that. He won't actually eat you."

"Strange hobby."

Lincoln looked to Nathaniel. "Hey, how about instead of eating people, how about words? How about Nikki? Can you say Nikki?"

Lincoln once again pointed to Nikki, repeating her name. Nathaniel seemed to have tuned out Lincoln, reaching for Nikki's bag. She frowned until she realized the lemon pin was glittering in the sunlight.

It had been a gift from Taryn during the local's summer harvest celebration and was one of her few possessions. She was tempted to unclip it for Nathaniel, but the idea of him attempting to eat it held her back.

"Lemon," she said, turning the shiny pin toward him.

Nathaniel's eyes widened and he clutched his stuffed monkey tighter, pinching his lips…almost like he was tempted.

"Lemon," he said. "Pwetty."

"Yes! You did it!"

Lincoln's face quickly hardened. "Well, he's going to the OHS now…so it doesn't matter. And maybe it will be better to have him away from me. I'm the person who almost gave in to the evil immortal lady trying to end the world or something. You'd be a much better fit with all your mighty Aguirre power."

Nikki knew he was trying to cheer her up with the nudge, but it just made her blood go cold with the reminder. She swallowed hard. "I don't think Aguirre has anything to do with this—"

Before Lincoln could question her, the front door of the car swung open. "Why hello, fellow passengers!"

Ray plopped down in the driver's seat.

Lincoln's jaw dropped. "Hold up! There is no way *you're* driving!"

"You're right," Lawrence said, practically dragging Ray out by his jacket collar and plopping down in the front seat of the auto.

Ray laughed as he made his way to the passenger side.

"We should leave now if we want to beat this storm and make it to Neuartig," Matteo said, plopping in beside Nikki.

Nikki clutched Fidelis closer, hoping not to poke anyone with the big metal shield. Matteo didn't seem bothered, scrolling through the doc on his tablet.

"Sounds good to me," Lawrence said. "Is Nathaniel prepared?"

Nikki couldn't help but stare at Lincoln as he kept his face stone cold. "Yeah. I guess so."

"Good. Then this should go smoothly." Lawrence started the auto down the road.

Nikki knew that Cole and the others wouldn't be too far behind, but the goal was to make sure the two weren't associated with each other to make it easier for Nathaniel to get into the OHS, and for them to get out.

Like Lawrence said, it *should* go smoothly.

So Nikki tried to relax. Lincoln's words repeated in her mind. Even Lincoln thought her being an Aguirre made things…different? It didn't. She was still the same Nikki from a year ago when they'd met.

Sure, she'd learned more words, learned punching people wasn't an appropriate greeting, and almost died, but she wasn't any more high and mighty just because she was an Aguirre.

She took a deep breath, reaching into her bag to pull out the NMA disc.

She'd considered turning it on only a few times in the past six months. The idea she might be able to hear her mother's voice again was oddly tempting. What had been so important that her family had set aside this specific file for?

"That black auto's been following us for a while now." Matteo's quiet voice drew her back to reality.

"It's a two-way road. I doubt they're following us," Lawrence said.

Nikki unbuckled, getting to her knees on the seat and looking out. A strange black auto seemed to be slowly moving around other cars, steadily approaching them.

Odd.

She looked back through the front window. They were approaching a large, suspended red bridge spanning over the river that branched into the ocean.

The black auto sped up.

Lawrence said it was nothing to worry about, but the windows were too tinted for her to be sure. The upcoming bridge seemed like an all-too-perfect way to make sure they couldn't escape.

But how?

Nikki didn't even have a moment to think.

The next second, the world was spinning. She'd slammed into someone. Something shattered. And then they came to a halt.

Nikki's mind quickly assessed the situation, her instincts flooding over everything else.

The windows had shattered. The auto was upright, but now *facing* the river. Alarms were going off. A car was flipped upside down. The driver had gotten out and was trying to run.

Lawrence was conscious with only a cut above his eyebrow. Nikki tuned out his instructions, quickly turning to Lincoln.

His eyes were closed, blood dripping down the right side of his face.

Nathaniel looked too dazed to notice. "Ouchie," he mumbled.

Nikki quickly scooped him up, pressing his face into her shoulder.

"Lincoln!" Her shout broke the silent bubble around her.

To her relief, his eyes opened in a daze. Blood dribbled down from his hairline. "What-what—"

The black auto had slammed into the back of their auto and sent them spinning. Her mind was still spinning, even though the car had stopped. They'd crashed through the barrier on the bridge and now were hanging over the river.

"It's a Defender!" Matteo cried out.

Out of everyone in the car, he looked the least affected.

Nikki looked out the back window, now shattered. Matteo was right. A Defender had stepped out of the auto. He wasn't dressed like the North Cordell Officers, or even like Taryn in her full Sergeant gear.

Nikki's eyes widened upon seeing the Defender step closer, a sword strapped to his back, wearing a helmet with the visor over his eyes. He wore a slick metal chest plate and armor for his arms and legs. His belt was riddled with knives, devices, and other weapons.

Lawrence cursed, digging through the cup holders and clamping on two metal bracelets.

Matteo sunk down in his seat, one word escaping his trembling lips: "Agent."

Nikki's eyes widened.

An elite special force of the Defending Department. One her own parents were a part of.

The Agent whipped two long knives out from his belt, flipping them in his hands. They cracked with electric bolts as they landed in his grip. He spoke down into a wristband. "Targets acquired."

"Show off," Ray grumbled.

Nikki didn't think it was the most appropriate response, seeing as they were teetering over the side of a bridge.

"We have reason to believe you're accomplices in smuggling a highly wanted person, along with an illegal child. And since I can see our suspect peeking out the window…you might as well turn yourselves in now."

"Nikki!" Lawrence hissed.

Nikki ducked her head. Too late now. They knew about Nathaniel.

"Bad guy," Nathaniel whispered. "I fight."

"No," Lawrence scolded. "You no fight."

Nathaniel pouted.

"We need to get out," she said. "I'll go and fight them."

"There's no way you can take on an *Agent*, Nikki," Lawrence said. "And what about Lincoln and Nathaniel?"

Nikki swallowed hard, turning back to Lincoln, who was

gazing off, the blood now staining the shoulder of his precious green jacket. Her heart swelled. She turned back to Lawrence.

They needed Cole.

"Ray, teleport Nathaniel to safety," she said.

"I don't want to abandon you," Ray said. "I could use my sword and—"

Lawrence shut him down quickly, reaching over to take Nathaniel. The auto creaked below them.

"Don't make me come in there. I'm giving you a chance to resolve this peacefully!" the agent shouted.

Peaceful? The Department that had arrested Giles and taken in Taryn?

"No!" Nathaniel protested as he was passed off to Ray. "Stay! No! Linc!"

Ray held him tightly. "Try to stay alive."

And with a salute, he jumped, teleporting away with Nathaniel.

The auto tilted under them. Nikki smothered a scream, grabbing onto the seat.

"The Oquelite just teleported with the Aguarious," the agent spoke into his earpiece. "Agent Aalto reporting."

Nikki's heart dropped. They knew what Oquelite were? And Nathaniel?

"Your chances are up, kids," the man, Aalto, sighed, starting to jog toward them. He jumped on top of the auto, and with one swift kick, he shattered the sunroof.

The weight shuddered the entire auto.

Nikki's heart plummeted to her stomach. The man was perfectly balancing the auto from slipping into the river below. He flicked up his visor, curls escaping from his helmet. He was young, but still had a deep, faded scar down his forehead and across his nose.

He cocked his head. "So you're the girl," he said cooly, tucking away a blade to reach for her.

"Don't you dare touch her!" Lawrence jumped up through the sunroof, launching a kick at Aalto. The Defender quickly blocked the blow.

A fight on the roof of an auto teetering over the river did *not* seem like a good idea.

"Lawrence!" The auto creaked forward. The Agent

seemed to take notice, swiftly landing a kick to Lawrence's ankle and a solid fist to his chest, throwing Lawrence back.

Nikki grabbed her shield. She had to help him.

"No! Don't go up there!" Matteo said. "We can't risk you! Let me use your shield."

Nikki refused to stay put, but she handed over the shield. Matteo had grown up in an entertaining troupe with his siblings, and his rhythmic, methodic moves were great at avoiding near death…but his combat? It was far weaker.

Matteo joined the fight on the roof, attempting to throw the Agent off balance with the shield, but the Agent quickly sidestepped. Matteo nearly toppled off the edge. The auto creaked forward, off balance. Nikki tried to hold onto the seat, but she fell backward, slamming into the dashboard.

She heard Lawrence curse. The Agent grabbed Matteo by the shirt collar and easily tossed him to the other side of the auto. The auto balanced upright. He whipped out his blades again.

Lawrence was back on his feet, ready to fight him back.

All he had were his fists, and Matteo with a shield he barely knew how to use.

They were doomed.

The Agent once again masterfully twirled his knives, almost like this was fun for him as he slashed out at Lawrence. Lawrence barely avoided it, scratching his bracelets together.

He was going to reveal his abilities to a Defender?

A spark formed, and Lawrence quickly controlled it, the flame growing rapidly as he clasped his hands together to blow back the blades.

The Agent wasn't fazed, moving side to side, dodge after dodge. Lawrence began to turn. It was merely self-defense. Matteo tried to come in from behind with the shield, but Aalto quickly threw one of the blades, which sparked with a bolt of electricity as it nicked Matteo's shoulder.

He cried out, his foot slipping.

The blade flew right back into the Agent's hand with a smirk. The shield fell from Matteo's grip, sliding back through the sunroof and inside the auto.

Avalon began to vibrate against Nikki's chest.

You insist on doing nothing? There's no need to listen to that foolish Ywondie boy.

Lawrence had said to stay put. And Nikki trusted him…even if he was totally embarrassing himself up there. She held onto the seat with her life, looking up at the fight above her.

Aalto grabbed the collar of Matteo's shirt, tossing the dazed boy so he rolled to Lawrence's feet.

The auto creaked forward, leaning toward the river. The hair on Nikki's neck rose. Aalto's eyes met hers before switching back to Lawrence and Matteo.

"You try to attack, and you go into the river. If you let me retrieve the fugitive, you'll live…of course, most likely with a little jail time for assaulting an Agent of law." He adjusted his grip on his blades. "If you let this go easy, maybe I'll take a few weeks off."

Nikki could take him, couldn't she?

After he'd so easily beat back Lawrence and Matteo?

He was an Agent like her mother and her father. Who was she to think she was anywhere close to being able to defeat them?

She glanced at Lincoln, still slumped over in his seat, bleeding.

Would he hurt Lincoln?

She couldn't go with him. She couldn't. Then the Defenders would learn who she was.

How much was it worth to keep this secret?

The Agent stepped toward the sun roof. He peered down, meeting Nikki's eyes. He drew out a knife, and a meaty hand reached down for her.

And then a boot came flying, hitting the Agent squarely in the face.

"I have another one and I'm not afraid to use it!" Matteo said.

The Agent scowled. "You made the wrong choice."

Nikki's eyes widened. What were they thinking? It wasn't worth it—

Aalto tucked away his blades, jumping from side to side.

With one quick thrust, Matteo toppled off the roof of the auto and into the river.

Nikki screamed. "Matteo!"

The auto tilted downward. Lawrence lost balance, sliding down the auto, clawing to stay on top. He grabbed the edge, hanging on for his dear life over the river.

"I'll give some credit," Aalto said. Nikki heard him step forward. "You're incredibly stubborn and almost honorably loyal…but loyalty can be your own personal downfall."

"I'm guessing you mean that quite literally," Lawrence said with a breathless laugh.

Aalto scowled, slamming his foot down on Lawrence's hand. "I guess you'll find out."

Nikki screamed her cousin's name as she watched him disappear over the edge. "LAWRENCE! NO!"

In that moment, a flame lit in her chest, tightening around her heart. It hurt. She grit her teeth, clenching the seat.

Fidelis was right there.

Aalto walked smoothly toward the window, the auto creaking back into balance. If she could just reach the shield, she could activate the blade and send it deep into his—

She caught herself. That was terrible. She wouldn't. She couldn't. She just wanted peace.

"Come on out, little girl." Aalto kneeled down at the window. His dark brown eyes pierced into hers.

"There's no need to be afraid," he said, his voice jaded and harsh. "We just have a few questions, and from the looks of it, it'll be quick." He scoffed. "To think a skinny little girl was really some Aguirre. I doubt it. Doesn't that sound ridiculous? We could get this over real quick."

To think a skinny little girl was really some Aguirre.

Her mother had instructed her to run from people like this.

She would show him what Reyna's daughter would do when he hurt her friends.

For the first time, she saw concern flash through Agent Aalto's eyes.

She grabbed Fidelis and, with a cry, threw her weight toward the front of the auto. The auto fell off the edge of the bridge.

The world was falling out from under her, racing toward the icy, cold river.

PART THREE

THE OUTOWN

25

THE WORLD WAS spinning, but she could feel the fire.

It burned in her chest even as the auto hit the water.

For a moment, she thought she was going to die a second time. Water seeped through the windows as the auto bobbed back up, floating on the surface.

Nikki's mind spun as she buckled the shield to her back. "Lincoln!"

"Nik?" Lincoln said, his words slurred. He was lying on the backseat of the auto.

She scrambled into the back of the auto as it rocked underneath her. She slipped her arm under his, trying to push him to his feet.

"Can you walk?" she asked. There was no way she could carry Lincoln. He was almost a foot taller than her.

Lincoln nodded, though she wasn't sure how much she trusted it. "Everything's blurry," he said, wiping the blood from his face, but it just smeared worse.

Nikki swallowed hard.

This wasn't going to be good. The water was slowly leaking through, and it now reached their ankles. "We need to get to the top of the auto," she said. "We're sinking."

"Where's Nathaniel?"

"He's safe. But you're not going to be!"

Lincoln stumbled after her. She crawled out of the sunroof window. He grabbed her hand for guidance as he slowly picked himself up onto the seat. His fingers fumbled to grip the roof.

Nikki's heartbeat quickened as she glanced back to the bridge.

Agent Aalto stood with his long knives in hand…just watching as they drifted further.

Her face hardened as she unclipped Fidelis. She activated the blade, slamming it into the roof of the car. She wrapped one of the leather straps to attach the shield around Lincoln's arm.

Usually he was the one helping *her* out of predicaments like this.

"Hold on! Pull!" Nikki said, desperately pulling at his other arm, praying his weight wouldn't pull her down.

Lincoln's senses might have been shaken, but his strength was not. In a heave, he was able to hoist himself up, toppling over on Nikki.

She grabbed his shoulder, trying to steady him. "Any wrong move, and we go into the river."

"That's fine," Lincoln said, his words tired with a stupid dazed grin. "We can just swim to shore."

Nikki swallowed, pushing him off her. "We'd drown."

"We'll be fine," he said, eyes drooped.

Nikki was quick to slap him. "Stay awake!"

"Why?"

"You hit your head really hard. You're bleeding." *Help! Anyone!* She screamed mentally.

She could already see Agent Aalto moving for his vehicle. He could easily drive to the next bridge and intercept their floating auto…if they hadn't sunk by then.

"I'm not bleeding. I'm just tired."

He was the one who'd instructed her about concussions, back when she'd fallen off a moving mail truck. He'd been the one lecturing then. Lincoln didn't yell when he lectured. It was actually almost exactly the same as him rambling about his inventions, just his brows were furrowed and his eyes were looking everywhere.

Nikki grabbed his face, forcing him to look at her. "Do. Not."

Lincoln looked almost genuinely surprised as his face softened. "You have blue eyes."

Nikki frowned. "Yeah. You have black eyes."

He didn't mention this part in his lectures.

The auto creaked below them. They grabbed onto each other. Nikki braced for the auto to flip. Instead, the auto began to sink faster.

She imagined this would be a moment where Lawrence would curse. There had to be another way! At this rate, they wouldn't even reach Aalto. They'd just be succumbed to watery graves. They'd never see the fields of North Cordell again.

What if she tried removing a seat and floating on it? The current was too strong. She'd meet Aalto faster...or go straight over and into the ocean.

Her throat and chest began to tighten. Just like in those horrifying moments after Silas had stabbed her. As she lay in the snow, unable to breathe. Unable to die.

Trapped.

They were trapped.

"We'll just swim," the delirious Lincoln said assuredly.

Nikki felt her eyes sting. "I-I can't."

"You can do it. You can do anything!" She wished she could believe his slurred voice.

She shook her head. "No, I can't. I can't swim! I don't remember how! When Kathryn messed with my head, she made me forget!"

Lincoln went quiet. He almost looked like he genuinely understood. Maybe he did. His bloodstained hand reached into hers.

She would not cry.

Lincoln believed in her. Who was she to let him down? Even if Kathryn had stolen some of her memories to insert her own torture, they'd won in Algery.

They were one step ahead. They'd completed the Curatrix machine, and they'd gotten the NMA file!

Nikki's sweat went cold.

The file.

She pulled away, desperately feeling in her pockets and her bag. It was gone. She looked at Lincoln. "Stay here!"

She took a deep breath and turned back to the open sunroof of the auto.

And she jumped back inside. The water had filled up to her mid-thighs.

The auto sputtered beneath her. She heard Lincoln call after her, but she couldn't turn back. Water was rushing in by the second. The disc had been right here.

It couldn't have drifted off.

Nikki took a deep breath and ducked her head under the water.

Her eyes widened, seeing it lodged between the two backseats. She quickly tugged it free, pushing herself out of the water with a gasp for air.

Her hands were shaking.

She'd almost lost it. The last thing her mother had meant to give her. What was throwing her off her guard?

She quickly tucked the disc back into her ba crawled to the top of the auto. "It's all good. I found—"

Nikki looked around. Lincoln was gone.

She jumped to her feet. "Lincoln!" she screamed.

Fidelis was left abandoned, the leather strap left in the water. Nikki felt the burning tears return. No. This couldn't be happening.

Her knees threatened to buckle under her.

He couldn't really be— She'd failed. How could she? They were all dead? And it was her fault? Because she'd sat back and did nothing.

All because of who she was.

She screamed Lincoln's name, her voice raw. This couldn't be happening.

She pulled Fidelis out of the auto's roof, turning to face Aalto at the bridge. He was gone. Her veins burned like the hot tear that rolled down her face.

She'd seen death.

She wasn't afraid. She'd destroy him if she had to, just like he murdered her—

The auto shuddered below her. Nikki slipped, hitting the top of the car with a slam.

No.

The water swallowed the windows.

It was too late. She wouldn't even reach Aalto at this point. She tried getting to her feet, but the auto shook again.

The dark water mocked her as it rapidly approached. *Die in this watery grave beside your friends.*

"Nikki! Watch out!"

Nikki didn't even have a second to spin around, before she collided with a pair of arms…and was lifted off her feet.

She couldn't remember anything clearly, except she was probably screaming and anticipating death…and that the sky did look pretty cool so if she was going to die, at least it was kinda pretty—

She hit the ground with a roll. She laid on her back, gasping for air. The solid earth was below her. The sky was still there. She dug her fingers into the sandy soil just to make sure it was still there.

"Nikki! Are you okay?" Matteo's voice echoed in her ears, his blurry face appearing above her.

Her eyes and throat burned. She could feel herself shivering against her will. She held her legs to her chest, wiping her hair and bangs from her face, trying to calm the rocking sensation that controlled her nerves.

She wasn't in the water anymore. She wasn't going to drown.

Wait.

She wasn't in the water anymore?

Her eyes widened. She spun around, facing Matteo sitting in a circle of singed grass, his shirt missing.

It took her mind half a second to realize what had happened.   "You   flew!" She jumped to her feet, nearly toppling over.

Matteo's face flushed, with a small nod. "It was kinda an instinct. I've never really carried people. I think I almost ran Lawrence into a tree—"

"No, Matteo, that's incredible!" she said, wanting to rush over and hug him. But then his words finished processing. "Wait. Lawrence?"

"Are you alright?"

Nikki spun around to see Lawrence, scratched up and soaked. Lincoln sat dazed beside him. Nikki didn't hold herself back this time. She threw herself into her cousin's arms, burying her face into his shoulder, trying to hold back sobs.

"I-I thought— I-You're alive! You-you're all—"

"Sh, Nik. It's okay," Lawrence said gently, hugging her back. His arms were warm, and she didn't want to leave them. Her heart was beating rapidly against her chest. She couldn't remember the last time she'd felt so shaken.

"I-I'm sorry," she said.

"Nik, you have nothing to be sorry for."

She should've been better than this. She *knew* she was better than this. Nikki didn't panic…and yet here she was, struggling to breathe.

She wriggled out of Lawrence's arms.

"Do we need to check you too?"

Ray's voice. He was okay too. He was now beside Lincoln, Nathaniel sitting a few feet away, his eyes puffy from angry tears.

Nikki quickly rushed to the toddler, dropping to her knees beside him. He clung to his drenched green stuffed monkey as he looked into her eyes. She brushed back his red curls and showed him the sparkling lemon pin on her bag.

"I'm fine," Nikki insisted.

"We all saw you fall back into the auto," Ray said.

Lincoln laughed deliriously. "Nikki doesn't fall."

"We need to take care of him quickly," Lawrence sighed before turning back to Nikki. "If you didn't fall, then why in your right mind would you jump *back* into the auto? That was extremely dangerous, and not to mention reckless!"

Nikki swallowed hard. She opened her bag, not saying a word as she drew out the NMA disc, which glitched in her hand.

Everyone went quiet. Even Lincoln.

"Oh," Lawrence whispered. "I'm sorry, Nik."

Nikki jumped, feeling Nathaniel's little hand on her thigh. He looked at the disc with wide eyes, reaching out a small hand.

Nikki frowned, expecting him to grab it, but instead he froze, his brows furrowing as he stared at the disc.

"Nat?" Lincoln said.

"What's he doing?" Ray said, frowning.

Nikki looked away from Nathaniel and back to the disc.

Her eyes widened: The disc had stopped dripping.

The droplets were instead rising up and slowly dancing toward Nathaniel's outstretched hand.

Nikki's lips parted, not daring to move and break Nathaniel's concentration.

Nathaniel furrowed his brows, and a burst of droplets exploded from the disc, rushing and hitting Nathaniel in the face. He fell over backwards in a fit of laughter.

The disc glowed back to life.

Everyone was silent.

"Great job, Nat," Lincoln said, hanging his head with a breathy laugh. "You saved the day! You can control water!"

Nathaniel beamed, crawling over to Lincoln and curling up into his lap. "Water!"

Ray quickly had to go and shake Lincoln to keep him awake.

Nikki stared at the disc and back at the toddler that had fixed it so effortlessly. She grasped the disc with both hands, holding it up to the sun as she got to her feet. "Our plan won't work."

"What?" Lawrence said. "Because of that Agent Aalto guy?"

Nikki looked back to Nathaniel, sitting in Lincoln's lap, squealing with excitement as Lincoln revealed the stuffed monkey from his jacket.

She looked back to Lawrence.

"He can't go to the OHS now. If the Defenders know who he is…he can't hide *anywhere*."

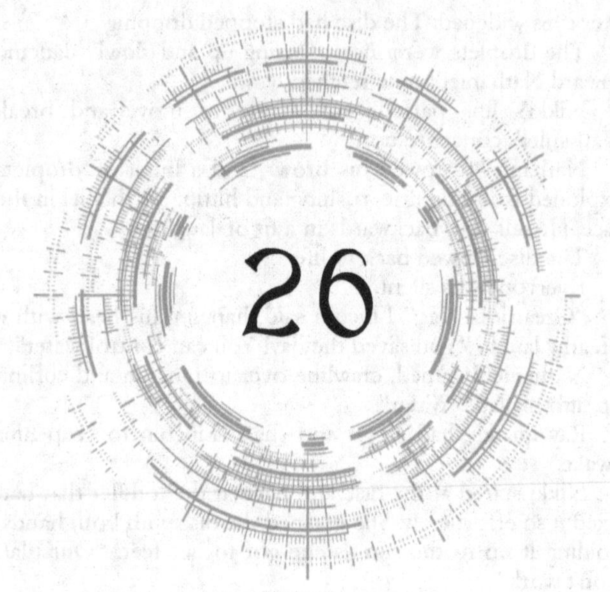

26

Nikki hated that she was right.

Even though she knew she hadn't caused it, just the fact she'd pointed it out made it feel all the more real and heavy on her shoulders. And the fact they now had a literal Defending Agent hunting them down made it all the more chaotic.

She corrected herself.

Agent Aalto wasn't hunting *them* down.

He was hunting *her*.

And from what she saw, he didn't seem to really care who got hurt…or even died…in the process. It took hours for the adrenaline to wear off, even when they'd reached the safety of the trailer.

Lincoln was forced to rest and take a medication recommended by a very worried Dr. Mathews. He was currently knocked out with a napping Nathaniel in the back of the trailer.

"What?" she shouted through the Comm once Lawrence had finished relaying the story.

Nikki had thought he'd made it sound better than it actually was.

"You fell off a bridge?" Dr. Mathews said, exasperated. "If Lincoln *wasn't* an Aviduous, you'd have much worse than a concussion on your hands. And is Nikki alright? Was the toddler hurt? I knew I should've gone after you. These are no conditions for a—"

"Mom, he's okay," Ray said. "He's asleep with Lincoln in the trailer. And Nikki really only had a few cuts and bruises."

Dr. Mathews gave a long sigh. "What about mentally?"

Everyone went dead silent.

Mentally? Nikki had never felt so…all over the place. She wished she could crawl away and join Nathaniel and Lincoln.

"I've seen worse," Lawrence said with a shrug.

He wasn't lying.

Dr. Mathews groaned. "No, no. That's terrible. You shouldn't have to see worse. Lawrence Williams, we're going to talk about this when you all get back, safe and alive."

Lawrence frowned, getting to his feet. "I'm good, thank you."

"Don't think you can escape my mom," Ray said. "She'll track you down and find you."

"He's right," Dr. Mathews said. "Now, I expect to hear a report of a full night's sleep and no attempted arrests tomorrow. Do you understand?"

"Will do, Mother," Ray said.

"What are your plans moving forward?"

"Our last two hopes are the Market and the Believers," Cole sighed, running his fingers through his blond hair that was beginning to grow long. "The Believers live underground in an abandoned region. Sister Lillian said they work as a small research facility and might be able to take in Nathaniel and bring him to another hidden community. And the Market…well, it's the Market. They're the best at staying off the radar."

Dr. Mathews thought on it for a moment before letting out a long breath. "Alright. Where are you planning to stay tonight?"

"We're staying at a motel in the middle of nowhere. In a background search, it's usually vacant. As long as Nikki just stays in the trailer and we use face disfigurers, we shouldn't be recognized and if we are, we'll be able to escape before any authority shows up."

Nikki hoped Cole was right.

"This is an Agent we're talking about. You've always been lucky to have Defenders on your side, but now the tables have turned," Dr. Mathews sighed. "Be careful…if you understand what that means."

Much to Lincoln's distress, he had to be dragged from his sleep early because Dow had ordered a virtual meeting about Nathaniel.

"Meet us in the room in ten," Cole said, once Lincoln had gotten down, still delirious from sleep and refusing to move from the couch.

"Fine," Lincoln grumbled. "Make it fifteen."

At least his usual grumpiness was back.

Nikki sat up, waiting for him to notice her.

Instead, Lincoln's eyes were focused on Nathaniel, who seemed just as grumpy to get up, still half asleep. He stuck his stuffed monkey's foot in his mouth before he noticed Lincoln's tired stare. He crawled over to him, offering the monkey to Lincoln's mouth, insisting it was "yum yum." Lincoln just shook his head, patting Nathaniel's red curls.

"Nik! Come! Come! Hurry!"

The earth was wet below her bare feet. The small hand clinging to hers was strong, and would've pulled her over if she didn't know the worn path like the back of her hand.

"Nik! Nik!" came a toddler's voice from the present.

Nikki's head jerked up as she gasped for air. She'd slipped into the past without warning. She hadn't even been able to warn herself.

She looked up and saw Nathaniel tugging on Lincoln's sleeve, pointing to Nikki.

"You okay, Nik?" Lincoln said, his eyebrows raised, his eyes wide and awake.

She straightened herself. "I'm okay," she said.

"You keep doing that," he said.

"Doing what?"

"Your eyes. They roll down, and then you go really still," Lincoln said, narrowing his eyes at her. "Are you getting sick?"

Nikki blinked. She'd only gotten sick *once* since being with the Council. Taryn said it was just a cold, but Nikki thought it was the worst thing known to humanity. Her throat hurt no matter what she did, and she couldn't breathe through her nose. And apparently, it was can-conta—she could spread it to other people, so she wasn't allowed to work.

"I don't think so," she said. "I can breathe through my nose."

Lincoln smiled. "Good," he laughed, rubbing the bandage on his forehead.

"I don't know what's going on," she admitted, pulling her legs to her chest. "Sometimes I see stuff…like Nathaniel, and then I start feeling stuff and hearing things."

"Like Kathryn?"

Nikki shook her head. "No. Like…me."

"You?"

"Little me."

Lincoln lips parted. "You-you're seeing your memories?" he stammered.

"Maybe? I don't like it."

He jumped to his feet. "Nikki! That's awesome! How are you doing it? How are you triggering it? Does it work quickly? Do you think you can show me?"

He quickly regretted it, wincing as he grabbed his head with a groan.

Nikki instantly felt guilty. She wasn't the only one with a forgotten past…and here she was *upset* that memories were trying to force their way back.

"I don't know," Nikki admitted. "It just happens."

Lincoln's face softened. "Oh."

Nikki got to her feet, rushing to grab his shoulders. "It's okay!" she tried to reassure him. "If I figure it out, I'll tell you! Maybe we can find your Ma and Da too."

Lincoln cracked a forced smile. "Maybe they'll be mega famous Agents too."

Nikki rolled her eyes. "Or maybe they're super nice and normal and like…make cool arrows too."

Lincoln laughed, even through his pained winces. "While that would be amazing, I highly doubt it."

"You never know."

She studied his face. Even with the cuts and the growing bruise on his jaw, his dark eyes still looked as if they contained so many secrets. It was as fascinating as the first time she saw them over a year ago.

Whoever Lincoln's parents were, Nikki had no doubt they were amazing. They had to be. He had to have gotten those genius genes from somewhere.

Lincoln blushed. "I should probably get going to this super important meeting with a headache that'll never go away," he said, clearing his throat, rubbing his forehead with the palm of his hand. He turned back to Nathaniel, who was still lying on the floor, his eyelids drooping and the monkey in his clutches. Lincoln turned back to Nikki. "Do you mind watching him?"

Nikki blinked. "Nathaniel?"

"Yeah. I don't know if I feel safe with him out there."

They both looked out the window to the rickety, broken-down motel sitting in the fog. "And I don't know if Dow would really like a toddler interrupting his super secret meeting with us."

Right. Dow probably wasn't allowed to be in contact with them right now.

"He's a pretty deep sleeper, and I have his food in the fridge, and if he pulls a meltdown, you can just call me—"

Nikki squeezed his arm. "It's okay. I can do it."

Lincoln gave a relieved smile. To her surprise, *he* hugged her. "Thanks, Nik."

He scooped Nathaniel up in his arms, gently cradling him as he brought him over to the couch at the end of the trailer, settling him in the pile of pillows. He brushed back Nathaniel's curls before quietly stepping back.

"You're getting good at that."

Lincoln went red again. "It's part of the mission," he whispered, signaling her to be quiet. He crept to the door, reminding her to call him if anything went wrong, before slipping off.

The door closed behind him, and Nikki locked it with a click.

Nikki let her head rest on the door, her eyes closing as she slumped to the floor.

She was so tired.

On top of her body fighting to survive, her mind seemed to fighting against itself.

She'd almost drowned. *Lincoln* had almost drowned.

For a split second, she'd believed he'd died and there had been a burning inside her like nothing she'd ever felt before. She rubbed her chest, trying to smother the knot forming.

What was that feeling?

She didn't want to feel it…so there! She just wasn't *going* to feel it.

She picked herself up, her eye catching the NMA disc lying at the center of the coffee table.

That was the reason she'd jumped back into the auto. Even if she couldn't swim.

She picked it up. Her fingerprint triggered the machine, causing the disc to slide out unharmed. Taryn had labeled it in her neat handwriting: *NMA File (for Nikki).*

Nikki wished she could go to Taryn and tell her the voices in her head were getting worse. Maybe they could fight it off, or Taryn could give her a hug and do her best attempt at advice that Nikki found amusing.

Your mother gave this to you.

Taryn said the NMA file was meant for Nikki. Nikki knew how much her mother, Reyna, had meant to Taryn. For her to hand over the NMA disc to Nikki must have been hard.

It scared Nikki to open it…but maybe since she was now a fugitive, it wouldn't be the worst idea to know what was inside.

Her mother was an Agent, after all.

Maybe she'd have some insight to help them get away from Aalto.

She pushed the disc back inside and crawled onto the couch bed, careful not to disturb Nathaniel. She crossed her legs, taking a deep breath as her heart beat against her chest.

With shaking hands, for the first time, she hit the play button.

A cheap, blue hologram appeared.

Realization hit her like a winter storm.

"Hello, Nikki."

Nikki had seen Agent Reyna Wents Aguirre's face more times than she could count.

Her dark hair, tanned skin, unusual violet eyes paired

with a muscular build and the instantly recognizable uniform were plastered all over net videos and occasional tabloids.

But no matter how many times Nikki had been told "That's your mother!" it had never struck her until now.

Not until she saw the woman staring back at her, with her long wavy hair pulled up into an imperfect ponytail, fidgeting with a mic in her ear. She didn't wear a uniform. She wore a tank top that revealed a jagged scar on her shoulder.

Despite the cheap film, Nikki felt like she could see her. She hugged a pillow to her chest, tempted to hide.

This was the Reyna she remembered.

"If anyone else is watching this…they shouldn't be unless you've been given strict permission," recording Reyna said. *"This file has been the result of multiple years of research and work. And let me tell you, it's hard to keep stuff this classified hidden from Cadissa Dean."*

Even though Reyna laughed, a lump formed in Nikki's throat.

Her mother didn't seem afraid at all. As if the world's most powerful woman was simply an inconvenience. It made her feel…safe. Reyna's face quickly softened.

"But if you are Nik watching this, then I'm afraid more unfortunate circumstances have come up," she said, seeming to meet Nikki's eyes. *"I don't know how old you are now, or who you're living with, or even how much you know…and I really hope I'm not too far away. As much as I wish it could be otherwise, you're a part of something so much bigger."*

Nikki knew that now. Seeing the hopeful smile on Reyna's face made her lower her pillow defense.

Reyna sighed. *"But I guess we all know that, and I hope I've properly prepared you. Per your request, you wanted this file to be named after you: Nikki Maria Aguirre. And because you'd probably throw a mud ball at me if it were named anything else, that's what NMA stands for…if you were wondering."*

A mud ball? An interesting choice of weapon from her younger self.

"In this file, I have my plans, theories, probably pointless rambles…. The important thing is: If the Defending Department rejects the past and tries to destroy full-bloods, it won't be in any way prepared for the Shadow Soul. Dean doesn't believe in using her brain. Everything is politics with her, even if it isn't in the best interest for the Defenders…or the world."

Her mother went on a list of other files, all full of various resources and documents. Nikki tuned it all out, unable to take her eyes from the hologram. The way her mother talked felt so familiar. So comforting. The way she moved her hands trying to explain, and once again fidgeting with the mic.

She looked so real…like maybe she wasn't far away.

"And, I hope it never becomes needed, but there's one last file," Reyna said. Her posture became stiff. *"If it does happen that…we die—"*

Nikki's hair raised on her neck, and her heart began beating in her throat.

"I want to be able to explain everything to you. I know what you need to prepare for. I want to be there for you, but Dean will stop at nothing to kill us Curatrix. I won't let that happen to you, Nik."

She sounded like Taryn, both gentle and firm, as she looked straight into the camera.

"If I die, I highly doubt it'll be by execution. The public outrage would be a little too much for Dean."

Reyna tightened her fists. *"So if Dean wanted to bypass execution…well…someone would have to murder me."*

Nikki's body reacted before her mind could. She slapped the disc player, and the hologram disappeared.

The room went quiet and grew dark as Nikki sat in silence, only the sound of Nathaniel's breathing to be heard. That, and the beating of her own heart.

She felt a warm tear touch her lips.

She blinked in surprise, realizing her eyes were overflowing with tears. She quickly tried to brush them away. She lay down, hugging herself. How could she miss someone so bad when she barely remembered?

It was fine. There was nothing to be sad about. But then why did her heart ache?

She didn't want to remember the past. She didn't want to go back.

Murder.

The echoes turned to youthful screams. Arms held her back.

She dug her fingernails into her skin. No! She wasn't going to think about it.

She wasn't going to think about how a small part of her wished Reyna was right. That her parents were not far away.

But they were.

They were *dead*.

And they had been this whole time. She couldn't change like that.

"L-Lem…"

Nikki's eyes burst open, her mind dropping silent. Nathaniel tossed in his sleep. "L-Lin—Lem—"

She rolled closer, tucking in the blanket under his chin and running a gentle finger against his cheek. Something in her memory told her it would work. Nathaniel stopped rustling, his small hand tightening around her arm.

Nikki froze.

The world felt still around her. She heard light rain begin to tap against the windows, and Nathaniel's warm little hand held her down in reality.

She took a deep breath, forcing herself to shut her eyes, falling asleep with the sound of her mother's voice echoing in her mind.

27

MERCY ADJUSTED THE collar of her jacket as she stood outside the trailer.

She was a terrible person! And this was a terrible idea.

She should just turn around and walk away now.

No! It was just a friendly conversation...with Nikki. Who she'd never attempted friendly one-on-one conversation with before. Council bonding.

You're planning on stealing her necklace.

She scolded herself. She wasn't planning on stealing it. She was planning on...borrowing it.

Somehow, that didn't make her feel any less like a thief. She was doing this for the Council. She was going to contact the Founder Association and find out how to glow. And then she could finally be helpful!

She took a deep breath. No backing out now. She knocked on the door, bracing herself.

Nothing.

She grimaced as she tapped in the code to the door and pushed inside.

Before Mercy had a moment to process, her feet were knocked out from under her and she was slammed to the ground. The sharp blade of Fidelis was held to her throat as Nikki's eyes pierced into her. Mercy's scream was stuck in her throat.

Nikki eyes widened in realization as she stood up and retracted the blade. "It's just you," she said.

Mercy rubbed her throat, getting to her feet. "I-is this normal for you?"

Nikki tilted her head, raising a brow. "Normal?"

That was an awful first impression! Great going, Mercy!

"To-uh-attack people as a greeting?" Mercy said, shoving her hands into her hoodie pockets. *That was such a weirdo thing to say! Of course it wasn't!* Unless it was…she didn't know what Nikki etiquette was!

Nikki's face softened, shaking her head, setting Fidelis aside. "No. I'm sorry. I wasn't expecting anyone." She pushed her unkempt bangs out of her face. "Sleep was kinda bad."

She didn't need to say that again.

Nikki's hair was fluffier, and frizzier, than usual, her bangs bent up from sleep. She was still wearing her jeans from the day before, and she was missing a sock.

Mercy's wasn't much better. "Am I interrupting something?" she asked.

Shoot. How was she supposed to make *actual* conversation from this? Nikki was as bad at talking as she was.

Nikki shrugged. "No. Go ahead and do what you wanted."

She picked up a disc player from the couch, where Mercy noticed Nathaniel wrapped up, asleep. Her back was turned to Mercy as she fiddled with a piece of tape.

Just get it over with!

"Are we friends?" Mercy blurted out.

Nikki didn't hesitate, looking over her shoulder. "Of course."

"Oh," Mercy said. Really? Was this how it worked? Did Nikki think everyone was her friend? "I-I mean we've never really…talked, ya know? But I guess it makes sense. I'm a Council Member. You're a Council Member. But like a cooler Council—"

"We're friends," Nikki assured her, turning to face her now. "Not just because of the Council."

Mercy eyes widened, and she swallowed hard. "Oh. That's…cool."

Nikki really thought that?

When did the "friend" thing happen? She was unaware of it.

She was tempted to walk out of the trailer right then and there before she burned with embarrassment. But Nikki watched with curiosity, not a crease of judgment in her brow.

"Well, since we're friends," Mercy said, clearing her throat. The word felt weird. There was no way *Nikki* thought she was her friend. "I-I had a question."

"A question?" Nikki's eyes lit up, setting down the disc. "For me?"

"It's—er—about the Curatrix Team."

Nikki's face fell. "Oh. It's usually about them."

Mercy panicked. How had she not considered that this was a sore topic? Mercy hated being asked about her dad and her grandmother. It seemed like constantly people were asking Nikki about her parents. Like they were no longer Nikki's *dead parents* because they were celebrities.

"It's about Zita," she quickly clarified. Nikki had said they were friends, and Mercy wasn't going to make her uncomfortable. Is that what friends did? "Do you know much about her?"

"I do." Nikki walked over to the kitchenette, tapping the button on the tea kettle. "Lemon tea?"

"Uh…sure?"

Nikki took out two bags from the cupboard. "I don't remember a lot, but she was an Aguarious like Nathaniel. Do you want a green or yellow cup?"

Nikki's eyes demanded Mercy join her, and Mercy was relieved to not be awkwardly standing in the doorway.

She knew about three things about Nikki, and one of them was that she loved yellow.

So she took the green.

"Nik!" The little voice caught Mercy off guard, causing her to nearly stumble back as she noticed a sleepy Nathaniel pop his head up from the couch.

The pot flew off the counter. Nikki barely dodged the

hot water, which splashed her front side.

"Food?" Nathaniel said, now wide awake, rubbing his groggy eyes.

Mercy jumped to her feet. "I can get him food!"

"Thanks," Nikki said with a breathy laugh.

Lincoln treated Nathaniel's meal plan like another project. He'd bought little color-coded containers and bottles at a convenience store in a small town they passed through, and he spent the late nights putting them together.

"I needed to change anyway," Nikki sighed, ruffling Nathaniel's hair.

He gave her a dirty, I-don't-want-be-awake look.

Mercy's heart dropped as she watched Nikki unclip the Stone from around her neck and set it on the counter. She shuffled through her bag, grabbing a fresh shirt before disappearing into the bathroom.

Mercy beside Nathaniel sat on a chair, as he began eating his cereal by the handfuls.

"You were asking about Zita?" Nikki called through the door.

Mercy filled up the pot, her eyes glued on the Stone on the counter. "Yes. An Aguarious," she said. "And did you know she had a Stone like yours…but for Agarious?"

"Really?"

Nikki was actually interested? Mercy's heart sped up. She was expecting to get brushed off. "Yeah! I got a replica back in Manifest!"

But you need to contact the Founder Association.

But Nikki was being so nice to her. It was like…she didn't have to prove anything.

She shook herself.

You need to learn to glow. You're worth nothing to them without your powers.

Mercy swiped the Stone off the counter, careful to only grab the chain, and slipped into her pocket.

Her insides twisted. What had she done?

"Wow," Nikki popped out the door. "Could I see it?"

"Sure."

Mercy hesitantly handed Nikki the keychain, trying to keep her hands from shaking.

It wasn't like it was the real deal, but that plastic blue

stone felt like the closest piece to being useful.

"And I thought...well, I don't know.... It might be too out there." Mercy took a deep breath. It wasn't a lie. "What if it's the Aguarious artifact? Like your Stone?"

Nikki blinked. The kettle went off. She looked back at the keychain and handed it back to Mercy. "That would make a lot of sense."

She poured the steaming water into the cups. "And what's your plan after that?"

Mercy swallowed. Plan after? She hadn't gotten that far. The Council usually didn't listen to her plans.

"I-I'm not sure."

Nikki offered her the green cup. Nikki sat in the booth, cross-legged, with her yellow cup cradled in both her hands.

She looked so...small when she did that.

Much less like the mysterious, fearsome, quiet warrior Mercy had assumed she was.

"Well, from what Ray told me, artifacts enhance their Impure abilities, right? Like you kinda get power with the Ewyon Stone?"

"Only when Avalon wants to," Nikki chuckled. Her eyes suddenly lit up. "So you're saying maybe it'll do the same for Nathaniel? Wait! That's an amazing idea!"

Mercy jumped, startled. "Really?"

"Nathaniel's abilities are all over the place, and if we could find the Aguarious artifact, it might be able to help him stop the storms!"

Mercy peered over Nikki's shoulder to see Nathaniel making a bubble out of his yogurt and exploding it in his own face. "I-I thought we were trying to find him a home and not drag him into Council stuff?"

"True," Nikki said. "But if that Leviathan situation gets worse...Nathaniel will be the only one who can stop it. No matter where he is. That stone would be a page changer."

"A page changer?" Mercy frowned.

"Yeah, like...what we're doing, and something changes it to go our way."

Mercy couldn't help a smile. "Oh! Do you mean game changer?"

"Yes, that!" Nikki shrugged.

Mercy held herself back from laughing, taking a strong

sip of tea. "So how do we get it?"

"Zita had it last."

"Yeah, but Zita's kinda…" Mercy's voice trailed off. "Not available."

That proved to be a significant roadblock.

"Where did Zita die?" Nikki asked, as if it wasn't an extremely weird question.

"Her home in Sulfur," Mercy said, her eyes widening, realizing what she was asking. "Are we passing through Sulfur?"

"If we're lucky; it really depends on him," Nikki said, catching Nathaniel right before he dumped his bowl over his head. "Hey! Nat! No!"

Mercy sighed. "Oh, right."

"Don't be disappointed," Nikki said. "Even if he doesn't pass through it, there's still a chance Taryn will clear a mission there."

"But she hasn't cleared *any* missions," Mercy said. "And she's under trial. Our only chance is now."

"Taryn will get off trial," Nikki said, her face hardening. "She survived the Curatrix Assassination. She can survive anything."

"That's a good point," Mercy said. She still didn't feel too confident. Somehow, being back in North Cordell felt like she'd failed. Right now was the only chance she had to contact the Founder Association to fix her abilities.

She thought getting the Ewyon Stone would make her feel relieved.

But looking at Nikki seriously sipping her lemon tea while studying her with her big blue eyes, and her messy, frizzy hair, she felt like she'd swallowed a rock.

Nikki felt like she was genuinely interested in her idea.

And that made her feel…really good.

She would make it up to her.

"You're right," Mercy decided. "The Sergeant is durable. Just like you. You both survived the Curatrix massacre."

Nikki shrugged, her face unchanging. "I don't remember it."

Her gaze suddenly sank into her tea.

Mercy thought it would've been a compliment. Why in the world did she think bringing up not-dying-when-your-parents-were-assassinated was a good COMPLIMENT?

"I'm sorry," Mercy said, quietly. "About what happened to your *mere*. And *pere*."

Nikki traced a circle on the wooden table. "It's okay. You didn't do anything. It just kinda…feels weird." She rubbed circles with her palm on her chest.

"My *mere* died too," Mercy said.

Nikki looked up.

Mercy's heart leaped. She was…listening to her?

"I know how that feels," Nikki said.

Mercy nodded. "Except I-I never met her. She died the day I was born. You're lucky you got to meet yours."

Dang it! Where were these words coming from? Nikki's mom was dead too! That was such an insensitive thing—

"I am. She was very kind, and headstrong. A bad cook." Her eyes drifted off, a small smile curling on her lips. She snapped herself back to reality. "Do you know what yours was like?"

Mercy's face heated. "Well, I know she was confident…a lot more brave against my grandmother's rules."

"You are brave too."

"You think so?" A lump formed in Mercy's throat. She wasn't brave. She could hardly talk to the Council Members, and she ran away from danger.

"Yeah. Ray told me all about how you escaped the lake, and you're trying to help solve the storms. I think that's pretty brave," Nikki said with a small smile.

Mercy held her head a little higher, for almost a split second.

Nikki nodded, reaching up to her neck. She stopped, frowning. "Huh. That's weird."

The twist in Mercy's stomach returned. "W-what's weird?"

"I must have misplaced it," Nikki said, scanning the trailer. "My Stone."

Mercy swallowed hard. She should take the Stone out her pocket right now and give it back and confess that she'd only come here to steal it, but she hadn't expected to genuinely enjoy talking to Nikki—

"I'll find it," Nikki shrugged, turning back to Mercy. "So, we find the Aguarious Stone in Sulfur? Together?"

28

"NIKKI'S STONE IS **missing**?"

In the past year of knowing Nikki, never once had Felicity seen her without the glowing green Stone.

"I'm sure it just fell through a crack somewhere," Felicity assured Nikki, who had now torn about an entire sofa and was sifting through the cushions. "There's not many places it could go."

The trailer was so crowded it was pointless to even search.

Nikki sat up with a huff, shaking dust from her hair. "I just can't believe I lost it!"

"We all lose things," Tabitha shrugged, biting into a granola bar.

"You lose things more than others, Tabs," Cole said, over the Comm. "How many socks have we found in various places in the Inn?"

"Socks are a totally different story. I haven't lost Taryn's knife yet!" Tabitha pulled the beloved knife from her sheath just to prove it.

Felicity sighed, smothering a smile.

Nikki plopped down on the pile of cushions on the floor. "Maybe Nathaniel tossed it somewhere."

"That's highly likely," Felicity said, turning to the toddler, who was currently being given a bath, which was a three-person job and included getting absolutely soaked.

"Wherever it went, I'm sure we'll find it. Right, Mercy?" Felicity rolled back to include Mercy, who was huddled up in her usual booth.

She jumped at being addressed.

"Nikki told us about your Aguarious Stone idea," Felicity said. "It seems pretty smart."

Mercy perked up. "Really?"

Felicity frowned. Instead of seeing excitement spark in Mercy's eyes, she saw her eyes twitch away…as if she was hiding.

Mercy was always hiding. It was nothing new…but this felt—

"We're approaching the Pryvt Market!" Cole announced over the Comm. "Echo and Cecileo gave me very specific instructions to get in. No one do anything crazy."

Felicity's heart leaped. It had been months since she'd last been to a Market. She had fond memories of the rugged counter culture Marketeers that lurked in their hidden cities all across the world. They'd fought to defend her against the Exerticus and had helped train Cole.

And now, she prayed they could help them again.

She tapped her headband, feeling the whir of power flow through her braces. She forced herself to stand up, an uncontrollable shiver taking over her. She shook it off and ran out the door.

The city was old. You could tell they'd tried to mix the crumbling buildings of the pre-EarthShaker world and new higher tech buildings. In the evening, it didn't seem like a soul was stirring, except for a few older model autos pulling up to a bar with its door propped open by a sparkly pink bot.

Cole turned down an alleyway until they approached an enormous wall. Cole got out of the truck to face the wall, untucking the Medallion from his neck.

The Council flooded out from the trailer and truck.

Cole rolled his eyes back, holding up the Medallion.

"Uh…we know you're here, Market."

"That was your plan?"

"Look, when Cecileo says address yourself to the wall, I wasn't really sure what he meant," Cole whispered, clearing his throat. "I'm Coleson Johnson, the Illuminate Member of the Council and friend of Pater Cecileo and Mater Echo. This is Felicity Bentsworth, Guardian Member of the Council."

For a moment, nothing happened.

Were they just talking to a random wall? Did they have to talk to every wall? That could take days! *Felicity, you're being irrational—*

The cracks between to glow.

Felicity shouted, jumping back as the wall began to separate, creating a small, narrow pathway.

We better hurry, Cole announced telepathically. *The path will close soon.*

"The truck and trailer won't fit through there," Felicity said, biting her lip anxiously.

Cole let out a sigh, and ran for the tunnel. "Then we'll have to make this trip quick."

Felicity shouted after him, but he didn't wait. She took a deep breath and chased after him, trying not to think about how at any moment, the wall could close in on her.

She broke out on the other side, nearly pushed off her feet by Lincoln.

He quickly caught her arm. "Sorry!"

She laughed breathlessly. "It's alright."

It took a moment for her eyes to adjust to the sight. This Market looked just like the one in Liberty. It felt smaller and more confined by walls, but the jewel-toned fabrics and tents were all the same. Little children stopped in their tracks to stare, and market vendors whispered among themselves as the wall closed behind them. The air smelled strongly of freshly baked ham, and the tune of a flute played in between the hum of voices.

"Ah! We've been expecting you!" A man stepped out from the crowd. He had a peg leg and a golden tooth, but a friendly smile. "And Johnson, is it?"

Cole nodded.

Felicity decided it was best to hide behind him.

"You might remember me from Elery Market. Tony?"

"It's the guy with the squeaky voice that was totally over-shadowed by Cecileo," Tabitha whispered loudly before she was shushed.

"I do," Cole said, cringing. "It wasn't…the most pleasant Market experience."

"Of course, of course," Tony said, quickly clearing his throat. "But the relations between the Council and the Market are much different now. I see we're *both* now wanted by the Defenders."

He laughed to himself, but Felicity found it hard to agree.

Tony cleared his throat. "Anyway, I'm the secondhand correspondent for Cecileo. I help manage regions he's not present in."

Felicity's face fell. "So Echo and Cecileo aren't here?"

Tony sighed. "Unfortunately not. If they'd known you'd be here, I'm sure they would've tried their best to meet you."

"Yeah, I'm really curious to meet this guy who dyes his hair half white," Ray said.

"That's a question we'll never have the answer to," Tony sighed. "Glimmer's been expecting you."

"Glimmer?"

"She helps run this Market when Cecileo's not here."

Tony led them down the streets. Felicity followed closely behind Cole.

"Nathaniel! No!" Lincoln swatted away a bubble containing a toothy, bloodthirsty-looking fish.

"Friend!"

"Not friend!"

Nathaniel sighed, dropping the fish back into his container. "Linc no friend."

Felicity hated being stared at. She'd experienced it since before she could even remember. It was like she could feel every individual eye burning into the back of her neck.

They turned the corner, and Tony pushed through a curtain of paper lanterns. Felicity held her breath as they approached an enormous velvet tent with metal trinkets dangling from the golden tassels.

Tony slipped off his shoes.

Cole did the same.

The others stared, confused. "It's a thing," Felicity whispered loudly. "This is the tent of their leaders."

No one questioned it.

Nathaniel insisted on not being left out, which left Lincoln struggling to unbuckle his tiny shoes.

Felicity stepped through the curtains. The sweet aroma put her at ease as she followed Tony and Cole into the main room of the tent.

There a woman sat in the pillows at the low-standing table. She had curly blonde hair adorned with silver ornaments. Her lips were painted a bright blue that matched her eyes.

She jumped to her feet immediately with a small curtsy. The little bells at the end of her shawl rang as she moved. "So this is the Phoenix Council?" she said with a small smile on her lips. "I extend the Pater and Mater's welcome. I'm sure they're discouraged that they missed the opportunity to meet you all."

Echo and Cecileo being there would've made Felicity's stomach feel much less twisted.

"My name is Glimmer DeFage," the woman said, tossing a blonde curl. "Please walk with me."

Felicity didn't like all this walking. Why couldn't they just stop and get down to the yes or no question?

Glimmer pushed through the flaps of the tent. Felicity's eyes widened as the smell of old books filled the room. The back part of the tent was exposed to the air. Tables were crowded full of Tabitha's favorite thing: Paper.

Tabitha immediately gasped, quickly picking up a yellowed page.

"Careful," Glimmer warned. "Some of these are ancient."

A few other Marketeers seemed unphased by the large group of teenagers as they shifted through the stacks of books.

"Did Echo and Cecileo receive our message?" Cole asked.

Glimmer stopped in her step. "Yes, they did. About the young Aguarious?"

Everyone turned to face Lincoln and Nathaniel in the carrier, chewing on his tracking necklace.

"Unfortunately, they've declined to take the child."

"What?" Felicity spun around. "They don't want him?"

Of all people, she would've expected Echo and Cecileo to want to adopt Nathaniel.

"It wasn't a personal decision," Glimmer said, clasping her hands behind her back. "I'm sure under other circumstances they would've been thrilled to take him in, but the problem lies in how dangerous keeping a Council Member in the Markets would be. The Exerticus already caused much damage before, and the people of the Market come first."

Felicity's heart fell.

Cecileo and Echo would've made the perfect parents for Nathaniel…but Glimmer had a point.

"Anywhere he goes makes him dangerous," Glimmer said bluntly. "I don't think anyone could protect him from the Exerticus."

Felicity swallowed hard, looking over the documents spread out over the tables.

"We've been collecting old documents from abandoned EarthShaker buildings," she explained as Felicity stepped nearer.

She spread the pages out.

A cool wave entered her mind, the low moan of the sea creature beckoning her.

Not now, Craig.

Her fingers brushed on the paper with an inked illustration. She frowned. A circle with twelve smaller circles, all leading to the center.

The words were etched in a strange dialect, yet the words almost seemed to fall in place.

"The First Council…"

"Wait," Glimmer snapped. "You understand that?"

Felicity's heart jumped to her throat. She spun around, clutching the paper to her chest. "I-I— Yes?"

"That's an unknown script," a Marketeer scoffed, getting up from across the room. "How could she possibly know?"

Felicity glanced down at the paper.

It couldn't be. She understood it. The words were simple and strange…but it made perfect sense.

"It's about the Shadow Soul curse," she breathed, turning the page around. "The circle represents the First Council. Where did you find this?"

"It was one of Cecileo's thievery finds," Glimmer said, frowning. "How can you read it?"

"It must be written by a Shifter," Felicity said, her face burning as she thought of the reality of her non-human state.

"What does it say?" Nikki rushed to her side.

Felicity turned back the table, her hands running across the symbols. "It doesn't say much. It just goes on about what we already know. The First Council curses the Oquelite for creating their own version of immortality. As punishment, an Oquelite hybrid will become the Shadow Soul, an immortal being who can't be killed and will destroy the world and take the Oquelite with it."

Felicity began to dig through the papers. Many were written in the same hand, often with the same Council diagram.

"There has to be more. If there's information on the Shadow Soul here…maybe we can find out why Kathryn's creating that storm…why she wants our blood so badly." Felicity spun around. "We need to search."

Glimmer blinked. "I-I guess there's no problem with that."

"You heard Felicity," Cole said. "Look for the papers with squiggles on them!"

"Great plan, Goldfish."

The Council immediately began shifting through the papers. Felicity sat down on a cushion, sorting through the growing pile as the Council excitedly began to collect.

The Council has the power to curse.

The Council is twelve Members.

The Council is connected to powerful artifacts.

So much of it was information that wasn't new, but the author was thrilled with the discoveries.

Centuries ago, it seemed like this was all fascinating information.

Night began to fall, and Glimmer brought out candles to the room and offered to bring food. The Council eagerly agreed. Something that wasn't charging station food sounded amazing to the others.

Felicity wasn't hungry.

She looked at the tall stack of papers before her, tossing aside another useless parchment.

How could she understand this when the others couldn't?

She knew for certain her parents had never taught her this.

"Do-do you need any help?"

Mercy's voice piped up behind her.

Felicity jumped, looking over her shoulder. "Oh. I'm alright. You can go enjoy dinner."

"I'm not hungry," Mercy said, staring at the floor.

"In that case, I guess you could stay with me. No promises I'll be much fun."

Mercy's eyes lit up as she sat down a few feet away from Felicity.

"How's it going?"

Felicity gave a frustrated sigh. "It's useless. None of this information is new to us."

"I doubt it's useless," Mercy said. "You can read it when no one else can. That's super cool."

"I guess so."

"You said to loosen up, remember?" Mercy said. "Maybe that will help."

"You sound like Giles," Felicity laughed, tears stinging her eyes from thinking of him.

"Well, maybe he's right."

Felicity sighed. "Maybe he is."

She closed her eyes, taking a deep breath. Giles was on trial right now. His life was being threatened. She had to get back and save him. She had to do *something*. Kathryn was going to do something disastrous if she didn't figure out these storms.

Sinni's words echoed back to her.

Felicity didn't want to figure out her feelings. If she did, would she break and fall back into the Felicity who was too scared to go outside?

Think. Craig's long moan beckoned. *Feel, Guardian. To feel.*

Felicity tensed, squeezing her eyes and clenching her jaw.

She was angry at Silas.

Even thinking about him made her want to scream.

You loved him.

The words were her own.

She could feel a hot tear trickle down her face.

Silas had betrayed her. She had placed her trust and vulnerability in him and he'd gone and shattered in into a million tiny, unrepairable pieces when she was crammed into that tiny cell.

A gust of wind slammed into Felicity, and her eyes burst open. The papers were swirling around her.

"No, no, no!" she shouted, panicking as she and Mercy scrambled to collect the papers.

Felicity's hand slammed down on a paper.

Blood Theory.

Felicity stopped, moving her hand and picking up the paper. Her heart skipped a beat.

A drawing of the Council symbol was on the page once more, but now drawn in red.

A theory has grown with my comrades that perhaps the blood from the Council is enough to harness a fraction of their power.

Felicity's heart quickened. "Mercy! This is it!"

Felicity continued to read. "This theory has thus been discarded from practice. The power of the Council is so great that it requires twelve members to harness it. Someone attempting to harness the blood of the Council alone could break the Shadow Soul curse."

Felicity swallowed as her eyes grazed over the last line: "But the unharnessed power could destroy the Void and timeline of the user."

"Wait, wait. So Kathryn wants to use our blood to try and recreate the Council's power and therefore destroy the Void? That's a stupid idea!"

Tabitha stared at the scribbles only Felicity could read, wishing more than anything she could decipher it for herself.

The Council was crowded in the small cushion room around Felicity, who held her hands in her head.

"She doesn't want to," Nikki said, holding her legs to her chest. "She wants to break the Shadow Soul curse of immortality."

"And it seems like she'll do it at any cost," Lincoln groaned, Nathaniel asleep on his chest.

"So what do we do?" Lawrence said. "Do we kill her?"

The room dropped silent.

Tabitha was usually in line with Lawrence's intensity…

but something inside her squirmed, and she couldn't figure out why.

"We can't kill her," Tabitha said.

"It doesn't feel right," Matteo agreed, fidgeting with his earbuds.

"I agree. Planning to kill isn't comfortable, but Kathryn is planning on possibly destroying the world if we don't!"

"No, the problem is that's exactly what Kathryn wants," Cole said, getting to his feet. "Killing Kathryn would be ending her curse...a curse that was created by the First Council."

"She wasn't meant to be killed," Ray said, quietly looking up. "Other-Ancient-Council made that clear. There has to be another way. The First Council couldn't have just doomed us like this!"

"The First Council had all twelve members and was made up of a bunch of old people," Lincoln said. "We only have ten Members, and one of us is like two years old! How in the world were they expecting us to figure this out? Kathryn's centuries older than all of us!"

Tabitha hated it when Lincoln was right.

"Our immediate threat is that Kathryn is using Craig for something," Tabitha said, chewing on her lip. "She's using Craig for the storm, but why?"

"She's trying to get our blood," Nikki said.

"But how does a storm help her?" Matteo said.

"She *wants* us to stop her," Tabitha realized, her jaw falling. "She's trying to cause chaos because she knows that inevitably, we'll come stop her."

"But then what do we do? We can't just...let her complete her evil plan?" Felicity said. "But if we do, we're walking right into her hands."

They were helpless.

They were just a bunch of kids. Tabitha loved saving the world, but she was tired. And she was scared. She just wanted to go back to North Cordell.

But she couldn't appear weak. She straightened herself, forcing her lips into a firm straight line.

"Council!" Glimmer pushed through the flaps of the tent, followed by two Marketeer men, all out of breath.

They all jumped to their feet.

"Our scouts have reported Defenders in the town,"

Glimmer said. "You can't stay here any longer."

Lawrence cursed. "Aalto."

"Let's hope not," Felicity breathed.

Tabitha's stomach dropped. "The trailer! The trailer's just out there unprotected!"

Tabitha barreled between the Marketeers and out the flaps of the tent. She scooped up her shoes but didn't bother to put them on.

"Tabitha!"

Tabitha weaved between confused traders and merchants, her heart hammering against her chest. She dove under a cart full of fabrics, scrambling back into a run down the street. She pumped her legs.

They couldn't lose the trailer.

Cole couldn't lose the trailer.

Their entire life was currently in that vehicle.

She approached the wall they'd entered through, sealed up and unopened. How was she supposed to get out? She couldn't wait for Cole.

She glanced over her shoulder. One of the tent stalls caught her eyes, a fire escape ladder directly above it. She tied the laces of her shoes together and slung them over her shoulders.

She ran for the tent, pulling herself up the pole. She leaped and caught the bottom rung of the ladder.

Tabitha ignored the shouts below. She could feel the screws beginning to give way under her weight. She began to climb, her heart hammering into her ears.

The ladder suddenly ripped from the wall, the bolts on the top of the creaking for dear life.

Tabitha hardly had a moment to scream, using every inch of momentum to fling herself to the edge. Her hands clenched the edge of the roof.

Don't look down. Don't think about anything.

Tabitha pulled herself up onto the roof, catching her breath. She ran to the other side, relieved to see the trailer unharmed in the alley. She could now hear the distant sirens.

She needed to buy the Council time.

Think, Tabitha! Think!

Her eyes widened. That was it. Her impulse buy was about to pay off. She scaled down the wall, running to unlock the lower storage of the trailer, pulling out two long, bright purple fireworks.

This had to be her stupidest idea yet…and she had a lot of stupid ideas.

Tabitha ran out of the alleyway and into the road.

The headlights began to come closer and closer.

She skidded to a stop, and set the explosives down into the dirt road.

She dug through her pockets, cursing herself as she threw out a granola bar wrapper and four receipts before she finally found her lighter.

The autos weren't stopping.

Tabitha's body threatened to freeze like a deer in the headlights.

No! Don't you dare!

She pulled herself into motion and lit the ends of the fireworks.

"Tabitha!"

"Run!" she screamed, turning and sprinting.

Bang! Tabitha was knocked off her feet, slamming into the gravel. She groaned, her ears ringing, her vision rocking.

"Tabitha!" Cole's voice was distant as he dragged her to her feet. Tabitha stumbled as Cole easily swept her off her feet. "Lawrence, drive!"

Tabitha felt Cole run up the steps into the trailer. The door slammed shut. The vehicle lurched backward at a full speed.

Cole held onto her tightly, and Tabitha tried to remember how to breathe, blinking her vision back.

Cole looked back at her. "Tabitha!"

"Cole?" she croaked.

"That was so— so reckless!"

"But it worked. Is everyone here?"

"Yes, it worked…but what does that matter if you got hurt?"

The vehicle took a harsh turn. Everyone shouted as they tripped and slammed into the wall. Tabitha could breathe with relief, knowing the Council was alive.

She lay on the floor, staring at the ceiling as her vision slowly returned. She felt Cole's fingers intertwine with hers. Tabitha wished she could stay in that moment, drown out

the ringing in her ears and forget her troubles.
And she did.
She closed her eyes.
Just for a minute.

"CONGRATS TABITHA! YOU'RE on the news!"

Tabitha groaned as Ray flipped the tablet over to face her. She slammed it down. "I don't need to know this."

Nikki couldn't blame her.

"Teenager from Imperial causes Pryvt explosions in run in with Defenders," Ray said, laughing. "Yikes."

Tabitha spoke into her Comm. "How much longer, Cole?"

"It should only be another fifteen."

The closest safe house listed in the plan had led them along a bumpy road for the past two days without a soul in sight.

Nikki didn't like the sound of it…or the feel of it.

The news broadcast shifted. "Storm conditions worsen in Liberty…"

Video clips showed drone footage of the rain clouds crowded around the Liberty Dome, lighting sparking through the crowds. Tabitha bit down on her lip as she watched the waves crashing down on the docks that she'd seen many times in her childhood.

Lawrence shut off the screen. "We have to take on one problem at a time."

Kathryn creating storms seemed pretty high up there.

"So what we've gathered is that the Defenders *think* Nikki might be an Aguirre, but they're not sure about it?" Lincoln said, pacing with Nathaniel on his shoulders.

"That guy seemed pretty fine with straight up murdering people to get the job done," Lawrence snorted, somewhat salty that Aalto had cut through his only good shirt he'd packed, meaning he had to resort to wearing his least favorite thing: T-shirts.

It made the nasty cut on his arm even more visible.

Nikki cringed. "Agents are some of the most highly trained Defenders."

Lincoln groaned. "Why is everything trying to kill us? First, Kathryn and her Oquelite and Exerticus, and now the literal Defenders?"

When put like that, it really didn't make their chances look too good.

Nikki scrubbed the edge of her shield harder. That strange burning feeling warmed itself inside her. Maybe she should ask Lincoln about it.

But looking up and seeing the scratches on his face, it made the feeling worse.

She instead looked out the window. Across the empty, dying fields stood a huge circular forest of tall, strange trees. In fact, they were nothing like she'd ever seen before. A river looped through the fields and into the little forest as the truck bumped along the road.

"Are we sure this is a good safe house—"

A bang went off, and before Nikki had a chance to process it, the trailer spun, sending them all crashing to the wall. Everything came to a screeching halt.

Nathaniel began to cry, and Nikki turned to see Lincoln holding him in his arms on the floor, trying to soothe him.

Lawrence opened the door. He cursed. "Did we research this safe house, like, *at all?*"

Nikki's sweat went cold. Out of the trees came a dozen, if not more, uniformed Officers. Her hand twitched to grab Fidelis.

One walked up to the door as another approached the main truck.

"Authorization," the Officer said. Nikki couldn't miss the pistol in his hands.

"We can just turn around and leave—"

"Now." The gun raised to Lawrence's head.

Lawrence scowled, seeming only inconvenienced by the weapon. He pulled out his Comm. The Defender scanned it with his wristband.

Nikki held her breath as rows of text began to scroll out on the screen.

She braced herself, ready to attack. She wouldn't back down this time.

"Get out of the auto," the Defender demanded.

Lawrence opened his mouth to argue, but a click from the pistol made him begrudgingly obey.

The Defender turned to companions. "Unload the others." He turned back. "Just listen, and no one gets hurt."

Nikki had just watched a Defender attempt to murder her friends in cold blood. Somehow she doubted that.

She reached for Fidelis, but Lincoln shook his head.

"I said get out!"

Lincoln got to his feet, quickly turning to pass off Nathaniel to Nikki. She blinked. Why would he—

Act like he's your little brother! Something! We can't let them take him! I look suspicious!

Now she definitely couldn't punch anyone.

They exited the trailer slowly. Two strong hands grabbed Nikki's shoulders. *Don't fight, don't fight.*

A cloth was tied tightly around her eyes.

Nathaniel began to cry.

"Quiet!"

"He's only two!" Lincoln said, somewhere in the vicinity.

"Well, if he can't shut up, Officer Tendo will take him."

Nikki's heart skipped. "No!"

Panicked, she quickly unclipped the lemon pin from her bag and shoved it into his tiny hands. Nathaniel went quiet, taking the pin.

Was handing a toddler a pin a good idea? Most likely not. But he was quiet.

The guard prodded her back, pushing her forward. Her

heart was racing.

Where was Lincoln? Lawrence? Were they all going in the same direction?

She tried to wriggle her blindfold off, but it didn't prove effective.

She kept walking. She wasn't sure how long, or how far. A harsh hand in her hair pulled her to a stop. She heard a small beep before she was pushed forward again.

"Load them in."

Were they being arrested? They said they wouldn't hurt them.

Nikki almost screamed as a pair of arms picked her up and shoved her into a leather seat, pressed into someone else. A hand awkwardly grabbed her cheek.

"Let me guess? Ray?" Tabitha's voice.

"I'm Nikki," Nikki whispered, wrenching her face away from Tabitha's hand.

"Oh. Hi Nik. Having a fun time? Let me know if you're sitting next to Cole. I need to slap him."

"I don't think he knew we were walking into *this*."

The road bumped below them.

Nathaniel pinched her.

"Linc fight bad guys?" he said.

Nikki shushed him.

A slobbery hand touched her face.

The auto came to a harsh stop. The door opened, and Nikki was dragged out of her seat.

"Where is the Outown's protégé?"

It took Nikki half a second to remember that they were talking about *Cole*. The Outowns had taken a liking to him because their son, Aaron, had the same Medallion as him or something…

But what did that have to do with this?

"Don't hurt him!" Tabitha cried from behind Nikki, a struggle in her voice. "Are you so pathetic you'd fight a blind-folded teenager? He'd cut your head off in five seconds flat if—"

Tabitha was muffled.

Nikki felt the wind begin to pick up. She held her breath.

Her blindfold was torn off.

They were now in the middle of an enormous, circular

field, surrounded by the woods. A curious building stood in front of them, the corners of the roof turned upward. It stood about two stories tall, with singles painted a deep black against the rest of the building's shimmering blue that complimented the enormous lake behind it, streams breaking out into the woods.

She looked to her side, seeing all the Members lined up.

The door swung open, the Officer pushing out in front of them.

A woman stood in front of the porch steps. Her sleek black hair was swept up into a messy bun. Her skin was pale, and she wore a rich, violet, sleeveless tunic. Her eyes grew wide.

Cole was pushed forward. "Mrs. Shi-Outown?" he said, his voice trembling. "We're the Phoenix Council."

The woman didn't blink, a brow raising. "The Council? Here?"

How did Cole know her name? She was an Outown? Was anyone going to explain anything?

"Let me see! Let me see! Let go!" With a bang, a young boy raced out the door, rushing to the woman, followed by a breathless guard who stumbled out the door.

The woman clung to the boy.

He was definitely her son. Same eyes and dark hair. His legs were tall, mismatched to his torso. He had likely just hit a growth spurt.

"Did Ann and Ludwig send you?" the woman said, her voice gentle.

Ann and Ludwig. Miriam's parents? Matteo asked.

Yes. Lincoln responded.

Too many people to keep track of.

"No. I didn't know you were the one who lived here. I- I'm so sorry," Cole said, flustered.

Who is that? Nikki asked, looking to Tabitha standing beside her.

You don't know Rallie Shi-Outown? Tabitha frowned, bewildered.

Am I supposed to?

"We were being pursued. And we needed somewhere to hide and throw them off their tracks," Cole explained. "Miriam said this might be a safe place to stay."

Is she Miriam's sister?

What? No! Do you think they look alike?

I don't know! Me and Lawrence don't look anything alike!

"Why do you need a safe house?" Rallie asked, inching closer. "What are you hiding?"

Her face hardened, her voice holding an echo of authority.

Nikki stepped forward, holding out Nathaniel.

"He's just…a baby," Cole said.

"And that girl too. Isn't that right?" Rallie said, staring daggers into Nikki. "She's the fugitive, isn't she? I hear rumors she might be an Aguirre."

Nikki's blood went cold, trying to calculate how she could set down Nathaniel, beat up the guard to her left, and escape.

"Any Aguirre is a friend of ours," Rallie said, instead.

Nikki let out a relieved breath.

"Nathaniel's a full-blooded Aguarious," Cole explained. "Currently, both the Shadow Soul and the law are after him."

Rallie was quiet a moment. She looked hard at Nathaniel, and then back at the boy waiting for her on the porch. She sighed, jerking her head toward the guards. "Let them in."

The guards slowly moved away from the Members. Raindrops began to fall.

"Hurry inside," Rallie said, walking through the doors.

Nikki glanced at Tabitha, who simply shrugged. They followed her up the steps and into the house. Who was this woman?

"So he's really a full-blood?"

Nikki jumped, not noticing the young boy had snuck up beside her. He stared at Nathaniel.

"Y-yes," Nikki said, unsure what to say. "He can control water."

"What?" the boy shouted, looking up at her, practically bouncing. "That is *so so* cool!"

He held his hand out to Nathaniel. "Nice to meet you, super powered baby. I'm Eleazar."

Nathaniel simply showed off the sparkly lemon pin instead. Nikki was relieved he hadn't eaten or lost it. "Sparkly le-le."

"That's a lemon."

"Le-le."

Nathaniel smiled, turning to Nikki. "I'm Eleazar Out-own. Twelve. Imperial."

Nikki nodded. "Nikki. Sixteen. North—" Was she really from North Cordell? Nikki *Aguirre* was from Algery, but she didn't even remember it. "Somewhere. I'm from some-where."

"Me too," Eleazar said, sliding off his shoes, looking at Nikki as if he expected her to do the same.

She looked down the hall to see the group turning the corner without her. She sighed, setting Nathaniel down and sitting down on a bench to unbuckle her muddy boots.

"So you're an Outown too?" she said, pulling her boot free. How many were there?

"Yeah. That's my mom," Eleazar said, sounding suddenly much older as his face twisted into a worried expression. "I should be checking on her."

Nikki set her boots together by the door.

She began to reach for Nathaniel when Eleazar threw himself in front of her. "Can I hold magic water baby?"

"I guess. He might start screaming—"

Eleazar happily took up Nathaniel, and to Nikki's shock, Nathaniel said in his bubbly voice, "Fight bad guys?"

"Sure! Come on, Nikki!" Eleazar said, leading the way down the hall. "Do you have magic powers too?"

Nikki felt too filthy to be walking in the pristine halls, the walls even etched with golden accents, not a speck of dust on any hanging.

"No," she said, almost forgetting Eleazar had even asked a question. "Not technically."

Some would consider the P9F file in her blood a power, but in terms of the supernatural, not yet.

"Lucky. They're stressful."

Nikki frowned. "You-you do?"

"I'm an Outown," he said, exasperatedly flapping his arms. "Have that wing thing."

His voice did the shift again, going from the boy with such childlike wonder comparable to Charles, to a stoic fig-ure who spoke with absolute seriousness and held the weight of his words.

They entered the next room, which was an open living

space, with glass windows stretched all along the walls and a fire burning in an inner pit.

Rallie sat down on a low sofa, two guards on either side.

The Council stood in awkward silence as they lined up in the room...well, that was until Nathaniel began to fuss for Lincoln.

Lincoln took Nathaniel quickly from Eleazar, who ran to sit by his mother.

Nikki shifted in her place beside Lincoln, who *still* hadn't answered her question on who Eleazar was.

But Tabitha appeared too occupied with looking ready to punch anyone who came too close to her.

"You say you're looking for shelter?" Rallie said, her voice quiet and her eyes unable to move from Cole...or rather, the Medallion hanging from his neck. "How did you find this place?"

"It was listed as an Outown estate," Cole said. "It was on the Curatrix Machine database. And Miriam recommended it."

Rallie's brows furrowed. "The Curatrix Machine?"

"It was a creation of Agent Reyna Wents Aguirre."

Rallie's eyes widened, and Nikki's heart leaped.

"Reyna?" she said softly. Her eyes became glassy, and she turned to Eleazar, who spoke to her softly. She turned back to the Council.

"We're the Council. The Phoenix Council," Cole said "Er---the name is a...work in progress."

"The Phoenix is intriguing creature. Perhaps an overused metaphor," Rallie said, running her fingers through the Eleazar's hair. "But a beautiful one."

A moment of silence.

"I suppose you're the Council Jess always speaks of?"

"Yes. We are...you know the Sergeant?"

Rallie smiled, though her eyes were elsewhere. "Oh, very well."

Her face fell. "Not as well as Reyna did. Reyna would've died for that child Sergeant. Or Lyell. Or Zita. Or..." Rallie froze.

Nikki's heart panged. What was up with the constant reminders of her mother lately? It was almost comforting to be reminded of how close her mother had been with young

Taryn. Taryn didn't have much family, and she always talked about Reyna as if someone were talking about an annoying older sibling.

Taryn was the only person in the world who didn't make being an Aguirre feel so…daunting.

The world remembered a strong inspirational leader of a team, outspoken against every odd…but all Nikki remembered was a blurry warm smile and embrace.

The ringing of a gunshot.

Eyes that didn't close.

The heat of flames…not arms.

A tear escaped her. She shook herself, feeling her mind try to drag itself to the past. No! Anytime but now!

Pull it together!

Eleazar eyed her suspiciously.

"You must be exhausted," Rallie spoke again. "You may stay in the gardens. A change of clothes and showers might also be in order."

"Are we really that dirt—" Ray began to ask before Lawrence slapped a hand over his mouth.

Nikki had to admit that a shower sounded amazing after having to live with the tiny trailer one and its limited water supply.

Rallie rose to her feet, Eleazar offering his arm to his mother. "You are welcome to join us for dinner in a few hours."

"Thank you, ma'am," Cole said with a small bow. "We greatly appreciate it. I'll be sure to repay you any expenses. Just let us know."

Rallie gave a weak smile. "No need, Coleson," she said. "Not now, at least."

Nikki let out a silent sigh of relief as they were led out of the room and away from Eleazar's all-too-intelligent gaze. Today had been all over the place.

She decided in the end she liked Rallie, but something was off about her.

At least she hadn't kidnapped them, or tried to kill them. That was really nice.

"You okay?" Lincoln whispered as they walked down a dimly lit hall.

"I am very okay." She quickly scrubbed the wet trail of

the tear. "My brain is just being weird again. Who is Rallie?"

"She's Aaron Outown's wife."

Tabitha's voice sent Nikki's mind silent.

That finally answered her question.

Aaron Outown. A member of the Curatrix Team. Killed the same night as her parents. Miriam's older brother.

"No wonder she looks so sad," Nikki said quietly.

"She watched her husband be inhumanely murdered. You can't blame her for being a little shaken," Cole said.

The memory of fire threatened to roar back to life. Her eyes widened. "She-she watched him die?"

No one answered her.

No one needed to.

Nikki's own feelings terrified her.

She couldn't help but know that she knew *exactly* how Rallie felt.

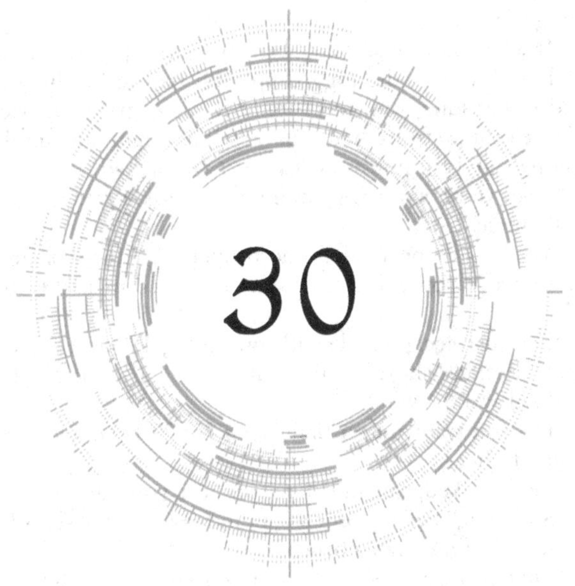

30

THE BEDROOM WAS like nothing Nikki had ever seen…which made sense, since it wasn't a bedroom.

The top story was an indoor garden, not dissimilar to the Bentsworths', just with less marble and more wood. The entire ceiling was glass, looking out toward the evening sky, where the light rain began to fall.

Mattresses were set up in the lounge sections of the gardens, the garden furniture moved to the side. It was obvious the house wasn't used to guests, as they were all offered the same change of clothes in two sizes: male or female.

They were sleeveless tunics and a simple pair of pants in a light gray-blue color. One large shower room was located down the hall, and it was decided that the girls would go first. In the meantime, the boys decided to attempt to bargain for their trailer back.

Nikki ran her thumb over the soft fabric of the shirt, a few sizes too big, but impressively made nonetheless. It was firm and tightly sewed together, but still breathable and functional. The stitching was so intricate and expensive it felt wrong to wear.

"It won't bite you, Nikki." Felicity rolled up to the mirror beside her, wiping the fogged-up glass before finishing the braid in her long, wet, red hair. "My father used to special order clothing from here for a while when my mother couldn't stand for polyester scarves." She sighed.

"They don't work very well either," Nikki said, slipping on the tunic.

"You've just never tied one properly," Felicity laughed. "There's a reason yours always fall off as soon as the wind picks up."

"I've just accepted that it's one thing I'll never understand." Besides, she'd lost the scarf a week after being given it…thanks to the wind.

"Do you want me to braid your hair?" Felicity offered, turning to her.

Nikki blinked, caught off guard. "I-if you want to."

"Sit down," Felicity ordered, pointing to a stool set off to the side. "Let me grab a brush."

Nikki brought the stool over, sitting down. Memories trickled back as Felicity's hands gently parted her hair.

"You know, if you took the time, you could have amazing curls," Felicity said.

Nikki stared into the mirror. A year ago, they'd been in almost the exact position, Felicity doing Nikki's hair for their first mission to Imperial. Her mind slowly began to drift…

"88, what are you doing?"

A painful echo of fingernails digging into her shoulder.

"This is unacceptable. It's not a plaything."

"She's just a little kid!" 88's voice echoed.

"We've gone over this. There is no human—"

"This is unjust!" Tabitha's voice saved Nikki from her mind. Mercy and Tabitha stepped out around the corner from the showers.

Nikki immediately saw the issue.

Tabitha's tunic fit her like a short dress, reaching to her knees, whereas Mercy's fit snugly and her pants came to her knees.

Felicity snorted.

"Like I said: Injustice."

Mercy squirmed and attempted to pull the pants down

further, but to no avail. Nikki had never seen so much of the marks on her exposed arms and legs.

"At least you'll be warm, Tabs," Felicity said, finishing Nikki's braid.

"If warmth was the concern, they'd have given us longer sleeves," Tabitha said, turning to sit under the wall dryer as she shook her wet hair.

"Are you alright, Mercy?" Felicity asked.

Mercy hesitated, looking surprised, as if she'd been hiding. She nodded. "Yeah, I'm fine," she said, rubbing her shoulders. "It just feels weird."

"You look awesome," Nikki assured her. "If anyone stares or says something weird, I'll punch them."

Mercy gave the tiniest smile. "Thanks."

With Nikki's hard-to-miss scar on the right side of her face, she could understand a little of how Mercy felt.

"I-I should be heading to dinner anyway."

"We *all* should be heading there," Felicity said, rolling to the door.

Tabitha leaped to her feet. "Food!"

"Then, I'll-uh— go find the boys and tell them the showers are free!" Mercy backed up to the door.

Tabitha frowned. "I can go with you if you want. I was meaning to tell Cole—"

"Nope!" Mercy said, rushing to the door. "I've got it! I'll let him know!"

Mercy had slipped out of the bathroom before anyone could stop her.

Tabitha frowned. "Uh…is she okay? She's acting distant."

"She's usually distant," Felicity said. "Just give her time."

"I mean, more distant than usual." Tabitha's brows deepened.

"We all take our own time to process things, Tabs." Felicity set a hand on Tabitha's arm before leading them out of the washroom.

Nikki followed the others out of the room. She had to admit, Mercy's behavior was confusing. Mercy had avoided talking to Nikki up until their conversation in the trailer over tea and talking about Zita.

The conversation didn't *feel* like Mercy was just using

Nikki for information.

It felt…genuine.

She didn't have much time to dwell on it as they had taken a wrong turn, and it took about twenty minutes for them to find the dining room.

Ray, Lincoln, and Matteo had managed to both shower *and* beat them to the dining room. The table was low to the floor, with cushions for seats.

Nikki quickly sat between Matteo and Lincoln.

"Where's Lawrence?"

"Why does everyone assume I know where he is?" Matteo grumbled.

"I'm guessing they're still at the showers," Lincoln answered.

Felicity stared at the table that was far below her chair. Ray and Tabitha didn't make a comment and helped her sit down.

"And they better hurry," Ray said as he helped her down. "I have a feeling those guards aren't really up for tardiness. I ran into a wall and they got mad at me."

Nikki frowned. "You ran into a wall?"

Tabitha burst out laughing. "Did that Agent Aalto take your brain cells too?"

"We almost died," Lincoln said.

"Look, you're not one to speak. You fell down the stairs twice in like two weeks." Ray smirked at Tabitha.

"Everyone does it!"

"Everyone does what?"

Lawrence and Cole stood in the doorway.

"Ray ran into a wall," Tabitha announced excitedly. "And you guys are alive!"

A small *ding!* rang through the room. Nikki froze.

"Stand up," Cole whispered harshly as he and Lawrence hurried to find seats.

Oh right. This was just like at the Outowns' house in Imperial.

Nikki stood up.

The curtains at the far end of the room opened. Eleazar walked out first, wearing a change of clothes in a bright red color that suited him well. His mother followed, still in the dark violet garment.

To Nikki's surprise, Eleazar sat at the head of the table. Everyone followed.

Bowls were passed around, but Nikki's stomach was tight. *Where's Mercy?*

Tabitha choked. Felicity went pale.

Everyone stared at each other.

I'm fine. Tabitha forced a smile at a frowning Rallie. *Ray, have you seen Mercy?*

His eyes were wide. *No! I didn't know I was supposed to be keeping track of her!*

She said she was going to look for you guys, Felicity said mentally.

We never saw her, Cole said, glancing at the empty seat.

"Is everything alright?" Rallie said.

"Yes. Everything's fine. We just had a bit of a crash earlier. They're still a little shaken," Cole said, straightening himself.

"I'll have some painkillers sent up then."

"Thank you, ma'am. I'm sure they'd appreciate it."

We need to get better at being more discrete with this telepathy thing. Nikki could almost hear a glare in Cole's voice. *They already don't trust us.*

Nikki felt her face grow warm, but she couldn't help it. Where had Mercy run off to?

"This is a very beautiful residence you have," Felicity said, tucking back a loose strand of hair. "I had no idea the Outowns had land here."

"Ann and Ludwig only acquired it ten years ago," Rallie said solemnly.

Eleazar stepped in. "It's seriously epic. You should check out the ground, and the woods if you get a chance! There's a bunch of cool pools and streams!"

Lincoln's eyes lit up, and he and Nikki both looked at Nathaniel.

"I didn't know the Bentsworth heir was making cross-ocean trips," Eleazar said, leaning toward Felicity. "You are Felicity…right? It would be kinda awkward if you weren't."

Felicity flushed, her eyes diverting to her bowl. "Y-yes. I am."

"Mama, the Aguirre is here too," Eleazar said, his voice becoming more gentle as he turned to Rallie.

Nikki's sweat went cold. *What?!*

No no no. Now was not the time for weird flashback memory things. She couldn't let that happen in front of everyone—

Rallie's eyes settled on Nikki. Nikki tried to hide behind Lawrence.

Lawrence shuffled out of the way. "The Aguirre you're looking for is my cousin, Nikki. Nikki Aguirre."

There was that name again, echoing so familiar and yet so foreign.

Rallie stared for a long moment. "Very interesting," was all she said before she turned back quietly to her food.

Eleazar looked at Nikki with a smile. He'd known all along.

"That's so cool! There aren't a lot of Curatrix kids," Eleazar said excitedly. "We could make a really cool exclusive club!"

Nikki smiled nervously. "I guess so."

"The only other Curatrix kid is technically Kate Oowatie," Eleazar said, taking a gulp of his tea. "Zita almost adopted her."

Nikki choked on a gasp.

"Almost adopted?"

Eleazar nodded. "Yeah. Zita died before it was official. After…the incident, Kate disappeared from authorities who went in for questioning. She was last spotted at Zita's grave in Liberty, never to be seen since…so she probably can't join the club."

Another Curatrix child? Someone with a direct link to Zita? Nikki's heart was racing. One step closer to the Aguarious Stone.

"That's nice, Eleazar. It's probably best to leave the Aguirre child alone." Rallie's gaze lingered for a moment on Nikki, a line forming between her brows before she looked away.

What had Rallie been expecting? Was Lawrence really a better alternative? Was Rallie disappointed?

Why did it make her feel like this?

The burning smoldered inside her. She quickly tried to stamp it out.

She wasn't a copy of her parents, and she didn't want to be.

Tabitha was happy to finally be free.

The dinner was best put as *awkward*. Rallie didn't seem all the way alive, and the guards seemed ready to kill if anyone dared to even breathe the wrong way.

She left early, claiming to have stomach pain. The real pain was finding where Mercy had run off to. Her relationship with Mercy was awkward roommates at best, but Mercy was still a Council Member, and Tabitha didn't leave anyone behind.

She walked down the dimly lit hall, straining her eyes. The house wasn't big, but there also wasn't much to fill it. It was dark and daunting, with countless empty rooms and photos draped with linen.

Focus.

But one frame was just so large and tempting, the curtain already pushed slightly back as if someone had already peeked.

Tabitha looked around.

No one was here.

She took a deep breath and peered behind the curtain.

The photo was a simple portrait. A man with thick, curly brown hair, his face freckled as his dark brown eyes stared at a small bundle in his arms. A sleeping child.

Tabitha let the curtain fall. Aaron Outown.

She'd seen his face enough on MEDIA broadcasts. But never like that. Never so personal and small. She felt a lump form in her throat as she turned away.

A creak caught her off guard. She stepped back, creeping to the end of the hall. There, a glass back door was cracked open. Tabitha frowned, sliding closer.

She slipped out the door, smelling the rain.

The steps creaked under her weight as she descended slowly. Her heart skipped a beat at seeing footsteps in the mud.

She narrowed her eyes. "Mercy!"

Her voice was lost in the emptiness. Tabitha scowled, breaking out into a run down the beaten path around the lake.

Had Mercy really attempted to run away? What was she thinking? There was an Agent after them. If he discovered she was associated with them…Mercy was as good as dead.

Tabitha pushed herself harder. She would never admit it to Taryn, but those hours of training sessions were paying off. She slowed as she approached the man made woods, the long skinny trees sweeping in the wind.

A glow caught the corner of Tabitha's eye.

Mercy ducked in the brush. She heard the soft crunch of footsteps.

Her knife had been confiscated, but she still had her venomous anklet.

"Hello?"

Tabitha's sweat went cold as she heard Mercy's voice echo.

She slowly peered over the bush, almost gasping as she saw the Ewyon Stone glowing as it hung from its chain in Mercy's hand.

Mercy had stolen Nikki's Stone?

What? Why? Was she working with Kathryn? Why in the world—

"Of all places, this sure was the most inconvenient." Out of the darkness stepped out a woman in a long tweed coat, wearing thick sunglasses in the dark, her hair tied up tightly. She wore gloves and combat boots.

Mercy stumbled back. "How did you—Are you—"

"Yes. I am a member of the Founder Association, and we have ears everywhere. It wasn't hard to track down your Comm signal. Not many try to reach us these days…especially with such a rare offering," the woman said, wiping the sly smile off her lips.

Tabitha ducked down. Oh no, no, no. Was this the rogue group Sister Lillian had been talking about? How did they get past the defenses? Were they going to take Nikki's Stone?

What in the world could Mercy possibly need from them?

"Surprised to see Virtue Faithful let her granddaughter out," the woman said, raising a brow. She reached her hands into her deep trench coat pockets. "She vowed to keep the Keyper line safe, even if it meant never letting them out of her sight."

Tabitha braced herself.

She totally wasn't vibing with this creepy group that apparently supported Mercy's terrible grandmother.

Mercy perked up. "So, you did know my grandmother! Does that mean you know how to activate Keyper abilities?"

While she stood straighter, Tabitha could see the shake in her hand as she held the chain.

She held back a gasp. Did Mercy not remember how to glow? No wonder she'd been so hurt after the storm.

Stupid Tabitha! You completely ridiculed her without realizing it!

The woman gaped in horror. "Do you know how difficult it was to sneak in here? Only for a stupid girl to ask how to use her *abilities*?" She scoffed. "A Keyper who can't connect a Council."

Connect a Council? Tabitha frowned. Is that what Mercy's abilities did?

Mercy's eyes diverted to the ground. "I-I'm sorry. It's just we're on our way to a Eidelis Believer facility soon, and I just want to figure this out before anything happens and—"

"Oh, enough with the whining," the woman sighed. "What do you want to know?"

Mercy peered up. "Well, it's kinda unrelated, but I saw a video…and my grandmere mentioned she knew Felicity had been born, and that Felicity was a Council Member. And then I think she leaked that information to the Shadow Soul six months ago to try to get rid of her."

The woman seemed unphased. "That would make sense. Our organization was trying to track each Council Member. Virtue must have found out about the Bentsworth's identity and used it as blackmail material."

What? So that's how the Exerticus had found out about Felicity?

How evil could one grandma be?

"Is there anything I can do? Will she try and hurt Felicity again?" Mercy said.

"If what you're saying is correct, there's nothing else she can do. The target has already been placed on Miss Bentsworth's back, and her blood has been taken. There's a reason the Exerticus were so adamant about getting their hands on Felicity's blood."

Tabitha's heart dropped. What?

"But-but Kathryn doesn't have all our blood," Mercy said, pursing her lips.

"You're so incredibly naive." The woman stepped closer.

"Felicity Bentsworth is the Guardian Member, a Lyntox at that, meaning she's a Mythic. A shifter creature."

"We-we know that," Mercy said.

"And yet, you have no idea why the Shadow Soul didn't choose until recently to find and get the blood of Bentsworth?"

"N-no."

"It takes the blood of the Mythic Guardian to awaken a Mythic sea monster." The woman laughed dryly. "The Shadow Soul got exactly what she wanted. Now all she needs is the blood of the Aguarious to control the creature."

Tabitha felt like she was going to vomit.

"Floods? Is there anything we can do? How do we stop Kathryn? The Aguarious Stone! Do you know where we can find the Aguarious Stone?" Mercy panicked, beginning to pace.

"You came here for answers about your powers."

"The world…my-my *friends* are in danger!"

"You only brought one artifact," the woman said, examining her nails. "So I was only required to provide you with one answer."

Mercy's eyes widened, the green Stone's glow reflecting in her dark eyes. "I-I thought the artifact was just a way to get your attention."

The woman raised a brow before giving a forced laugh. "No, child. There's a trade. I gave you the information. You give me the Stone."

"You hardly gave me anything!" Mercy said, taking a step back.

"Hand over the Stone." The woman held out her hand, her voice firm and demanding.

Tabitha's brows furrowed, and she braced herself, readying herself to tackle Mercy to ground for the Stone.

To her surprise, Mercy pulled her hand back. She took a deep breath before looking the woman straight in the eyes. "No."

The woman tilted her head. "No? Child, you've made a grave mistake. You have no idea what you're asking for."

"I can't give you the Stone."

"Well then, for your own good, I'll take it." The woman lunged for Mercy. Mercy dodged her. The woman's fingers grazed against the bare surface of the Stone. She cried out, falling back only for a second to spin back on Mercy.

"Get away from her!" Tabitha sprang from her hiding spot, throwing her weight at the woman, knocking her off her feet and slamming her to the ground.

The woman reacted quickly, throwing Tabitha off her with a kick to the stomach. Tabitha groaned, pushing herself up.

"You're rather small to think you can take on a trained professional." The woman wiped her lip, a bruise forming on her jaw.

Tabitha slipped a smirk. "Oh I wasn't trying to take you on," she said. She took a deep breath and screamed. "We're being attacked! Someone help! Please! Help!"

The woman's face went pale before shriveling to anger. "You little—"

"Have fun dealing with jail! Mercy, run!" Tabitha avoided the woman's grab, ducking and rolling to her feet. She broke out into a run, grabbing Mercy's arm.

She could already hear the guards' voices. She broke out onto the path.

"There!" She heard a guard yell. "A woman!"

Tabitha kept running, only tightening her grip on Mercy's arm. No guard stopped them. A breach into the Outown estate was enough.

As soon as they were out in the open fields, she slowed down, spinning on Mercy. "What the actual *heck* were you thinking?" Tabitha shouted.

Mercy flinched. "I-I-I didn't do anything."

"Don't lie to me. You stole Nikki's Stone!"

Mercy looked away, her hands tightening to fists. "I was trying to help."

"Hand it over."

Mercy begrudgingly handed Tabitha the chain.

"You probably just made things worse!" Tabitha continued, tucking it into her pocket. "We can't afford making enemies. We have the Defenders *and* Kathryn after us right now!"

"But—"

"You ran off without even telling us," Tabitha said. It was taking everything in her not to storm ahead. Gosh, now she was sounding like Cole! "How many other lies have you been telling? Your marks for one thing. You can't glow, so you went to this literal cult for answers?"

Mercy's face hardened, her brows furrowing. "Why does it matter to you?"

Tabitha blinked. "I'm part of this Council! Are you?"

"I was trying to help," she grumbled.

"Well, congrats! You almost screwed everything up," Tabitha said.

Mercy scoffed.

"You're going to return the Stone. And we're going straight to everyone and explaining this."

Mercy stopped dead in her tracks. "No."

"What do you mean, no?"

"I-I can't— The Council can't know."

"The Council deserves to know!" Tabitha huffed. What was her problem? "Do you know what it means to work as a team? Or do you just care about yourself?"

Mercy tore her fingers through her hair. "You're not my parent!"

"Well, you're acting like a child!"

"We're all children!"

"Well, maybe it's time you grow up!"

Tabitha caught herself. Her eyes grew wide, trying to comprehend what she'd just said.

She stood in the silence, staring into Mercy's eyes, watching them water.

What was she doing?

"Tabitha! Mercy!"

Ray's voice echoed through the darkness. She looked back over her shoulder to see him standing at the steps of the back door.

Mercy's eyes darted from Tabitha's to his, her brows raised, her lips parting. She closed her mouth and swallowed. She wiped her eyes and turned her face away before she ran to the door.

Tabitha scowled and ran after her.

Mercy pushed past, ran, and went down the hall.

"Apparently, there's been a security breach," Ray said, stopping Tabitha before she went through the door.

"I've heard."

"Guards are telling us to get the gardens," Ray said, shutting the door behind her. He frowned. "You doing okay? You look a little…pale."

Tabitha nodded. "Yeah, I'm fine. I think I'm going to head to the washroom."

"Okay. Just make sure to go up to the gardens as soon as possible. I'll let Cole know." He flashed her an encouraging smile.

She forced a smile and nod in return.

She reached the bathroom, lifting up her shirt to the nasty bruise spreading along her side. It was sore, but she'd just have to live with it.

But the words echoing in her mind, her *own* words, she wasn't sure if she could stand.

She walked down the hall and back to the gardens.

Her nightmares mocked her.

She entered the gardens. She tried to ignore the smothered sniffle of Mercy's tears. It made her chest hurt so tightly, Tabitha nearly gasped.

She kneeled down beside Nikki's mat, slipping the Stone into her bag. She clenched her fists, resisting the urge to tear her fingers through her hair. She couldn't tell the Council now. She couldn't do that to Mercy.

Tabitha looked back over to Mercy a few feet away, crying.

Because of Tabitha.

Because in that moment, Tabitha had acted just like her mother.

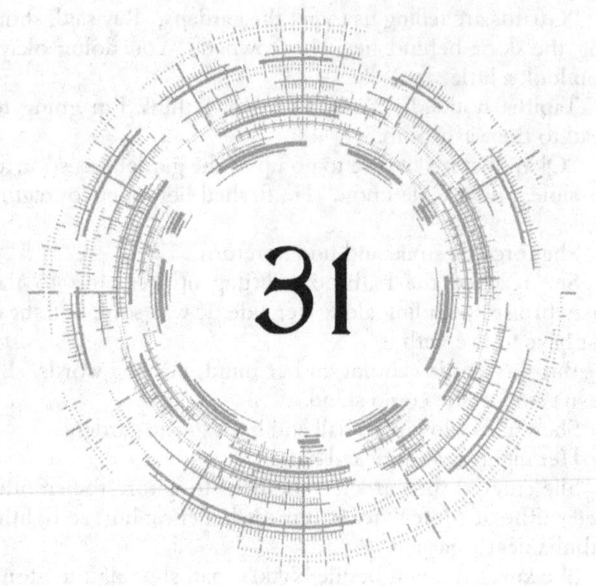

31

Nikki exhaled with relief as she closed the door behind her.

"We did it!" Lincoln said in an excited whisper. Even Nathaniel was jumping in his carrier on Lincoln's back.

Nikki did a quick check over her shoulder before racing after Lincoln down the path, a chill running down her spine in the cold morning air, the earth soft below her feet from the storm.

"I'm sure this will help clear your head and whatever weird things your brain is doing," Lincoln said, nudging her as he ran alongside her. "Fresh air is really helpful."

"I still can't believe I never noticed I put the Stone in my bag," Nikki said, shaking her head, clutching the Stone that was back to hanging around her neck.

Avalon scoffed.

"You need to relax, Nik! Just for a day."

"You want to help me *swim*. That doesn't sound relaxing," Nikki laughed, shaking her head.

But Lincoln did have a point. She did need a chance to

just…stop thinking. Her thoughts took up so much space. She'd found the Stone in her bag this morning. She'd panicked about it being stolen or lost at a stop, when in reality, she must've been so stressed out she misplaced it.

Lincoln had been excited as soon as he heard about the pools in the woods. The whole water and swimming thing wasn't her favorite, but if they didn't want a repeat of the bridge, she'd have to relearn.

So far, just being out in the stormy air brought Nathaniel to a new life.

His bubbling excitement made her smile as he reached up toward the air, his curls bouncing.

They followed the stream across the field, heading toward the trees.

"Do you find it odd that Aaron moved to practically the middle of nowhere?" Lincoln frowned.

"Maybe he wanted to get away," Nikki suggested. "I know my…the Aguirres did."

Lincoln's expression softened as he turned back to walk forward beside her.

"Right," he said softly. "I'm sorry. I wasn't trying to turn it back to them."

"It's fine. It's just that…I just keep…" Would he think she was crazy? "…You know how I have weird thoughts?"

Lincoln raised a brow. "Yeah."

"I keep seeing stuff in my head. Sometimes it's voice and feelings, or full-blown scenes." Nikki massaged her temples. "It's about my family. I can't control them."

Lincoln was quiet a long moment. "The memories again?"

She felt her face heat. "I'm sorry. I know you—"

"Nah. It's okay, Nik. One day I'll get them back." He adjusted his hold on Nathaniel's carrier. "Besides, Kathryn can't tempt me with them anymore. I've made my choice."

Though the glint behind Lincoln's dark eyes told another story.

"It's worth it," he said. "I'd do it a hundred times over. It was super creepy to have my eyes go *all* black anyway. You're so lucky you didn't have to see that."

"We'll get your memories back, Lincoln. I promise."

His forced humor broke. He pursed his lips and nodded.

"Thanks, Nik. And we'll get yours too."

He held her gaze for a long second before he looked away, his eyes lighting up. "Look, there's a pool!"

He didn't wait another moment, grabbing her hand and racing off the path and into the forest. Nikki squeezed his hand, finding her balance as they raced between the trees, trusting him to lead the way.

She missed this.

She missed following Lincoln blindly and learning every word he spoke. She missed the light feeling in her chest before the name "Aguirre" and its responsibilities weighed her down.

"There!"

They broke out into the clearing, down a small decline. The stream slowed into a pool, the dirt soft and fine around it. The tall, thin trees circled around it, sunlight shining in the little circle.

Lincoln dropped to his knees, unbuckling Nathaniel from his carrier. Nathaniel was squirming to get away from Lincoln's arms. "Calm down, Nat. One minute, kid."

He set the little boy down, and he instantly began to toddle away. Nathaniel slipped, falling forward in the dirt. "Water!"

"Hey!"

Nikki crouched, watching curiously as Lincoln took Nathaniel's hands and pulled him to his feet. "Here, come on, Nik!" Lincoln said, looking over to her.

"What do you need me to do?"

"Grab his other hand!"

Nikki wasn't sure what the point was, but she was happy to be needed, racing over and taking Nathaniel's hand. He gripped her finger tightly, his eyes set on the pool, pulling them forward. "Water! Water! Linc!"

Nathaniel wriggled free, balancing himself as he ran for the water proudly.

Lincoln shook off his boots, tearing off his shirt as he ran after Nathaniel. "You did it, you little monster!"

Nathaniel laughed, plopping down in the shallow water and splashing his hands. The water spun from the ripples and came up into a wave, crashing down on Lincoln.

Nathaniel thought he was a comical genius, not minding

that he'd just soaked Lincoln and himself.

"Never thought you'd be drenched by a baby," Nikki laughed.

Lincoln rolled his eyes, shaking his wet hair. He smirked. "Then why don't you get in here and face him?"

Nikki froze.

Lincoln's smile softened. "I won't let you drown, Nik."

She let out a breath. It couldn't hurt. She removed her boots and her tunic, wearing the silk undershirt that still felt too nice to get wet, but she wasn't turning back.

She stood up straight and marched toward the pool.

"Nik!" Nathaniel reached his hands out for Nikki.

She blinked in surprise. He was reaching for…her?

"That's *Nikki*," Lincoln said with an exasperated sigh, plopping in the water beside Nathaniel.

"Nik! Water!"

Nikki poked her toe into the cold water, glancing at Lincoln, unsure. Even with Nathaniel trying to climb him, he gave her a reassuring smile.

She took a deep breath and waded into the water. She was fine. She was standing and—

And she was doused with water.

She tripped over backward, splashing into the pool.

Nathaniel burst out laughing. Nikki blinked, her mind taking a second to catch up.

"Nat. That was not nice," Lincoln scolded.

"Linc!" Nathaniel shouted, popping a water bubble above Lincoln's head.

Lincoln glared at Nathaniel. "Betrayal."

"Linc!" Nathaniel shouted proudly to himself with a small squeal.

Lincoln laughed with him, hugging the little boy and spinning him around. "Yes! Yes, you got it! Linc! That's it!"

Nikki couldn't help but watch. A warm feeling grew in her chest that made her smile. It didn't burn. It glowed at seeing Lincoln so happy. It was so weird to think that a couple weeks ago he was denying and complaining about any attachment to Nathaniel.

Lincoln stopped spinning, setting a dizzy Nathaniel on a little island of earth jutting out from the pool. "Now stay there, and practice your 'Linc.'"

Nathaniel was content with patting the dry dirt and being fascinated by the little moss beginning to grow along a rock.

Lincoln turned back to Nikki. "Can you swim here, Nik? The water's pretty shallow."

He was right. The water only went up to his waist, but it was still deep enough to get lost in. *And* she was shorter than Lincoln.

But she wasn't going to let this be another thing Kathryn stole from her.

She took a deep breath, shivering as she moved deeper into the water.

Her mind echoed back to Felicity standing on the rocky shore, her eyes blank as she stared out into the ocean. How Felicity had slipped and almost fell into the water, speaking about some sort of creature. How she pulled herself out of the auto thinking that Lincoln had drowned. And the Agent watching from the bridge with his wicked stare.

Nikki dipped her head below the water, and she went blind. She couldn't open her eyes. She couldn't remember how to move.

"Punishment is the only way we can keep the subject submissive."
Struggling against a metal grip. A shallow voice.
"It's my fault! You don't have to do this!"
"Silence 88!"
Sharp pain in her shoulder. Water up her nose.
She was dying—

Her head was pulled above water. She gasped for air, throwing her arms around Lincoln's neck, holding onto him tightly. It's okay. She could breathe. She was okay. Lincoln wouldn't let her go. Lincoln wouldn't punish her—

"I'm sorry," she gasped, burying his face in his shoulder.

"Nik, it's okay," Lincoln laughed softly. "I'm really sorry if I scared you."

It was that stupid memory. Not Lincoln.

"I should be able to do this," she said quietly.

"Well, you can't. So stop forcing that idea on yourself that you *should*. We're going to figure it out."

Nikki opened her eyes. She'd never thought about it like that. "Okay," she said, out of breath.

She dared to step back in the water, her arms still wrapped around Lincoln. She met his eyes, and his face went red. She still hadn't figured out why it did that.

He cleared his throat. "What if we just practice not freaking out underwater?"

"O-okay."

"Hey!" Lincoln's eyes lit up, looking over to the little island. "What if you practice with Nathaniel? He's the master of water."

Nathaniel looked up with an excited "Huh?" at the mention of his name.

Lincoln moved over to pick up Nathaniel, Nikki still clutching his other arm. "Wanna hang with Nik?"

"Linc?"

"Close enough."

Nikki swallowed hard.

Lincoln looked back to her. "It's only for five seconds, and if anything goes wrong, I'll have your back."

She let out a breath, slowly moving away from him on her own two feet. Lincoln handed her Nathaniel, his big green eyes looking up at her. No fear or threat of tears, just genuine curiosity in his innocent gaze.

"Ready?"

Nikki gave a sharp nod.

She took a deep breath and dropped underwater. Her heart seized in her chest, waiting for another creepy voice from the past…but nothing. She cracked an eye open. To her surprise, she saw Nathaniel in front of her, not holding his breath.

Nikki panicked until she saw Nathaniel smile. He laughed, seeming comfortable and unfazed with the clear pool water around them.

Little colorful fishes swam along the ground, and long grasses had sprouted up among the pebbles swaying in the ripples of the water. It was oddly peaceful.

She burst above the water for air. "Nathaniel really can breathe underwater!" she sputtered.

Nathaniel didn't seem surprised whatsoever, simply raising a bubble of water out of the water, gasping at a little fish trapped inside.

"No wonder Kathryn wants his blood so bad," Nikki whispered.

Lincoln smothered Nathaniel to his chest protectively.

"She won't be getting him. Any of us." His eyes fell away. "Him staying with those scientist Believers is what's best. They'll protect him."

"You don't think she'll catch up?" Nikki said, sitting on the little island in the warmth of the sun.

"I don't know," Lincoln said. "And if she does, we can handle her. One on one."

"Two on one," she corrected.

Lincoln smirked. "We have a water-breathing toddler. Anything's possible. Now, Nik. Feel like you're up for another swimming try?"

Nikki gave a dramatic groan, but she couldn't help but laugh. The warmth in her chest grew, but it felt painfully good.

It felt rare now, but right now, it felt safe.

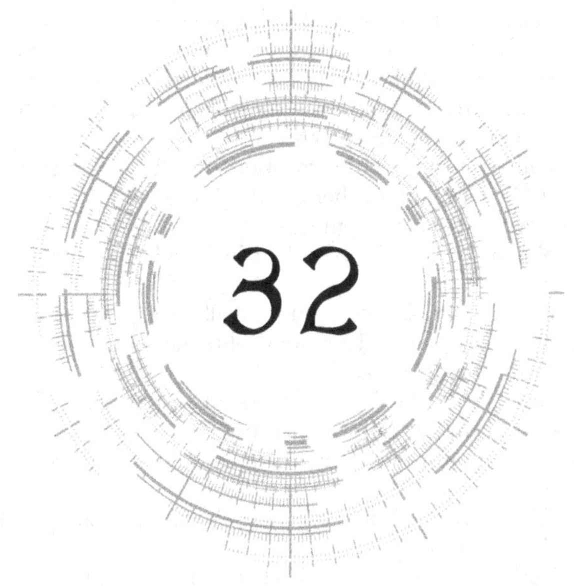

32

"So, we think that the Outowns are keeping Rallie and Eleazar hostage?"

"Tabitha, what?"

Cole looked at her like she was insane, but Tabitha simply shrugged.

"I wouldn't say *hostage*," Lawrence said. "We've seen how the MEDIA treats the Curatrix team. Nikki's just under *speculation* of being an Aguirre and we've almost died because of it."

Nikki hugged herself, trying to look small. She sat beside Tabitha on the mattress they shared. The rest of the Council sat awake throughout the garden.

Tabitha pursed her lips, wrapping a protective arm around Nikki's shoulders. "It's still awful they have to live like this."

"Ann and Ludwig seemed extremely close with their son. And Miriam has mentioned she received a lot of pushback from them when she wanted to become a Defender," Cole said. "They might think these measures are a way of keeping their remaining family safe. Besides, Rallie seems…lost."

"Controlling and watching over her just seems like a bizarre way to help her heal," Felicity admitted from the pad across the path. "It feels like something my aunt would be in the name of 'curing my psycho.'"

Tabitha scoffed at the mention of Olivia Bentsworth. She disliked Tabitha for being a third born and deemed Felicity crazy for her panic attacks.

Tabitha guessed the Bentsworths couldn't be *totally* perfect.

"Besides, Eleazar seems like a really smart kid," Lincoln added. "And he just takes care of his mom and hangs out with pushy guards all day."

Cole sighed, running his fingers through his hair. "Look, it doesn't seem fair to me either, but there's nothing we can do. It is their private family affair, and it's not our place to butt in."

"Why not? We butt into people's family affairs all the time!" Ray said.

"Yeah, our *own* family lives. That's way different," Lincoln said.

Cole sighed, rubbing his temples. "This is obviously going nowhere. We should just get some rest and try to talk those guards into giving us our trailer back tomorrow."

Rest didn't mean sleep.

And Tabitha was in the mood for neither. "I'm going to get some fresh air."

Nikki didn't protest as Tabitha got up from the mat and walked down the stone path that led out to the halls. She took Taryn's knife with her, strapping it to her thigh. She doubted she needed it, but it felt almost comforting to have such a notable weapon with her.

She took a deep breath. Nikki was right. Something did feel off here. But Tabitha wasn't sure if that was her lack of sleep or a true feeling. She walked along the hall and past the dozens of covered photos.

Aaron Outown, Miriam's infamous older brother, had moved to this remote location in Boli far away from his rich, well-established parents. Had he been trying to get away?

Tabitha's throat tightened. Her older brother, Lucas, had left home abruptly after an argument with her parents. She'd been twelve, and she'd only seen him for a few holidays.

She couldn't understand why he'd left without telling her goodbye in the middle of the night.

Had she ever considered it wasn't her who he was running from? Maybe her brothers also had problems with their parents...

She stepped into the enormous kitchen, fishing out a tin cup from the stack, turning on the faucet.

The sooner this mission was over, the better.

Her eyes drifted out the window. Tabitha blinked in surprise. Out on the porch sat a woman, her long hair undone as she looked out to the glassy lake in the moonlight.

Tabitha set her glass down.

Rallie Outown.

She needed answers about this creepy place. She didn't know why, but it felt deeper than just morbid curiosity.

She rushed out of the kitchen, making sure to be quiet as she creaked the door open and stepped out onto the porch. Tabitha held her breath. Rallie didn't move.

Tabitha creeped over to her. "Hello?"

Rallie remained still.

Tabitha slowly sat on the step beside her. "Are you alright, ma'am?"

"You should be asleep." Rallie didn't even look at her.

"It didn't...work out," Tabitha laughed half-heartedly.

A small smile tugged at Rallie's thin lips. "It seems every Council is haunted."

"It comes with the job." Tabitha surprised herself.

"The blond boy has Aaron's Medallion," Rallie said quietly. "Cole. He's close to you, is he not?"

Tabitha's face went warm, swallowing hard. "I guess you could say that."

Rallie gave a distant smile, her eyes never moving from the lake. "I loved a boy with that Medallion once too..."

Aaron. Tabitha didn't dare whisper his name.

"I thought it was gone forever." Rallie pulled her sweater over her shoulders. "And better for it. No one deserves the pain that comes with it."

The two sat in the silence of the night, the crickets humming a tune of the dark. "I'm so sorry," Tabitha choked.

"They all say that."

Tabitha's mouth was dry. "I-I'm sorry. I have no idea how that feels."

"I hope you never do," Rallie said, twisting the dark ring on her finger.

"Would you say I should...avoid him?" Her stomach twisted even thinking of it.

Rallie was startled by the question, tearing her eyes from the lake and to Tabitha.

Tabitha froze. Was she going to scold her for being so ignorant? And not avoiding him all along?

"Child, hold onto him." Rallie studied her face for a long moment. "I don't regret a single moment I had."

Tabitha could feel tears threatening her eyes. She blinked them away. "Even if it's wrong? If it hurts? Even if it...ends?"

"Everything hurts. Everything ends." Rallie pressed a cold hand against Tabitha's cheek. "Who's telling you these things?"

Tabitha's eyes widened, unable to move at the gentle touch. "I-I just want to know if I'm doing the right thing."

Rallie paused, running a soft thumb over a loose tear. Dang it. How'd that get there? "Aaron built this house. All of his own earnings from being an officer. He saved and learned for years to even get started." Rallie choked. "His parents weren't thrilled. He'd moved across the ocean for his own life...his own family."

"My mother threatened to disown me." Tabitha was so shocked the words had slipped out. She'd kept them so hidden, so tight inside her heart she'd sworn she'd forget them.

"Child..."

"She-she probably wasn't serious," Tabitha said nervously.

"It's painful to know the people who are supposed to love you could be the most cruel."

Tabitha felt boiling tears prick her eyes.

If you ever show your face here again, you won't be part of this family!

It was the last time she'd made the news for assisting Felicity. The publicity threatened to expose her mother. To expose her mistake. The third born child. The daughter she'd never asked for.

In that moment, Tabitha realized that her mother was serious about the disowning.

And so she took up Felicity's offer to go to North Cordell.

Tabitha reached up to touch Rallie's hand. "He left that life for…you?"

"He left for himself. He was free here. He had no past to hold onto for the first time in his life—" Rallie stopped, her face going blank again. She pulled away her hand, her eyes drifting back to the lake.

And then, he died.

Tabitha knew the details. Almost everyone did.

Buried on his parents' woodland property. His *parents*. He wasn't even buried at the home he'd spent the last years of his life making.

Is that how it would end for them?

Their names up in lights and the public shouting their praises, but in the end, they were just tragic results of a terrible accident in graves they never asked for?

"I-I don't know what to choose."

Rallie squeezed Tabitha's leg gently. "That's up to you, child."

Tabitha raised her eyes to meet Rallie, the smallest smile on the woman's lips.

"Choose your family wisely."

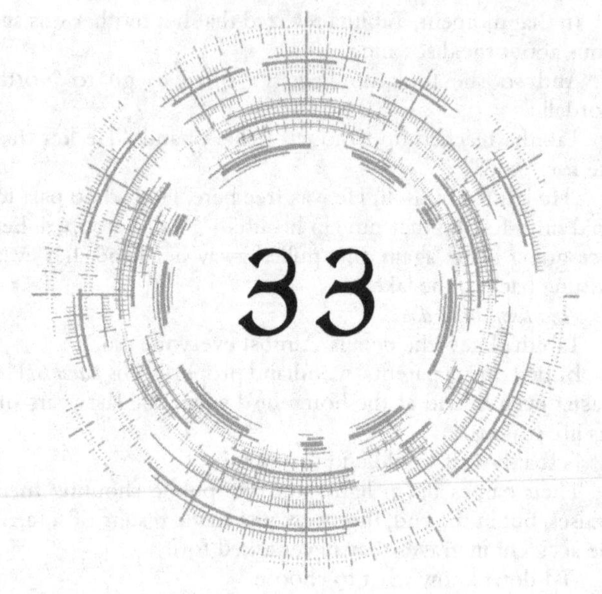

33

"WE LEAVE TOMORROW morning," was what Mercy had woken up to at noon when Ray shook her awake. "Glow Girl, it's noon! Stay up late partying without me?"

That got him shoved off the mattress.

Mercy sat up, rubbing her eyes. Noon?

Her heart skipped a beat. "I've been asleep for that long?" she squeaked, jumping to her feet.

"Sleeping won't kill you," Ray said from the floor.

She never slept in.

Ever.

"I'm falling apart," she whispered, squishing her face between her hands.

"You're not. Calm down."

She took deep breaths like Felicity instructed. Ray didn't know all the terrible things she'd messed up. What had she been thinking, contacting the Founder's Association? And now she knew Tabitha probably *hated* her.

Mercy groaned into her hands. "So stupid."

"Whoa, whoa. What's stupid?" Ray leaped to his feet.

"I think your brother hates me," she said, peering out from her hands.

Ray stared at her with a blank expression before bursting out into a fit of laughter. "Cole? Hate you? Are we talking about the same person?"

"I totally screwed up."

"Cole burned down a building and had a one-on-one battle with Tabitha. I doubt he'd judge."

Mercy blinked. "He what?"

Ray shrugged. "It's a long story. But I doubt he's angry. He's pretty terrible at hiding his emotions and he seemed fine this morning. Speaking of, I saved you a plate from breakfast…and lunch if you're hungry."

Mercy looked at him, frowning.

Ray smiled, offering her a hand. "Trust me, Glow Girl."

She sighed, ignoring his hand. She jumped off the mattress. "I should go take a shower."

"Okay, sounds good!" Ray began to walk down the path and out of the gardens before he turned to call back to her: "I think there was some sort of talk to have a fire by the lake tonight if you want to join!"

"Thanks!"

"Yeah! And you better be there, Glow Girl. No more sulking around!" He flashed her a smirk and jogged out before she could insult him back.

She sighed, now left alone to her own thoughts. She took an eternally long shower, deciding it was about time to treat her hair since it had been too long since she'd dealt with it. It was a true time killer. It was somewhat therapeutic in a frustrating-yet-satisfying way to watch each curl fix into place.

Her father had been the one to teach her. Her grandmother had always argued for him to chop it all off and keep it short like hers. And yet Mercy had always seen photos of her mother's and insisted she wanted it just like that.

It was one of the few things she'd ever fought for.

It felt so silly, but having control over at least this helped the spiral feel less dizzying.

The sun was setting by the time she creeped out into the kitchen to find a bowl of rice labeled with a holonote that melted away with her touch. She could see the reflection of the fire in the glass of the kitchen windows. She couldn't help but peer out, seeing that young Eleazar had made himself a seat.

They all fit so well together.

She turned away, sitting at the long table in evening light by herself. She could hear Cole's voice through the propped-open door, and the cool breeze that drifted inside.

The trip was almost over.

One more destination that would hopefully take in Nathaniel and they'd be back in North Cordell. Maybe she could convince Taryn to let her stay behind as the rest of the Council went to face the Leviathan storm.

They didn't need her.

Mercy finished her bowl and slipped out onto the porch. Once Cole had finished, she watched Eleazar run to a disc player he'd dragged outside, turning on music.

He said he'd promised to show Nikki how to dance before they left.

It was adorable to watch the preteen take Nikki's hands and attempt to show her the steps. Matteo observed the steps before forcing Lawrence along with him, and they produced an impressively smooth rendition...on Matteo's part. Lawrence was clumsy and looked about ready to blow something up. Ray excitedly shoved Lawrence aside and demanded to try, much to Lawrence's relief. "Having fun over here by yourself?"

Mercy jumped, slamming her hand over her mouth as she slowly turned her head to see Cole sitting beside her. She choked, breaking into a coughing fit with a strangled "sorry."

"I'm sorry," Cole laughed. "Are you good?"

"I'm fine," Mercy said, figuring out how to breathe again. Her face burned. What was she doing?

"Tabitha told me what happened."

Mercy knew it! Tabitha told him! "I'm sorry! I'll never do it again. You don't ever have to bring me on these missions ever ever—"

Cole frowned. "What are you talking about?"

Mercy blinked. "W-what did she tell you?"

"She told me you were having a hard time fitting in with this whole Council thing," Cole said, his eyes narrowing at her. "Did you think I was coming to get *angry* at you?"

She swallowed hard, itching to run for the door. "What else is there?"

"I just wanted to check in. We all know how it feels to feel like…you're trapped in this Council thing. You know, if you really don't feel comfortable with it, I could always arrange with Taryn—"

"No! I-I don't. I—" Mercy loved the Council. She thought they were some of the coolest people she'd ever met. "You're all really amazing."

No matter how much they argued or teased each other, she'd seen time and time again the lengths they'd go for each other. "I don't want to get in the way of that."

It wasn't a lie.

Cole's face softened. Did he think that too? Did he think she didn't belong with them? He couldn't throw her off the Council?

Instead, he offered his hand.

She frowned.

"Come on," he said, his eyes glimmering with a deep compassion in the dying sun. Something she'd seen in Ray's eyes before. She could see right then and there why Tabitha liked him.

She hesitantly took his hand.

Her heart skipped a beat as he pulled her toward the others. What was he doing?

He stopped, turning to her. "Care to dance?"

"Yeah, Mercy!" Ray cheered. "He's probably better than Lawrence."

"Everyone's better than Lawrence."

Mercy's face burned. "I guess so," she managed quietly, taking both of Cole's hands.

She took a deep breath, following Eleazar and Nikki's example. It was methodic and simple with Cole confident in his leading.

The music began to pick up.

Her heart raced faster, but she felt lighter as she focused on each step.

They began to move in circles, the sky growing darker and the glow of the fire more brilliant.

Cole gave her a quick smile as they began to spin faster. She held on tighter, the music racing faster.

And then it spun to a stop.

Mercy stumbled back into the sand, out of breath, choking a laugh.

"Pretty good for a first try," Matteo said, going back to restart the music. "If you didn't fall."

"Falling is the fun part," Cole said, brushing himself off as he walked back over to Mercy.

She wrung her hand. "What was that for?"

Cole shrugged. "Like I said…a little fun."

He ran back to Tabitha and Felicity on the other side of the fire.

Mercy's heart was still racing her chest. Cole was right. It had been…fun.

"Hey! Mercy!" Ray barreled toward her, a cup of a fizzy drink in hand. "Now that you've danced with my boring brother, you are required to teach me."

"I don't know how."

Ray took a large sip of the drink before zapping the cup away in his hand. "What a coincidence! Neither do I!"

She couldn't laugh as Ray pulled her back into the sand and into the music.

For one small moment, it felt nice to be wanted.

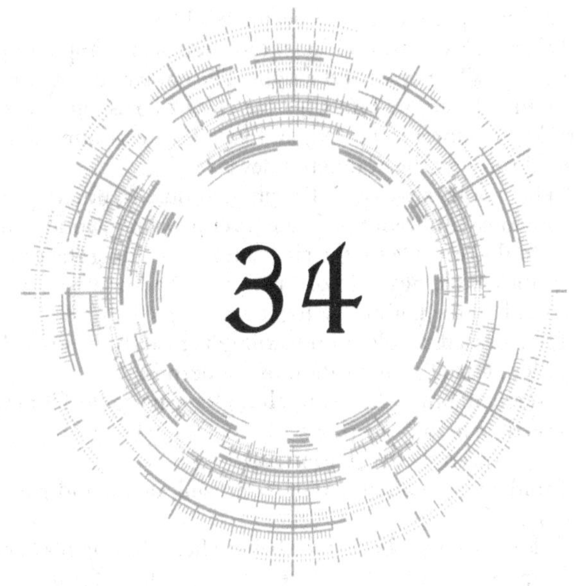

THE HOURS OF road were bumpy and empty.

The way to the abandoned city was long, and the landscape was empty, left untouched since the war. No one had come back to settle the land, going to bigger cities or more fertile soil.

Leaving the Outowns behind felt bittersweet. Getting out of the creepy, haunted environment and back into her regular clothes felt nice. But leaving Rallie and Eleazar felt like a crime.

Tabitha silently vowed to come back for them.

Choose your family wisely.

Tabitha's heart twisted. A tiny part of her did miss her family, as much as she hated to miss it. Her mother had threatened to disown her if she returned...but maybe things had changed.

Tabitha nearly dozed off against the window before her eyes caught sight of an enormous, long-forgotten sign in the distance as the auto bumped over the 300-year-old road. The sign was written in a language Tabitha didn't recognize, whole pieces peeled off and beaten by the sun.

Tabitha slowly turned her head, her heart flipping and her mouth falling open at the sight. The enormous city came closer and closer, the buildings the color of rust against the gray sky, windows shattered, and strange autos littered and crushed through the concrete sidewalks.

"The woods are close," Felicity said quietly, pointing out the obvious infiltration of the ever-growing woods that crowded the left side of the city, vines suffocating the crumbling brick buildings. Almost as if the supernatural shrubs were holding the nightmare together.

They passed a hologram warning for safety, but besides that, there wasn't an indication of modern life.

It seemed almost like something Ryynar would fabricate for a terrible night's sleep.

Cole slowed the truck to a stop.

Tabitha was suddenly tempted to sink down and plaster herself to the seat.

Cole opened the back door behind her, offering his hand. He stopped, noticing her face with a frown. "You good, Tabs?"

Her stomach flipped. She grabbed his hand, letting him help her out as she jumped down onto the sidewalk. It was so quiet it felt like a crime to breathe.

She didn't want to let go of Cole's hand.

You know I would not approve, you ungrateful child.

She didn't want to think about her mother right now. She was so tired. *Please don't take him away from me.*

When did her mother ever listen?

Her hand fell away from his.

"I-I'm great," she said, forcing a smile and finger guns for dramatic effect.

His brow furrowed. "Is it the dreams again?"

Dang it.

She opened her mouth to laugh it off, but her mouth went dry. She met his eyes, staring so intently into hers.

"If you don't want to talk about it, that's alright," he said with a small, worried smile. He tucked a loose strand of her hair behind her ear. "I'll be here if you ever do need to talk."

She could feel the tears burning in her eyes, half because she was so tired she could collapse, and half because she wished she could ignore all the stupid thoughts in her head and hug Cole.

"Thanks," is what she managed instead.

"Anytime," Cole reassured her, his hand still resting on her cheek before someone called his name. He gave a tired sigh, apologized, and ran off toward the call.

Tabitha took a deep breath. It didn't matter what her stupid dream mother said. Why did she keep letting it affect her?

She decided to ignore it and walked to the other side of the trailer, where the rest of the Members had collected.

"Alright, so quick refresher," Cole said, jumping up onto the hood of the truck. "We're looking for a bunker which the Believers have converted into a secret research facility."

"Cool. Got it." Ray turned to run off, but Lawrence caught him by the collar.

"We approach them. We tell them about our situation with Nathaniel, and then we hope that they'll take him and raise him in hiding with their families," Cole finished, catching his breath. "Now we got it."

"So where is the bunker?" Matteo asked, frowning as he looked up from his tablet.

"It shouldn't be too hard," Cole said, crossing his arms. "Bunkers are usually marked, and there should only be about one major bunker for a city this size."

"If the markings haven't eroded away in the past three centuries," Lincoln grumbled as he tightened the strap on Nathaniel's back carrier.

"What if we split up to cover more ground?" Tabitha said, stepping into the circle.

"That's a terrible idea," Ray said. "Have you ever watched a *single* net drama?"

Tabitha shot him a glare.

"There is an entire city to cover," Felicity said hesitantly, inching forward.

Cole bit his lip, thinking for a moment. He sighed. "Alright, we split up and search a block, and then regroup."

"Do we at least get to choose?" Ray said in defeat.

"What is this? Primary school?" Lawrence snorted.

"You never even went to primary school."

"I'll go with Felicity and Lincoln. They're the most vulnerable," Cole said, ignoring them.

"Hey!" Felicity and Lincoln shouted in unison.

"I have *two* weapons, unlike most of us," Lincoln said, patting the pack of arrows hanging from his belt.

"Yeah, but you also have our most valuable Member strapped to your back."

Lincoln grumbled something under his breath. Nathaniel thought this was a perfect time to grab Lincoln's ear.

"I vote I go with Lawrence and Matteo!" Ray said, teleporting between the two, throwing his arms around their shoulders. Lawrence quickly shrugged him off.

"Are we sure having all the Members with active abilities together is a good idea? I mean, how are—" Felicity looked around to the remaining three "—Mercy, Nikki, and Tabitha going to protect themselves?"

"Nikki's done more damage to Oquelite than anyone here," Tabitha said, shaking Nikki's shoulders. "Isn't that right, Nikki?"

Nikki froze. "I guess."

"And Mercy glows," Tabitha said, looking around for the tall, curly haired girl, finding her hiding in Cole's shadow.

She jumped at the mention.

"Don't worry. There won't be any need for glowing," Cole said, gently setting a hand on Mercy's shoulder.

Mercy looked to him, giving a small nod, her shoulders resting in relief. She walked over beside Tabitha and Nikki.

"Alright. Remember, we simply cover the block and meet back up at the end. Nothing more," Cole said, turning to the rest of them. "You got it?"

Everyone agreed, and Tabitha quickly took the lead as Cole assigned their group to the left. Mercy and Nikki followed her down the sidewalk in silence.

"What's got you two so solemn?" Tabitha said, walking backward to face them. "After this, don't you realize that we can go home?"

"This place…" Nikki said, clenching her fists. "…It's so quiet."

Even her small voice echoed off the empty, scorched walls, years of dirt and dust built up in the cracks. Vines twisted through the shattered first level windows. Tabitha jumped over a root that had cracked through the sidewalk.

She swallowed. "Yeah, so it's a little creepy?"

Mercy held her sweater closer. "Why would anyone want to live here?" she said, shivering. "It's overrun by the woods."

Tabitha rolled her eyes. "Well maybe they just like the spice of life here!"

"You didn't seem too 'spiced' when you first got out of the truck," Nikki pointed out.

Tabitha deadpanned her. "Well, I was just…in shock."

Mercy raised a suspicious brow.

Tabitha rolled her eyes and turned back forward, breaking out into a run. "Let's spice it up even more and begin this search!"

"What if you don't like spicy cities?" Nikki called after her. "Just spicy food!"

"Oh come on, Nik!" Tabitha said. "Enjoy the rest of the mission while it lasts!"

That was the only thought keeping Tabitha from joining Mercy and Nikki in being terrified of this place. It was hard to ignore the abandoned suitcases, slowly decaying beside a crushed automobile.

The EarthShaker's peak is what gave it its name.

It stopped being a war the moment the near destruction of humanity came about. Tabitha had only heard stories passed down about how bombs had wiped entire cities off maps. Once the first had dropped, mass hysteria broke loose.

No one knew what city would be next.

Governments were disassembled overnight, and any civilian who could ran for a bunker as the world above burned into two decades of winter.

People's entire lives had been shoved into those suitcases before they were tossed aside and they made a run for it.

"The city was never bombed," Mercy said, talking to Nikki. "I wonder why no one ever moved back."

"Two decades of trauma might make a difference," Tabitha said as she passed the third hologram that indicated the area where bodies had been found.

She swallowed hard.

"They thought this was the end of the world," she whispered.

"Weird to think we might actually be approaching it for real this time," Mercy said.

"What?" Tabitha frowned.

"Kathryn," Mercy said, quietly diverting her eyes to the ground.

It was hard to be annoyed with Mercy when everything felt like a gruesome reminder of the past…and what was yet to come.

The Delorouses had thrived in the time of controversy. They'd moved quickly to the safe haven of Liberty, and on old money.

Something to do with politics, and the population proposal to instate the rule of two children in Liberty.

There was a reason her mother was so steadfast about it.

But Tabitha had never seen war of this scale…and she still came from wealth. Even if her mother despised her…and had said those terrible words before she'd left.

Tabitha had never been homeless and orphaned like Lincoln, and her University used to be paid for by her family, unlike Cole who had gone on an uneasy scholarship. She'd never had to move to a different region to help work and provide for a family like Ray.

But if her family had really cut her off…what was she?

She had to go back and beg. She needed the money. She needed to still be able to help the Council.

Even if it meant facing her mother again.

"Do you hear that?" Mercy's voice wavered.

Tabitha frowned. The city was dead quiet. What was she hearing? "What—?"

"Shh!" Nikki glared.

A small scratching. Tabitha slowly turned to see shrubbery spilling out of the shattered window across the street. A shiver went up her spine, and she flexed her hand, ready to grab the knife from its strap across her leg. And if it came down to it, she had an anklet around her ankle, the beads full of a deadly venom. A gift from Cole.

Nikki walked straight for it.

"Nikki!" Tabitha hissed. "What the heck do you think you're doing?"

"Investigating," she responded plainly as she kneeled beside the shrubbery.

Mercy and Tabitha exchanged glances.

Tabitha scowled. Right now was *not* the time for Nikki's

naivety.

Hadn't their multiple bad encounters with creatures in the woods taught her anything?

Too late. Nikki pulled back a branch. Tabitha pulled out her knife, bracing herself—

—And a blue kitten rolled out onto the sidewalk.

And another. And another.

"Blue kittens?" Mercy said.

Nikki slipped, falling to the ground with a laugh. "Ice!" she said suddenly. "They're ice cats!"

"Ice?" Tabitha's eyes widened, realizing that under the kittens' paws, ice had begun to spread. She and Mercy ran to meet Nikki.

Nikki scooped one of the kittens up into her arms. It sneezed, a little snow cloud bursting in her face.

They were gray with blue streaks, ice forming along their back.

They were tiny.

And oddly so cute.

"Ice cats! Just like Fire Wolf!" Mercy laughed, bopping one of the kittens' noses, crouching down to their level. "They're so little."

"They're adorable and all, but we have to keep searching for the bunker," Tabitha said, crossing her arms.

"And leave all these adorable little things here?" Mercy said, scooping up two into her arms.

"I'm sure they have a mother nearby. Leave them."

"Now you sound like your boyfriend," Mercy grumbled.

"I'm older than both of you!"

"But shorter," Nikki said.

Tabitha looked at her, horrified. "Hey—!"

A long, deep rattle cut Tabitha short. All three of them froze. Tabitha turned around slowly, her sweat going cold. She cursed under breath.

An enormous repitox creature scuttled over the rooftops of the nearby buildings, the weak brick structure quaking. Its huge beady eyes flashed in the sunlight.

Tabitha could hear Ryynar's laugh echo, flashing back to his snake appearance.

She shook it off. It wasn't him.

The city! It's infested with Mythic creatures! Tabitha shouted.

Tabitha spun to Mercy and Nikki, quickly looking to the window the kittens had crawled out of. *Get in there! Now!*

Mercy quickly collected the kittens in her satchel, Nikki having to drag her inside.

Tabitha shoved herself in after them. It was tiny, branches poked into her neck, Nikki's elbow in her side, and she could feel the ice melting below her. She held her breath, closing her eyes, tightening her grip on the knife.

The hissing tickled the air.

She could feel the quiver of the ground.

We think we've found the Bunker! Cole's voice broke into her mind. *How's you guys' creature situations going?*

Fine! Lawrence said, in a very not fine voice.

Very…squished, Nikki replied.

The earth trembled again. Dirt began to crumble above them. Tabitha's heart clenched in her chest. She cracked open an eye, staring up in horror as a crack began to grow on the ceiling in the shrub-infested room.

Giant snake creature, or have a building collapse on them?

Not very lovely choices.

Tabitha made hers. With a cry, she leaped out of the hiding space, tearing out the knife as the enormous creature whipped around its enormous head.

Lawrence had told her they were only as tall as his five-year-old brother Charles, not big enough to fill the first story of the Inn.

"Tabitha!"

"Mercy, Nikki! Run!"

"We can help!" Nikki shouted, pulling out Fidelis in front of her.

"No! You need to protect Mercy—"

"Tabitha!"

The repitox dove for her. Tabitha dove and rolled out the way, skidding on the loose dirt road. She jumped to her feet, brandishing her knife and staring the creature in its beady eyes, imagining Ryynar and his stupid sunglasses. "I said go!"

She didn't look back, only hoping they'd listened.

The repitox opened its enormous mouth, diving down on her. Tabitha ducked, slicing her blade under its head, before rolling out. The creature gave an ear-piercing screech.

She ran, glancing down at the sticky black blood that ran down from the blade to her fingers.

Tabitha dared to look over her shoulder and back at the beady eyes that now looked at her with a reflection of ferocity.

Tabitha's blood went cold.

She turned down the alley and ran, catching sight of a metal staircase bolted to the side of a building. She raced over, grabbing onto the railing and spinning herself up onto the steps, and ran.

The creature raced for her at an impressive speed, ramming its massive skull against the staircase.

The entire structure creaked. Tabitha held onto the centuries-old railing for dear life.

Thunder rattled in the sky.

The creature paused. Tabitha looked up the sky. It was almost as if the storm clouds were chasing them. It grew faster than the woods…

The wall suddenly exploded. She didn't even have time to process it as she scraped across the asphalt below. Pain exploded down her back. Dust stung her eyes. Where the wall once stood were twisted, growing branches. Small reptile creatures scrambled up the branches.

She pushed herself up, trying to blink away from the tears, holding her bloodstained knife in her shaking hand. She turned around slowly, waiting for the creature to emerge from the dust. "Come on, you big dirt snake."

As if it understood, it came diving out of the dust, racing in a circle around her.

Tabitha braced herself, her heart beating against her chest, her entire body shaking.

It gave out an ear-splitting screech, rising, and all in one swoop came down and—

The creature cried out, blood suddenly slashing across its eye. It pulled back, crying in pain.

Tabitha screamed as a blood-stained shield lodged itself in the dirt at her feet. She looked up as a girl emerged from the dust, running toward her.

"Come on! We have to get to Cole!" Nikki shouted, pulling Fidelis from the ground.

The serpent shook its head to the sky. Tabitha's stomach

twisted. Nikki grabbed her hand and pulled her down the side alleyway.

"Where is Mercy?" Tabitha shouted, letting go of her as they broke out into the opposite street.

"She went ahead?"

"Alone?" That girl was *so* annoyingly stubborn.

Nikki didn't clarify. The two took a turn down the block, weaving between the abandoned autos.

The sky cracked with lightning.

The city was no longer quiet.

35

MERCY CLUTCHED THE bag of kittens to her chest.

She felt awful leaving Nikki to go help Tabitha alone…and even worse, having Tabitha basically acknowledge Mercy was useless, but she reminded herself: *That's how it always goes. You're always in this alone.*

She ran until she spotted a familiar face standing in the middle of the road. She held back every urge to run at him full speed and hug him. Ray was safe.

She jogged up to him, hoping it wasn't obvious she was on the verge of tears. "You're okay."

"I'm fine," he said, glancing over her and inspecting a scratch on her shoulder. "Are you okay?"

She shrugged him off, opened her bag as a blue kitten popped its head out. "I-I have kittens."

Ray frowned. "Wha—?"

"There!" Lincoln jumped down from a van, lowering his bow. Nathaniel enjoyed the ride with a cheer. "I see them!"

Mercy's heart leapt, looking back to see Tabitha and Nikki turning down the street in a full run. Her eyes widened, seeing blood down the right side of Tabitha, her arm and leg bleeding.

"Tabitha!" Cole pushed past them toward her. She nearly slammed full force into him, unable to catch her breath. "What happened?"

She flinched as Cole's hand brushed against the graze wound.

"A scrape," she choked out. "I got blown off a building."

"A bomb?" Matteo said, his mouth hanging open.

Mercy turned, her eyes skipping past Lawrence and Matteo and instead focusing on the door next to them that opened to a passage leading downward. The words "Leave now, or you'll meet your Creator" were spray-painted across it.

"The woods," Tabitha breathed. "They're taking over this city."

"No wonder it's not a tourist destination," Mercy said under her breath, trying to crack a joke.

Ray gave her an uneasy smile. "Just our kind of fun."

"And the storm. Is it just me, or is it getting worse?" Tabitha said, hugging herself.

They all looked up toward the sky.

"It seems like no matter where we go, it's following."

"Maybe it's not following," Nikki said, quietly. "Maybe it's growing."

The thought made Mercy shiver, not from the cold. If Kathryn's storm was this big…then finding the Aguarious Stone was becoming a much bigger deal than for just herself.

"Got it!" Lincoln shouted from the door as a bolt driver retracted into his Cube. Lawrence helped haul the door to the bunker open.

Mercy swallowed hard. Tabitha had said that after this, the mission would be over. But her doubt was beginning to grow faster than the storm.

"It's going to be fine," Ray said with a short, forced laugh. "It's just like a…really big basement. And if anyone here should have a fear of creepy basements, it's me."

"That was not a funny time." Mercy didn't like the reminder that her grandmother had chained him up in the cabin basement with a shock collar.

All while Mercy did nothing.

This time would be different.

But that didn't mean she wasn't relieved that Lawrence was the first one to step down into the dark halls.

A kitten butted its head up through the pouch, looking up at her curiously. She patted it head, gently pushing him back inside. She pulled away with frost on her fingertips.

"Huh, ice cats," Ray said, chuckling to himself. "Fire Wolf will love them."

Lincoln and Matteo followed in after. Mercy looked over her shoulder, seeing Tabitha reluctantly take a jacket from Cole to cover her wound.

"Are you coming, Mercy?" Ray called, snapping her attention back to see Ray and Nikki waiting down the steps into the bunker.

She tightened her grip on her satchel and followed them.

The hall smelled like dirt, dust, and age, but the floor squeaked underneath her shoes.

"Anyone have a light?" Lawrence called out from further ahead.

"Mercy's a human glowstick!"

"Ray, don't make me run over your foot." A light switched on from behind them. Felicity held out a glowstick. She was standing, her leg braces visible as she stood forward.

Mercy felt her face heat.

"You're not even in your chair," Ray said.

"Just you wait," Felicity said, pushing past him. She tossed Mercy a glowstick. She cracked it.

Lincoln insisted he could see in the dark, but the others took them from her graciously.

"Bunkers used to be some of my favorite places," Ray said, running his hand along a pipe that was bolted across the wall. "That's where I met Nikki, actually. In a small bunker under the utility store."

"Oh cool, you met Nikki in an underground ditch in North Cordell. How special," Lincoln teased, his voice echoing.

"Aw, he's just jealous because he almost shot her the first time they met," Ray said, with a mischievous smirk. "Honestly, very rude, Linc."

Is that really how their friendships all started? It felt somewhat relieving. It hadn't always been sunshine, rainbows, and lemons.

It reminded her a lot of meeting Ray.

"To be fair, I did smack you and grab your ear," Mercy said. It was almost funny to think about now. "But I didn't kill you."

"You just killed my dignity. And I saved your life!"

"You smashed my tables! And you were just *asking* for the short jokes."

"I'm not even that short, okay?" Ray said, crossing his arms. "And sometimes, the smallest Members are the best Members. Right, Tabitha?"

"Speak for yourself," came Tabitha's pained voice behind.

"Be quiet!" Lawrence snapped. The line came to a halt. "I think I found something."

That was the fastest Mercy had ever seen them all shut up.

They all hurried to meet up with Lawrence. The light from the glowsticks revealed a metallic yellow sign on an enormous steel door, a freshly installed keypad keeping it locked shut.

Cole translated it to mean one simple word: Welcome.

It looked well taken care of, just like the freshly mopped floors. People were definitely here.

"They'll know who the Council is," Cole said, moving his way to the front. Lincoln was already trying to break the keypad.

"I'll introduce us as the Phoenix Council, and we go in with whatever terms *they* have. No talking or annoying commentary. This could be Nathaniel's only chance."

And Mercy's last chance to prove she belonged in the Council.

A click echoed through the hall. Mercy froze, holding her breath as the keypad flashed green.

Lincoln stood up, dusting off his hands. "Success."

There was the same excitement in his voice. Mercy couldn't miss the pinched look he gave as he turned back to look at Nathaniel, who was peering out from under Lincoln's hood.

The door slowly creaked open.

Out of the corner of her eye, Mercy caught the Ewyon

Stone glowing from around Nikki's neck. Guilt swelled in her stomach.

Lincoln stepped back from the door, reaching a protective hand to Nathaniel.

Cole took the first step inside.

Mercy glanced at Ray. He looked unafraid, almost excited to race through these halls. She wouldn't show weakness.

The first hall was eerily quiet, the white light lights dim and flickering as they stepped inside. Mercy forced herself to swallow, finding comfort in the fact she was surrounded by other Members.

"Search the Bunker. Use telepathy or ear comms if it's really urgent to communicate. We'll group as soon as we find the Believer lab."

Mercy was the only one quick to dig her ear Comm out of her bag. She had to rub off the thin layer of ice thanks to the kittens, but she stuck it in her ear.

Her throat was too tight to point out that their splitting up plan didn't work too well last time.

Ray met her eyes, but she looked away quickly, slipping around the corner into the nearest hall.

She took a deep breath. She just needed to clear her head. She was almost through this. She worked better alone. No one could watch her mess up anyway.

Thud!

Mercy jumped, slowly turning to see if anyone had turned to join her. Nothing.

A small meow broke through the silence.

She muffled a scream, nearly tripping backward over the ice kitten, which was rubbing its prickly frozen fur on her ankle.

It stared at her with its glowing red eyes.

Just like Fire Wolf had when she'd failed to ignite.

She sighed, picking up the little kitten. "You nearly scared the living daylights out of me, you little rascal. Hey! Don't you even think about freezing my fingers."

She shook the frost from her fingernails, beginning to put the kitten into her bag when she heard a creak. Even the kitten went still in her arms.

"Hello?" Mercy said, her voice wavering. "We-we come in peace!"

She held out the kitten in front of her, as if that would be any threat. Mercy inched forward, down into the darker section of the hall.

A little glass window was in the wall, protecting a red lever. In bold Anglish letters, it read "DO NOT TOUCH." That was then followed by the same warning in multiple languages.

The lights flickered down the hall. If someone lived here, why hadn't they fixed them?

Maybe she should've waited to find a partner before bursting down this freaky hallway alone. Ray had supernatural abilities, and Nikki was levels beyond her in combat. Even with Felicity, she'd feel safer.

She shook off the thought.

She had to prove herself first. Her grandmother had been the one to endanger Felicity, and Mercy had to make it right before she ruined everything she had between them. She could risk…

"Ah!" Mercy's foot slipped from under her. She hit the ground with a thud. The lights flickered off.

The ground was slippery…slimy below her. She reached her foot out, slipping over and falling onto her back, her shirt dampening. She scrambled to sit up.

The lights flickered on above.

Blood.

Mercy was sitting in a pile of blood.

She couldn't scream. She slowly got to her feet. All she saw was an ominous push door a few feet away, the streak of red seeping underneath.

The kitten curled up against her chest.

She had to run. Something was wrong. Something was horribly wrong.

She swallowed the pain in her throat and moved forward, pushing through the door.

A thin sheet hung from the ceiling. A fractured hologram lay broken on a smashed table. Mercy wiped clean her shaking hands and picked it up.

A half written net message.

"Location compromised. Founder Association gave out info—"

And then the screen had been smashed. She slowly

moved behind the table. She held her breath and drew back the curtain.

Mercy almost vomited.

She turned away, touching her ear piece. She couldn't speak.

"Who's Comm is on?"

"Not me."

"It's Mercy's." Lincoln's voice.

She'd found the lab. She'd found the lab.

The hologram slipped from her hand, its projector shattering on the floor.

"What's going on?"

"Mercy, we have your location," Cole said. "Are you okay?"

Overturned tables, smashed projectors, scorch marks in the ceilings. And bodies, most lazily covered in the sheets.

Mercy turned and threw up.

She stumbled back, covering her face, but the image would never leave her mind.

The sound of glass crunching sent the hairs on her neck standing straight up.

She slowly raised her eyes up, her heart seizing in her chest. At the end of the room, standing on a desk was a Defender Agent, a scar across the bridge of his nose. He unsheathed two long electric knives.

"Mercy!"

Ray dropped into the room.

"Ray! Watch out!" Mercy screamed.

"You all rely far too much on that Oquelite hybrid," the Agent sighed, jumping down from the table dand racing for them.

Ray didn't hesitate. He grabbed her, and within a second, they were teleported to the hall. He pulled out of the Shadow Blade.

Mercy found the lab! His voice boomed mentally. *But it looks like our Agent friend got there first...*

He met Mercy's eyes, only holding her gaze for a second. She could see the horror in them as they slowly grew glassy. "Run! Go! Now!"

"I'm not leaving you!"

His golden eyes sparked, his brows furrowing. "Mercy."

The door exploded, sending both Ray and Mercy sliding across the floor.

The agent walked through the rubble. Mercy could only see his silhouette and the sparks of his blue blades.

Ray scrambled to his feet, sending a blast of purple energy straight for him. "Envelope!" he shouted, spinning the Blade.

Mercy would never be used to the literal shadows peeling off the walls, bouncing off Ray's blade and weaving through the dust and enveloping around the Agent.

He turned to Mercy. "Get out of here!"

And then he charged after the Agent.

Mercy pushed herself to her feet, and something came flying from the room, slamming into a wooden chair and it burst into flames. She scrambled back.

This would be a *really* good time to ignite, she begged herself.

Ray was pushed back out into the hall. Mercy tried pointlessly to stamp out the flaming chair.

Ray jumped to his feet. The Agent came running for him. His speed was unmatched. Ray could hardly keep up, having to teleport in and out to avoid being shocked.

He managed to hit the Agent's shoulder, but the Defender armor bounced him back. Ray disappeared before dropping out of thin air, slamming the Agent against the wall, the Blade held to his throat.

The Agent scowled at him, smashing a glass window in the wall, and pulled down the "DO NOT TOUCH" lever.

Instantly, sirens went off.

"Extraction Gas activated. Sector #014"

The Agent smiled wickedly before Ray knocked him hard in the head with the hilt of his sword.

"Mercy, hurry! He won't be out long!"

He ran, reaching out for her hand before he stopped, stumbling.

Mercy coughed.

The air began to smell sweet…too sweet.

Ray cursed. "Stupid gas," he wheezed, holding onto his ear Comm.

"Ray?" While he was struggling to get to his feet, Mercy could just *smell* something weird.

A deep, throaty laugh sent a shiver down her spine. The Agent pushed himself off the ground, a bloody gash bleeding down the side of his head. "Extraction gas was meant to keep Purizies out of the bunkers," he said with a small smile. "And you probably know exactly who Purizies are by now."

Oquelite.

The gas was made to kill Oquelite.

Mercy's blood went cold, her eyes falling back to Ray.

"I guess I'll be the first to die," he said with a forced laugh.

"This isn't fair!" Mercy shouted, her blood burning as she whipped around to face the Agent. "You're a Defender! You're supposed to protect people! He didn't do anything wrong!"

"Don't cry, child," the Agent said. "No one else has to get hurt if you just hand over the Aguirre and the Aguarious kid."

"Fat chance," Ray said with a shallow laugh, shooting a purple blast from his hands, sending the Agent sliding across the ground.

Mercy rushed to him, pulling his arm across her shoulders to help him run.

Ignite. Ignite. Come on, Remembrance! Glow!

She began to feel her head grow lighter. The gas might not kill her like Ray, but it certainly wasn't leaving her alone.

Um, guys? Tabitha's mind broke into Mercy's. *Cole's on the verge of passing out.*

"Even people with just Oquelite blood? Wow. These people were efficient," Ray said with a half laugh.

Mercy wanted to kick him. They broke out into the main hall. She wasn't sure if the hallway was actually hazy with gas or she was just panicking.

A hand grabbed onto her. She gave out a weak scream until she recognized the glint on his glasses. She let Lawrence's warm hand lead her forward.

Ray slumped over against Mercy, but Lawrence was quick to catch him, resorting to slinging Ray over his shoulder.

We made it outside. Lincoln's voice.

Lawrence turned to Mercy. *Don't say anything. Speaking will increase your intake of the gas, got it?*

She nodded. Mercy almost tripped as they approached

the steps, her stomach wanting to revolt as they ascended.

Light.

And fresh air.

She could breathe—

She broke out of the bunker doors.

"You found them!" Felicity cried out, rushing to hug Mercy before turning to Lawrence and Ray.

Lawrence gasped for air, almost dropping Ray.

"He's out," Lawrence said, looking pale.

Mercy tried not to cry. It was a terrible time to cry. What happened to the Mercy who never cried?

Would Ray die?

She looked over to Cole, who was at least still on his feet.

"I'm fine," Cole drowsed, though his eyes were clouded. He clasped his hand over his mouth before turning away.

"We need to go!" Mercy shouted. "Before the Agent finds us!"

"The Agent?" Nikki eyes widened. "He's here?"

"He's the one who triggered the gas!"

"Get to the trailer!"

"But Cole can't drive!" Tabitha shouted, helping Cole regain his balance.

"I'll do it!" Lincoln said excitedly.

They didn't have much of a choice as a gunshot rang out from below.

The Council ran. Lincoln unbuckled Nathaniel as they ran, handing off the confused toddler to Nikki. "Sorry, Nat. This is for the good of the world."

Nathaniel looked betrayed as Nikki slung his carrier over her shoulders. He clutched his stuffed monkey and pouted. "No Nik."

They turned into the next street. The trailer stood untouched. Mercy couldn't be relieved yet even as they loaded into the trailer.

Ray was thrown as gently as possible onto the couch.

Cole threw up before he was dragged into the trailer with an injured Tabitha.

Without warning, the vehicle was sent flying forward. Everyone screamed.

Tabitha cursed, pulling the door closed.

Nathaniel began crying. The trailer took a harsh turn,

sending everyone slamming against the wall.

The city raced past the windows.

Mercy shook with adrenaline. They bounced out onto an open road. The woods grew higher around them. Mercy cringed at an enormous crack growing from the rising trees not too far in the distance.

"Oh no…"

Matteo's voice came from the back of the trailer as he stared out into the road behind them.

Mercy dared to move to the window.

Her heart plummeted.

There was Agent Aalto in the slick black Defender truck, racing at full speed after them.

The trailer erupted into chaos.

"What do we do?"

"I could throw fire?"

"That's a stupid idea!"

"We need to do *something!*"

"He's gaining on us?"

"How about Mercy?" Felicity's voice piped up. "She has the ability to enhance things with her touch when she glows!"

"You think you can do that?" Lawrence asked, spinning on her.

Mercy's throat tightened. She knew Felicity was trying to be nice and give her the spotlight…but this was an awful time! She couldn't do this! "Y-yes."

"You might just be the one to save us," Lawrence breathed, running a hand through his hair as someone rummaged through Lincoln's bag and pulled out an explosive arrow.

She took it nervously, trying not to show her uncertainty as they opened the latch to the top of the trailer. She took a deep breath. This was her moment.

Cole had said she was a part of this Council. She was going to prove it.

She stuck the arrow between her teeth and crawled up on top of the counter, pulling herself up to the top. She nearly slipped off from the sheer speed.

Lawrence grabbed her. "The closer it gets, the more of a chance we have!"

Mercy steadied herself, the speed beating behind her. The truck took a harsh turn and she nearly slipped, screaming. She and Lawrence grabbed the trailer's ceiling door.

The truck turned the corner with grace.

Mercy took a deep breath. This was her one chance to *really* prove herself. Otherwise, the entire mission was compromised.

Glow.

Glow.

Glow.

Come on!

She could feel the stares. Why wasn't it working?

"Mercy, throw it!"

"Why isn't she glowing?"

"It's getting too close!"

"Give me my shield! I'll do it!"

Mercy squeezed her eyes shut, trying to remember the two times she'd ignited. It was blurry, and she wasn't sure if it was from tears or fear. Or both.

Why couldn't she do it?

She had to save them.

Nothing was coming.

She couldn't feel *anything*.

Aalto's auto smashed up against the trailer. Lawrence and Mercy were knocked back through the hatch, hitting the floor with a *thud*.

All of a sudden, the world was spinning. She hit the ceiling. Pain exploded in her ankle. The lights went dark.

She couldn't tell if she was screaming. Her mind was blank till she hit the window, which shattered as the trailer skidded across the ground.

Her body was trembling, and she could feel blood dripping from her cheek.

She couldn't get up.

She could hear the gunshots.

But nothing compared to hearing Aalto's booming voice and knowing she'd failed.

"Well, well. It looks like The Council has finally met its match."

PART FOUR

THE RAGE

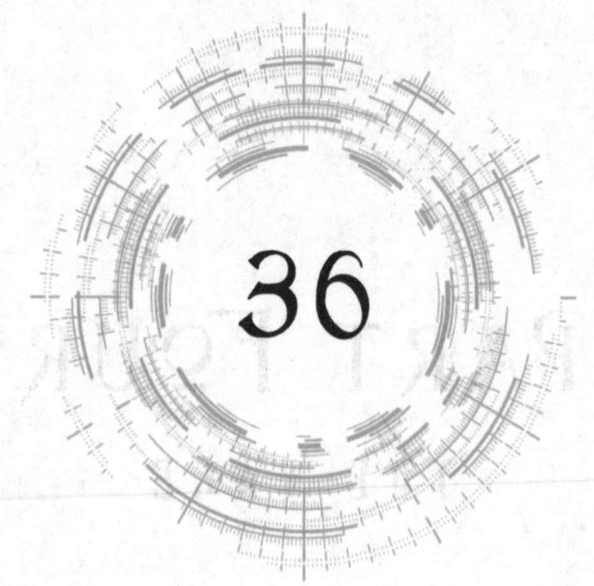

36

"DON'T LET HIM get inside the trailer!"

Nikki leaped to her feet, glass from the window crunching under her boots. She unbuckled the shield from her back. The trailer was turned on its side, but that didn't stop her from running, launching herself off the cabinet and crashing through the door, and pulling herself up onto the top of the trailer.

She activated the blade on her shield, holding it out in front of her.

Agent Aalto stood out in the road, blood streaming down his face. He tightened his grip on his blades. "You finally ready to turn yourself in?" A smile creeped onto his lips as he stepped forward. "You aren't going anywhere with your Oquelite out of commission."

Nikki clenched her jaw, the fire smoldering in her chest.

"Stay away from her!"

Nikki's heart jumped at the sound of Felicity's voice as she raced from the truck. She held her spear, looking unharmed except for a cut on her arm and her jeans ripped from the braces, exposing parts of her bruised legs.

"Oh. A stick." He looked unamused, racing for Felicity.

Felicity jumped out of the way, spinning around and catching the weak spot under his breast plate, spinning back to avoid the swing of his blade before sending the butt of the spear into his face.

He scowled, swinging and missing Felicity's dance around him before he finally swung out a leg, catching her rhythm and knocking her off her feet.

Nikki couldn't sit back anymore.

She was sick of being protected.

Everything inside her burned to protect.

She raced for Aalto. His eyes grew wide at seeing her before his brows narrowed with a glimmer of a smirk. He wasn't Kathryn. He wasn't even Oquelite.

"Felicity! Help the others in the trailer!"

She could feel Avalon's energy muster inside her as the blinding instinct took over and she swung the shield at him over and over, dodging back and forth.

The voices echoed in her mind, but they only fueled her.

Strong arms dragged her across the forest as she kicked and screamed. She could still see the streak of smoke in the sky where home once stood.

His blade grazed her shin. She cried out, using the pain to thrust the shield at his jaw, sending him stumbling back.

"They're dead. All gone." She sat in a cold room, her hands strapped down to the table.

She shook off the horrifying memory, marching toward him as he braced himself, flicking his blades to bring the sparks back to life.

"Maybe I take back what I said earlier," he said with a hoarse laugh. "You do have the Aguirre attitude."

"Nobody tries to kill my friends." She grit her teeth and charged at him.

The memory of Aalto knocking Lawrence over the edge and into the river. The moment of horror when she'd thought her cousin had died. The moment she'd thought Lincoln died.

And by a *Defender.*

Someone she thought they could trust.

She beat him back over and over and over again. Every

hit she took just drove her further, the burning overcoming her. Her vision wasn't even her own.

Her shield came down on something hard.

She heard a scream of pain.

She just wanted him to...

"Nikki! Nikki, stop!"

She felt Lawrence wrap his arms around her, holding her back.

"What are you doing?" she shouted. "He's going to get away! He's going to kill you! He's going to—"

"I don't think he's going anywhere, Nik." Lawrence held her tighter as her vision came back into focus.

Aalto kneeled on the floor, a hand against the ground and the other hand...

Nikki's stomach leaped to her throat.

Her eyes burned. *No, no, no.*

"I knew this would come in handy." Cole stepped out, fog still in his eyes as he clamped one of the Oquelite shock collars around Aalto's neck.

Nikki couldn't look away. The adrenaline was racing inside her, burning to continue.

Take his other hand, Avalon taunted.

She shuddered at the idea, wanting to hide in Lawrence.

Cole unsheathed the Illuminate, his hand trembling.

"What are you going to do?" Aalto laughed, though his blood-streaked face was contorted in pain. "Kill me? You don't look like you have the guts."

"How did you find us?" Cole said, his voice firm.

"Why don't you ask your Keyper over there?" Aalto said, cringing in pain.

Nikki blinked, turning to see Mercy standing with the others a few feet back.

"Oh, don't look so confused," Aalto said. "Some Founder Association gave us a tip on your next location. Said you gave it to them."

"Mercy..." Cole's voice was low and unreadable as he looked at her.

"I-I didn't know this would happen." Mercy stepped back, her eyes flooding with panicked tears. "I-I'm so, so sorry."

"She wanted to help," Tabitha stepped in. "It was an incredibly risky idea, but she couldn't have known this would happen."

"You knew about this too?" Cole said, his jaw dropping.

"I didn't think—"

"Tabitha! Why didn't you tell me right away?"

NIKKI!

Nikki perked up, her mind drowning out the sounds of the Council. The voice sounded so strained. So distant…like it was being pulled. She saw Felicity leaning on her spear as Mercy attempted to cower behind her. Matteo stood on guard with the bag containing their sole pistol, and Lawrence stood on guard beside her.

Ray was still out of commission.

Was he okay?

Had someone checked up on him?

NIK! BAD GUY! NIK!

Nikki nearly stumbled back. Nathaniel was contacting her?

"Lincoln!" she shouted, breaking through their argument. "Where's Lincoln?"

Nikki ran for the woods.

She had to find Lincoln.

She screamed Lincoln's name.

Was he okay? Had a Repitox found him?

Her heart pounded against her chest. *Had Kathryn found him?*

She broke into the patch of twisted trees. Faster. Faster.

"Lincoln!" she screamed at the top of her lungs, her voice ragged. "Nathaniel! Where are you?"

Out of nowhere an arrow whizzed back, scratching her face, through her jacket and into the tree behind her. Her mind went blank, her veins on fire for a split second before she doubled over, hanging by her sleeve pinned to the tree.

It took her a second to catch her breath and realized she'd been tazed.

Lincoln stepped forward, his bow in hand, the other lifting to draw another arrow.

"Lincoln? What are you doing?" Nikki shouted, her throat growing dry as she met his eyes…or what used to be his eyes, but were now empty voids of black.

So that's what Lincoln had been talking about his eyes going all black—

"Little Aguirre, we meet again." His voice was hollow. Nathaniel was crying in his carrier, clinging to Lincoln.

Lincoln raised his bow. Nikki reached for her Fidelis before she paused.

She couldn't hurt Lincoln.

That is not Lincoln.

"Lincoln! Please! It's me, Nikki! Snap out of it!" she cried. She thought he'd rejected Kathryn. What was happening?

"The Lincoln you remember isn't here," said a hollow voice from Lincoln's lips. "He may have rejected me, but that doesn't mean he didn't give me his name…in his struggle…in his panic in Algery."

Not-Lincoln smirked, letting go of the string. Nikki braced herself, ready to tear away, but the arrow landed its mark on her other sleeve, this time cutting into her arm. She cried out in pain, the burning in veins zapping through her, her knees buckling.

Her eyes burned. "Lincoln!" she screamed.

He lowered his bow, folding it and clicking it onto his belt. He removed Nathaniel from his carrier. Nathaniel looked to Nikki, reaching out his hands and screaming "Linc!"

He began to cry inconsolably.

It echoed through her mind.

The cries of her younger siblings caused her to stop. Her mother pulled on her arm, the smell of smoke only growing stronger. "You have to run, Nik!"

Tears began to race down her eyes as she pulled against the arrows, pain shooting down her arm. "Nathaniel!"

Out of the shadows stepped another pair of glowing eyes. The woman's dark skin and long white braid were painfully familiar.

Lincoln walked toward her, holding up Nathaniel wriggling wildly in his hands.

Nikki's eyes widened in horror. She screamed. "No! Lincoln, stop!"

She threw her entire body weight forward, ignoring the pain that tore up her arm as she stumbled, grabbing the shield with her good arm and throwing it between them.

Sergia stepped back, the shield landing in the tree, and she turned with a quick jump to the air, a gust of red energy thrusting her to the ground. She clenched her hand, Nikki feeling the mobility draining from her body as she was slammed back against the tree.

She couldn't even scream as Nathaniel was placed in Sergia's free arm. Senseless tears streamed down her face. *NO! NATHANIEL!*

Nathaniel waved his arms around wildly, but not even water could save him.

Sergia tore the tracker from Nathaniel's neck. She crushed it in her hands.

Nikki watched all their hard work crumble to the ground.

The tiny, helpless eyes of the Aguarious toddler she'd grown to love met hers. "Fight!"

He reached out to her, his stuffed monkey slipping from his hands and hitting the ground. He tried to bite Sergia. She placed a finger between his eyes, and Nathaniel fell unconscious.

Sergia turned, looking Nikki dead in the eyes. "Your Council has seven days to turn themselves over, or Liberty sinks."

She flicked her hand in the air and disappeared into the shadow.

Her hold on Nikki and Lincoln left with her. The two both collapsed to the ground.

Nikki gasped for air, repeating Nathaniel's name over and over under her breath. He couldn't be gone. He couldn't. Her whole body hurt as she tried to bite back a rising sob.

"He's…gone."

Nikki turned her teary eyes toward Lincoln, his hands against the ground as he stared blankly. She picked herself up, clenching the wound on her arm.

She could barely form his name as she collapsed beside him. They both sat on their knees watching the darkness where they'd last seen the little boy's eyes.

"I did this," Lincoln choked, his shaking hands picking up the little stuffed animal. "This is all my fault."

He turned to meet Nikki's eyes, tears falling freely.

"She found out my name, Nik. She found out my name. She controlled me and I-I—" He stared at his scarred hands before balling them into fists. "Nikki, she's known all along," he choked.

Nikki leaned her shoulder against his. She'd been so close. She'd met Nathaniel's eyes. If she'd fought a little harder…just a little longer…if she'd just been paying more attention.

"We'll find him," she whispered, her voice hoarse.

Lincoln angrily wiped away his tears with his dirt-streaked hands. "I'll do anything," he said through grit teeth. He turned to Nikki, his brows furrowing. "I-I—"

He didn't finish. Instead he hugged her, burying his face in her shoulder. She hugged him back, wanting to feel anything but the burning inside.

The flame in her chest grew as Lincoln apologized over and over again through his tears. She hugged him tighter as the fire inside grew to a blaze.

The voices in her mind taunted her.

She's known all along.

They hadn't been a step ahead of Kathryn.

They'd played right into her trap, and Aalto had been the perfect distraction.

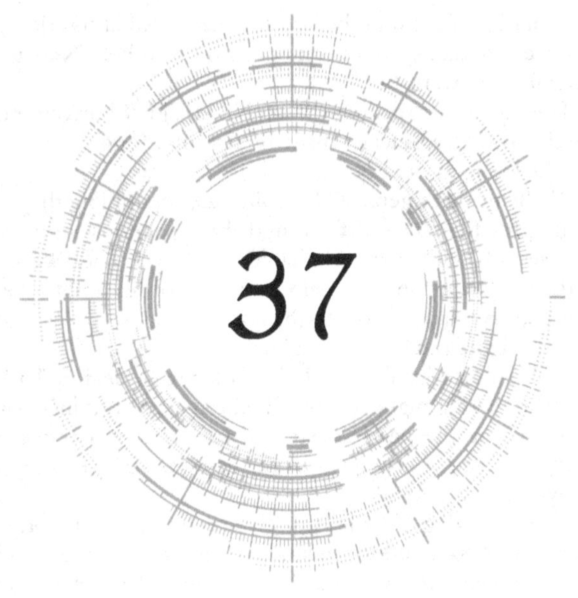

37

"KATHRYN'S GOING TO flood Liberty."

Felicity's mind went numb.

Every head turned to her.

"That's where I saw the vision," Felicity said quietly. That's where she'd seen Silas. "And where the news reports show the storm being the worst."

It all made sense.

Aalto looked like such a small problem now. They'd contacted the Outowns, and the guards had taken it from there with the promise they would somehow convince the Department that Aalto had broken the Defender code.

He had slaughtered an entire organization in cold blood.

The thought chilled Felicity to the bone.

Mercy sat close to her on the bench inside the station, hugging the only surviving ice kitten to her chest, her eyes darting up to Felicity's. And Mercy had witnessed it.

"Do you think the Aguarious Stone is in Liberty?" Mercy piped up quietly.

"The Aguarious Stone?" Lincoln frowned.

"Zita had the Stone before she died," Nikki interjected. "We were thinking about trying to find it to help Nathaniel control his powers, but…"

Felicity's heart sped up. "Wait. Nikki, didn't Lincoln track you down with a bracelet made of Ewyon Stone?"

The Council went quiet.

"Felicity, that's genius!" Lincoln said, scrambling through his bag for the Cube. "If we find the Aguarious Stone, we can use it to track down Nathaniel! And then when we save Nathaniel, we'll use it to help him control his abilities and stop Kathryn from flooding the city!"

And figure out what 'Craig' was.

Cole rubbed his forehead, the dark circles clear under his eyes after a long night of SpeedRail travels and trying to get them to take the nearly destroyed trailer as an overweight transport item. It was obvious the gas was still wearing off, his eyes begging for sleep.

"We can't all go," Cole said. "We need to get to Liberty as soon as possible, and those kinds of tickets will be *expensive*. We already have to take a Rail back to North Cordell because of the trailer since lugging it around would only make it worse and ugh! …and Taryn."

And Giles.

The pit inside her stomach grew bigger. They hadn't heard a word about the trial since Sinni's home.

Felicity tried to push down her emotions. Giles was a Defender. He was innocent. No matter what it was. He *couldn't* be executed.

"I'll go to Liberty."

Felicity startled at Tabitha's voice. Tabitha got to her feet. Tabitha? Tabitha Delorous, of all people, wanted to go to Liberty?

"I'm going too," Nikki said.

"So am I!" Lincoln said after her.

"We can't risk that," Nikki said, turning on him. "If Kathryn knows your name…she might try and use you again."

Lincoln opened his mouth to argue, hesitating before his lips twisted in frustrated defeat.

Nikki turned back to the others. Ever since yesterday, her eyes felt distant, and it almost scared Felicity. A spark of her wide-eyed innocence had died when she'd hacked Aalto's hand off.

That was all that was left of him.

"Remember a year ago when we infiltrated the Glass Tower?" Nikki said. "It was just the girls. We're less suspicious, a smaller group, and far more experienced now."

"I don't know," Cole said, biting his lip.

"You scared you'll lose your women folk?" Tabitha teased.

Cole deadpanned her. "My *friends*. It just seems incredibly risky to send just four of you on an incredibly time-sensitive mission while an immortal is out for our literal blood is using a supernatural toddler and a giant sea monster to flood a city?"

Tabitha put her hands on her hips. "Exactly."

"Felicity's home is one of the most secure places on the planet. The Exerticus have failed to break in there *twice*," Nikki said, now standing beside Tabitha.

Both times, however, did end with poor revelations.

Felicity shivered.

"Who will expect a bunch of snobby Liberty girls to thwart the Exerticus?" Tabitha said.

"Fine. That's the only plan I can think we can scrape together in time," Cole said, smothering his face in his hands.

Tabitha cheered, attempting to high-five Nikki who just stood, staring confused at her hand.

Felicity tried not to panic. Back to Liberty? Back to Silas?

This time there was no Giles.

"We'll get him back." Nikki's whisper was so quiet that Felicity nearly missed it. Nikki had sat down beside Lincoln, who was holding the little monkey stuffie. Lincoln didn't even look at her.

Felicity's heart sank. Right. It didn't matter if she had choice words with her family. Baby Nathaniel was in grave danger.

She took a deep breath. "Let's do this, then."

She looked back to Mercy, whose eyes lit up. She gave a tiny nod, and Felicity gave a small smile back.

The train whistle went off, and the sleep deprived, beaten-up Council pushed themselves to their feet. Felicity had to rely on Cole's support to get into the traveler car. Her wheelchair had been unsalvageable in the wreckage, and her braces lacked charge.

She tried not to panic thinking about them completely dying before reaching a safe space.

They loaded into the car with leather peeling off the worn seats, and they crowded in with the other passengers, many drenched from the storms.

She settled on the window seat beside Cole, where she could see the ocean already waiting as they sped by. Across from her was Lincoln, who was staring out to the ocean. His eyes were red, but he'd deny ever crying. She doubted he even slept, as he'd been so anxious trying to get the Cube to track Nathaniel's location.

She wanted to comfort him, but she couldn't even think of what to say. She couldn't even imagine the pain and guilt he was feeling.

The rail car began to move, and Felicity held her breath as they rocketed into the ocean tube.

Hours passed, and Felicity had begun to doze off against the cold glass window, the glimmer of the ocean rushing past them—

A roar racketed through her skull.

She jumped, grabbing at her chest.

"You okay, Felicity?" Cole asked.

The creature, Craig. It was back.

Tabitha looked up at her, knowingly, nudging Nikki. Felicity shooed away their stares. "I'm fine."

"What's up with you guys and saying 'it's fine' when it's obviously not?" Ray said, mimicking a feminine voice with a crack from the seat behind them.

"You're totally guilty of that too," Lawrence scoffed.

Ray gave a horrified gasp. "I would *never*, Edge Lord Himself."

Felicity tuned them out. *What now?* she asked. She still wasn't totally on board with the idea of mentally communicating with the creature.

It always seemed to reach out near water, she recognized.

It gave a sad moan in return.

We have to save our little Aguarious, Nathaniel…Maybe you'll see him. He's in Liberty too.

A loud roar pulled Felicity from her consciousness before she could even scream. It was painless, but her entire body went numb. She couldn't feel the seat beneath her, just empty space around.

"Let me out!" she screamed into the void. "What's going on?"

The creature gave a long, low whistle. *Flood! Coming! Prince!*

She could only give a frustrated huff, stomping her foot. Her heart flipped. Wait? She couldn't usually move her feet?

"What is this?"

The creature groaned, sounding annoyed.

You.

The world changed around her, throwing her back to the docks in Liberty at sunset. Silas once again stood at the dock, this time lacking his worn-out cape, his thin tunic showing his muscle tone…and yet he looked smaller.

He had a busted lip and a cut by his eye.

The same Exerticus woman stood beside him. "Perhaps you should put up less rebellion. You're lucky you're not sent with the others underwater."

Others? Underwater? Felicity frowned.

"She promised night would be my own. She wouldn't control my mind at night." His words trembled…childlike as he spat. His hands balled to fists.

"You have your own mind now," the woman said. "Just do your duty and we can be back. If you didn't pick such a fight every night—"

"I don't care. I'll keep fighting. You have *my* kind working till they die like tools!"

The woman raised a brow. "Fighting for what exactly, Idicous?"

Silas paused before turning away with a grimace.

The woman gave a small smile. "You remind me of your sister."

"Curse my sister," Silas growled. "I'm nothing like her. I don't even understand why you stand by her, Sergia."

Sergia stiffened. "She hides more than you know."

"What? What is she hiding?" Silas said, unconvinced and with a scoff. "There's not much to hide besides a dingy old warehouse. She could at least steal one of the submarines—"

"Quiet," Sergia said, slapping her hand over his mouth. "I can feel it listening."

"It's a giant lump of meat and seaweed. Who's it going to tell?" Silas pushed Sergia's hand away.

"You underestimate the intelligence of Mythic creatures," Sergia said, wiping her hand on her cape. "We need this creature for the flood. Only its power is capable of such destruction. Kathryn even has her limits."

"It's just a dumb fish," Silas scoffed.

"You should know what it's like to have your intelligence questioned."

"We're not going to start talking about me now." Silas waved his hands, beginning to untie his tunic. "Nope! End of discussion!"

This was the Silas Felicity remembered. The one with spunk and a smidge of personality behind his stoicism.

"You're like your sister in the way that you're not what your family intended," Sergia said, following behind him as he started down the dock.

Silas tore off his shirt, pretending not to hear her as he moved to the edge.

"That's why they made you keep your hair white, isn't it?" Sergia said. "They want you to stand out. They want everyone to know you're the mistake of your father."

"I'm a prince!" Silas shouted, standing at the edge of the dock.

"You're a broken *child* on Oquelite terms! Why won't you accept that?"

"Like you said. I stand out! I'm my father's joke." Silas began to walk backward, his hands held out dramatically. "And if I reject that…Everyone will see me for what I really am." He laughed. "I can't risk that."

And then he jumped into the waves.

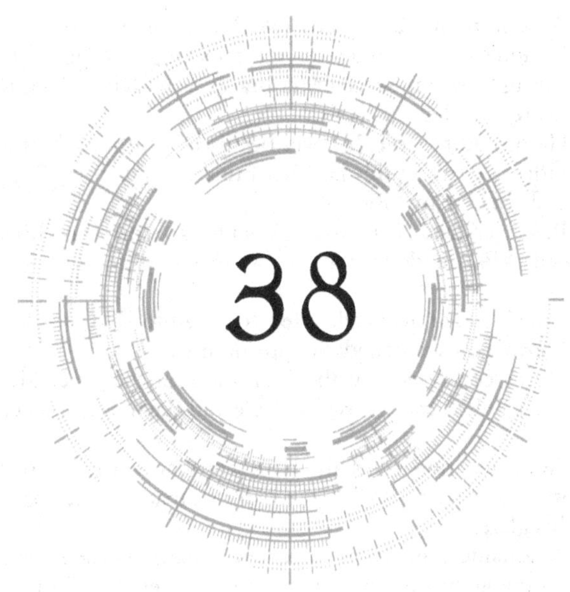

38

"Sulfur?"

Mercy nearly ran into Ray as he stopped dead in his tracks in front of her. She stumbled back, turning to look up at the hologram proudly spelling out the region's name: SULFUR.

Her heart leaped.

No. She couldn't, could she? She'd already messed up so bad. She'd gotten people killed. She needed to just stick to the sidelines.

But wasn't Sulfur the region of Zita's home? It would be the perfect place to start their search for the Aguarious Stone.

Ray spun around, his face pale. "No, no, no. We can't stay."

Mercy frowned. Ray was panicking now? They couldn't turn back, and they hardly had enough savings to get them to their next destination.

"We need a power source and a proper night's sleep," Felicity said, clinging to Cole. "I need to contact my family."

"And hop on the next possible Rail to Liberty," Cole said.

It didn't take a genius to see the flicking red lights glowing through Felicity's jeans. Her braces were dying. Even Ray had to realize that.

He turned to Cole, his eyes begging. "Not now. Not like this. Please don't let this be what I think you're doing."

Cole held firm. "Ray—"

Ray clenched his fists, glancing around, his breath rushed. "Please don't tell me we're going to your dad's house."

Cole lowered his head. "He's your dad too."

Mercy's eyes widened, her lips parting.

Mercy could see that the realization hit the other Members too. Sulfur was the region Cole and Ray's dad was living in?

"Ray, we don't exactly have another choice." Mercy stepped in, avoiding Cole's gaze. Her stomach twisted at seeing his glare.

"Nathaniel's in danger and every darn moment we sit here arguing, he's getting further and further away!" Lincoln pushed his way forward. "And you're here sulking about your dad?"

The two boys stared at each other, both with their own glimmer of rage. Ray finally turned away, muttering under his breath. "Not like this. It wasn't supposed to be like this."

He didn't say another word, following Cole's lead.

Mercy tried to give him an empathetic look. "It'll be fine."

He scoffed.

Not a word.

She swallowed hard.

The streets of Sulfur were destitute compared to the glorious, industrious cities of the past regions they'd visited. The roads had a patchy paving job. Vendors and trucks had stands set up outside of the stations, advertisement bots racing around arriving passengers' ankles.

The further they went down the main street, the more motorized bikes she saw, and little children playing on the curbs, taking turns sliding on a discharged traffic bot, only stopping to stare at the large group of tired, beaten teenagers.

Mercy clenched her jaw, dying to say something to Ray, but the words wouldn't form. She hugged her jacket tighter to herself. Mercy hadn't seen her father in exactly twenty-one months. For Ray? It had been a whole decade.

Did he not miss him at all? Mercy missed her father more than anything in the entire world. She'd never had to prove to him her love, despite what Grandmere said.

But she knew what it was like to feel betrayed. She remembered vividly the morning she'd woken up and come down the stairs to an empty house. At first, she'd convinced herself her father had gone out for errands or a jog…and then he'd never come back.

She'd called her grandmother, frantic. Maybe he'd been kidnapped. They needed to call the Defenders. They—

"You're an awful lot of work for one man."

Mercy swallowed hard. Her father hadn't run away. She wouldn't believe that. She shook it off, playing with the keychain in her pocket.

"We're almost there," Cole called. "He still hasn't responded to my message."

Mercy glanced at Ray. He was tense, staring at his boots as they walked. Ray was usually the upbeat, annoyingly encouraging one. How was she supposed to do the same?

She remembered flowers had always been her father's favorite. She'd collect them from the back fields of the motel as a child.

Flowers won't make Ray feel better, she scolded herself.

Cole stopped in front of one of the beaten-down brown stucco buildings, insisting that Felicity let him carry her up the stairs.

Cole had grown up…here?

Mercy followed the others up the concrete steps to the second level. Cole set Felicity back on her feet. He pressed his thumb against the sensor, and the door clicked open.

They hurried inside. Thunder shook the sky above.

The "house" hardly consisted of much more than room. A kitchenette was connected with a greater living room, a small table and two chairs, and two doors, one open to reveal a tiny bathroom.

Cole's Comm notification dinged.

Ray jumped back, nearly ramming into Mercy's shoulder.

Cole pulled out his Comm. He gave a long sigh. "He's off on a work trip this weekend. He said it's fine if we stay here."

Ray leaned up against the wall, catching his breath. Mercy hesitated a moment before placing a gentle hand on his arm.

He flinched and instantly, her face heated. She stepped away.

"We should be looking for food," Cole said, crossing his arms. "I don't think my dad will have enough for the ten…" He stopped himself. "…nine of us."

"Is there anywhere near here?" Tabitha asked, pulling out her tele.

Mercy zoned them out, dropping her bag at the door and sneaking off toward the bathroom. She closed the door behind her, taking a deep breath. She flinched as she turned to see herself in the mirror. She'd traveled with a dirty streak on her face. She quickly rushed to scrub her face clean.

She stopped, looking up to meet her reflection in the mirror.

Her face looked slimmer, and her curls were in desperate need of proper treatment. Her shirt was wrinkled, stained with blood on the collar of her hoodie.

She didn't look like a Council Member.

You're hardly even pretty compared to the others. She shook herself. That wasn't fair.

She opened the bathroom door. The apartment was mostly empty now. Felicity sat on the weathered couch, her braces charging.

"You doing alright, Mercy?" she said with a kind smile.

Mercy only managed a nod before she made her way through the kitchen and out the sliding door to the tiny balcony. She took in a deep breath of the dirty Sulfur air.

But it was still better than being cooped up inside with her feelings.

"Glow Girl?"

Mercy's heart jumped so high she thought it was going to topple her off the edge. She spun around to see Ray huddled in the corner of the balcony. "Rapheal? What are you doing here? You-you didn't go shopping with everyone else?"

He shrugged. "I didn't feel like it."

His eyes drifted down to the street below.

Mercy swallowed hard. *You can't comfort him! You mess every-*

thing up. He's not really your friend—

Mercy sat down beside Ray, squished between the wall and the railing. "Do you want to…talk about it?"

Ray didn't say anything. He rested his head against the wall.

She sat in silence beside him, just happy he didn't tell her to leave.

"I could've lived here," he said quietly. "I could've lived with him."

"Did you want to?"

Ray hesitated, meeting her eyes for a moment before looking away. "I-I guess I wanted a dad."

"You can still have one," Mercy said, quietly.

"I know." Ray hugged his legs and drew them to his chest. "Mercy?"

His voice dropped to a whisper.

"Yes?"

"I'm scared. I'm scared to meet him again."

Something about Ray's trembling eyes looking into hers made her heart twist. Ray, the bubbly, outgoing, always-dives-in-headfirst Member, was scared.

"I'm scared he won't like me," Ray admitted. "Why would he? The only thing I've done is be under Kathryn's mind control. I haven't done anything heroic or noteworthy. I don't know why I care so much. I-I just want him to be proud of me."

Mercy was speechless. Ray thought he wasn't worthy? "Ray. You *are* a hero. And even if you weren't, he should love you regardless. You're his son. And you're witty, loving, and always trying to do the right thing. If he won't realize that, then he's not worth it."

Ray peeked out from his arms. "Where did that come from, Glow Girl?" he said, trying to crack a joke, but Mercy could hear the emotions cracking in his voice instead.

"You'll never know until you face him," Mercy said, squeezing his shoulder.

Ray was quiet for a moment. "I guess you're right, Glow Girl."

Mercy felt like she really could glow. *You'll never know until you face it.*

Who was she to talk? All she'd done this entire trip was

run from her fears of the Council, and it had all ended in disaster.

Not again.

No more running. She was going to find that Aguarious Stone.

"You really look like a real Council Member with that mischievous smile." He gave her a friendly shove.

Mercy hadn't even realized she'd started smiling. She dropped it, tempted to hide in her hair. *A real Council Member?* "I-I'm working on it."

"That's the attitude."

Ray raised up his fist. "Here's to working on it."

She couldn't help another smile, pumping his fist. "Working on it."

39

"Zita's house is only a ten-minute walk from here," Nikki said by Comm light. The girls sat in the kitchen, their voices whispers as the boys had fallen asleep over an hour ago, and even Tabitha was dozing.

Mercy was simply happy to be included, and after her talk with Ray, she had the tiniest smidge of…hope. Maybe she could do this.

Just maybe.

"So we get there. We look for Stone. We go?" Felicity asked.

"Seems simple," Nikki said.

"Too simple." Ray's voice came from the darkness.

Mercy's heart leaped as she spun on him. "You're supposed to be asleep," she hissed at him.

He sat up, pushing away his blanket, letting his dark hair fall in his eyes that were focused on the floor. "Can't sleep."

"Because this your…Da's house?" Nikki lifted her head.

Mercy didn't understand how she could have such sadness in her wide eyes. The girl didn't even know her parents, yet she looked pained.

Ray glanced up with a sigh. "That's off topic. Back to Mercy's fantastic plan."

"That didn't sound sincere."

"Am I ever sincere?" A half-hearted smirk rose on his lips. "Once you get to Zita's place, how will you get back in time to catch your Rail?"

Mercy paused, frowning.

He had a point.

"Um…" Mercy looked to Nikki for support, but she only shrugged. "Call a bot to ring a taxi?"

"Wrong!" Ray said in an obnoxious, over-the-top voice. "You're late for Rail. You're late to Liberty, and the Bentsworths burn you at the stake!"

He jumped out at her, but she swatted him in the face and he fell back to his seat. She rolled her eyes.

"Fine. I guess I don't really know how we'll get back on time," she admitted begrudgingly.

Now, a real smile lifted Ray's head. "How nice is it that your good ol' bestie can teleport?"

"But if he teleports, we have to bring him with us?" Tabitha said, who apparently wasn't asleep, and Mercy tried not to groan.

"What? And you don't want my hot face with you at all times?" Ray said with a fake whimper.

"Why are you hot?" Nikki frowned. "It's kinda cold in here."

"No—I mean—Nikki, why are you like this?"

"Like what?"

Mercy swallowed down a laugh with a cough. "Ray thinks he's good-looking."

Nikki pursed her lips as she studied Ray a moment without saying a word.

"So, am I?" Ray said, leaning forward.

She shrugged. "You look like Ray."

"What is that supposed to mean?" Ray groaned.

"It means go to sleep," Tabitha said with a yawn. She plopped down on her pillow. "If you sleep, we'll take you."

"This is my mission. I get to decide if Ray goes or not," Mercy said.

It was petty to argue with Tabitha, she knew it, and she

went warm remembering Ray was watching. He didn't look much like his brother, but he still reminded her of Cole's kindness and faith in her.

And here she was still being rude, unfeeling Mercy who pushed people away.

But that Mercy felt safer.

But that Mercy gets people killed.

"So, do I get to go or not?" Ray said, turning to Mercy with an exaggerated smile, and pleading eyes.

Mercy sighed. "Fine. You can go. But sleep, like Tabitha said."

"Can't guarantee that," Ray said, his smile faltering as the lantern shut off as Tabitha kicked the sensor.

"Just think about happy things," Nikki said.

"It's not that simple, Nik." Ray's voice became quieter.

Mercy sank down, settling her head on her pillow. Ray was right. Happy thoughts didn't make anything better. Every night, she would still see her grandmother's face. She'd still wake up in a cold sweat just to make sure Grandmere hadn't found her. She would still think of her father's face, wondering what her grandmere had done with him, and trying to remember her mother's eyes…and not the image of her blood sprayed against the back wall of the motel.

Nikki sighed in the dark. "No, but it's better than letting the nightmares smother you."

Her voice echoed through Mercy's mind as she drifted off to sleep.

Mercy didn't take Nikki's advice, and therefore was already awake before the sun had fully risen.

She threw off her blanket, finally having enough of staring at the ceiling. She rubbed her eyes, looking around carefully. The boys were spread out around the main room. Not a single one stirred.

Ray was closest to her, and to her relief, it looked like he had managed to fall asleep, his cheek against the pillow, his black hair fallen across his face. His expression was relaxed, showing the dark circles underneath his eyes.

She hesitated before kicking him.

Ray's eyes opened as if he'd never been asleep at all, wincing in the light. "What do you want?" he said, his voice cracking as he rolled over to cover his face.

Mercy shushed him, crawling over to shake his shoulders. "This mission, remember?"

Ray froze a moment before dropping his hands from his face with a dramatic sigh. He sat up quickly, scrubbing his face. "Right. Get the others ready.."

He didn't give Mercy another moment before getting to his feet for the tiny bathroom, expertly jumping over his sleeping friends without a creak.

Mercy woke up the others. Nikki was a light sleeper and woke up without Mercy even having to say a word. Tabitha utterly refused to accept being awake, and it took Felicity to soothe her awake.

They were dressed quickly.

A Comm message lit up as Mercy reached for her backpack.

MESSAGE FROM MATHEWS*

I'm outside. Meet me at the bottom of the stairs.

Getting an early start at teleporting, she guessed. She ushered the other three after her and they snuck out the front door. Immediately, Mercy felt the Sulfur chill as it crawled through her skin. The sky was gray and the streets were quiet, besides a few tired and not entirely sober Foundation Field workers going about. She spotted Ray on the sidewalk at the bottom of the stairs, and she rushed down to meet him.

Ray turned to greet them, tucking away his Comm. "You all ready for this?" he said excitedly.

"I still don't get why we're doing this," Tabitha grumbled.

Felicity elbowed her.

"What? It just seems far-fetched," Tabitha shrugged. "How are you feeling anyway? You sure it's worth using your energy for?"

"I'm charged enough," Felicity said, adjusting her headband, moving to Mercy with a squeeze to her shoulder. "Besides, even if it turns out to be nothing…it'll be a cool trip?"

Mercy didn't want to waste anyone's time, especially Felicity's. If they wasted her leg brace's power…she would be unable to move herself until they got to Liberty.

She smiled back for Felicity's sake.

"Are you sure you can teleport us there?" Nikki asked, pushing forward.

"I know where it is."

"You've been?"

"Well, I saw it on a map and that's good enough." When they all gave him a long stare, he sighed. "I did it with Algery six months ago, remember?"

Tabitha groaned.

"Well, let's hope it works," was all Mercy could muster with a shaky laugh.

"Great!" Ray said, holding out his hands. "Time to grab on and enjoy the ride."

"Enjoy is maybe the wrong word," Nikki said as she grabbed hold of Ray's shoulder.

Mercy blushed as Ray quickly grabbed her hand, but she didn't wrench away for the pure purpose of transportation. He took Felicity's hand and looked around excitedly. "Ready?"

"Just try not to rip us into a billion pieces in the Void," Tabitha sighed.

Mercy's stomach flipped. "Wha—"

Before she knew it, her thoughts no longer made sense. Her head was spinning and so was the world around her. And then she hit the ground.

She toppled over, her hand slipping from Ray's, nausea rocking over her. It wasn't as bad as her first time, but it was awful.

It took a moment to get in deep breaths of fresh air as she looked at their new surroundings. Fields of lilacs grew in the quiet along the dirt road.

And then a small, weather-beaten house with a holographic sign floating nearby.

Ray helped her up. "Not exactly what I was expecting when I thought 'famous Curatrix member house.' Even the Aguirres had a bit more security."

She was surprised too. "Hopefully we're at the right place?"

They all exchanged glances and moved down the road. The sign glitched, but the closer they got the more clearly it read "The Residence of Zita Klirkpatrick" and in small print below "Walk-Ins Welcome!"

"Not like the Aguirre residence at all," Nikki said quietly. "We needed government passes to get into my own house."

Her laugh was quiet and distant.

Zita's house was simple. It was painted a light blue with white trim and a wrap-around porch. It hadn't been cared for much, weather slowly eating away at the board-and-shingled roof.

A middle-aged man sat in the tiny booth set up out front.

He perked up, seeing them approach. "I didn't hear anyone coming," he said with a bubbly laugh as he leaped to his feet. "Do you have an appointment?"

"N-no," Mercy stammered out.

"Would you like a tour?" he asked excitedly, grabbing a stack of mini projector frames.

"No tour needed," Felicity said, stepping forward and opening her tele, showing the man.

His face went white. "You're-you're— Oh my goodness, it's an honor to meet a Bentsworth! Let me tell you, your sister's net channel is amazing, and oh my your—"

"We'll just take our own tour," she said, holding her hand out for the projector frames.

He handed her the frames, and she dug a few coins from her pocket, which made him even more ecstatic. "Feel free to go in. Don't touch anything signs say not to, but I'm sure you knew that." He stood half-frozen in starstruck awe.

Felicity gave a queasy smile before they rushed to the porch of the Zita residence, handing out the projector frames. The frames were the same size of a tablet, but with a double tap to the side, a much cheaper hologram filled the frame.

The tour guide looked like it was typed up in an amateur online document creator, with an awkward font and the photo of Zita taking up most of the front page.

Not that Mercy minded that.

The photo of Zita had a beauty to it. It was her official Defender portrait Mercy had seen a hundred times. Zita was smiling brilliantly, her long blue braids to the side, her jacket fit perfectly to her small frame.

"So, any of you ever been before?" Tabitha asked, daring to be the first to push the door open.

All of them quietly responded with a *no*.

They stepped inside. It was remarkably clean. Almost everything was plastered with red signs screaming "DON'T

TOUCH."

"It looks like they preserved literally everything," Ray whispered, looking at a cased display of a broken set of dishes and a smashed chair.

It felt wrong to even speak in a place like this.

A place where...

"Nikki," Felicity hissed. "You can't go upstairs."

Nikki only looked at Felicity before leaping over the red sign and creeping up the steps.

"What have you all done to our sweet, innocent Nikki?" Felicity sighed.

"She might be onto something," Tabitha said. "She knows Curatrix better than all of us."

Literally.

Mercy took a deep breath and followed Nikki upstairs. Her heart pounded in her chest. Breaking rules wasn't Mercy's thing. It wasn't even her grandmother's rule, but she still felt guilty.

The upper level was tiny, with only two doors with a small hall and window in between.

Mercy opened one door and was stopped with the youthfulness of it.

Posters of an unfamiliar MEDIA star were taped to a mirror. A hand sewn rug was on the floor, and a stack of tablets collected dust by the window.

She glanced down at her hologram frame, swiping through.

Kate Oowatie - OHS Resident of Zita Klirkpatrick.

A photo of a teenaged girl, dated over a decade ago, was shown. She had short hair and clips to hold her overgrown bangs. Her face showed indifference, and her clothes were creatively put together in a hand-stitched fashion.

The girl Zita had almost adopted. Her heart clenched in her chest. It all made sense. Zita had been in the OHS herself as a child, and she was very involved in the program.

And she'd almost given another child a home.

"I can't find a sign of an Aguarious Stone anywhere," Nikki said, rushing out of the room.

"You guys almost done?" Ray called from below. "Your Rail leaves in less than twenty minutes."

Mercy knew she'd been too hopeful in thinking this

would be easy.

She rushed down the steps. "Search the cupboards," she ordered.

No one argued, rushing to break even more rules. The cupboards were mostly empty besides plates and dishes, a singular blue coffee cup that looked to be routinely used, and a few holo chip games.

Nothing.

Mercy's heart pounded as she pulled out her frame, flipping through the pages. Where else could it be?

The pages stopped flipping.

DEATH SITE

Mercy's heart leaped, her eyes slowly trailing out the window to the lilac fields. She didn't bother to read the description. She raced out the back door.

"Mercy!"

She bounded down the steps, her heart beating in her chest, trying not to think about the fact that this must have been the very path Zita was dragged along to her death.

She heard the others race after her.

She narrowed her eyes. She could see a hologram marker up ahead. Her heart hammered in her chest. She broke through the last of the lilacs out into the clear.

HERE ZITA KLIRKPATRICK TOOK HER LAST BREATH.

SHE NOW LIES IN LIBERTY.

Mercy sank to the ground, catching her breath, before panicking and scrambling back up to her feet and wiping the dirt off her hands. She knew it had been a decade, but the ground still felt so unholy.

"Oh…" Tabitha's soft voice approached from behind.

No one dared speak a word.

Mercy slowly lifted her frame.

Zita Klirkpatrick was killed behind her home in Sulfur, and plans were made for her to be buried there. Upon special request of the OHS, she was buried near OHS's main base in Liberty.

Mercy shut off the machine with a sigh. "A dead end."

"Her gravesite might be our second chance," Felicity said, looking to Mercy with a squeeze of her shoulder. "Don't give up."

"We're running out of time. Nathaniel doesn't have much

longer…and how are we even going to get in there? I imagine it's pretty heavily guarded."

"Why weren't the Curatrix buried where they were requested?" Ray asked suddenly, cutting Mercy off.

Nikki squirmed at the mention of it.

Her family had been buried near their house in Algery, but from what Mercy had seen, it wasn't impressive. Odd, considering Agent Reyna Wents Aguirre had been one of the most publicized.

"We'll find a way," Felicity sighed, though her face was pinched. "I hope."

"Guys, your Rail leaves in ten minutes, and Cole's probably going to kill me if we don't show up like right now."

They began to head off, but Mercy couldn't help but look back over the haunted lilac field.

A lead should have excited Mercy, but instead she just felt the pit in her stomach growing deeper.

The brutal murders. The orphaned children. The screwed-up burials.

Who had done this to the Curatrix Team?

She kneeled down, tearing out a bunch of flowers. She turned and raced back toward the grounds and beside Ray, who was lagging behind.

"You good, Glow Girl?"

Mercy held out the bunch of flowers, her throat too tight to try and explain herself.

Ray blinked. "For me?"

Mercy cleared her throat, nodding. "I-I— Uh. My father used to like flowers when he was upset."

So dumb. What are you thinking?

Ray's face softened, taking the lilacs from her hands. A small smile crept on his lips. "Thanks, Mer. That's really sweet."

Mercy's face heated. "Really?"

Ray gave her a side hug. "Just relax, Glow Girl."

It was easier said than done…but she tried to listen and take a deep breath.

No more mistakes.

No more blood.

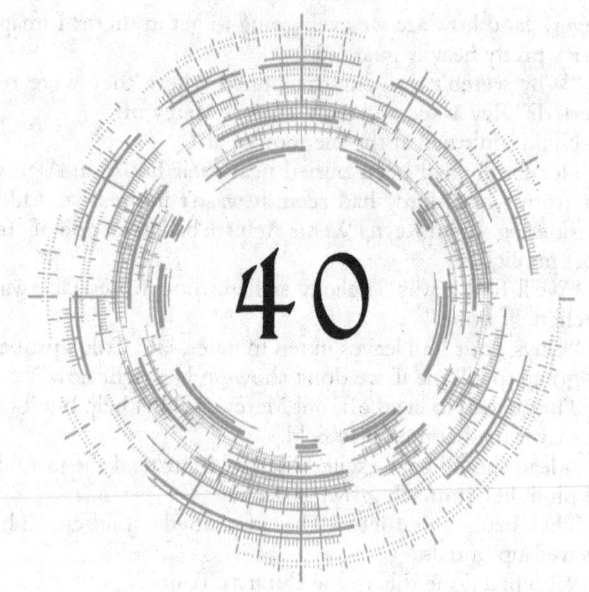

40

LINCOLN HUGGED NIKKI so hard that he lifted her off her feet.

She wheezed for air, giving Lincoln a pat on the back before he set her back down. She knew it was taking everything for him to stay composed. His face was stone cold, but she knew it was only to make sure nothing else slipped.

He clutched the torn stuffed monkey in one hand as he took a deep breath. "If you find him before I get there, give this to him for me."

Nikki took it gently. "I will."

"Stay safe."

She would be getting Nathaniel back. At any cost.

Lincoln only managed a small nod as he let her hand go, and Nikki ran for the Rail after tackling Lawrence with a surprise hug.

She leaped through the doors, which shut quickly behind her.

She pressed herself against the window, watching the large, ragged group of teenage boys grow further and further away until they were plunged into a dark tunnel, racing far away from the region of Sulfur.

"I hope Ray gets the kitten to North Cordell safely," Mercy said, quietly.

"I hope so," Tabitha snickered. "I bet he's going to have some trouble babysitting an ice-powered kitten."

That part was true.

Nikki was amused by the idea.

"So what's the new plan?" Tabitha plopped down in her seat, tapping her knees.

Nikki turned to face the crammed car, squeezing into the bench beside Mercy. "We find Nathaniel."

"And the Agurarious Stone," Mercy said.

"And the Leviathan, and whatever Silas is doing," Felicity added.

Tabitha blinked. "Okay…uh…that's a lot."

"They're all connected," Nikki said. "To an Agurarious."

"But how to find any of them?"

"The Exerticus are connected to Silas," Felicity said. "I saw him with the Exerticus, Sergia."

"And we know for a fact Sergia is with—" Tabitha's voice lowered. "—Kathryn."

"And the Agurarious Stone could help us find both of them," Mercy said. "If it's connected to Nathaniel."

"Alright, so first priority is finding the Agurarious Stone to find Nathaniel…and uh…hope that the storm Kathryn is forcing Craig the sea monster to make isn't a big deal?" Felicity forced a smile.

"Real foolproof plan we have there," Tabitha joked.

"I think it's alright," Nikki said, trying to lift the mood.

"We just have to really hope that the Leviathan won't destroy anything, and we'll be fine?" Tabitha said.

"I like that idea."

Tabitha sighed.

Felicity took a deep breath. "Let's take it one world-ending crisis at a time, shall we?"

Nikki could see Felicity's hands beginning to shake. She reached out to clasp hers on top with a small smile. "One crisis at a time."

Nikki had only been to two Golden Regions in her memory,

though she wasn't sure if Imperial counted since it had been burning down then.

Even stepping out into the Liberty SpeedRail station, the air felt fancier.

Everyone around had bright shades and uptight looks. Pencil skirts and colorful pants and colored hair twisted up, or in what seemed like a very popular style of bob.

Nikki sat straight, paranoid that any wrong move would cause her disfigurer device to glitch and reveal her face.

Tabitha froze as she stepped out, her eyes searching the place.

Nikki was startled. She'd never seen Tabitha like this. "Are you alright?"

Tabitha jumped, taking a moment to settle on Nikki. "Y-yeah. I'm fine. Let's just get moving."

She pushed past her quickly, her head down.

Nikki exchanged a confused look with Mercy.

What was into her? Another dream?

Nikki decided against asking, and she and Mercy followed Felicity up the enormous staircase to the doors. Felicity had drawn up her hood of the jacket Lawrence had lent her before they left. Nikki slipped in front of her to help her cover.

Her jaw dropped as they pushed through the glass doors.

The city was literally sparkling. It was nothing like she'd ever seen. Clean autos gliding on multiple air space levels, the streets full of the same sparkly people, and buildings that soared into the artificial blue sky.

"Gross," Tabitha mumbled, her nose wrinkled. "The air is so stale…"

She had a point. While it was refreshing, it was nothing like a breeze back in North Cordell or Algery.

A flash through her mind.

Sitting among the trees, closing her eyes, taking in the sun and mountain air.

Nikki blinked the flashback away.

It wasn't the time.

With you, it's never time, Avalon grumbled.

Nikki didn't respond. "How long until we get to your house?" she asked Felicity.

"Manor," Tabitha corrected.

"A fifteen-minute walk," Felicity said, her voice becoming very small. "Fifteen minutes to not get recognized."

They stood out like a sore thumb in their weather-beaten travel clothes, jeans, and long hair.

But Nikki couldn't help but stare right back at the eyes they attracted.

They thought she looked weird? Did they see themselves? It was so impractical to walk around in a skirt that hugged your legs to the point of shuffling around.

But it did look fun.

"How far are the docks from your house?" Nikki asked, pulling the strings of her hoodie.

"Close enough to run to," Tabitha chortled. "We'd escape homework sessions to watch the submarines."

"You can see the ocean?" Mercy frowned. "What about the Dome?"

"The Dome actually reaches about a mile or two out into the ocean," Felicity explained. "That way it keeps the docks, the ships, and the submarines safe."

The crowd started to thin out, and the road became more windy. A cool little arc went over the road, a few men standing around it with thick sunglasses.

A man dressed in a white suit grabbed her shoulder. "This is a restricted area."

She almost punched him, but Felicity pulled her back, whipping out her tele. "Felicity Bentsworth. Nineteen. Liberty."

The man's eyebrows raised as he scanned her tele.

Felicity held her breath as it dinged.

"I'm so sorry, madam," the man said with a small bow, shouting over to his fellow guards to grab an auto. "We'll inform your family of your arrival...and these are?"

"Mercy Remembrance. Sixteen. Kennedy," Felicity said, looking to Mercy. "Oh, and of course, Tabitha Delorous. Seventeen. Liberty."

Tabitha cringed.

"And—" Felicity stopped on Nikki. "—Nikki. Unknown last name. Sixteen. North Cordell."

Nikki Aguirre. Sixteen. Algery.

The man didn't dare question Felicity, tapping all the information quickly into his wristband.

A strange auto sped through the arc. It looked like a cart a few farmers had, but it was bigger, painted a shimmery white, with padded seats and a roof. They loaded up into the back row of the cart. There was enough room for them to spread out, but it felt safer to huddle together.

Felicity still kept her hood up, and Tabitha kept her eyes down.

Mercy and Nikki both seemed to have an equal awe as the enormous white manor pulled into view.

The cart stopped in front of the massive doors. Men in the white suits scrambled to form themselves for the unexpected arrival.

Felicity couldn't have cared less, rejecting the hand as she stepped out of the cart. She stood up straight, taking hold of Tabitha's arm as they walked up the steps.

Nikki and Mercy didn't say a word, racing to keep up after them.

Nikki couldn't believe her eyes as the door opened.

Enormous windows. A fountain in the middle of the room. Three staircases leading to glass elevators. Her footsteps echoed as she walked across the pristine marble floor.

This was more magnificent than the Outowns' by far. Nikki felt right out of one of the fancy palaces in Kathryn's flashbacks.

She shuddered at that thought.

While pretty, those palaces had been filled with blood, death, and vengeance…and a society that had driven Kathryn over the edge.

She shook it away.

A woman stood right in front of the indoor fountain, dark purple hair drawn up in an impossibly tight bun. She gave a small bow. "Miss Bentsworth. Miss Delorous."

"Renee?" Tabitha gasped. "Holy cow. She still works here?"

Felicity raced up to the woman to grab her hands. "We need help."

"I assumed. You don't come to visit twice in a row by your own will," the woman said.

Tabitha laughed. "And her jokes are still as stale as ever." She nudged Nikki. "You'd get along."

The woman, Renee, eyed Tabitha. "It is good to see you

too, Miss Delorous. And good to see you ditched your purple."

Tabitha ran her hands through her short hair. "Yeah, it turns out I know a really good barber."

"And I've seen you've made quite the mark on recent MEDIA news stories."

Tabitha went red. "Oh, really?"

"The fireworks stunt? Impressively stupid."

"I'll pretend that was a compliment."

Renee gave an amused smile before her eyes settled on Nikki and Mercy. "I don't believe we've met. Renee Kitts," she said, holding out a hand.

Nikki high-fived it. "Nikki."

The woman frowned at her. "Nice to meet you Miss… Nikki?"

"Her last name is confidential…actually, it's worse than confidential," Felicity said, squeezing Nikki's shoulder and looking at her. "It's okay. We can trust her."

"Uh, Liz…" Tabitha started.

"What's confidential?"

Nikki spun around, her breath caught in her throat at the sight of a young teenage girl sitting on the railing to the staircase. She was no doubt a Bentsworth, with her fiery red hair swept up in a purple bandana and purple lipstick.

Everyone was frozen.

"Great," Tabitha sighed under her breath.

The girl jumped down from the stair railing, her eyes widening. "Felicity? You're back? Where's your Mullet Defender?" She spun to Tabitha. "And Tabitha? Liz, did you bring Cole here too? Who's this? Isn't it kinda hot to be wearing a jacket? And why is her last name confidential? Wait, is that the girl from—?"

Nikki's sweat went cold.

"Veronica, shush!"

This girl talked more than Ray.

"Uh, hi Veronica," Tabitha said before Felicity could process. "This is Mercy, and that's Nikki."

"Wait. Didn't she die?"

Renee gaped. "What?"

"I did die," Nikki said.

"Only for two weeks," Felicity butted in.

"But now she's not," Tabitha said.

Veronica and Renee had identical twisted faces.

"Anyway." Felicity cleared her throat. "I'm back on important business. They're here to help, and that's all. I don't intend to be here long."

Veronica had completely tuned Felicity out and was staring at Nikki with her mouth hanging open. Nikki tried to pretend she didn't notice. Was she going to turn her in?

"You're emphasizing the 'not here long' because you intend to tell me not to have you meet with your parents, isn't that right, Miss Bentsworth?"

Felicity's face reddened, her eyes falling for a moment. "Renee, I—ah!"

"Felicity!"

Felicity stumbled back with a pained cry.

Nikki rushed to support her. Felicity squeezed her, taking in a deep breath.

"She can't be on her braces too long," Mercy said quickly. "She needs a wheelchair."

"I can do that," Renee sighed. "You're not getting out of this conversation, Miss Bentsworth. I will be informing them of your arrival."

Even in her pain, Felicity managed a scowl.

"Miss Veronica, please assist them and keep from chitter-chatting about this," Renee said with a sharp nod and turn.

"I don't chitter-chat," Veronica said, in a mock impression of Renee's accent, before spinning to face them again. "Right this way! Man, this is so epic!"

Nikki wouldn't exactly call helping a limping Felicity to a floating caged elevator "epic."

The cage gave a small swing as the five of them stepped inside. Veronica's fingers flew over the keyboard before turning with a mischievous brow. "Now, last time you lugged a friend here, our Manor got broken into and you got really mad at Mom and Dad for some reason…and now you're with three."

"It's not your business, Vers," Tabitha said.

"Please. I helped your Cole friend through his whole mission. I'm qualified for secrets." Veronica gave a puppy dog pleading smile.

The girls exchanged looks.

Nikki, for one, found the girl suspicious, not in the 'she works for Kathryn' way, but in a way she couldn't figure out. All the purple, a chain hanging around her neck with the number 53…

"Maybe later. Just pretend like we're here on vacation having lots of tourist fun," Felicity said, rubbing her forehead.

"Tourist?" Veronica's eyes lit up. "I can help with that!"

"Tourist what?" Nikki said.

"Girl-who's-supposed-to-be-dead-and-has-a-confidential-last-name, Liberty is the best tourist experience you're ever going to get," Veronica said with a wink.

A ding went off and the elevator came to a stop. The opposite doors opened up, revealing a large, lit, marble-floored hall.

Felicity nudged her forward, and Nikki stepped out onto the immaculate floor.

"Are-are you all staying in Felicity's room?" Veronica said with a frown as Tabitha and Mercy unloaded after them. "We have guest rooms up a level."

They all looked to Felicity.

After being crammed into a trailer with ten people, nothing felt too small. An empty room meant more time for memories.

Memories she couldn't fight.

"They'll all stay here," Felicity said.

"Am I invited to your epic sleepover?" Veronica gasped, a teasing glimmer in her eye.

Felicity snorted but followed with an almost endeared, "Maybe later, Onica."

"That wasn't a no."

Felicity turned, leaning off of Nikki's support.

Veronica moved to click a button before her eyes met Nikki's. "I've got my eye on you."

Before Nikki could say a word, the elevator door shut.

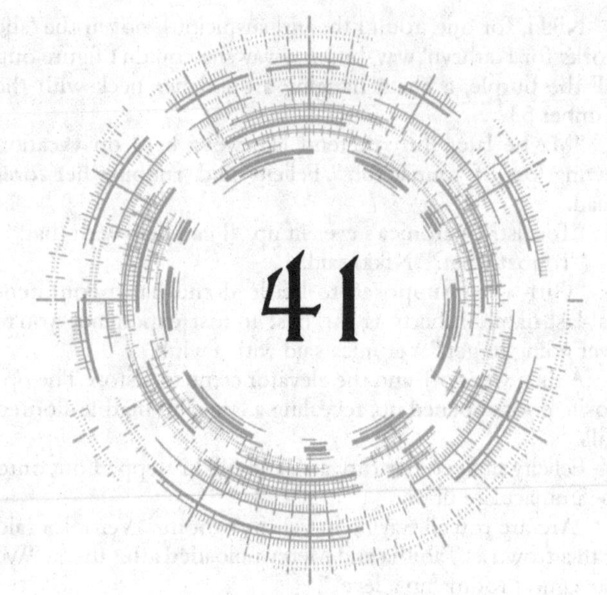

41

TABITHA WAS USED to Felicity being anxious.

She was used to the long rambles, the occasional crying, and the frustrated rants. She was used to calming her down.

But what she wasn't used to was Felicity trying to hide it.

She could see the all too familiar fear in her friend's eyes as she stared at her tele, sitting on the couch by the window of her parlor.

Tabitha had also forgotten just how big Felicity's room… or rooms…were. After sharing a room with Felicity and Nikki for six months, this seemed like a whole house.

Tabitha sat in the doorway to the hallway, waiting for Mercy and Nikki to come back, who had gone to join Renee for some security check-in and to retrieve a wheelchair for Felicity.

Tabitha trusted Renee, but Nikki's identity was too much to risk…especially right now.

She looked back to Felicity, whose head dropped, tossing her tele aside.

Tabitha's heart skipped a beat, and she got to her feet.

"Are you alright, Liz?"

Felicity looked up, startled. Tabitha made her way across the room, sitting next to Felicity on the bench. "Is-is it about your family?"

"No," Felicity said quietly, her eyes falling down to her hands.

"Oh."

"I mean my mom did…reach out." Felicity's hands hardened to fists.

"Did you respond?"

"How am I supposed to?" Felicity scowled. "Oh, hi mom! I just found out you're not human…which you've somehow hid my entire life. And now I'm also half-not-human-shape-shifter. Let's hug it out?"

She buried her face in her hands and groaned.

"I'm sorry, Liz."

"It's fine," Felicity sighed, dropping her hands. "Besides, I'm trying not to think about it."

"Then what's actually bothering you?"

Felicity's face reddened as she slowly turned to look at Tabitha. "The Defenders."

Right. Tabitha hadn't heard anything about the trial since Sinni's. "How's that going?"

"Giles said it's not looking so great," Felicity said, tugging on a loose strand of hair. "I-I'm afraid…this is my fault."

Tabitha frowned. "Felicity, what? How could this possibly be your fault? Mullet Man is responsible for his own screw ups."

Felicity flinched. "He mentioned knowing something…-something acting Commander Dean forbade him from mentioning. He-he said he could be executed for it."

"And somehow that's your fault?"

"I just feel like it's too coincidental. It's like he was trying to warn me and I didn't see it soon enough."

Tabitha was about to send another jab at Giles before she saw a glimmer of tears in Felicity's eyes, and her face softened. She placed a hand on Felicity's. "Hey, Liz. Don't cry. Don't worry. Giles isn't going to die. He's too stubborn for that."

Felicity squeezed Tabitha's hand. "I keep telling myself that. I keep trying to think about that creature…anything I can help to distract from the fact there is absolutely nothing I can do to help him."

Rallie's words flashed through Tabitha's mind. The woman's lost, broken eyes that had seen more horrors than Tabitha could imagine, staring into her soul.

"You're doing the right thing," she said, looking into Felicity's eyes with a small smile. "And I think you have the right idea. Try and focus on what we can control."

"Like avoiding my mother."

"I mean…you do have a big enough house?"

Felicity smiled, a tear escaping down her cheek. "Good to know you'll always support bad decisions."

Tabitha laughed. "Isn't that what I'm here for?"

The ding of the elevator interrupted them as Renee's voice rang down the hall. "Miss Bentsworth, your chair has arrived."

Renee walked into the room, her hands on the handles of a basic wheelchair, nothing like the one Lincoln had put together with all its knacks and pockets, but Felicity seemed relieved nonetheless.

Nikki and Mercy followed, lanyards around their necks, and Nikki appeared totally fascinated by the card attached.

"Are you sure you'd all like to stay here?" Renee asked, looking around the room.

"It's fine," Mercy said, raising her voice.

"There's more than enough room," Felicity said, eagerly pushing herself forward in reach of the wheelchair.

"Could I at least get you all something to eat?"

"I'll take free food!" Tabitha leaped up, taking the wheelchair from Renee to glide over to Felicity, and spun back around to face Renee. "And don't forget the—"

"Hot sauce."

"Yes! Aw, you remembered."

"How could I forget?" Renee said with a sigh, turning for the door. "Please call if you need anything tonight, all of you."

"Wait!" Felicity called out from her new wheelchair.

Renee stopped.

"Did you see my mother?"

"She's out for the new harbor opening banquet, but I did inform her of your arrival."

Felicity gave a small nod, and Renee took that as a sign to leave. The room was quiet as they heard the creak of the elevator leave.

Tabitha coughed.

No one seemed to get the signal.

"You all are so stiff," she grumbled with a dramatic sigh.

"A two-year-old got kidnapped? An unkillable immortal is raising a sea monster from the ocean to flood the city?" Mercy raised a brow. "Not exactly a party."

Tabitha's eyes lit up. "Maybe that's exactly what we need. Tomorrow, we're visiting Zita's grave and searching for the Aguarious Stone."

"Tabitha, we're not throwing a party."

Tabitha ignored Felicity, throwing her arms around a confused Mercy's and Nikki's shoulders. "We're practically already having a sleepover, so why not make it fun?"

Mercy and Nikki both looked at her blankly.

"What's a sleepover?" Nikki whispered.

"Well now we have to do it," Tabitha said with a smile. "How about you, Mercy?"

"Never been," she said, stiffly, shifting out of Tabitha's arms.

This was going to be harder than Tabitha thought.

"Oh, come on Liz, you've had your fair share."

"You didn't like those very much," Felicity said, with a raise of an eyebrow.

That was true. Felicity invited a bunch of older girls who thought Tabitha was weird, which was probably true, and sat around playing games that often involved talking about boys they considered hot. It often ended in Tabitha sneaking off to play net games in Veronica's room.

"Yeah well, this is different. I actually like Mercy and Nikki," she said, crossing her arms. "It's a requirement now. No backing out."

Felicity laughed. "Fine."

"It sounds fun," Nikki chimed in. "Whatever it is."

"As long as we get food," Mercy shrugged.

Tabitha smirked. "You will not regret this."

Even Felicity's water felt rich.

Nikki wasn't sure if she'd ever felt so clean. The bathroom alone was two times bigger than their cabin. She walked out of the shower room wearing an oversized shirt and the baggy leggings Taryn had "gifted" her months ago, and she found Tabitha already making plans, which included a nervous-looking Mercy with Tabitha's hands in her hair.

"Are you sure you've got this?" Mercy said, looking up anxiously.

Tabitha removed a bobby pin from her teeth. "I'm doing exactly what you told me. Don't worry, Glow Girl."

Felicity rolled her eyes. "Don't worry, Mercy. I won't let Tabitha ruin your beautiful hair."

Felicity was right. Mercy's hair was nothing like Nikki had seen before. So long, and curled in tight coils that practically floated around her shoulders.

Apparently, Nikki had curls too like her cousin, Lawrence, but she was too impatient to sit down and figure them out. It was easier to just deal with fluff.

"Oh Nikki! You're done," Felicity said, patting the bench in front of her. "Tabitha said this was mandatory."

Nikki didn't mind it being forced. She always liked the feeling of hands in her hair…just as long as no memories came along with it this time.

"So any solid plan for Zita's grave?" Tabitha asked.

Nikki watched Mercy bite her lip. "We…uh…go in. See if the Stone is there. Take the stone."

"We're grave robbing?" Felicity said, startled.

"What? No! Yes…I mean…" Mercy took a deep breath. "I don't know."

Everyone was quiet.

"It's okay," Nikki said. "I don't know anything most of the time."

Mercy cracked a small smile. "Yeah, but you have a valid excuse."

"I don't think any of us grew up having to make life-saving mission plans," Felicity said with a comforting smile.

"Nope…that was all done for me." Mercy's voice was quiet as her eyes drifted off.

Mercy's grandmother.

Mercy was so quiet about where she came from that Nikki had hardly thought about it.

"Well, it's different now," Felicity said. "Now you're free

to make your own decisions…maybe too free."

Mercy's face fell again. "My father is still out there," she said. "I-I just…Never mind. It's selfish, seeing that Nathaniel is missing."

"It's not selfish to miss your family," Nikki said before she could stop her tongue.

What was she saying?

Did she even know?

Felicity nodded. "And I miss Veronica, even though I know where she is most of the time."

Mercy seemed to loosen with a small nod.

Tabitha's face remained firm on her job, without a word.

"Speaking of family, have you spoken to Mechanic—I mean Lucas—since Ray gave you his ID?" Mercy asked.

Tabitha's face twisted. "Not really."

"Lucas is great. He's helped me out ever since he moved to Kennedy," Mercy said, her eyes becoming lost to her mind. "I was twelve when he first moved in, and he helped me and Papa set up our first projector."

A smile escaped Tabitha. "He always did have a way with machines. He helped me set up a recording program on my tele, and we totally weren't allowed."

That was the first time Nikki had heard Tabitha speak somewhat positively about one of her brothers.

"And he used to drive you over here…also when you totally weren't allowed," Felicity teased.

Tabitha laughed. "Not sure if it was even legal."

Nikki couldn't help but also smile.

They finished up with Tabitha's hair expedition, and Mercy seemed to somewhat approve of Tabitha's curl job with an uneasy nod.

The next thing on Tabitha's mental list was building a fort, and much to Nikki's surprise, it was an ordeal that Mercy took very seriously. She instructed them to remove all the sofa cushions and helped Tabitha push over Felicity's desk from the window. Nikki was floored when she opened Felicity's *blanket* closet. Who needed a blanket in every color?

She chose every yellow blanket she could and returned to the fort making.

Art history tablets were fished from the shelves and used as weights to keep their blanket roof up. Tabitha found a string of purple fairy lights that seemed to have been stolen from Veronica and added the finishing touches.

Somehow, picking out a MEDIA film proved more difficult than building a pillow fort.

There was also a strict rule of no films with Tabitha's other brother, Clarence, in it. Everyone insisted Nikki couldn't do romance, and wouldn't answer her when she asked what that was. Tabitha suggested something called "horror," to which Mercy and Felicity heavily disagreed.

Finally, Felicity clicked off the projector.

"Any other ideas?"

"You're not very good at this, Delorous."

Tabitha threatened to chuck a pillow. She groaned. "Why are we so much better at running for our lives and fighting supernatural murderers than having a simple, classic sleep-over?"

"It seems much harder," Nikki said, inspecting a strange plate of what appeared to be potatoes and a strange orange sauce.

"Nacho potatoes," Tabitha explained. "I touched them up with my favorite spice as well."

"So you *can* cook," Nikki said, raising a brow.

"I'm a selective chef." Tabitha winked.

Nikki was still impressed, though from the taste she wasn't sure if she could live simply off this strange orange sauce.

"Any suggestions, Liz?" Tabitha said.

"Well, we typically did a game of pestering each other for secrets about our boy classmates. A less formal version of our dare and truth game." Felicity's face twisted. "Though I never liked it much."

"Gossiping about our boys isn't even fun," Tabitha said.

"Yadea thinks they're pretty swoon-worthy."

Mercy snorted. "Who?"

Nikki wasn't even sure why someone would even consider it. The male Council Members weren't exactly secretive or swoon worthy…just sleep deprived.

Felicity explained how she had an acquaintance who, per her last visit, had expressed some weird sentiments about Cole's looks.

"Yaeda was focused on the wrong Members," Tabitha

said. "We're obviously far superior. We have Glow Girl, a rich Bentsworth heiress, me who needs no explanation, and—" she lowered her voice to a comic whisper, "—a freaking Aguirre."

Nikki rolled her eyes. "Veronica might hear you."

"And then Veronica with her super hearing will come and snatch you up and keep you in her own personal case." Tabitha attempted to tickle Nikki, which just resulted in Tabitha being tackled off the bed.

The two girls collapsed onto the ground in laughter. Tabitha was fairly easy to pin to the ground. It wasn't like she gave much resistance.

"You're going to wake up the whole manor," Felicity said, obviously trying very hard to stay stern.

"Your room alone is bigger than our level in the Inn. I think we're fine," Tabitha said, shoving Nikki off of her.

Nikki happily collapsed to the ground. "So I'm guessing that game is a no?" she said, catching her breath. "Unless we all ask questions about Giles."

Felicity almost choked on a pretzel. "You don't know what you're asking." Felicity gagged, her face going red.

Nikki sat up. She didn't really. She was confused why her friends seemed to get so shaken when things like this came up.

"I'm worried about him," Felicity said, tugging on the end of her braid. "That's all. We have a big day tomorrow. We should get some sleep."

"Is this your way of avoiding the question?" Tabitha smirked.

Felicity deadpanned her.

"What if I dared you…"

"There's nothing to comment on," Felicity said.

"Well I guess that just means you lose the game and you don't get any of my hot nacho sauce."

Felicity's face was even redder now. "I-I don't know. We have so many more important things to prioritize, I haven't even *tried* to figure this out."

"Okay, let me adjust my dare." Tabitha cleared her throat. "If Giles survives, you two use your healthy adult communication skills and figure it out."

"I-I— Fine," Felicity said, defeated.

"Why are your feelings so complicated?" Nikki asked, raising a brow.

"Stay that way," Tabitha said.

"Are we going to sleep?" Mercy piped up.

"What? Do you not want to be questioned too?" Tabitha teased.

Mercy hid underneath a pillow.

Felicity chuckled, shaking her head. "Alright, now we really need to sleep."

Nikki couldn't help agreeing. As she hugged her knees to her chest, her eyes drifted around the room. She felt the strong air conditioning beat down on her, and the strong smell of chemical cleanser filled the room.

Not super comforting.

The chemical clean smell nagged at the back of her skull.

"We can all sleep in my bed," Felicity suggested.

Tabitha leaped her feet, tumbling over into Felicity's enormous bed. "Even better sleepover material!"

Nikki preferred the company of her friends than the empty space and eerily familiar smells.

She couldn't even imagine one person needing a bed this big. She tried to imagine a tiny Felicity sleeping here and not being lost, but it didn't fit.

With a quick voice command, Felicity shut off the lights.

The only light was the light seeping under the crack of the bathroom door. Nikki curled up under the covers, trying to focus on the breathing of the others.

Tabitha gave an enthusiastic goodnight, which got her another pillow from Mercy.

Tabitha was satisfied and the room was quiet.

Nikki's heart raced in her chest, but her entire body was heavy with exhaustion. She needed to find Nathaniel. She couldn't sleep. Stay awake. Stay alert.

If you sleep, they'll hurt you.

Her eyes drooped, ignoring the murky, shattered memories of the drowning and the shocks, and she let herself be comforted by the warm, familiar thoughts of her mother, just this once.

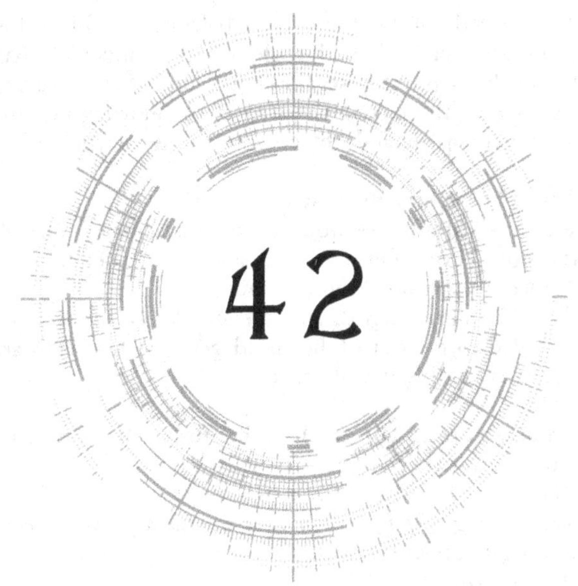

42

IT WAS RARE that Tabitha fell asleep without being woken up by the force of a nightmare.

But the buzz of her Comm might have been worse.

She didn't remember the last time her sleep had been so dreamless…so peaceful. All to be ruined by her Comm buzzing away on the dresser across the room. She wished she was still a heavy sleeper to have ignored it, but lying awake and staring at the ceiling while it went off would drive her insane. She wriggled out from under Felicity's arm, quietly slipping off the bed and creeping across the carpet to the dresser, snatching the Comm up.

4 MISSED CALLS FROM LUCAS

She snorted. Just her obnoxious older brother.

That's what she told herself. She wanted nothing to do with him or Clarence. And yet here she was, tempted to press on his voice message. She glanced back over her shoulder to her friends sleeping soundly in the bed.

She sighed.

Just delete it, Tabs.

She slipped out the doors to the balcony, careful to close them behind her. The marble tile was cold under her bare feet, and the night chill sent a shiver through her. Tabitha leaned against the balcony, staring at the glowing city that she'd grown up in and yet couldn't bring herself to call home.

It was home though, wasn't it?

She was Tabitha Delorous. Seventeen. Liberty. The obnoxious third born, never graceful and never quiet.

Why does that boy even like you?

Tabitha's heart leaped, and she shook off the thought. She needed to get out of her head. She grit her teeth and clicked on Lucas's voice message.

"Hey Tabby."

Tabitha's breath got caught in her throat. It was just her stupid older brother's voice.

"I know it's been a while since we've talked, but I know you've been getting my messages. Did you forget that a Comm notifies you when you see a message?" Lucas laughed.

Tabitha groaned. *Shoot.*

His tone grew more serious. *"I know none of us left on good terms…or at least, that's what Clarence told me about you."* He was quiet. *"Tabitha, I really wish I was there when you left."*

But he had been in Kennedy, where he'd left abruptly the year before when Tabitha was thirteen. All she knew was that it included a lot of yelling. She'd hidden under her bed, a pillow pressed so hard against her ear that it hurt to drown it out.

She never said goodbye to him, or to either of her brothers. Clarence probably didn't even care. And Lucas was regions away when she left after Felicity to North Cordell. She was surprised he even knew what region she'd ended up in.

"Then why weren't you?" she gritted through her teeth. No one could hear her, but the words festered to be spoken.

Lucas cleared his throat. *"Anyway, I'm in Liberty now. I-I had to get a new shipment that's been delayed for months in the harbor, so I just decided I might as well come and get it myself since Clarence suggested I just come stay here and pick it up myself—Anyway, I'm getting ahead of myself."*

Lucas was here? In Liberty?

"What I'm trying to say is that maybe you could visit too. I know

it's a far SpeedRail trip from North Cordell, but I'd be willing to help pay. This is a rare opportunity to maybe put some things in our family to rest."

Lucas wanted her to go visit their family again? All of them in the same place? For the first time in four years? The thought alone made her throat tighten up.

The nightmares echoed back.

"Just message me if you think you can come anytime soon. Yeah.... *Bye."*

The voice message ended abruptly, leaving Tabitha alone in the cold, shaking, and her mind louder than it had been before. She wanted to let the Comm slip from her hands and watch it fall to the ground far below and break into a million pieces.

Just say no. Get it over with. Leave them behind.

Why did she feel like she wanted to cry?

She scowled, trying to rub away the tears crowding in her eyes. "I'm fine," she told herself. "I'm totally, one hundred percent fine! I-I don't care! I don't care!"

But she did.

Hearing Lucas's voice again after all these years made her want to curl up like a child. She didn't like thinking about her family, and especially her brothers. It was too confusing.

She tore her fingers through her hair, trying to breathe. Why couldn't she breathe? Everything inside her felt tight. What was happening to her?

She couldn't let herself crack. She couldn't be soft. That wasn't her.

"Hey, are you okay?"

Tabitha's heart seized in her chest as she slowly turned to look over her shoulder to see Mercy standing at the doors to the balcony, hugging herself in the cold.

"How-how long have you been standing there?" Tabitha tried to snap, but she was out of breath.

"I just...I couldn't sleep," Mercy said, staring at her feet. "But-but I heard you crying—"

"I was not crying." Tabitha cleared her throat, crossing her arms. "I have no idea what you're talking about."

"It's okay," Mercy said, her eyes opening wider. "Just breathe, Tabitha. Take deep breaths. Focus on counting your breaths."

Tabitha wanted to snap at her, but she listened to Mercy's instructions, hugging herself tightly.

One. Two. Three. Four…Nineteen. Twenty.

"I'm okay," Tabitha stammered, turning her back to Mercy. "Thank you."

The two were quiet for a long moment.

"Look, I'm sorry for…contacting the Founder's Association," she said, her voice cracking. "You didn't have to keep it a secret. What I did was awful and I know it. I understand why you don't like me."

Tabitha stopped. Did Mercy think Tabitha was angry with her about that still?

"This doesn't—"

"My grandmother used to tell me I should keep my emotions to myself, and then I totally spiraled and thought maybe they'd give me the answers on why my powers weren't working. And I stole from Nikki, and I made you and Cole argue…and he was so nice to me and I didn't even deserve—"

"Mercy!"

Mercy stopped in her tracks, her eyes wide with fear.

Tabitha sighed. "I'm not mad at you."

Mercy blinked. "You-you're not?"

Tabitha felt too tired to try and make some snarky comment. She was having a hard enough time hiding the fact she was struggling to breathe as it was. She pushed herself up, sitting on the balcony railing. "I lost my temper. I do that a lot," she said, laughing hoarsely. "There were things I said I shouldn't have…. What you did was stupid and reckless, but I've done the same in the past. It's terrible that we're so young with so much power. It almost feels like we're not allowed to make mistakes."

"I lose my temper too," Mercy said quietly.

"Yeah, but it's okay. Just acknowledge the mistake, apologize, move on. Story of my life," Tabitha shrugged. "Just…don't contact sketchy groups again."

Mercy's eyes widened as if the information was brand new to her.

"You ever heard of making mistakes, Remembrance?" Tabitha laughed.

Mercy shook herself back into focus, clearing her throat.

"Yeah. Of course…"

Tabitha turned her back on Mercy, letting her legs hang dangerously off the edge. Not that it mattered. She'd done it many times before. The Bentsworth Manor had been more of a home to her than her own.

Her own home she would have to return to.

"Are you sure you're okay?"

Tabitha opened her mouth to respond, but she almost choked on her words. She nodded, clutching her Comm. She could feel Mercy walk to the end of the balcony, keeping her safe distance as she leaned on the railing beside her. "I'm not really good with feelings…if you want me to go away, I will."

"That makes two of us," Tabitha sighed.

"So something is wrong."

"Something is always wrong with us."

Mercy studied Tabitha intently, which was somewhat intimidating considering Mercy was a few inches taller. Finally, she looked away and back out into the night sky.

Mercy didn't say a word, and neither did Tabitha, but she silently enjoyed the company.

She took a deep breath, exhaling slowly like she used to instruct Felicity to do when she was panicking.

The irony.

"So you have grandma issues?" Tabitha said, turning to Mercy.

Mercy flinched. "If that's what you call them."

Tabitha shrugged. "I got mommy issues, daddy issues, and brother issues. The whole golden trio."

Mercy shifted uncomfortably. "My grandmother killed my mother," she said quietly.

Tabitha blinked.

Way to go, genius. Complaining away.

"But it's fine," Mercy laughed hoarsely. "I guess. She's not here anymore. I'm free from her."

She forced a smile as she looked off to the night sky, but Tabitha knew the quiver in Mercy's smile too well. Tabitha had all too often forced a smile, and all too often it went unnoticed.

"You don't feel free from her, do you?" she said gently.

Mercy tensed, opening her mouth before slowly shaking her head, sinking her face into her hands.

Tabitha quickly moved to put a hand on Mercy's shoulder. "Oh Mercy, I didn't—"

"It's okay," Mercy said, scrubbing away a loose tear. "It's fine. I keep telling myself it's fine. I keep telling myself I'm free, but she's always there."

"Always in the back of your mind, criticizing your every move?"

Mercy slowly met Tabitha's eyes with a small frown. "Y-yeah. She's always telling me…telling me that having friends is dangerous."

"That nobody would like you? And if they did, they're probably lying and are going to do something terrible to you?"

Mercy snorted. "I guess so."

Tabitha smiled. "Hopefully that isn't true."

Mercy shrugged. "Sometimes it feels like it. You all are so close…and I have no idea how you do it. I don't want to ruin it."

Tabitha slipped off the balcony, standing beside Mercy, both hands now on her shoulders. "Nah, you couldn't ruin it. You're one of us now."

Mercy rolled her eyes. "You sound like your boyfriend."

Tabitha gasped in mock disgust. "Ew."

"I admit he's not that bad."

Tabitha gave her a teasing smile. "His brother isn't that bad either."

Mercy blinked in surprise. "What-what brother? What are you talking about? Ray?"

Tabitha broke down laughing.

"Tabitha!"

"What?"

Mercy glared at her, taking everything to keep her smile from blossoming.

"Maybe you need some sleep, Remembrance," Tabitha said, faking a yawn, grabbing her Comm and walking back toward the doors to Felicity's room. "We have a big day tomorrow."

"You're seriously going to end it with that?"

Tabitha glanced over her shoulder. "With what?"

"I take back what I said about your boyfriend. You will never hear the end of my teasing about him."

"Great. I'll join you."

Mercy couldn't hide anymore. She broke down laughing. Seeing the stoic girl laugh made Tabitha smile. It reminded of her Nikki, who had taken weeks to do the same around them.

Mercy was growing on her.

The two snuck back into Felicity's room, and almost as soon as Mercy's head hit the pillow, Tabitha heard her slow, rhythmic breathing. As for herself, she was back to the lonely darkness.

She took another deep breath and pulled the Comm out of her pocket.

Life is full of choices.

She clicked on Lucas's contact and sent him her first message: *I'm in. Where and when?*

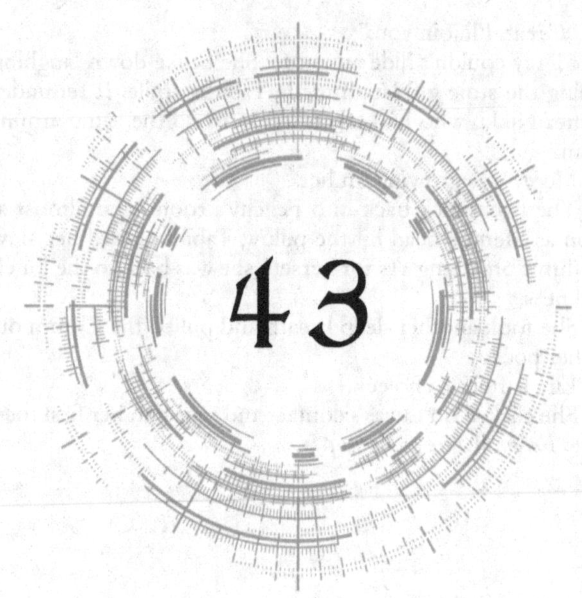

43

FELICITY HAD NEVER seen someone so confused by the functionality of a skirt than Nikki the next morning.

Not that she'd ever needed to make use of one in North Cordell, but now in Liberty, blending in was their most vital asset.

And Nikki's weather-beaten jeans and too-big T-shirt wouldn't make the cut.

She wore a short checkered pleated skirt, a simple short-sleeved black blouse, tights, and boots. The boots were the only thing familiar to her, and Felicity couldn't tell whether she was in favor of the disguise or not.

"So, thoughts?" Felicity asked, not able to bear the silence anymore.

"Looks…different," Nikki said, looking up to Felicity and playing with a loose hair, which had been pinned up tightly in the same fashion as Felicity's. "Not very good for running in."

"The plan is to not have to run away from anything," Felicity said.

"There's always something to run from." Nikki shrugged, turning to look back in the mirror. "I like it. It's very interesting."

"That's a word for Felicity's closet." Tabitha came bounding out, her hair up in an attempt at a ponytail that just struck straight out, wearing the closest to formal shorts Felicity could provide for her, a button-up blouse that the sleeves had already been rolled up on, and a sweater vest.

Tabitha insisted on wearing her beat-up sneakers, and Felicity wasn't in the mood of trying to argue.

"And what about Mercy?" Felicity frowned, wheeling backward to peer into the walk-in closet.

"I don't know about this," Mercy squeaked behind the door.

"Oh come on, Glow Girl," Tabitha said, racing into the closet to drag Mercy out from behind the door to present her to the world. Mercy hid her face in her hand.

She wore a sweater vest and slacks with boots similar to Nikki's, her marks proudly displayed down her arms. Her curly hair was up in two buns.

"Aw," Felicity said. "You look adorable!"

"I look like I'm five."

"The cutest five-year-old," Tabitha teased.

Mercy elbowed her.

"As long as we're out of anyone's notice, we're fine," Felicity said. She took her tele out of her skirt pocket. "6:12. If we move quickly, we can avoid confrontation with any family members."

"Imagine having a house so big you can actually avoid people in it," Mercy snorted.

"You can't even wake up in the Inn without running into someone," Tabitha added.

Felicity shook her head. When did they start getting along? And Mercy was joking now? "You two together is a dangerous mix."

The four of them moved quickly to the elevator. Felicity checked her pack twice, making sure her face distorter was in the right pocket and her tele was properly situated.

She didn't dare look down and out the golden caged elevator.

It was unlikely, but the very thought of her father or

worse, her mother, standing waiting for her made her nauseous.

What would she say?

How did someone bring up the fact that their mom was a shapeshifter?

Felicity gripped the arms of her wheelchair. A gentle hand rested on her shoulder.

She looked up to Nikki, who gave her a small, uncertain smile.

She gave a small smile back. She wasn't in this alone.

The elevator hit the ground floor, and Felicity held her breath as the doors opened up.

The grand room was empty, the fountain's trickle the only sound.

Felicity let out a breath of relief as she rolled out into the main room, looking back over her shoulder, ushering the others after her.

They all shuffled out, keeping quiet.

They must have felt it too.

Nikki got the door, and Felicity rolled out first only to come to a harsh stop before the stairs.

She groaned.

Stairs were slowly becoming her worst enemy.

"Want help, Liz?" Tabitha asked, stepping out behind her.

"If it doesn't include carrying me."

She should have known better. Of course the plan was for the other three to carry her wheelchair down the stairs as Felicity held on for dear life.

Once she was back safely on the ground, she was quick to move across the circular driveway to the gate. "Renee will be waiting for us outside," Felicity said.

"Why does your house have to be so big?" Mercy said, out of breath. "It's a whole journey to the end of the driveway."

"Richest family in the world problems," Tabitha said.

The gate was already opened, and Felicity relaxed on seeing a familiar long black auto, with a tinted window down. She rolled up to see Renee scrolling through a tablet, not looking up. "You're late, Miss Bentsworth."

"Well, then, we better get a move on!" Tabitha said, banging on the door. "Let's get this party started, Renee!"

Renee sighed, setting down her tablet and tapping the holographic screen on the steering wheel. The door flew open and sent Tabitha toppling backward. "She really hasn't changed much, has she?"

Getting into the auto was another unpleasant experience. Unlike Cole's trailer, the fancy auto wasn't equipped with a ramp, so her friends once again had to hoist her up into the auto.

Finally, after what seemed like an eternity, they were on their way.

Felicity tried not to think about the auto moving. She played with the button the cuff of her sleeve, trying to remember Giles's advice...but thinking of Giles made her feel sick.

"You don't think anything...bad is going to happen to the Defenders in Imperial, do you?" Felicity asked quietly.

Nikki's eyes grew wide. "Taryn said nothing would happen."

Tabitha looked at Felicity. "Look, I trust the Sergeant. Nothing bad is going to happen to them. She wouldn't let anything happen to them...especially your favorite Mullet Man."

Felicity couldn't bring herself to laugh. She just pressed her lips together firmly and nodded. "You're right," she breathed. "We need to focus on the mission."

"We get to Zita's grave and look for the Aguarious stone," Mercy said.

"And if we take it?" Nikki said, excitedly.

"Nikki, that's stealing."

"But we need it."

"Yeah, but I don't really want to go to jail for grave robbing."

"Maybe we can just explain why we need it?" Mercy said.

"Yeah, I'd like to see how that goes down," Tabitha snorted. "Oh yeah, there's this giant zombie sea creature being controlled by some angsty immortal woman and we need that to help a two-year-old control it."

Felicity sighed, rubbing her temples. "Whatever happens, happens. We'll figure it out."

Mercy raised a brow.

Felicity tried to pretend not to notice. They hadn't exactly thought this through. She quickly changed the subject. "Nikki, Lawrence called you this morning, right?"

Nikki nodded. "They're on their way. They said they should be here by tomorrow evening at the latest."

"Just in time to crash your parents' party," Tabitha jumped in. "They're going to be in for a real treat."

"Hopefully we leave before that," Felicity laughed nervously.

"Is this 'party' a bad thing?" Nikki asked.

"You don't know what a party is?" Tabitha said, wrinkling her nose.

"Look, I thought I caught up on knowing things until I got here," Nikki said, tugging on the Stone around her neck.

"In her defense, I've never been to one before either," Mercy said.

"Let's just say you don't want to experience this one," Felicity quickly butted in. "Fancy stuff, lots of elites. Really boring. You're not missing out."

"What are you talking about? They're the best," Tabitha said.

Felicity flushed red. "Look. We're just here to get Nathaniel back and stop Kathryn from wreaking havoc with that— that creature. That's all."

Everyone was quiet until Renee pulled the auto to a halt.

Felicity didn't complain as they helped her out the door. She stuck the face distorter under her chin, clicking it on.

"I'll be only around the corner. All you need to do is contact me," Renee said, with the closest thing she got to a smile, tipping her sunglasses.

Felicity forced a smile back. "Thank you, Renee. For everything."

Renee just nodded in return, climbing back into the auto.

Felicity turned back to the building before them. Among the steel and glass stood a stone building with an engraved sign above the entrance: *Liberty Defending Department Memorial.*

And the infamous gravesite of Officer Zita Klirkpatrick.

"Let's do this," Felicity breathed.

To her luck, there were no stairs included and the doors opened themselves, leading into an open lobby room. It was empty except for a tourist couple poring over a brochure from the front desk.

A hologram hovered over the desk, listing out instructions on how to link a map to your tele and the rules of silence, no touching, and the fact that the place would be decked out with Defenders.

But seeing how scarce the place appeared, Felicity wondered how true it was.

Mercy tried to get the map to show up on her Comm, and after arguing with Tabitha and attracting a few weird stares from the couple, the two figured it out.

Felicity confiscated the map from the two.

The memorial wasn't enormous. Seven halls led to a singular courtyard, where Zita's gravesite lay.

"Don't do anything suspicious, and we can be in and out of this place," Felicity said in a whisper. "Stay close behind me."

No one seemed to argue, so Felicity started off down the closest hall out of the lobby.

To her relief, the halls were empty besides a few small bots wiping down projector lenses. The lighting was dim, and the only sound was the wheels of Felicity's chair and the click of the girls' shoes.

Plaques of names filled the walls.

"Wow," came Tabitha's breathless whisper.

Lists and lists of fallen Defenders occupied each plaque, a small photo file attached to each name.

"Nikki, what are you doing?" Felicity said as Nikki stopped, studying the wall closely as they passed. "Don't touch it!"

The girl didn't respond, just moved quicker down the hall.

Felicity glanced to Tabitha. Tabitha shrugged. "Maybe she's looking for her parents?"

That was plausible.

The Aguirres had to be one of the most famous Defender deaths.

She couldn't imagine them being listed here, but it was always plausible—

"I found him!" Nikki stopped, Felicity's heart leaping as she tapped on a name on the wall.

Instead of alarms going off and all the bots turning around with machine guns, a hologram popped out of the plaque with a small profile.

Felicity sighed with relief, rolling to catch up with Nikki.

A man's profile was projected on the wall. A typical Defender headshot of a man with brown skin and curly dark brown hair was attached to a few basic facts.

His name was Ulysses Akash.

He was an eastern Bōli native and a North Cordell Officer.

It listed his date of birth, the date of his Trial completion, and the date of his death.

He'd been twenty-seven.

"Do you know him?" Felicity asked quietly.

Nikki shook her head. "Taryn did. Very well. She was going to marry him."

Felicity blinked. She's almost forgotten Taryn had been engaged at one point. "This is him?"

Nikki nodded, not saying a word. Her eyes that usually were windows to Nikki's thoughts were clouded, like even Nikki wasn't sure how to feel.

"Isn't he the one who allegedly is the reason Taryn didn't die that day?" Tabitha said, her voice suddenly serious.

The story went that Ulysses had told Taryn to not struggle against the assassins and play dead. The details were far more gruesome, but it worked.

"And all he gets is a tiny picture in a memorial?" Mercy said. "Doesn't seem fair."

Felicity swiped away the file. "Nothing is fair here," she sighed. "We should keep going."

No one argued or dared to wander to another file.

Felicity had never even heard Taryn mention Ulysses. She'd only heard about him from Lincoln.

That's how it was with Defenders. They picked up and moved on.

Don't think about Giles. Giles is not going to die.

"There!" Nikki's voice broke the stale silence as light poured into the hall. Felicity glanced down at the map.

Nikki was right.

They'd arrived at the courtyard.

Felicity turned the corner, and her breath caught in her

throat.

The courtyard was in a circular shape, the floor made of brick and marble pillars holding out the shade around it, lavender growing at their base. In the center of the courtyard, where the sun spilled in, was a stone casket.

Felicity tried to remember how to breathe as she rolled out into the courtyard.

A few people were scattered about, looking at the information boards projected on the walls or the few glass cases of exhibits.

In the silence of the early morning, the grave was beautiful, left to a lonely peaceful eternity.

A metal sign indicated for silence to be kept, and that the entire courtyard had been funded by the Sulfer OHS.

"We should split up," Nikki whispered.

"What?" Tabitha said, a little too loud, attracting every single eye in the yard. She flushed red.

"So we can cover more ground and get out faster," she said, her eyes settling on the casket. "I don't want to disturb this place more than we have to."

Felicity agreed. "Nikki and Tabitha go right, and I'll go with Mercy left."

There was no argument as they split up. Mercy kept close, making it difficult for Felicity not to run over her foot.

Felicity looked around, trying to spot anything remotely blue or glowing.

Nothing so far. Just old uniforms and photos.

Nothing left but memories.

Was that what this Council was also destined to become?

"Fourth time this week!" Felicity stopped in her track, her ear twitching as she picked up the voices of the employees scrolling through a list. "She donates flowers more than anyone here."

The fellow employee chuckled. "Klirkpatrick's really saving the memorial money."

Felicity rolled back. Klirkpatrick

"Felicity!" Mercy squeaked, Felicity running over her foot.

Felicity cringed. "Sorry. Do you hear them?"

Mercy frowned. "Hear who?"

Felicity gestured to the two employees.

Mercy frowned. "It's too loud in here."

Felicity swallowed hard. She didn't like the idea of having sharper senses. *You're not human.*

"What about them?" Mercy whispered.

"I don't know…but I have a feeling."

The two exchanged glances, moving toward the screen in the wall as the employees went off to their break. Felicity approached the screen, which was left open.

It was a volunteer and donation log.

As the employees stated, a woman's name was listed four times in the past three days for flower donations and midnight volunteer hours.

Navi Klirkpatrick.

"Klirkpatrick?" Mercy frowned. "Like Zita?"

"It could just be coincidence?"

"Maybe." Mercy's frown deepened as she selected the flower donation.

Lavender Arrangement from ARIANA'S FLORAL.

"Do you know where that is?" Mercy said.

"Ariana's Floral?" Felicity frowned, biting her lip. "It must be a smaller shop. I haven't heard of it."

She pulled out her Comm, plugging in the name.

"It's only ten minutes from here," she said, her heart leaping.

"Well, then? What are we waiting for?"

"What are we going there for?"

"I worked in the service industry," Mercy said. "We keep tabs on our customers, especially returning customers. They must have some sort of contact information on her!"

"But what if she's not helpful? Just a devoted Zita supporter?"

"Didn't Eleazar tell us about someone who went missing in Liberty?" Mercy said, with a sparkle in her eye. "Someone very close to Zita?"

Felicity's heart jumped. She'd never seen such a smug look in Mercy's eyes. "Zita's adopted daughter."

"*Almost* adopted daughter."

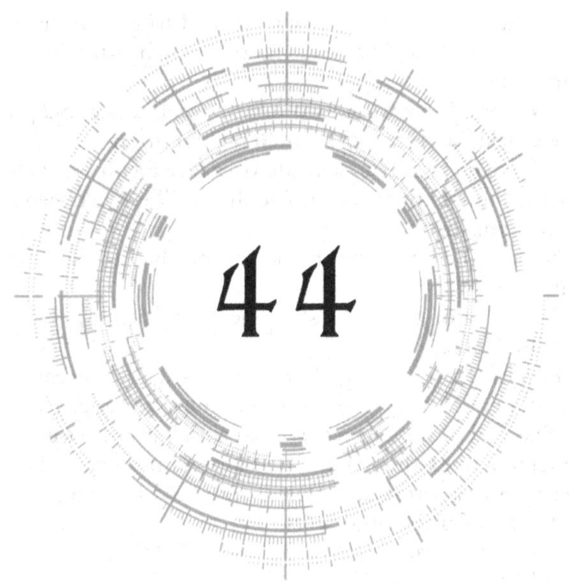

44

"SOMETHING BOTHERING YOU, NIK?" Felicity asked as they loaded back into the elevator.

She'd noticed Nikki stare intently at the poster on Veronica's door. A woman with dark skin and a purple suit, matching its violet top hat. "Does…she look familiar?"

"She's a famous film star, it's hard not to notice her," Mercy snorted.

"Veronica just loves Viv since she's a classic rags-to-riches story," Felicity explained with a sigh. "Viv seemed to come out of nowhere and out of nothing. Some say she did shady things to get there, but I just think that's spread around to cause drama."

Felicity couldn't help but notice Nikki's eyes linger on the poster as she pulled away.

"Hey! You can't go judging Viv when I got you the entire history to Ariana's Floral shop!" Veronica said, proudly skipping out beside her, her T-shirt blasted with the actor's photo as well.

The group crammed into the elevator. Felicity's stomach

felt twisted in a knot. They just needed to get to the floral shop, find this 'Navi' person, and then maybe find the Stone from there?

She prayed this would work. The week was coming to a close quickly, and the boys would be here soon.

"Nikki, make sure to activate your face distorter," Felicity said, the thought popping into her head. "We don't need anyone recognizing you."

Nikki sighed, tapping the device attached to the bottom of her jaw.

The elevator came to a stop, the door opening.

"Oh! Hello."

Felicity's insides leaped to her throat, her sweat went cold, her entire body going stiff, her mind screaming to run.

She looked up to see a woman sitting at the base of the fountain, a scarf draped and tied around her head. She was wearing a long dress and gloves, short red hair curls pulled out from under the head scarf.

"Hi," Nikki said.

Felicity tried to roll back.

The woman got to her feet. "You should have told me you were bringing friends, Liz."

Felicity's cold sweat was quickly replaced by a fire burning inside her. She tightened her grip on her armrests, her eyes narrowing into daggers that screamed: *I know what you are.*

And then a thunderous, high-pitched roar of laughter broke the silence for her.

That was the final straw.

She couldn't do this.

She turned, immediately trying to slam on the elevator buttons.

"Oh my gosh! Veronica was right! Lizzie is here!" A group of colorful-haired girls walked out into the main entrance.

"I'm going to kill her," Felicity groaned.

Tabitha scowled, balling her fists.

"Who are they?" Nikki whispered. Mercy shrugged.

"Felicity's really awesome higher education friends," Tabitha said.

"Why'd you say 'friends' like that?"

Friends was a broad term. After the stunt Yaeda had

played, Felicity wasn't putting up with this anymore.

"And hello, Mrs. Bentsworth," one of the girls giggled as she ran closer, her heels clicking against the marble floor.

Felicity rolled out of the elevator with defeat, Mercy stepping out nervously behind her. She tried not to meet anyone's eyes.

"Oh my gosh Liz, when did you get a wheelchair?" one of the girls squeaked. Nikki was having a hard time telling them apart. "That's so sad!"

They were making it really hard to keep the flame inside from growing.

"It's lovely to see all of you. If you wouldn't mind…"

"Why are *you* here?" Tabitha butted in, her fists clenched.

"Why are you here?" Felicity heard one of the girls snicker.

Felicity bit her lip to keep from snapping. She'd always been aware her old classmates disliked Tabitha…but now, she couldn't stand it.

"I invited them," Mrs. Bentsworth stepped in. "I thought you'd be lonely…you didn't tell me you were bringing others."

Felicity felt torn. That was a nice gesture, but entirely unhelpful.

"Thank you," she said, begrudgingly, glancing at Tabitha, begging for help. "But we really should be going."

"Yeah. The almighty Bentsworth has places to be," Tabitha said, clearing her throat.

"Did you hear you're a suspect for a crime?" one of the girls said. "Blowing up Defender autos with fireworks?"

"Sounds like her."

"Yeah, whoever that was sounds pretty cool," Tabitha said.

How do we get rid of them? Nikki said.

Felicity was glad she wasn't just being dramatic. *Ariana's Floral is in a Plaza. I'm sure we can give them a detour.*

Tabitha groaned mentally.

For Nathaniel.

No one argued that.

Felicity drowned out the chatter as they made their way to the enormous auto, trying to avoid her mother's lingering stare.

It was an awkward ride as Felicity tried to keep her answers to their questions shallow and amiable. For Nathaniel.

"So does your little friend speak other languages?" Nevada said excitedly.

Nikki looked up, surprised. "No."

"Yeah. Where is she from? Her accent is funny."

"Leave it alone," Felicity snapped.

The group of girls went quiet before one started snickering. "Wow. Someone's got snark."

"Well, I wasn't exactly expected to be dropped upon this morning," Felicity said.

Dang it! What was she thinking? She couldn't talk like this.

Tabitha smirked proudly.

"Veronica said you were back," Nevada tried to say innocently. "And we were all going to meet up with you last time, but you apparently had some weird freak out with Yaeda."

"We've arrived," Renee's voice announced over the speaker, saving Felicity.

She quickly rolled out of the auto, facing a pink steel building, a sign hand-painted above a violet door: *Ariana's Floral.*

Felicity glanced over her shoulder.

The group of girls chattered among themselves. Nevada frowned. "What are we doing here?"

"You like flowers, don't you?"

"If you like flowers, Felicity, I do!" A short girl Felicity hardly recognized squealed.

Felicity forced a smile. Tabitha shoved through the group. "Alright then! Let's go get some flowers! Whoo!"

The door automatically swung open, the group making their way into the shop. Felicity took a deep breath, feeling a small bit of comfort with the earthy fragrance.

A tiny bell went off.

An employee popped up from under the counter. "Can I— Oh! Miss Bentsworth!"

Maybe Felicity should've worn her face distorter too.

She smiled nervously. "Hello!"

"We're her friends!" The short girl jumped in front of Felicity. "Huge fans of your shop!"

Felicity, you're going to have to be a distraction, Tabitha said.

There's no way we're going to get what we need with them around.

Felicity sighed with defeat. "Yes! Oh, my! Look at this rose display!"

Immediately, the group flocked to the roses.

Felicity pretended to hear their chattering conversation as she peered over her shoulder to see Tabitha talking to the woman over the counter.

The woman frowned, tapping a few buttons on her screen.

Felicity let out a breath of relief as a paper printed. She tore it off and handed it to Tabitha.

Tabitha turned around with a grin and a thumbs up. *We got an address! On the condition that you give her Veronica's autograph.*

That's how easy it is to coerce people into breaking the law?

What do we do now? Nikki asked. *There's no way we can take you to visit Navi.*

Felicity sighed, disappointed. Nikki was right. She was too recognizable, especially with this entourage following her around. *Mercy and Nikki should go.*

She saw Mercy's eyes widen.

You'll be fine, Mercy. You'll have Nikki.

You say that like Nikki's a little guard dog, Tabitha laughed.

We don't have much of a choice, Felicity said. *Can you do it?*

Mercy nodded.

Nikki took the paper. *For Nathaniel.*

Nikki and Mercy headed out the door, and Tabitha stepped in beside her, watching the girls load their arms with roses. "You know you're going to be buying *a lot* of flowers."

Felicity sighed. "I know. I guess it's the least I can do to thank this shop for their help."

She could see Tabitha's less-than-thrilled face as she growled, "I can't believe we have to deal with this again."

Felicity studied Tabitha's face. She'd seen it so many times before. But she could tell the difference of Tabitha being angry and Tabitha being in pain.

"Don't worry, Tabs," Felicity said. "I won't leave you behind this time."

Tabitha's eyebrows raised, before her face softened to a smile.

"I wasn't worried."

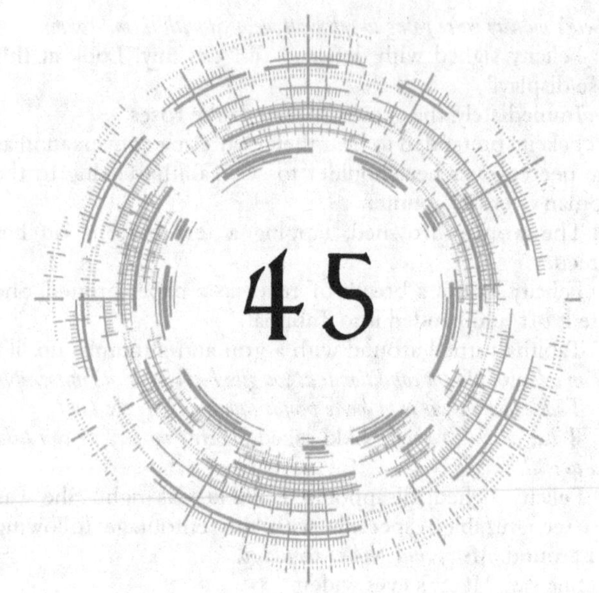

45

MERCY WALKED QUICKLY, staring down at her Comm, weaving through the morning crowd on the streets of Liberty.

"The storm is growing," Nikki said quietly as she forced herself beside Mercy, her eyes stuck on the sky above.

Even the simulation of the Liberty dome couldn't hide the darkening sky.

Kathryn's threat loomed in Mercy's mind.

"You don't think it's really…going to happen?" Mercy asked, looking to Nikki. How could they stop a storm of that scale?

They'd done the impossible before, but this seemed so much bigger than that. This time so much more was at risk than themselves. Regions could be destroyed.

"I don't know," Nikki admitted, her eyes falling, before straightening herself with a forced smile. "But we're going to figure it out! We're going to meet this Katie…Navi person, and we're going to get Nathaniel back and go to this part-tee."

Mercy could only stare at Nikki's forced enthusiasm.

"Just admit it. You're as hopeless as we are."

"Never."

Mercy rolled her eyes. "Alright fine, Miss Sunshine and Rainbows."

The nickname didn't fit Nikki's little tailored vest and boots Felicity had chosen for her to wear. Her hair was braided back, and Nikki looked more professional than Mercy had ever seen her.

Her words said optimism, but Nikki's eyes stared at the ground, unreadable and distant.

Mercy didn't ask.

The two moved quickly down the Liberty streets. Most people went about their business without a second glance at anyone nearby, zooming by on floating scooters, enamored by their teles or the person next to them, or just seeming to be making it their life's mission to try and run them over.

Nikki seemed to navigate it fine, but Mercy was not as small and nimble. She glanced down for only a moment to check the address when someone rammed into her, spinning her off track. Her Comm flew out her hand as she tripped on her undone shoelace.

Mercy caught herself, her breath flying from her as she stared, dazed, at the out-of-pace world around her. "Nikki!" she cried out without thinking.

Where was the Comm?

She was alone.

She couldn't see Nikki anywhere.

Had Nikki abandoned her? Just like Grandmere said. You can't trust anyone. You can't trust—

"Mercy!"

Pushing through the stream of people, Nikki reached out, holding tightly to the Comm.

Mercy's heart slowed.

Nikki held out the Comm, catching her breath. "You almost lost this," she said.

Mercy tried to keep her hand from shaking as she took the Comm from Nikki.

Nikki took Mercy's hand, making her heart leap into her throat.

"So we don't get lost again," Nikki said, with a small shrug. "We're running out of time for that."

Mercy focused on the directions, trying to ignore the incoming storm and the feel of Nikki's hand in hers.

They just needed to get to Katie, and then this could all be over.

They turned the street. The further they walked, the quieter it became. While the streets were still nice, most of the action was happening above them as gliding autos assisted shoppers to the upper-level shops, leaving the ground street level mostly vacant for the few lower housing units.

Was this what they considered poor in Liberty?

How did people even get to the higher levels?

She didn't trust one of the flying hover autos not to drop her, anyway.

Nikki hurried her along.

"It's not too far," Mercy said, scanning over the numbers nailed to each door, her heart leaping with every step.

"There!" Nikki pulled Mercy into a run. Her heart rammed against her chest as they barreled across the street and up the concrete steps to a chipped blue door.

Mercy opened her mouth to breathe.

"We're here," Nikki said excitedly, letting go of Mercy's hand. "Can I knock?"

"Uh…" Mercy could barely fumble a word out to respond to Nikki. She managed a nod.

Nikki spun on her, raising her fist. There was a split second before Nikki knocked gently on the wood. Her excitement was smothered as she stepped back in place beside Mercy.

"No one's home!" a voice shouted from inside, followed by a crash and a click from behind the door.

"We can hear you," Nikki said.

"You're just hearing things. Going crazy."

Nikki looked at Mercy, confused.

Mercy swallowed. She should've known this wouldn't have been easy. "We need to talk to you. We know who you are."

"Yeah, you really do sound crazy."

"We're running out of time," Mercy said, stepping toward the door, trying to swallow her fear. *Pretend it's just Ray being stubborn.* "We need your help. We need Zita's help."

"Zita's dead."

"Why are your feelings so complicated?" Nikki asked, raising a brow.

"Stay that way," Tabitha said.

"Are we going to sleep?" Mercy piped up.

"What? Do you not want to be questioned too?" Tabitha teased.

Mercy hid underneath a pillow.

Felicity chuckled, shaking her head. "Alright, now we really need to sleep."

Nikki couldn't help agreeing. As she hugged her knees to her chest, her eyes drifted around the room. She felt the strong air conditioning beat down on her, and the strong smell of chemical cleanser filled the room.

Not super comforting.

The chemical clean smell nagged at the back of her skull.

"We can all sleep in my bed," Felicity suggested.

Tabitha leaped her feet, tumbling over into Felicity's enormous bed. "Even better sleepover material!"

Nikki preferred the company of her friends than the empty space and eerily familiar smells.

She couldn't even imagine one person needing a bed this big. She tried to imagine a tiny Felicity sleeping here and not being lost, but it didn't fit.

With a quick voice command, Felicity shut off the lights.

The only light was the light seeping under the crack of the bathroom door. Nikki curled up under the covers, trying to focus on the breathing of the others.

Tabitha gave an enthusiastic goodnight, which got her another pillow from Mercy.

Tabitha was satisfied and the room was quiet.

Nikki's heart raced in her chest, but her entire body was heavy with exhaustion. She needed to find Nathaniel. She couldn't sleep. Stay awake. Stay alert.

If you sleep, they'll hurt you.

Her eyes drooped, ignoring the murky, shattered memories of the drowning and the shocks, and she let herself be comforted by the warm, familiar thoughts of her mother, just this once.

said. "We're obviously far superior. We have Glow Girl, a rich Bentsworth heiress, me who needs no explanation, and—" she lowered her voice to a comic whisper, "—a freaking Aguirre."

Nikki rolled her eyes. "Veronica might hear you."

"And then Veronica with her super hearing will come and snatch you up and keep you in her own personal case." Tabitha attempted to tickle Nikki, which just resulted in Tabitha being tackled off the bed.

The two girls collapsed onto the ground in laughter. Tabitha was fairly easy to pin to the ground. It wasn't like she gave much resistance.

"You're going to wake up the whole manor," Felicity said, obviously trying very hard to stay stern.

"Your room alone is bigger than our level in the Inn. I think we're fine," Tabitha said, shoving Nikki off of her.

Nikki happily collapsed to the ground. "So I'm guessing that game is a no?" she said, catching her breath. "Unless we all ask questions about Giles."

Felicity almost choked on a pretzel. "You don't know what you're asking." Felicity gagged, her face going red.

Nikki sat up. She didn't really. She was confused why her friends seemed to get so shaken when things like this came up.

"I'm worried about him," Felicity said, tugging on the end of her braid. "That's all. We have a big day tomorrow. We should get some sleep."

"Is this your way of avoiding the question?" Tabitha smirked.

Felicity deadpanned her.

"What if I dared you…"

"There's nothing to comment on," Felicity said.

"Well I guess that just means you lose the game and you don't get any of my hot nacho sauce."

Felicity's face was even redder now. "I-I don't know. We have so many more important things to prioritize, I haven't even *tried* to figure this out."

"Okay, let me adjust my dare." Tabitha cleared her throat. "If Giles survives, you two use your healthy adult communication skills and figure it out."

"I-I— Fine," Felicity said, defeated.

The words felt like a punch to Mercy's gut. She flinched. "Y-yes, but she lives on. She still has Katie Oowatie."

The woman went quiet. Mercy could hear her own breath in the cold wind.

"Katie died with her."

"But—"

"Now go! Before I call the Defenders on you kids!" She banged the door, sending Mercy stumbling back.

"Katie isn't dead," Nikki spat, her eyebrows furrowing as she stormed up to the door. "Katie doesn't die when Zita dies. The Curatrix Team doesn't die as long as we remember it!"

Mercy blinked.

What was Nikki thinking? Yelling at her wasn't going to fix this. They were so dead. They didn't have the law on their side, especially not with the North Cordell Defenders on trial—

A chuckle. "Who's your dangerous little friend?"

"Nikki." Nikki swallowed hard. "Nikki Aguirre."

"Nikki," Mercy snapped, her sweat going cold. "You can't just—"

The door cracked open. The woman peered out. "The Aguirres didn't have a Nikki. They had two children, the twins, who died in a fire."

Mercy saw where Nikki was going.

Nikki was one of the last living remainders of the Curatrix team. The only link they had to Katie.

"They did have an older one," Nikki said.

The woman's brow lifted. "But-but it can't be. The Ewyon kid was killed before its term…it can't be…"

She pulled the door all the way open, her hair disheveled and her jaw ajar.

It was no doubt Katie. She looked older than her photo at the Klirkpatrick house, but she had the same arching nose, which now was pierced, and same dark brown eyes. Even her hair still held its thick waves, kept out of her face with bobby pins.

The woman looked back and forth between Nikki and Mercy before she settled on Mercy. "How on earth did you find me?"

"Flower shop," Nikki said. "We found your name through

your donations and got your address from there."

The woman blinked, cursing under her breath as she rubbed her temples. "You know that's illegal."

Mercy and Nikki exchanged looks. "Yes?"

"You really are Sergeant Hunter's kids," she groaned. "I just didn't think...I just...A living Aguirre." She shook herself awake. "You better get inside."

Nikki and Mercy exchanged glances.

They couldn't lose a moment. They ran through the door, all the things that could go wrong swirling through Mercy's head.

Keep alert.

The woman closed her door, closing a series of locks, before pacing into a small living room right out the left doorway. She ran her fingers through her hair, muttering under her breath.

Mercy looked at Nikki.

Nikki was staring firmly at the woman, her unreadable, hard expression back.

The woman felt dangerous. Mercy couldn't trust her, even though the echoes of Zita were etched in her mind.

She plopped down on a stool near a dining table, which had a vase of lavender in the center.

"So who are you?" Nikki said.

"Like you," the woman sighed. "If what you say is true, of course. Zita always talked about an Aguirre child as if she was alive. I just thought it was her way of comforting Reyna."

Mercy's eyes widened. "Wait, Zita knew about Nikki?"

Nikki nodded. "I remember her. She used to help look after me and my siblings."

"Right. You were saying that," Mercy said, her nerves beginning to clash with her excitement as she tried to hold herself back from pacing.

There was a stiff silence as the three watched each other. The woman finally cleared her throat. "Take a seat. I'll have some coffee made."

Nikki and Mercy cautiously sat down on the stools at the table as the woman swiveled around, clicking a remote for a small tabletop bot to roll across the counter, beginning to heat up water.

She set down the remote, turning back to them.

"I guess since you put in all the work of finding me, you ought to know I'm now legally Navi Klirkpatrick," the woman said, her shoulders heaving. "Katie was a name given to me by OHS. Zita used to promise I could change it as soon as the adoption was finalized..."

Navi's eyes trailed off, lost for a split second before she shook herself back to reality. "But that's behind us now. What do you two want from me?"

The kettle went off, the little bot speeding to pick up the pot.

Mercy straightened herself. "We-we're here for the Aguarious Stone."

Navi's eyes narrowed. "Why? You don't look Aguarious. You have the marks of a Keyper."

Mercy's face immediately went warm, her instincts telling her to cover them.

"The Keyper is a fascinating role. It's pretty useless on its own, but when put with the others...well, I'm sure it's very flashy and cool." Navi smirked.

"So you do have the Stone?" Mercy said, clearing her throat. She didn't want to dwell on her glowing-ness.

"Again, that depends on why you want it?"

"Kathryn's coming," Nikki said.

"Nikki, she doesn't know who Kathryn is."

"Is she another one of you kids?" Navi said, raising a brow, taking a steaming cup from the little bot.

"Not exactly...she's a prophesized immortal who's quite literally out for our blood?" Mercy said with a forced smile.

Navi blinked. "Well, that was...unexpected."

"The name Kathryn is misleading," Mercy agreed. "But she has our Aguarious...friend. He's only two years old, and if she gets all of our blood...the consequences could be dire...like ripping a hole in the Void!"

Navi listened intently, lifting the cup to her lips.

Nikki followed, though she pulled back at the bitter taste.

"She gave us a deadline," Mercy said. "And if we didn't turn ourselves over, she'd flood Liberty."

"So why not deceive her? Turn yourselves in, and then take her out?" Navi said.

"We don't have all the Council Members. Even if we did

surrender, we couldn't give her what she wants." Nikki shook her head. "We're still looking for the Oquelite and Sublinight."

Navi let out a breath. "That is…complicated. And the Aguarious is two, you say?"

Mercy and Nikki nodded.

"How'd they manage to catch him?"

Mercy cringed. "Well, our friend…he accidentally gave Kathryn his name. And her whole thing is controlling people by their name."

"Ouch."

"In conclusion, we need the Stone," Mercy said. "I wish I had more to prove. I-I know this must be disruptive after living your life in hiding—"

Navi laughed, getting to her feet. "Zita always talked about the future Council. She would be thrilled to hear they're children." She sighed, her face hardened. "Personally, I still don't know whether to trust you, but Zita would give you the Stone."

"So you have it?" Mercy said, jumping excitedly to her feet.

Navi's face twisted, and Mercy's blood went cold.

"I don't," Navi sighed, setting down her cup. "The artifacts don't stick around with people they're not meant to stay with."

Nikki fiddled with the Stone around her neck. "I remember finding the Stone…very vaguely. I was trying to run…and then something started glowing and calling out to me."

Navi nodded. "If the Aguarious Stone is truly still out there, it would've found its way to this two-year-old by now."

"But how?" Nikki said.

Mercy bit her lip. Nathaniel was found in a box. Everything he owned, they'd given to him, except for…

A boom shattered the window.

Mercy wasn't sure who screamed. She just dropped to the floor. Her heart beat against her ears.

"What did you do?" Navi shouted.

"It wasn't us!"

Nikki jumped to her feet, running through the door.

"Nikki!" Mercy screamed. It was too late.

Nikki was off down the hall.

Mercy spun on Navi. "Are you okay?"

"I'm fine—ah!" Navi staggered as she pushed herself up, clutching her bloody side, the shards of glass from the broken window around her.

Mercy couldn't breathe. "Navi? Are you—"

"I'm fine," Navi breathed, like she was trying to convince herself, looking at the blood staining her shirt. She turned to Mercy. "Run! Find the stone."

"But-but what about you?"

"I'm expendable," she said with a forced shrug.

Why were her eyes burning? She couldn't cry now. Stupid.

She couldn't tear her eyes from Navi.

"Go!" Navi demanded. "You can do this!"

Mercy flinched, nodding, and ran for the window. She leaped through, ignoring the shard that scraped through her leggings, and ran. *You can do this.*

She tried to scream mentally.

Tabitha! Nikki? Anyone! Can anyone hear me?

It was useless. She couldn't do telepathy.

Felicity? Are you there?

She couldn't even glow.

So much for being a supernatural Member of the all-power Council.

I need help! Please! I think I know where the Stone is!

She had no choice but to run. Run faster than she ever had before, and ignore the brewing storm above her and the echoes of the thunder that rang Kathryn's warning back loud and clear.

Nathaniel's stuffed toy!

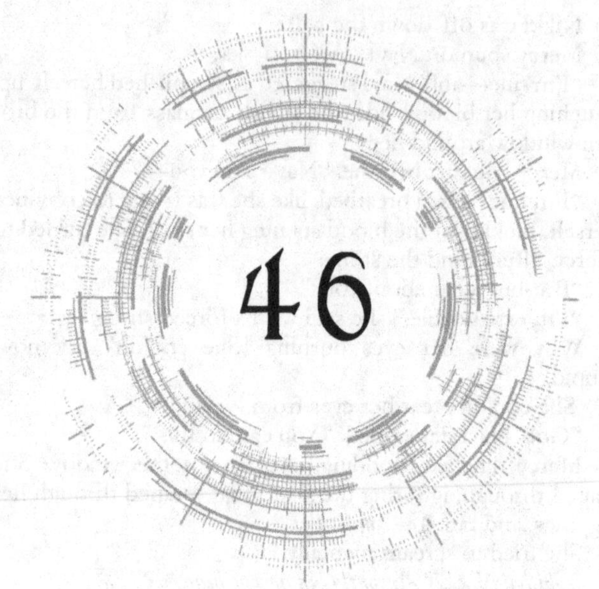

46

NOTHING FELT MORE natural to Nikki than running.

Her instincts took over, and it was exhilarating when danger sounded. She wasn't entirely aware of it, but it was comforting in a way. Overthinking wasn't required when she barged into the front room, bracing herself.

She shouldn't have been surprised to see a long red cape, a braid of white hair facing the shattered window. Nikki didn't hesitate. She grabbed the vase off the table and leaped soundlessly toward the Exerticus.

The Exerticus spun around with a blast of energy, shattering the vase and sending Nikki slamming against the floor.

Nikki's heart skipped a beat as she met the Exerticus woman's eyes. She was so familiar.

The Exerticus's glowing eyes bore into Nikki's soul.

But it wasn't possible. She'd seen Kathryn's memory. She'd seen her cut by glass shards in a bloody death.

"You're Sergia." Nikki's voice was hardly a whisper.

The woman's face hardened. "And you're the Ewyon. Just as the mind-controlled Aviduous said."

Lincoln.

"What did you do to him?" Nikki scrambled to her feet, grabbing a chair. It was pointless. She knew it was no use. An Exerticus's power could easily snap it.

But Kathryn's only known friend walked around Nikki, not paying her much notice.

Nikki couldn't let her get to Navi and Mercy.

So she took her chance and threw the chair.

Just as she suspected, Sergia shattered it with red energy that zapped from her fingertips, giving Nikki a split second to charge for her.

Sergia reached for her blade.

Nikki rammed herself against her.

The Exerticus staggered, shoving Nikki back.

Nikki grabbed hold of her cape, spinning back in control. Sergia twisted her legs around Nikki's ankle, but Nikki took her down with her, snagging the sword from Sergia. Nikki rolled to her feet, grabbing the hilt of the blade. Sergia got up, catching her breath.

She cracked a small smile, brushing away a drop of blood from her nose.

Dozens of scars littered her bare arm.

Nikki didn't have a second more to plan as Sergia sent a blast across the hall. Nikki ducked, the picture frame shattering behind her and the smell of burned drywood flooding her lungs.

Nikki jumped to her feet, swinging the blade.

Sergia dodged, slamming herself into the door of Navi's room, smashing it open.

Nikki's heart sank in her chest.

She raced after her.

Navi was on the floor, trembling as she clutched a bloody wound, though her face was hard in defiance. Where was Mercy?

Navi snorted. "Oh, lovely. You did attract some."

Sergia lifted her arm.

"No!" Nikki whipped the sword.

Sergia sent Nikki and Navi flying against the wall. Navi gave a pained grunt as she hit the floor. Nikki gasped for breath.

Sergia didn't kill Navi.

Navi had been right there…and Sergia hadn't killed her. She hadn't seen an Exerticus show any sign of mercy before.

Or maybe she was just giving this one too much credit.

Nikki scrambled for the blade, but Sergia's foot slammed on her wrist. Nikki bit back a cry of pain as Sergia leaned down to scoop up her sword before kicking Nikki in the face and racing for the window.

Nikki's entire world flashed white, spinning as pain cracked though her mind.

You don't have time for this! Avalon shouted.

Nikki pushed herself, tasting blood as she ran, her vision blurring as she leaped out the window, grabbing onto Sergia's cape…

…and everything flipped upside down.

Nikki had broken her wrist, been impaled by a deadly Oquelite blade, underwent an allergic reaction to a deadly acidic file, and yet she'd never been in more pain than the split second Sergia had teleported.

It was nothing like Ray's.

Nikki pushed herself up, her head rocking. Her eyes began to adjust, her heart leaping as out of the corner of her eye, she saw the ground far below her. She scrambled back, her heart ramming against her chest as she slammed against the railing. She looked around. The building was enormous, the walls tall and metal, with suspended mental walkways lining the place.

An empty warehouse building.

Just like what Felicity saw in her mind.

Mostly empty. Nikki could feel the essence beating down on her senses. She could feel power pulsing around her. They weren't alone.

"Nathaniel!" Nikki screamed, running to the side. "Nathaniel! Are you—"

Sergia grabbed her from behind, shoving a hand over her mouth. Nikki fought against her, kicking and shoving.

Sergia laughed hoarsely. "You're quite stubborn. You remind me a bit of her."

Nikki's sweat went cold as the smallest echo of a cry was heard. A child's cry. Across the building on another swinging passageway, she saw the lanky figure of an Oquelite man, clutching a small child to his chest.

His eyes were gone, no pupils to be seen, his white hair growing out at the roots to a natural brown. His uniform was tattered, and he looked thinner.

Nikki tried to scream Silas's name against Sergia's hand, scraping her nails into Sergia's skin. Sergia cried out, Nikki lunging forward against the railing, tears pricking her eyes as she reached for the crying toddler. "Nathaniel! Silas, don't do this! She's controlling you! She'll kill everyone! She'll kill—"

Pain seared through Nikki's skull. Sergia grabbed the collar of her shirt, shoving her to the ground.

Nikki cried out as Silas disappeared, still hearing Nathaniel's cries as they grew further and further away.

Her mind began to swirl, echoes of the past begging for her attention, refusing her the ability to focus, her entire world swaying. All that time pushing them away, and they were coming back roaring at full force.

Nikki struggled to lift her face, Sergia standing in front of her. "I thought you were supposed to be good," she choked. "I thought you were trying to stop Kathryn from killing."

Sergia was quiet.

Nikki's mother's voice echoed for her. The memories were taking over her mind. It was not gentle. It was a pained crying, a dying scream. Scenes of the past flashing before her eyes, dragging her back. Chanting for her to remember, remember, remember—

AVALON, MAKE IT STOP.

Avalon didn't say a word.

"I follow her, and I will die for her countless times," Sergia said, her voice soft. "Violence isn't my preference, but it's only a temporary solution."

"Give back Nathaniel," Nikki choked, her head falling. It was useless.

"I'm afraid she won't permit that," Sergia said with a sigh. She turned, the click of her boots shaking the walkway, leaving Nikki alone and unable to get up.

Her entire mind swallowed her whole as she was sent back to her six-year-old self, crouched in the corner of a hallway in horror as her mother stumbled over.

And all she could do was sit there and watch and beg as her mother uttered the words that tortured Nikki ever since she'd stepped foot in North Cordell, dragging her back to relive her memories.

Run. Run and never look back.

47

For the first time, Felicity heard Mercy's voice in her head, loud and clear.

The Aguarious Stone…in something that was with them all along?

It made sense.

It was the only item Nathaniel had come with and kept this long. Felicity prayed Mercy was right.

Felicity was only relieved for a split second before she heard her name being screamed through the crowded side-walk. Mercy barreled toward her, her arms clutched to her chest and a cut across her cheek.

The group around her sprang back with a scream.

Felicity's heart lurched. "Mercy!"

Mercy nearly collapsed beside her, out of breath. "The Stone— But-but Navi! She's hurt—attacked. We were at-tacked. Nikki-Nikki— oh my gosh—"

"Whoa, whoa. Calm down," Tabitha said, rushing to her and steadying her shoulders. "What happened?"

Felicity began to back away. "We need to move out of here."

"We don't have time."

"Liz, what's going on?" Felicity had almost forgotten about the entourage of girls.

"Oh, would you just scram?" Tabitha snapped.

"It's alright, girls!" Felicity cleared her throat. "We just have important matters to attend to."

"Ooohh, like the harbor party this weekend?"

"Exactly!" Felicity began to move quickly down the street, not stopping for anyone in her way, Mercy close behind.

She opened her Comm to message Renee.

The signal was down.

She could see confused faces around her. But they weren't looking at her. They were staring at their devices. Holograms glitched in store windows, bots were stopped halfway through sidewalks.

Felicity hadn't seen an auto pass in the last five minutes.

Her stomach sank.

Can anyone hear me?

I can hear you! Tabitha's voice erupted. *This is the most fun I've had all week, ditching your crummy friends.*

Not important. We need to get back to my house now. The Dome is intertwined with the power of the city. If the signal is down, the Dome is getting weaker.

What about Nikki? Tabitha said. *Mercy's really worried. We need to get the Dome back up and this flood taken care of!*

You say it like it's easy, a new voice mentally scoffed.

Felicity stomach flipped, Ray's voice throwing her off guard and causing her to nearly ram into an unsuspecting person's ankle. *RAY?*

We told you we were here. I guess the message didn't go through.

"Kathryn wasn't joking," Mercy said as she caught up with Felicity.

Felicity gave a hoarse laugh. Did anyone ever think she was?

Ray, can you teleport us to the Bentsworth Manor?

Where are you?

We're a block away from the SpeedRail station. Can you pick us up there?

Can do.

"Except not me." Tabitha panicked suddenly, stopping.

Felicity pulled back on her breaks. "Tabitha, what do you mean? Last time you tried to pull some solo stunt, it did not end well."

"Look, I made an appointment, and I cannot miss it," Tabitha said, beginning to bounce.

This was unusual. Tabitha wasn't exactly the one who really kept appointments. Something was off.

"We don't have time for this," Mercy said. "The longer we stand around, the longer the Stone is in danger."

"The longer Nikki is in danger," Tabitha said, staring straight at Felicity.

Felicity swallowed hard. Either way, she was putting her friends in danger. "Fine. Go."

Tabitha nodded, sprinting across the street in the panicking crowd.

Felicity tried to control her racing heart, trying to count her breaths like Giles instructed. She could see the massive crowd spilling out of the SpeedRail station. The noise was unlike anything she'd ever heard in the usually peaceful, ordered region of Liberty.

Never before had these people experienced such a phenomenon.

And if they didn't hurry and figure out something soon, they'd be experiencing so much worse.

"Do you see Ray?" Felicity shouted to Mercy, who was scanning the crowd.

Felicity couldn't hear Mercy's response, her voice drowned out by the screams and shouts. Her chair rolled over something—

"Ah! Felicity! My foot!" Ray jumped back, trying to shake off his foot. "Holy—"

"Language, Ray Mathews. We have things to do." Felicity was overjoyed to see his face. It had only been a short time, but she wished she could jump up and hug him and all the rest of the boys and never let go.

But in her own words, they had things to do.

"Rapheal!" Mercy said, her face lighting up. "We got the Stone!"

"What? That awesome, Glow Girl!" Ray said, pumping his fist. "I knew you could do it."

As adorable as their excitement was, Felicity cleared her

throat.

"Right." Ray grabbed Felicity's hand and put an arm around Mercy. Ray took a deep breath as he looked at Felicity. "You know if I teleport in public, it'll cause an uproar, right?"

"I think they have bigger things to worry about," Felicity laughed hoarsely.

Anything went now. As long as they stopped Kathryn from drowning the city.

Ray took a deep breath and nodded, closing his eyes.

The entire world warped. Felicity was already too tense from anxiety to feel sick from teleporting as they dropped onto the floor of a room in the Manor. The main parlor.

Felicity immediately felt nauseated, seeing the crowd gathered of security personnel, Renee among them.

"Where are the others?" Felicity asked, looking at Ray.

He shrugged. "I dunno."

Renee's head turned, catching sight of Felicity as her eyebrows rose.

Felicity tensed.

"You've arrived, Ms. Bentsworth."

"Oh my, Alla is here?"

Aunt Olivia pushed through the crowd, pale and visibly trembling. Felicity wouldn't be surprised if she was forcing herself to shake just for the act of it.

"How could Hannah let the poor girl out of the house at a time like this?" Olivia cooed. "Oh, it was Hannah, wasn't it?"

Felicity tried to keep the burning knot in her stomach down. This wasn't the time to snap.

"We have a bit more import—"

"Olivia, this is not the time." Felicity's father's voice struck her speechless. She'd hardly even had a glimpse of him in her past visit, and seeing him step out of the crowd, placing a hand on his sister's shoulder, made the burning pit go cold.

He turned his eyes to meet hers.

A simple brown, nothing at all like hers.

In fact, she didn't have many features of her father's, besides the flaming red of his hair. She was a striking resemblance of her mother.

Her parent who wasn't even human.

"Felicity, we need to get you and your friends to the bunker until this blows over. Your other friends have already been escorted," Gordon Bentsworth said, turning toward his daughter, his back straight and his face unfeeling as if what he just said had been the simplest of things to ask.

"The ordeal wasn't—"

"What?" Mercy said under her breath, slowly backing up.

"I advise your friend to not attempt to run away."

Whatever you do, find a way out. We need to get Nikki and the Aguarious Stone safe. Felicity swallowed hard.

Ray and Mercy broke through the door, the Defenders rushing for them.

Felicity's heart leaped, and she rolled in front of the door. "No! Please, you don't understand, you can't!"

A Defender pushed her out of the way. The fire erupted back through her. "No!"

The tiny voice in the back of her mind wanted to pounce.

She settled for throwing her weight, knocking herself out of the chair and hitting the floor. She rolled back, throwing her hands out.

The Defender stepped back, stunned.

Felicity struggled to breathe as pain crept up her side. "Let them go," she gasped. "You don't understand what's about to happen. Please, just let me explain!"

"Someone, get her off the floor before she has another one of her freak out episodes," Olivia said, her fearful act dropping for a scoff of impatience.

Her father just stared at her, not saying a word as the Defenders roughly pulled her up.

"Father—Dad, just listen to me!" Felicity felt tears burning, her throat closing up. "Just this once, stop hiding from me."

The slightest hint of emotion rose in her father's brow, his shoulders shifting uncomfortably.

She wanted to yell so much at him. She wanted to ask him why they'd avoided the truth of her mother, why they'd rather send her away than deal with her anxiety, and why they'd sent her off to a Marketeer instead of trying to face the fact that she was paralyzed.

"This family taught me to run away from things," Felicity said, swallowing hard as she forced herself to straighten in the Defender's tight grip. "But I am sick and tired of running away. The only good thing you ever did for me was send me to North Cordell. At least they taught me I don't away from my problems!"

She was out of breath. She hung her head.

The room was silent.

Felicity knew she'd messed up. Olivia would finally have her way, and Felicity would be in a psych ward for all they knew.

"Leave us a moment," Gordon Bentsworth said.

"And the others?" an Officer asked.

"Leave them. Prioritize securing the perimeter," her father said.

The Defenders agreed soundlessly, the two holding Felicity setting her back in her wheelchair, walking past her out the door.

Renee hesitated before leaving the room, looking at Felicity for a moment of assurance. Felicity managed a queasy nod.

Renee slipped out the door, and it felt like it took everything she had in her to turn her head to see her mother sitting on the parlor couch, staring at the floor, and her father watching her.

"Get down to it. Enough of all the standing around wasting time on her," Olivia said, her perfectly-combed black hair falling out of place as she spun on Gordon Bentsworth.

He didn't look at her. "Olivia, please see yourself out."

"Gordon, I am an owner of this estate and you—"

"This is my child," he said, the tiniest bit of anger flickering in his dark eyes.

Olivia shut her mouth, turning and storming out of the room with a wicked look in Felicity's direction as she slammed the door behind her.

Felicity couldn't breathe.

Her father had just called her his child.

"Come closer," Gordon Bentsworth said as he took a seat beside her mother, but not close enough to touch her. Just enough space to keep the professionalism he'd always had.

She rolled over to sit accross from them. There were so many things spinning in her mind that she wanted to say, but she felt like any word would break the tears she was trying to hold back.

"While I know you disagree, the best course of action is to stay in the bunkers until this blows over. If you don't trust the durability, remember it's what housed hundreds during the EarthShaker, and it has been upgraded in recent years with comfortable accommodations—"

"I don't want comfort," Felicity choked, her fingernails digging into the arms of her wheelchair. "Father, I know you know what I am. You must have if you married Mom. I'm part of a group that's the only thing that can stop this storm. Who can stop a literal immortal from tearing apart the world! I won't let innocent people get hurt."

Her father was silent as he exchanged glances with her mother. "How…" her mother whispered.

"How do I know that you're a shapeshifter? It's a long story," Felicity scoffed, though a tear escaped just seeing the horror in her mother's face. "Did you ever plan on telling me?"

Felicity hoped and prayed it had all been a mistake. That maybe, just maybe, it wasn't true, and if it was, her parents had just forgotten to tell her about it.

But from the look on her mother's petrified face, Felicity knew the truth.

"You weren't going to tell me, were you?" Felicity breathed.

"Felicity, I-I didn't know that it would ever become relevant."

"But your own people prophesied you'd be the one to have the Guardian Member!"

"They are a superstitious kind, Felicity. When given the opportunity to leave, I ran. It was better if they believed I was dead. I wouldn't be their pawn for power."

"And yet you married the wealthiest man on the planet?" Felicity couldn't help but give a tired laugh.

It was all so selfish.

"We can't deny the truth now," Hannah Bentsworth said, unclipping her headdress.

"Hannah, please don't," Felicity's father said.

Hannah ignored him, letting the scarf fall away.

Felicity only had vague memories of her mother's full

face, but it looked nothing like she remembered it. Her mother had sharp ears, her hair more frizzy and wild…like Felicity's, with curled marks up her cheekbones and down in her collarbones.

"I didn't think it would hurt you too," her mother said, rolling back the sleeves of her blouse.

Along with the markings, there were blotches of blue and purple swelling around her mother's arms…just like Felicity's legs.

"You-you knew this would happen to me?" Felicity gasped, rolling back.

"It's what happens when a Shifter doesn't shift for long periods of time," Hannah said.

"So what's going to happen to me if I don't figure out how to…shift?" Felicity forced herself to breathe.

"I-I'm not sure. There's never been a case like this," Hannah said, wringing her skirt.

"But you were such a normal-looking child," Gordon Bentsworth jumped in. "No one expected you to be…one of them."

"You married one of them!" Felicity said. "Is that what this family is all about? Hiding and running away all in the name of comfort?"

Her parents were silent.

Felicity couldn't breathe, brushing away her tears. "Well, like I said, I'm not running away anymore. I won't hide like you did. I'm going to do everything I can to save this city because that's what I was born to do."

Hannah looked up with a small nod. "Then you better hurry. Your friends are on the base floor."

Felicity's heart flipped. Her mother…agreed?

Her mother got to her feet, squeezing Felicity's shoulder. "You're right. All our lives we've been running. *I've* been running." Her mother pursed her lips. "Once you handle that storm, I'll teach you to shift. No more secrets."

Felicity felt like she could glow. She smiled with a firm nod. "No more secrets."

"Be better than I was," her mother said softly.

Felicity didn't take another moment to race for the door.

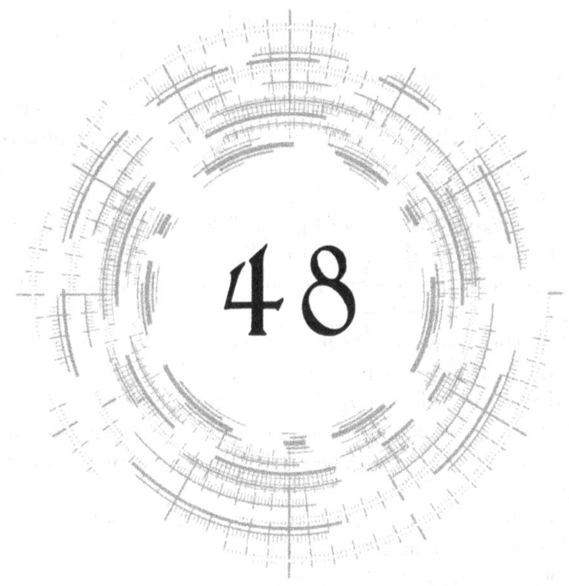

48

IT DIDN'T TAKE longer than five seconds to convince Veronica to let Ray teleport them to the location of Nikki's tracker.

Mercy picked up the little stuffed monkey with shaking hands from Nikki's satchel.

"So how do you intend to test your theory? Ripping Nathaniel's precious stuffed monkey's head off?" Ray smirked.

"We don't have time for this," Mercy said.

She acted like it didn't make her blood cringe when she ripped the seam of the monkey stuffie. The inside was stuffed with old rags. Mercy swallowed hard. *Please. Please. Please*—

She searched inside with her finger—

Zap!

Mercy fell back with a cry, her fingertip singed.

Her heart raced against her chest.

The monkey lay on the floor. Ray crept closer to the toy. Mercy's eyes widened as a blue light began to spill out of the stuffed animal.

Ray scooped up the little stuffed monkey, tossing it into a bright purple bag of Veronica's. "Very cool. Extremely dangerous, powerful stone in a cute little monkey."

"Can you guys hurry up?" Veronica groaned. "Nikki's tracker stopped at the docks. I told you using practical private networks was superior," Veronica said, offering her hand to Ray.

"Just wait till you meet Lincoln," Ray snorted. "You two will nerd your heads off together."

Veronica's eyes widened with a mischievous smile. "One genius versus the other."

Ray rolled his eyes. "Okay, you can challenge Lincoln to a nerd off after we jump out this window."

Mercy clipped the bag shut. "Sounds like a plan."

"Placing any bets on who will win?" Veronica said, excitedly looking at Mercy. "Has your friend ever built an entire system to watch deleted net files?"

"He did make the device that lets Felicity walk."

Veronica groaned. "Aw, man."

"Miss Bentsworth?" The voice echoed down the hall.

Mercy snapped back into focus. They had to get out before a guard came to retrieve Veronica. "Okay! Out the window we go then!"

She grabbed Ray's other hand, not having enough time to feel weird about it as they raced for the open window. Mercy screamed as her foot pushed off from the window sill, and Veronica cheered.

They were swallowed by the darkness and came stumbling out onto a hard concrete sidewalk. Mercy rolled to her knees, catching her breath and scrambling to check on the Stone in her bag. It still glowed brightly back at her. She got to her feet.

The air was thicker here.

It smelled…different.

"We're at the docks," Veronica breathed, getting to her feet, her excitement fading.

Mercy dared to turn and look.

Her heart did a flip.

There was sea only yards away, churning and tossing up and down violently against the Dome. The dark clouds were so much more visible here as a raging storm rained down on the Dome.

It was only a matter of time before it broke through.

"Where does the tracker say Nikki is, exactly?" Mercy said, turning to Veronica.

Veronica pulled her tele out of her pocket, her brows diving to a frown. "The signal's not working here."

"So much for your advanced tech," Ray sighed. "Any theories?"

Mercy looked around them. Dozens of enormous warehouses were lined up at the docks.

Mercy's eyes widened. "Wait. Felicity mentioned seeing that Silas guy always walking about at one of these warehouses at the dock."

"Felicity saw Silas?"

"Mentally."

Ray blinked.

"Oh come on, you can turn yourself invisible and walk on walls, and seeing events in your mind is where it gets you?" It was Mercy's turn to roll her eyes.

"But how…and why?"

"We haven't figured that out just yet," Mercy broke out into a run. "Maybe we can try mentally communicating with Nikki?"

"Whoa. You guys can do that?" Veronica squealed, racing after Mercy.

Mercy laughed nervously. "Totally."

Ray eyed her suspiciously.

She swallowed hard and ran forward.

She could hear Ray's echoes in her mind, calling out for Nikki as they ran.

She needed to try.

You already have the Stone. Isn't that all you needed to prove you're capable?

NIKKI!

She'd failed last time she'd tried.

A wave crashed up against the Dome, causing it to shake. Shadows scattered through the dying afternoon light. Mercy's stomach flipped. *NIKKI? WHERE ARE YOU?*

It was useless.

Her Grandmere had said she shouldn't have personal connections.

That's all she'd ever known.

But she'd felt a connection with Nikki before. She felt the tiniest smidge of fear that Nikki was hurt…or worse, dead. She'd felt a connection with Ray when he'd hugged her as she cried on the kitchen floor all those months ago.

Nikki believed in her.

"Your mother is looking for you, kid. We can take you to her."

A flash of a little girl's face, smudged with dirt and soot as she balled her fists, wavering with hesitation. "My ma is dead."

Mercy gasped, stumbling. The echoes of the voices in her head were unfamiliar, but the young face.

There was no way.

Nikki? Nikki, can you hear me? she shouted in her mind.

An echo of a child's scream flooded back. Flashes of the forest floor, strong arms holding the child down. It was all flashing by quickly. Mercy's vision blurred.

The scene switched.

A woman stood in front of a large truck, her hair tinted silver and her suit white, with long red gloves as she stared down, unfeeling. "Welcome, 53."

Mercy stopped, trying to catch her breath, shaking her head, trying to pull herself away from the strange images flashing through her mind.

"Mercy, what's going on?"

"S-seeing things," she gasped.

The power was pulsing through her mind.

Connection.

It was a connection. Mercy gasped, her vision still hazy, the voices still echoing.

"Nikki is here!" she said, turning toward the nearest building.

"How do you know?"

"I don't," Mercy admitted, running anyway.

"Are you aware of the effects the injection has on the mind?" The little girl looked up at the two medics, standing on either side of the calculating woman and her silver hair.

"Are you aware that this isn't a neural operation? We're here for results in the blood. Whatever happens to the subject's mind is none of our concern."

The door to the warehouse was torn off its hinges.

That was a good sign.

The three of them rushed inside. The place smelled of fish, oil, and dust, the air colder than the outside. Suspended walkways rose up throughout the warehouse.

"Nikki?" Mercy shouted out the empty warehouse, her voice echoing back. She ran for the nearest staircase, ignoring as it swung underneath her.

"You know, 53, water is good for you." A young woman with dark skin, a beautiful face, and a long braid looked into the child's eyes with a forced smile. "I promise Nano didn't put anything in this. It's safe."

That's when Mercy spotted the small girl crouched over, holding onto her head, lying trembling.

"I found her!" Mercy shouted, running toward Nikki. "Nikki!"

The ramp swung under her feet as she dropped in front of Nikki, shaking her.

"Nikki, wake up! Snap out of it!"

A person in a full white suit stood with a baton, a mask covering their entire face. Her entire body ached, but pain wasn't allowed.

"NIKKI!"

The images came to a harsh stop, everything going quiet.

Nikki shot up, gasping for air, her eyes rolling back. Once they'd focused, she stared at Mercy for a long moment before tears began to well, and she slumped over onto Mercy, crying softly.

Mercy instinctively wrapped her arms around her, just like Ray had.

She soaked in the silence for a few seconds, remembering how to breathe before her grandmother's reminder struck her. She stiffened.

She couldn't get too close. *You're not their friend.*

But she wanted to be. She wanted to make sure Nikki knew she was safe.

"Were those your memories?" Mercy whispered gently.

Nikki didn't respond, but the hollow look in her eyes confirmed the images.

Ray's footsteps caused the walkway to shake.

Mercy pulled away, and Nikki turned to face him, pushing herself to her feet.

Her hair had fallen out of the braids, her coat was missing, and the first few buttons of her shirt were undone, but Nikki's face was hard in an emotion Mercy had never seen it in before.

"Nikki, are you okay?" Ray said, grabbing her shoulders.

She pulled away. "They have him," she choked out.

Mercy's face softened. "Nathaniel," she breathed. "You saw him?"

Nikki nodded. "Silas had him."

"Silas?" Ray looked to Mercy. "You were right."

"We have to get to the docks then before they break the barrier," Mercy said, her heart pounding against her chest. "We don't have much of another choice."

Nikki nodded, tightening her fists, glaring at the empty space in front of them. "Then what are we waiting for?"

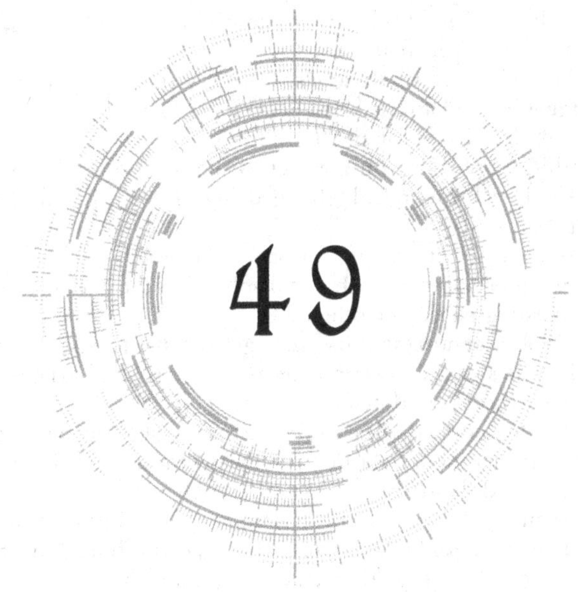

ALL HER NIGHTMARES had led her here.

Tabitha wouldn't let her family drown.

The entire world was chaos around her as she stood on the steps of her family's penthouse.

She held her breath as she raised her fist to knock, but her hand just stayed there, suspended. She couldn't force it forward. She drew back, pulling out her Comm and messaging Lucas.

T: I'm here at the door.

She waited, staring at her Comm, trying to focus on breathing. She wouldn't have another almost panic attack like the other night.

She remembered standing in the same place, looking at the door before she turned to follow Felicity down the hall, thinking she'd never return.

Never.

The door swung open. "Tabby!"

Tabitha's heart leaped to her throat as she glanced up. Lucas stood right in front of her, looking older than the last time she saw him, his jaw more defined and his blonde hair grown out longer than hers.

He didn't say anything else before stepping to her and hugging her so hard he lifted her off her feet.

Tabitha gasped for air. "H-hi Lucas."

He set her down on her feet as she recovered from the attack. Her brother had…hugged her? Even after all this time?

"Aren't you dressed up for once?" he teased.

She choked on a laugh, for a split second forgetting she was wearing Felicity's clothes.

"We better hurry if you want to get a chance to talk," Lucas said. "The storm evacuation seems to be reaching this area."

That wasn't good news.

Tabitha nodded, clearing her throat as she followed her older brother though the door of the penthouse. He shut the door behind them.

Tabitha felt like she'd been slammed into a brick wall.

The main hall looked exactly the same as when she'd left.

Same red walls, gold accented carpet, and hologram portraits on the walls, and the eerie violin music wavering through the speakers.

Nothing out of place, glittering in its peaceful finery… that was, until Tabitha rested her eyes on Lucas again, and his scruffy, oil-stained jacket and frizzy long hair.

But he was smiling. She didn't remember such life in her brother's eyes.

She only remembered the hunched-over boy with buzzed hair who kept to himself unless Tabitha dragged him in on a technical problem.

Her mother insisted Lucas looked better with a buzzed head…and here he was with his long golden hair tied up.

"You look good," Tabitha managed to breathe. "Kennedy was good for you."

Lucas smiled, ruffling her hair. "North Cordell was good for you too, kiddo."

Tabitha laughed, playfully swatting him away. "You have muscle now."

"Aw, you noticed?" Lucas said, with a smirk. "You're looking a bit bigger yourself."

"I've been working on it."

"Come on. Clarence has been waiting for this," Lucas said, excitedly grabbing Tabitha's arm and running down the hall like he wasn't a twenty-three-year-old man.

Her heart raced as they went up the winding metal staircase, the dangling chandelier above her. She remembered vividly breaking one of them when she'd attempted to throw a tablet at Clarence for fun when she was six.

She'd spent a week grounded, and she'd had a very long one-sided shouting match with her mother going on about a "troublesome third child" as she sat on the edge of the stairs, bawling her eyes out.

She shook it away. She wasn't going to remember that.

They reached the top of the stairs, the wide hall bright with the glass ceilings as Lucas rushed through. Tabitha held her breath. If anywhere she was going to run into her parents, it would be here.

She had to be prepared.

A good impression was vital. They were her parents, the people who'd brought her into this world no matter how much they regretted it. They would have to have some sympathy for her. At the end of the hall was the parlor that sat on the edge of the building, smelling strongly of peppermint, overlooking the dazzling city of Liberty, usually glowing and at peace as the waves swam calmly at shore.

But now, all of that was flipped upside down.

The waves crashed against the Dome, casting shadows down on the buildings below. Echoes of the nightmare returned.

"Clarence, look who decided to show up!"

Tabitha swallowed hard as she lowered her gaze to the living room and the hovering furniture to see her second eldest brother look up from his tablet, his face going blank.

Clarence looked almost the same as when she'd left him, or maybe that's just because he was unavoidable when scrolling through the net with girls fangirling over his pretty face and recent film releases.

Clarence was her parent's perfect child. The one they'd wanted, and the one they'd created to be the perfect image. The well-groomed hair and perfectly fitted suit. He was an internationally acclaimed public figure. Everyone's dream boy.

Tabitha could feel her stomach twisting, remembering

the jealousy she'd had as a child against him.

Clarence had gotten everything she never had.

He'd gotten her mother. The fame. The attention.

Tabitha wanted to step back, but Lucas was still holding onto her arm.

Clarence got up slowly, setting down his tablet. "H-hey, Tabitha."

Tabitha gave an awkward wave. "Hey."

"Been a while," Clarence said with a forced laugh.

Tabitha noticed his hands shaking as he shoved them into his blazer pockets.

"I think it's been a while for all of us," Lucas said, pulling Tabitha closer, hugging both Clarence and Tabitha's shoulders. "But hey, that's changing now, isn't it?"

Tabitha glanced at Clarence, who was also squished against Lucas's chest. Was it?

Lucas let them go, and Tabitha cleared her throat. "How's everything been?"

"Normal," Clarence said quickly. "You know, besides the raging storm outside?"

Tabitha laughed nervously. "Yeah. That's a bit of a problem."

"You know our sister here has been one of the people dealing with those problems, right?" Lucas said, excitedly shaking Tabitha's shoulders.

Clarence gave a small smile. "I've seen."

"What is going on here?"

Tabitha went rigid, her hair on her neck rising, her sweat going cold. She suddenly couldn't breathe. *Remember what Mercy said. Count your breaths. Count your breaths—*

"Mother, Father," Lucas said, even his cheery voice dampening. "I-I brought Tabitha."

Tabitha slowly turned, unable to breathe as she met her mother's eyes, a crystal turquoise much like Clarence's, and so unlike Tabitha's.

She couldn't even muster a hello, just a nod. Lucas squeezed her shoulder. She was going to faint. This wasn't a dream. She could breathe. Focus on breathing.

Her father stood passively to the side, his face pale as he glanced from Lucas to Clarence.

But not at her.

Tabitha felt her stomach sink, her arms pressing into her sides as she wanted to slink back. She was a fool to think things had changed. She couldn't breathe still, but this time because her insides burned. The nightmares had tortured her for nearly a year, mocking her with her mother's voice, promising a small chance at love.

But now, she was finally awake.

Her fingernails dug into the palm on her hand.

"In these conditions, you thought it was best to show your face again? With your face plastered all over MEDIA reports? Associated with a felon? Blowing up Defender autos?" her mother scoffed, flipping her hair and gently rubbing her temples with her long nails as not to ruin her makeup. "Lucas, you've always been so thick-skulled."

"It's not his fault," Tabitha snapped. Lucas just wanted to reunite their family again. "He didn't know this would happen."

"But apparently you did," her mother scoffed, marching forward, shoving Tabitha aside as she moved to the glass wall. "The condition you went to North Cordell under was that you'd keep under the radar and out of the way! And what does this look like to you?"

Her mother tore out a live news report, Tabitha's blurry face in the heading.

"M-Mother, there's danger coming!" Tabitha forced out. "You can't stay here long—"

"I know you've been running around the regions, gaining yourself quite the name with the law! My one condition! You broke it! You foolish, selfish—"

"If the waves crash through the Dome, they'll drown the entire city!" Tabitha gasped.

Her mother blinked, taken aback. "Don't you dare shout at me, young lady! You've caused enough damage to our reputation!"

Her mother stormed toward her, and Tabitha couldn't move. She was frozen, just like she'd been at the bottom of those steps eleven years ago.

"How was she supposed to know?"

Tabitha's breath was stolen from her as Clarence stepped between them. "All she's done is gotten her name in a few news articles, Mother. It isn't worth the rage. It's not her fault."

"She is putting your reputation on the line," her mother spat in Clarence's face. "All the work I've done for you, and you'd have that soiled knowing your lawless third sibling is running about."

Her mother pushed Clarence away, his face pale.

Tabitha held her ground, her mind still reeling. Clarence had stood up for her?

"The city is going to be destroyed. You need to get out of the city," Tabitha said, her voice weak, unable to breathe as her mother's eyes burned into her.

"Oh! And now you run around playing hero and have the audacity to show your face here? I hear that crazy Sergeant of yours is on Trial. Maybe I should have you arrested as well!"

"Mom!"

"Lucas, would you be quiet!"

"You can't arrest her. This isn't the time for overreacting!" Lucas said, his face growing stern, his shoulders straightening.

"Overreacting?" Her mother gave a strained laugh. "Even if that wave destroys Liberty, she still will have destroyed our family!"

Tabitha's face burned.

Destroyed our family.

Not Tabitha's family.

Their family.

Lucas's lips parted with shock. Clarence stood, awkwardly uncomfortable, his eyes darting for one painful moment to Tabitha.

Tabitha stepped back, trying to hold back the tears burning at her eyes. "B-but I'm still your daughter."

"If you dare say another word, you legally won't be," her mother snapped. "I will keep good on my threat."

Tabitha felt as if she'd been forced underwater, everything becoming echoes.

"That's a little far, darling," her father said, his voice shallow and fearful as her mother glowered at him.

So all the times her mother had ever given her the smallest smile for sitting still at Clarence's performance had been nothing.

Lucas thrust forward. "That's insane! You didn't disown

me when I left!"

The agreement when Tabitha had gone to North Cordell with Felicity, and when she'd listened to Tabitha excitedly rattle off about the music program.

When Tabitha had thought she maybe cared.

"You won't disown her," Clarence said. "She just showed up, Mama. Just let her prove herself—"

Tabitha's raised her eyes, straightening herself. "No."

"What did you say?" Her mother snapped her head in Tabitha's direction.

"No."

The room was silent.

"You have messed up too far, child," her mother sneered. "Don't you ever think of showing your face here again."

"Don't worry. I don't intend to."

Tabitha turned and walked down the hall.

She could hear her brothers calling her name. She heard Lucas try to run for her, but her mother called him back.

"Tabitha!"

It hurt. It felt like her heart had been ripped out of her chest.

She wanted to run and take her brothers with her.

They didn't deserve it either.

She'd let her mother turn her against them.

Even Clarence…. All these years Clarence had been trying to protect her, not steal her spotlight.

Tabitha broke out into a run.

She could hear the echoes on the walls.

Don't you ever think of showing your face here again.

She pushed through the front door, racing down the halls and the stairs. This was her childhood home. Was it home?

She broke out the doors into the storm.

"Miss Delorous! It's dangerous out there!" she heard the front desk manager shout at her.

She didn't respond, letting the doors shut behind her as she ran through the drenched streets. No one could see the tears streaming down her face. What was she even mourning?

She wasn't Miss Delorous anymore.

She was just Tabitha.

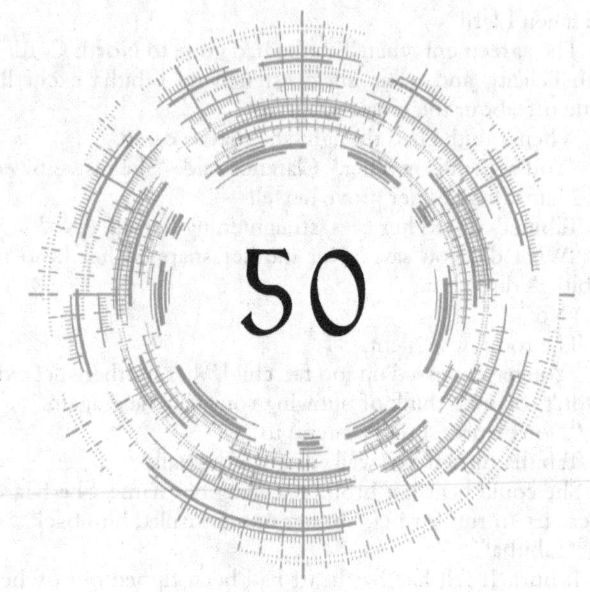

50

Rain poured down.

The streets were upended in chaos as people tried to figure out what was happening. Rain had never penetrated the Dome when it wasn't scheduled.

And here was Tabitha, soaked down to the bone in Felicity's nice clothes, trying to not audibly sob her eyes out as she pushed through the streets, not caring who she shoved over in the process.

The storm in her mind far dominated the one around her.

She approached the Bentsworth gates, the path beginning to flood. The guard didn't bother to check her as she pushed through the door into the backway of the manor.

That's always how it happened.

After some big fight or disappointment, Tabitha would always come through the backway in the Bentsworth manor. Felicity never seemed to mind. Tabitha would just sit on a sofa by the window, wrapped in a blanket as Felicity would talk and go about her homework, not ever making Tabitha feel awkward or unwanted.

Tabitha ran through the rose garden, normally perfectly tamed but now with the sculpted hedges flailing in the wind. Puddles splashed under her feet as she ran.

The last time it rained in Liberty, Tabitha was leaving the Bentsworth manor, angry with Felicity over the pettiest thing. Felicity had cut her hair to fit in an unsavory group of popular classmates.

She'd never felt more guilty that night when she'd opened her Comm to see the news that the eldest Bentsworth daughter had been in a lethal auto wreck.

Tabitha was only fourteen at the time.

Yet she'd felt like she'd been hurting forever.

Hadn't she learned her lesson yet?

The realization almost seemed strike her out of nowhere as she pushed through the gate with a gasp for air—

"Tabitha?"

Her heart skipped a beat, hearing Cole shout above the storm.

Cole?

She turned, seeing the backside courtyard empty except for the truck, and Cole standing drenched, looking as confused to see her and she was to see him.

She tried to breathe in, stand up straight, and force a laugh and punch a joke. *Oh wow, I forgot you were coming back so soon! Surprised to see the truck survived! Ready to go risk our lives once again, like old times?*

Instead, Tabitha began to cry.

Her knees buckled, and she collapsed to the ground. She wrapped her arms around herself and sobbed.

She couldn't hold it back anymore. She felt like every part of her had been torn apart, and like her chest might burst if she didn't scream.

"Tabitha!"

Her vision was blurry, her whole body shaking. She felt so numb. She just wanted to lie down and never get up.

She felt a warm coat draped around her shoulders and strong, comforting arms cradled her. She'd missed this touch. She just cried, not knowing what else to do but bury her face in his chest as he ran his fingers through her hair.

They sat alone in the rain for a moment before Cole

slowly helped her to feet, letting her cling onto him as he led her to the truck. He opened the door and picked her up off her feet, setting her down gently into the backseat before climbing in after her, shutting the door on the storm.

The rain pelted outside, and Tabitha could finally hear herself breathe.

Or struggle to as she tried to wipe away her tears and snot.

She felt so tired and out of breath. Her lungs burned, and it made her eyes burn with tears again.

"Tabs?" Cole placed a hand on her knee. "Is everything okay?"

It's fine. I'll take care of it, she was tempted to say.

Tabitha sniffled, swallowing hard. She gave the tiniest shake of her head.

Cole was quiet, not saying anything, leaving Tabitha alone to her thoughts. But she didn't like the emptiness. There was too much in her head that echoed against it. She couldn't stand the rain and the chaos. She grabbed his hand, squeezing it. "I went to see my mom."

That was the truth. She hadn't gone to see her brothers. Definitely not her father.

She'd gone because she so desperately needed her mother.

Cole's eyes widened, waiting for her to finish.

"I tried to warn them about the storm, but she wouldn't listen," she choked.

"Oh, Tabitha…"

"It's fine," Tabitha said, forcing a laugh, scrubbing away the tears that dared fall. "She disowned me anyway."

"What? Are you joking—"

"Nope," Tabitha choked with a shaky breath. "She was dead serious." Just like last time.

"That's insane," Cole whispered. "I'm so sorry, Tabs."

"It's fine," she repeated, squeezing his hand harder. "I didn't want to be part of that family anyway."

Even as she said it, tears fell, a new sob threatening to choke her.

"That isn't true. You know it," Cole said gently, running his thumb over her hand. "She was still your mother, and you are her child. No matter what, you're going to love her, even if she doesn't. That isn't fair to you, Tabs. You deserve so much more than that."

She just laughed. She had no idea what else to do. She felt so empty, the pain felt so raw, but she felt like she could breathe. She took a deep breath, letting herself loosen. "I want to be angry so badly, Cole. But I just feel so…sad. And I know that's stupid. The entire city is in danger and I'm here feeling all emotional and—"

"We've dealt with cities in danger before. Not everyday you…get disowned."

This time she genuinely laughed. A small one, but she felt lighter.

"Family is supposed to be there for you. They're supposed to care for you, and tell you the truth even if it hurts." He took a deep breath. "It's hard to accept, I know…that maybe your biological family wasn't as great as you thought it was. You were born to love them, and the fact that they didn't love you is painful, but you couldn't control that."

Tabitha leaned her head against his shoulder. It wasn't her mother who would take care of her when she was sick in the middle of the night.

It was Lucas who sat with her in his Comm light.

And Clarence who'd say he wanted *all* his siblings on his business trips.

It was Felicity who comforted her when the kids in her class ridiculed her, and Renee who'd bandage her knees with no questions asked.

Why did her mind feel so cluttered and clear all at once?

"But your family is great," Tabitha said.

"I'm lucky that they care for me," Cole scoffed. "I always thought my mother was some sort of angel…but I know now why my dad doesn't really like talking about her."

Tabitha's raised a brow. She didn't press him.

"That's a perfect example though. Like Dr. Mathews isn't my biological mother, but she's the closest person I have to a mother."

"By showing up at your trailer, making sure you did your dishes?"

"Dishes are irrelevant."

Tabitha laughed. She knew it was the worst time to do so, when the city was on the verge of being destroyed, but it felt so good. "You're a lot smarter than you give yourself credit for," she snorted.

Cole rolled his eyes. "Why, thank you."

Thunder split through the sky, throwing Tabitha back to her senses. She shook herself. "We have to get to the harbor," she gasped. "We have to stop Kathryn. We have to get to the Council."

"Felicity's gathering them as we speak," Cole frowned. "Are you sure you can handle this?"

Tabitha smirked, feeling a loose tear trickle down. "We were born for this, Johnson."

He smiled back, pulling the Illuminate from under the seat, opening the truck door for her. "Right behind you, Delor— Well, I guess you're not Delorous anymore."

Tabitha crawled out first, shrugging as she stood in the rain. "It's just…just Tabitha."

Cole jumped out after her. "Good," he said with a smile. "I like just Tabitha."

He slammed the truck door shut behind him, tossing Tabitha her knife, before strapping his sheath to his belt.

She looked down at Taryn's sheathed knife, rain pouring down on them. She tightened her grip on the hilt, daring to pull it out an inch, seeing her blurry reflection staring back at her.

Tabitha staring back at her.

She sheathed the knife, taking a deep breath as she strapped it to her belt loop. She looked up to Cole, her breath catching in her mouth as she met his eyes.

It had been so long since she'd let herself study them.

She could hear the echoes of her nightmare mother telling her that it was wrong, but she didn't care anymore. She was tired. She was exhausted, and she just wanted to turn and look at Cole in his bright green eyes that were staring, waiting for her.

She wouldn't let the nightmares stop her again.

She grabbed Cole's face and kissed him.

He didn't pull away. He wrapped his arms around her and kissed her back.

She pulled back, out of breath, her face suddenly feeling warm. "I've been waiting forever for that."

Cole went red. "Well, I've been here the whole time."

"Please stay," she said. "Forever."

He smiled. "I'll try."

"Tabitha's here?" Lincoln's voice broke through the courtyard as the mechanical whir of the back garage door lifted. He stepped out into the rain with his bow in hand. Tabitha's heart quickened as Lawrence, Matteo, and Felicity followed. Matteo had an extra sweatshirt tied around his waist, no doubt coming in handy if he used his wings, and Lawrence fidgeted with Lincoln's goggle invention.

Felicity was standing on her own two feet, leaning on her spear, her headband glowing with life. "You good, Tabs?"

"Never been better."

Felicity looked to Cole. "On your command."

Cole nodded. "To the docks."

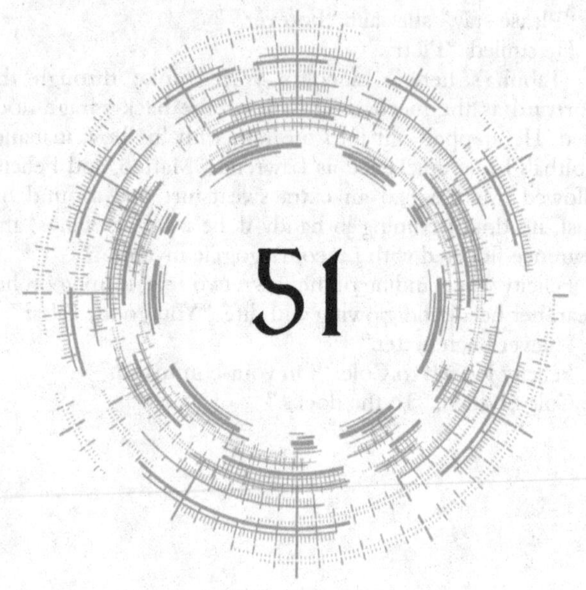

51

"Use the left exit!" Nikki called over the raging waves, and dozens of dazed port workers spilled from the building.

The Defenders hadn't arrived, most likely held up by the chaos in the rest of the city, leaving three over-competent teenagers and dock shift managers scrambling to evacuate the dock.

It only took Ray teleporting one of the managers to safety from a falling light pole for them to start taking them a little seriously.

Veronica had been given a massively oversized coat and made to sit at a tollbooth office entering the dock. She wasn't exactly pleased to be excluded, but none of them liked the idea of getting another Bentsworth daughter in the chaos.

Mercy knew for a fact they couldn't afford it…literally.

"So what exactly is breaking through the Dome?" a grown man asked Mercy, fear in his eyes as he held onto the hood of his raincoat to keep it from flying off.

Mercy was almost his height, but she still felt infinitely underqualified to be explaining anything. "A giant sea monster," she said with a queasy smile.

The Dome glitched again, the lights of the dock going black. Mercy's heart stopped. Screams broke out before it flickered back to life.

The waves crashed hundreds of feet in the air, covering the entire port in shadow.

Mercy stood frozen, trying to remind herself to breathe in.

Nikki ran up next to her, out of breath, as the wave came crashing back down. "The Dome isn't going to last," she said, turning to Mercy. Her hair was wet, her bangs sticking to her face, her jagged scar over her right eye now clearly visible.

Once again, Mercy was struck with the unfamiliar sight of a threatening Nikki. A girl with a stone-cold face, and a rageful determination as she clenched her fists, turning to face the Dome.

Ray appeared beside them.

Mercy was too busy being worried about dying in the next ten minutes to be startled.

"We cleared out the south part of the harbor," he said, his jacket now missing, completely soaked.

"But that still leaves the whole north," Mercy sighed, daring to look at the struggling ships trying to speed over the rising waves. Their hover mechanics weren't built for these conditions. "They're not going to make it in time."

Her voice fell to a whisper.

She could feel Nikki and Ray's eyes burning a stare into her.

"We have to at least try," Nikki said, the quiver in her voice evident. "We can't let them die."

"What do you suggest we do?" Mercy said, looking at Nikki, whose eyes were now studying the horizon...or where the horizon should have been.

"Give me the Stone," she said.

"What?" Mercy said, stepping back defensively. "Why?"

"We need to calm the Leviathan," Nikki said. "The Aguarious Stone is the closest thing we have."

Mercy inquisitively clutched the case in her pocket. "But why? Doesn't anyone that isn't an Aguarious who touches it get harmed?"

Nikki hadn't been the one to find it. What if Nikki lost it? What if Mercy lost the only thing she'd done right? What if Nikki got hurt?

You can trust her!

This was too important.

You've already messed up too much!

Nikki looked over at her, her frown deepening. "You're not an Impure full-blood. I am. I know how the artifacts work. Even if it does hurt me, it will be better than this whole city drowning."

"But I-I'm the Keyper, and that means I like..." What did that mean? "I connect everyone, right?"

"I don't like the idea of either of you dying, how about that?" Ray butted in, laughing nervously.

Nikki still raised a suspicious brow, and Mercy looked away, her face burning. Why was she having such a hard time letting go of the Stone? Nikki was her friend, wasn't she?

But Mercy had to prove herself. She couldn't let anyone else mess up.

A crack broke through the chaos of the storm.

Mercy whirled around to see the boarding bridge sinking into the water, sailors and dock employees scrambling up the incline.

"The cord snapped!" Mercy shouted, seeing one of the thick metal cords that kept the bridge upright whipping violently in the air. "Those ships will have nowhere to unload!"

If they didn't sink first...

The three Members broke out into a run toward the bridge. Mercy racked her brain. How in the world were they supposed to fix it? Yeah, she could maybe fix a dishwasher in her free time, but a whole bridge?

Not like it mattered if the Dome broke.

Then it would all be gone.

They reached the dock, racing up the steps as everyone fled around them, no one paying them a second thought as they ran straight toward the enormous sinking bridge. Internally, Mercy was screaming. Everything in her body told her to run the other way. She couldn't control this. It wasn't safe. She had no plan. She was racing onto the biggest bridge she'd ever been on in her entire life that was dipping into the deep, green, churning waters of the stormy Liberty ocean.

The moment her foot left that level ground onto the slick steel bridge, there was no going back.

"Ray, you need to teleport them off of here!" Mercy shouted.

Ray nodded, quickly spotting around, grabbing unsuspecting victims to safety on the level land.

Nikki kept running, becoming more blurry as she ran into the mist and pouring rain, only identifiable by the bouncing green glow of the Ewyon Stone.

The awful grinding sound caused Mercy to pause in her tracks. Fear took over, processing the snap of the second cord before her mind did.

The bridge tilted, and Mercy slipped off her feet. She couldn't hear herself scream as she slid into the mist, knowing in only a hundred feet were the violent waves.

Her body slammed into something hard. She gasped, clinging onto the metal structure, letting her vision adjust to see a check-in station embedded into the bridge.

She could feel the power of the waves, the wind slamming into her. She could hear the creaking of the bridge.

She was going to die.

She should have listened to her gut and stayed on land. She was going—

"Mercy!"

Mercy whipped her head around to see the mist clearing around Nikki, who was balancing on the nearly-sideways railing a few feet away. "Throw me the Stone!" she screamed.

Mercy's head whipped around the crashing ocean that seemed to be reaching for her.

You don't need her. You don't need anyone but yourself.

Then why was she terrified?

I want to trust Nikki, Grandmere. I want to trust her.

Mercy made up her mind.

She reached her shaking hand into her pocket.

She pulled out the purple bag containing the Aguarious Stone. "Nikki! Catch!"

A wave crashed against her. Mercy screamed, slipping. The Stone fell from the bag. She twisted her leg around the cord, throwing herself to catch the Stone.

Everything went quiet.

The ocean sprayed at her, drenching her in salty freezing

air. She clutched onto the Stone. It was blue and yellow now? Her vision was foggy. *She wasn't letting go. She was a Council Member. She could do this. She wasn't going to let her* friends *down.*

Her hand felt like it was on fire.

Why was this so confusing?

"MERCY, YOU'RE GLOWING!"

Mercy jumped, her grip tightening, the bag dissolving in her glowing fingers. She couldn't even cry from the pain of the glass slicing into her hands because the sensation of touching the Stone's surface was burning at the very core of her bones, her heart speeding up, pounding against her chest, aching. She couldn't let go. Her hand felt like it was on fire.

She cried out with pain, and the blue light vanished.

The pain subsided.

All that remained was Mercy's glowing fists, fast fading.

"Mercy! Mercy! Are you okay?" Nikki's screams overcame the waves.

Mercy pressed herself against the wall. *Just breathe.*

She didn't move till she saw the blurry form of Ray appear. She threw herself at him, clinging to him and squeezing her eyes shut before she felt solid land on her feet. She stumbled back, falling over, letting herself just sit on the ground until her vision adjusted and she could feel her heartbeat again.

Ray appeared again, this time with Nikki, who immediately rushed to Mercy. "Are you okay?" she repeated, out of breath.

She had a cut above her brow, but besides that she looked fine. Mercy couldn't dare look into her eyes or utter a word as she slowly opened her hand.

Mercy smothered a sob as she saw the broken blue shards in her palm, her hands bleeding from broken glass.

Ray let out a horrified, shuddery gasp.

Mercy could only stare.

She'd broken the Aguarious Stone. The Stone hadn't been too powerful for her, she'd been too powerful for it.

She could feel the hot tears streaming down her cheeks. Why was she crying? So pathetic and weak. She'd tried to do the right things. Grandmere had been right.

They would throw her out for sure now.

She'd doomed all of Liberty—

A gentle hand pressed underneath Mercy's, carefully collecting the shards of the Aguarious Stone and putting them into Veronica's purple satchel.

"Ray, do you think you can bandage her hand?" Ray crouched down beside Nikki in front of Mercy, taking her hand into his, and undid his satchel.

"I'm sorry," Mercy choked, the words slipping so freely now. "I'm so sorry."

To her surprise, Nikki hugged her.

Her heart jumped.

Nikki quickly pulled back, holding her gaze. "You didn't do anything wrong. Sometimes things don't work out. You tried."

If you'd just given it to her sooner…

"You can't just sit around and beat yourself up over it," Ray said as he guided the rain water to wash her hand. "It just makes things worse. Besides, at least you didn't betray everyone and then try to kill your friends and stuff."

Nikki rushed them, Ray struggling to bandage her hand as they went.

"Nikki's whole plan is messed up now, Raphael. We have no plan. And now I'm wasting time."

"You didn't mess up my plan," Nikki said softly, in the voice Mercy knew her best in.

It coaxed her to look up into Nikki's big blue eyes.

To her surprise, there wasn't the rage that Nikki had held before. They were pierced, pained as she studied Mercy. "We all have no idea what we're doing."

"I know, but I should have…"

"The Aguarious Stone is broken, and we can't change that," Nikki said, her voice a bit stronger now as Ray finished the bandaging. "But we do have a new advantage."

"We-we do?"

"Something you said earlier," Nikki said, getting to her feet. "Something about the Keyper being the one that connects us."

"Yeah, well, that's just what everyone says. I don't think that means anything important." Except for the fact she could break Stones.

Ray helped Mercy to her feet.

"But you found out how to glow again, right?" Nikki said.

Mercy retraced her steps. She hadn't *meant* to glow. Everything inside her had burned. Everything in her wanted to.

She was a Council Member. She looked down at her arms, for the first time feeling a small smidge of pride at the marks that decorated her skin.

She nodded firmly. "I think I do."

Nikki began to pace, similar to Lincoln when he was thinking. "Well, I guess we'll just find out," she said, stopping. "We should get to the others."

"What is up with you guys and having, like, no plans ever?"

"See, it's hard to stop supernatural storms," Ray said. "But we still have an entire city to keep from drowning."

Mercy shook herself, taking a deep breath. "Right."

And this time, she knew she couldn't do it herself. She was part of a team.

So she ran alongside Nikki and Ray toward the chaotic streets of Liberty to meet the other six, without a plan…and this time, as a Council Member.

Felicity wasn't used to running.

Her legs having virtually no feeling in them didn't help her in the slightest either. But she pushed it to the back of her mind, trying to call out for the others telepathically.

Ray! Nikki! Mercy!

We heard you the first time, Liz. Ray's voice. *Outside the docks. Lucky for us, your sister is there waiting at the checkpoint!*

Craig moaned excitedly. They were close.

Felicity would've tripped over if it hadn't been for Lawrence throwing a hand out in front of her. She stumbled. "Veronica's there?" she said out loud.

"As in, your sister?" Lawrence frowned, though it was hard to tell with his goggles.

"All the more reason to hurry," Lincoln shouted, running past them.

"We'll get her out," Lawrence said with an assuring nod. Of all people, Felicity could at least find a little comfort in his words. She'd seen and heard firsthand the things Lawrence had put on the line for his siblings.

She'd never meant to get her family wrapped up into this…but apparently, her family was the one who got *her* wrapped up into this.

She tried not to think about it too hard.

They raced toward the docks. A place that, in all her years living in Liberty, Felicity had never truly visited. It went on for miles of warehouses, full of boats and mechanic bots. Most of the lower income Liberty citizens typically were dock workers, and Felicity never had reason to trek through the grease and sweat of the salty docks.

Never had she thought about how her father's entire business relied on it.

Liberty was a Golden region because it was the main port of shipping. Did Kathryn know that? Was that why she was targeting Liberty? Would she really take down the whole world to get to them?

This woman confused Felicity like nothing else.

She heard distant shouts of familiar voices, feeling a little looser as she ran into the fog toward the figures of Ray, Nikki, and Mercy.

They didn't have time for a reunion, and Felicity could tell they all knew it. No hugs or teasing.

"We need to calm that creature," Cole said.

"Did you get the Aguarious Stone?" Felicity said, spinning to Mercy.

Mercy looked down. "I-I sort of broke it."

"You what?"

"It wasn't her fault," Nikki jumped in quickly. "Either way, none of us are Aguarious, and it wouldn't have worked without someone getting hurt."

Felicity's mind was spinning, and for the first time in a long time, the monster threatened to crawl down her spine and freeze her in panic again, reminding her of all the things that could go wrong. That she should just give up now and hyperventilate.

Breathe. Giles said to breathe.

"Felicity, you're the one with the connection to this creature," Cole said. "What do we know?"

"Kathryn's using it…something to do with the storm." Felicity leaned against the frame of the gate to keep her balance. "I don't know if we can stop it," she whispered.

Beat.

"We-we have to stop it," Mercy said. "The whole city will

be underwater."

"And I personally like being alive," Matteo said.

Ray nodded. "It's a huge plus."

Felicity took a deep breath, rubbing her forehead. "I don't think the Leviathan is the problem so much as what's causing the Leviathan to act this way. Something is disturbing it. We cut off what's disturbing it, we cut off most of the problem. It's just us versus the Leviathan."

"Kathryn, most likely," Lincoln said. "That's pretty obvious."

"That's too broad. Kathryn is most likely who we'll face after we get the disturbance out of the way." Felicity bit her lip before her eyes widened. "It's been a while since we've seen an Oquelite."

"I just saw Silas," Nikki butted in, her face hardening. "He had Nathaniel."

"He what?" Lincoln shouted.

Felicity swallowed hard. It was starting to make sense. "That's just it. The Exerticus kept bringing Silas out every night to the water. The creature was obviously pained…what if the Oquelite have something to do with it?"

"How?" Lawrence frowned.

"It might be something like how Felicity has a connection to the Leviathan because they're both Mythics," Cole said.

Mythic was just a nice way of saying *Felicity and that sea monster are both magical, not exactly human creatures,* which was super comforting.

Felicity tried to brush it off.

"Maybe it has to do with the Void," Tabitha said. "Mythics come from the Void, and I remember Giles saying something about how the Oquelite source their teleporting ability from the Void."

"Wouldn't that be funny if there was just a bunch of Oquelite teleporting all over the place," Ray snorted, though no one laughed with him.

He blinked.

"Wait, you guys are being serious?"

"But where would they be?" Matteo said. "We clearly don't see Oquelite."

Felicity took a shaky breath as she forced herself back to

her own feet, staring toward the churning waves. She settled herself. Today, she wasn't running away.

"Where else? The only plausible option is underwater."

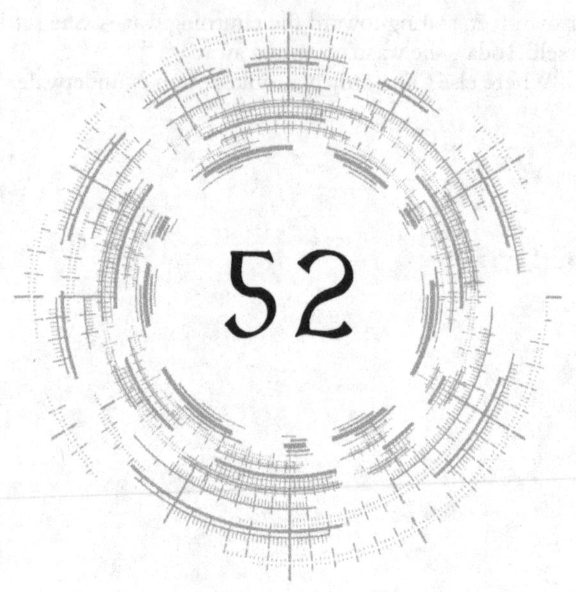

52

THIS HAD TO be the stupidest idea they'd ever had, and the Council had a lot of stupid ideas.

Tabitha had never seen them loading into a submarine as one of them.

Only one of the submarine boarding docks hadn't been entirely flooded yet. The submarine was Council size. Enough to fit ten people, and probably not much more.

The top of the sub was flat, perfect for walking on and looking out over the railing and into the ocean when there *wasn't* a giant-sea-monster-incited-storm happening.

Underneath, there was one detectable pod and a main room full of more buttons and switches than Tabitha had ever seen in her life. There were only two leather chairs bolted into the ground. The rest of the Council was left to their own devices.

The front window gave Tabitha a full view as they slowly sank into the water, red lights flashing and everyone screaming at Lincoln, who was desperately trying to figure out how to turn on the steering.

Typical Council dilemmas.

"Why didn't we figure this out before?"

"Don't touch any buttons!" Lincoln shouted at Lawrence, who was slamming down on every button on the wall, and the sub launched forward, sending everyone slamming to the ground.

Tabitha groaned. "Great going, Williams."

"More than any of you've done."

He had a point. Tabitha could feel the speed of the submarine below them.

The front window of the sub had also opened up.

Lawrence cursed. Everyone else was too stunned to scold him.

Felicity bit back a cry. "Craig is definitely nearby! He's saying *they're* pulling him closer!"

All around them was dark blue, and every so often a waft of foaming water would slam into them. It was eerie and never-ending as she could see the waves crashing above them and feel the rocking down to her stomach.

But that wasn't what terrified her.

Tabitha nearly stumbled back as she saw the haunting sight under the waves.

"You were right," Matteo breathed. "The Oquelite are here."

Flashing in and out of view like a blink were whatever remained of the mind-controlled Oquelite.

"That was such a stupid theory," Lincoln scowled. "I hate when Ray is right."

"So she *was* trying to create disturbances in the Void…to lure Craig?" Tabitha frowned. "Craig must be seriously powerful."

"Craig is a sea creature," Felicity said, almost defensively in her turn. "There's no doubt she's using him to create the Leviathan storm."

And this was the only idea Kathryn could come up with? Controlling and trapping the minds of these Oquelite underwater as they blinked in and out of the Void?

She tried not to focus on the bodies no longer moving.

"Does anyone see Silas?" Nikki said, pushing forward.

"I doubt Kathryn has him here," Cole said, his voice unsteady as he leaned on Lincoln's chair. "If Silas has Nathaniel, he's too important for her to risk."

Felicity scoffed. "I wish she'd just drown him."

Tabitha wasn't used to hearing her friend talk so bitterly. That was usually her thing. Felicity was dead serious, staring out the window.

Then a few Oquelite began to still, their pale faces turning to stare right at them. Tabitha frowned. Were they dying? Were they about to watch Oquelite drown themselves?

And then they started teleporting again sporadically…right toward them.

"They sense us!" Ray shouted. "Shoot, shoot, shoot. LINCOLN, GET THE SUB TO WORK!"

"I'M WORKING ON IT, GENIUS."

"Everyone, brace yourselves!"

Tabitha grabbed Taryn's knife, clutching it with her fist. She had very little patience for Kathryn's antics.

"Hit the pedal!" Mercy gasped.

"What pedal?" Both Ray and Lincoln screamed back at her at the same time.

Mercy pushed Ray out the way, jumping into the second seat beside Lincoln, slamming her foot down on the pedal at the foot of the seat.

Everyone was thrown to the ground again as the sub launched forward.

"Turn!" Tabitha shouted.

"The steering unlocked!" Lincoln celebrated, turning the wheel with a jerk, sending everyone slamming into the wall.

"I think you're doing us more harm than the Oquelite," Matteo grumbled.

"So it operates with two people," Tabitha said. Interesting.

"Lucas once worked on a hovercycle that could go up to six feet in the air. To get that leverage with full control he needed a two-person operator," Mercy said, out of breath, her eyes practically glowing. "Just like this!"

Tabitha felt a lump form in her throat. Lucas. Her brother.

Instead, she forced a smile. "Lucas is pretty great," she said. She was going to see him again. This time, she was going to make sure to let him know she appreciated him.

A bang echoed through the sub, and before Tabitha

could process what was happening, she was spinning through the air, lights flashing and her stomach threatening to overturn itself before they rolled back right-side-up.

"Lincoln!"

"It's not us!" Lincoln shouted, looking back over his shoulder. "It's kinda hard to outrun people who can teleport, remember?"

Tabitha racked her brain for an idea before her eyes landed on Ray. "Then let's use our teleporter."

"Underwater?"

"What other option do we have?"

Cole looked at Tabitha and then back to Ray. "Fine. That's our only option."

"This sub has to have a horn somewhere. If we can make a big enough disturbance, we can maybe snap them out of it," Lawrence said, as one of his most recent button smashes unveiled a door to a lower level. "Come on, 'Teo. Let's go do something illegal."

Matteo followed him without hesitation.

"In the meantime, we have to keep those mind-controlled, essence-hungry Oquelite from destroying this sub," Cole said. "Who's going with Ray?"

Immediately, everyone's hand shot up.

"You can't all go," Ray said. "There's only one pod for like, three people, and I doubt any of you can drive. Strong swimmers?"

Nikki's hand dropped.

"I'm the smallest," Tabitha said. "I'm a Humanic. I have no abilities and nothing those Oquelite would be attracted to."

"You can't drive?" Mercy pointed out.

"I can."

Tabitha's heart skipped a beat as Felicity stepped forward.

"I-I mean, it's been a while…but it can't be too different from an auto, right? Besides, I have a connection to Craig." Felicity's face was pale, her shoulders pulled back, her expression tight and unreadable.

Cole stepped to block her. "Tabitha, there is no—"

"Cole, you can't go," Tabitha said, sternly. "If we lose you, we lose this entire operation."

She could see Cole's face tense, his jaw clenching like he

had something to say but was fighting everything not to as he stared at Tabitha intensely. She could feel his pain. She didn't want this to be the end.

She wanted to hug him again. She wanted to kiss him again. She wanted to spend every aching hour proving her mother wrong with him.

But if any of that was going to happen, they had to actually live.

"Okay, are you lovers going to stop staring into each other's eyes long enough to actually do something?" Ray shouted.

Cole snapped out of his daze, his shoulders falling in defeat. "Don't die."

"Don't worry. I'm living out of spite," Tabitha said with a small smile, grasping her knife as she ran toward Ray and Felicity. "Ready?"

"Let's go buy us some time."

The three ran over to the door leading to the small, lime green pod. Lincoln opened the door and the three loaded in, quickly shutting it behind them.

Power flooded through the pod.

To Tabitha's surprise, there was only a lever, a pedal, and a steering wheel. No buttons or screens. Her stomach sank. A pack sat on the back bench. She unzipped it, finding two breathing tubes labeled with five-minute labels.

"Pull to initiate launch." A robotic voice commanded.

Felicity jumped into the seat, buckling herself. "Safety first," she breathed with a half-hearted chuckle.

She pulled down the lever, and the pod launched forward.

Tabitha flew into the small bench seat in the back, Ray slamming into her, both shouting as they sped into the water with the dark blue waves enveloping them. Felicity took a harsh turn, sending them crashing against the opposite wall.

Time froze. Tabitha couldn't breathe as she turned to look into the water.

For a split second, she was a child again, wanting to cry and run into her older brother's protective arms.

Even through the murky waters she could see the shadow of an enormous creature slowly moving toward them. There wasn't enough glass to see where Craig ended.

He had to be miles wide. Did he touch the ocean floor? And the two enormous glowing eyes.

It sent chills down Tabitha's spine.

"You didn't mention Craig was so *big*, Felicity?" Tabitha screamed.

"How was I supposed to know? Were you expecting a goldfish?"

"We don't have much time!" Ray shouted. "Stop wasting it screaming! Craig is getting closer!"

"Right!"

Ray turned to Tabitha. "You can swim well?"

"You better hope so." Tabitha stuck the breathing stick between her teeth, pulling the goggles over her head. Ray did the same.

Tabitha took his hand, unprepared for when the world slipped out from under her. Everything was dark. Everything was wet. It was cold. Heavy. She couldn't breathe. A figure was coming—

She bit down, oxygen flooding through her.

Don't look down. Don't look down.

Tabitha felt the dark deep below her. She couldn't see where the water ended. All she could see was the enormous sub in the eerie water as the Oquelite rushed toward it.

Everything was so quiet.

She couldn't scream.

She could only brace her knife as Ray blasted her forward with a gust of water.

She tried not to think about breathing as an Oquelite came flying for her. She was moving in slow motion, and they were speeding, flashing in and out of sight.

It was all about timing.

They were mindless.

They wouldn't stop their collision.

She counted, raising her knife.

If she got this wrong, the Oquelite would reach the sub, or the Oquelite would hit her. She didn't like those options. She could see the flashes of Ray's energy strikes as he raced another Oquelite toward the sub.

A blast ripped through the water as the Oquelite slowly appeared into the water.

Tabitha felt the weight pressing on her chest as her

Oquelite grew nearer.

Just.

A.

Second.

Longer.

She brought down her knife. The Oquelite just seemed annoyed, raising their hands of blazing energy. All Tabitha could do was helplessly try and slash at it with her knife as a flail before the blast struck her, sending her spinning through the water.

Pain exploded through her arm, Taryn's knife slipping from her grip.

She flipped over, ignoring the blood streaming from her wound to grab the handle. Her vision began to blur. She couldn't see the glow of the Oquelite getting closer.

At least she—

Tabitha collapsed on the floor of the pod in a puddle of water, gasping for air beside Ray.

"It's like fighting in slow motion," Ray sputtered, shivering. "We can't fight them all off."

Felicity rammed the pod into an Oquelite racing toward them.

Tabitha glanced at blood on her arm, pushing herself up. "We have to try."

They teleported back into the watery battle.

This time Tabitha held onto her knife, bringing it down on the Oquelite spinning toward her, and the blade hit its chest.

Its face went soft before slowly sinking into dust.

She turned around, kicking to stay upright. Her heart plummeted. More were racing toward her.

All of them are coming, she heard Ray's voice in her head.

She saw him pull out his Shadow Blade, the shadows of the ocean beginning to spin around it. She felt them begin to crowd around her, pulling her to Ray's side before they absorbed into his Blade.

She had to remind herself not to gasp.

You keep any who get through from reaching the sub. I'll try to take the majority out. Ray's face hardened.

Tabitha nodded. They only had a matter of seconds before they had to go back for air.

The shadows exploded from the Shadow Blade, slashing through the charging army of underwater, brainless Oquelite.

Tabitha's heart quickened as a few began to sprinkle through the explosion and Ray began to summon more shadow.

Tabitha counted down, hitting an Oquelite blind in the face, quickly swimming to stab another.

She didn't have time to remind herself of death.

It was either them or all of Liberty.

They flashed back into the sub for a split second before diving back into the ocean.

An Oquelite burst toward Tabitha. She tried to cry out for Ray, but a gust hit her face, sending her spinning into the ocean. Her mask slipped off and immediately, the world went blurry.

She almost screamed.

Hands tightened around her throat. She tried to struggle. She tried to cry out for Ray.

The world was so heavy. She was going deeper, and deeper, and...

The grip tightened and her body instinctively gasped for air, water filling her throat. She couldn't cough. Her eyes were burning. She couldn't breathe in or out. It was just water. She was trapped. She was dying. She knew it and she couldn't do anything about it.

She couldn't scream.

She could just taste her own blood and her own demise as her vision grew lighter and lighter and Ray further and further away.

Don't let go of the knife. Don't let go of the knife. Don't let go of the knife.

A horn erupted through the water. Everything around her rippled, and her ears felt like they were bleeding.

They did it.

At least I'll die knowing that.

She let her eyes shut, trying not to panic. Even the loud siren horns were distant.

Have you found your family yet?

I have, she responded to the voice in her mind.

"Tabitha!"

Tabitha shot up, turning to vomit up water before gasping for air. Lights were flashing red. Her arm was exploding with pain. She could feel hot tears streaming down her face, but she could also feel the hilt of the knife in her hand.

"Where's Felicity?" she coughed, looking around desperately. Felicity. She was supposed to protect Felicity. Had she—

The sound of a door clicking open. "I'm here!"

Hearing Felicity's voice, Tabitha's vision came into focus. Cole was crouched in front of her. She threw her arms around him, trying to keep herself from shaking.

The sub trembled again.

The lights flickered. It was Lincoln's turn to curse as he began to bang the steering wheel. Tabitha's blood went cold as the next sentence slipped out.

"It didn't work! They're still attacking!" Lincoln shouted. "It seems like the waves are worse. We have to get up to surface level!"

Tabitha stepped away from Cole, taking in deep breaths as she turned to meet the eyes of Nikki and Felicity.

It took everything in her not to hug Felicity too. Her red curls were frizzy, but the color had returned to her face. They'd failed. All that effort, and pain, and almost dying…And it didn't even work. She clenched her fists.

"How was being a pod captain?" she tried to joke.

"I'm never doing that again," Felicity laughed.

"Everyone on deck!"

Tabitha snapped into focus.

Lincoln jerked the steering up, the submarine launching above the surface, back into the stormy chaos of the world above, tossed by the enormous waves.

Tabitha stepped toward Felicity, wrapping an arm around her friend's shoulder.

"There's too many of them," Ray said as Matteo and Lawrence climbed back up and Lincoln and Mercy joined them from their seats. "And we don't have enough time to prepare, or resources to fight them."

"So how do we stop the storm now? And how do we stop them from destroying us?" Lawrence said, his voice strained. "Are we really just going to give up and die?"

If Lawrence was nervous, this was bad.

"What if we don't need to stop the storm…" Nikki's voice was quiet.

Everyone was arguing over her.

Tabitha flashed back to their time in the cave, a year ago when this all started. Nikki had been crouched in the corner, her voice tiny as she pitched her suggestion.

"Everyone shut up!" she shouted, turning to Nikki. "What do you mean?"

The boys stopped and stared.

Nikki bit her lip, looking around to the faces of the other Members. "Once Craig and the storm break through the Dome, that will be enough power to wipe the Oquelite out. Kathryn has no purpose for them, and they'll have no reason to try and kill us."

"Wait, Nik, you're saying we should let the Leviathan break in?" Lincoln said, blinking.

Tabitha didn't like it. Her gut said that was bad, and a big no. That's what Kathryn wanted and anything Kathryn wanted was bad. She'd done so much damage already.

But Nikki had a point.

The only way the Oquelite would leave them alone is if they completed their task of luring in Craig.

"But then what after that?" Tabitha said.

Nikki took a deep breath. "Then I say we face Kathryn."

"That's under the assumption she's with Craig," Cole said. "And how will she not just plow through nine teenagers in a sub with her personal sea monster?"

"What about Mercy?" Nikki said. "Navi said something about you being a key."

"That's a theory," Mercy said in a small voice. "I can enhance the objects around me…but-but we've never tested *people*. And my ability to glow is unreliable."

Tabitha grew excited, walking forward to the center of the circle. "If we can get Mercy to glow, she can power us all. She's the Keyper, she's what connects us physically."

"If I can glow," Mercy corrected.

Nikki smiled. "I saw you at the bridge. Whatever you did there works."

Mercy swallowed hard. "But I broke the Stone…"

"We need that power," Lawrence said, crossing his arms. "We need every last bit of that destructive power."

"I see where this is going. If we can take Kathryn head on, we can stop her up front. We don't have to worry about the barrier if we stop the problem trying to get through," Cole said, his eyes lighting up before he scowled. "There's a very low chance of this working, though."

"Do we have any other chances?" Matteo said, raising a brow.

No one said a word.

Matteo sighed. "I thought so."

Tabitha turned to Mercy, extending her hand. "Are you ready, Glow Girl?"

Mercy timidly stepped forward with a deep breath, the tiniest smile, and a glowing spark in her eye as she took Tabitha's hand.

"The real question is: How do you feel about glowing?"

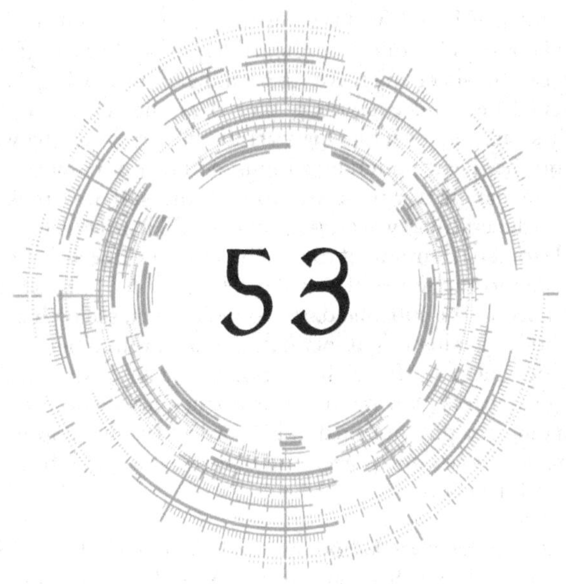

53

NIKKI COULDN'T HELP a gasp as Tabitha began to glow underneath her skin as soon as Mercy's glowing hand touched hers.

Mercy's marks began to glow brighter, strands of her hair going golden and defying gravity as it rose upward.

"Wow," Tabitha laughed, her voice now sounding strange and echoey. "This is epic. What are you all staring at? Come on!"

"Get to the top of the sub!" Cole shouted, snapping out of his daze.

Nikki's heart leaped before she tightened her grip on Fidelis. Perfect. They planned on facing Kathryn head on.

Mercy's eyes couldn't seem to focus on one place, either out of nerves or excitement as Cole led them up on land, screwing open the door. Water crashed inside, but Cole pushed through.

The ladder began to glow as Mercy touched it.

Tabitha gave a hoarse laugh as they rose up the glowing ladder.

Nikki swallowed as the ladder dimmed. She was going to

get Nathaniel back. She was going to make Taryn proud of her.

She ran and climbed up the ladder, nearly blown off her feet by the sheer might of the wind before a warm hand clutched her, and everything slowed as she felt her entire body swallowed by a tingling warmth, her veins surging with energy, her heart pounding a thousand times a minute.

The flat platform of the top of the sub was rocking above the crashing waves, but Nikki could hardly feel it.

It took her a moment to remember to breathe as her eyes adjusted to the waves. The wind felt like a cool breeze, her feet fixed to the sub. She dared to look down, seeing her entire body glowing bright, her hair floating around her.

She squeezed Mercy's hand, holding back a gasp at seeing the girl's marks glowing, her eyes bright yellow, and her hair levitating straight up. She'd only heard and seen glimpses of Mercy's "Glow Girl" power, and here it was, right in front of her, in full action.

"Nik!"

Lincoln had crawled out of the hole, the wind snatching at him. Nikki reached out, grabbing his hand, clutching it tightly as she watched the shock in his face as he began to glow as well, everything but his black eyes which looked around, very confused. "Holy—"

"A little help, our glowing friends!"

"Right," Lincoln said, turning to grab Matteo, and then Lawrence, and then lastly Felicity, who threw herself at Lawrence before a wave could take her.

That was the most strange feeling as an enormous wave came crashing down on top of them.

"Everyone, stay where you are!" Cole demanded.

It was against her very human nature to watch the rolling wave rise up above them. Nikki held her breath as it came crashing down. For a moment, she couldn't breathe. Her entire body felt perfectly still, though, her feet anchored to the ground, and her hair still floating gently around her shoulders as the wave rocked the sub beneath them.

She turned to Lincoln's dark eyes, which looked as lost as she felt.

She tightened her grip on his hand.

The wave passed, and everyone was left gasping for air.

"That…that was incredible," Lincoln sputtered, his voice

echoey and deeper than usual.

Mercy took a deep breath. "The Dome," she whispered.

Nikki dared to look up, watching another enormous wave crash against the Dome. It glitched, water seeping through.

"It doesn't have much longer!" Cole shouted over the wind.

"Way to state the obvious!" Lawrence shouted back.

"Is everyone ready?" Cole said.

"Well, we're all here and we don't exactly have any other battle option," Felicity said nervously, moving closer to Lawrence. She cleared her throat. "But yes. I-I'm ready. I was born for this."

They were all born for this.

They were all born for standing hand in hand as the most destructive force known to humanity broke down the Dome.

She'd never thought much about the fact that all of them were made for this purpose. They all had a place. It wasn't just chance that they'd all come together.

Nikki took a deep breath.

The Dome was glitching frequently now, sending sporadic flashes of light brighter than the lightning above them.

"Don't let go!" Cole shouted. "No matter what happens to the Dome: Do. Not. Let. Go."

Nikki held her breath, and the entire world seemed to hold it with her.

For a moment, the wind didn't rage, the waves almost calmed, and rain became lighter.

And then with an ear-ringing crash, the Dome flickered and fell, an enormous wave crashing down into the docks.

"DON'T LET GO!"

The water came rushing for them. Nikki's heart beat faster. She couldn't swim. She was going to drown. She was going to die, and she'd never get Nathaniel back—

The water swallowed them before she had the chance to panic any further.

The sub bobbed beneath them, though still her feet remained steadfast on it. She held onto Lincoln and Mercy's hands with all her might. She couldn't breathe. When would she breathe again?

She squeezed her eyes shut, trying not to imagine her

mother's dying face. The memories were back full force. She remembered everything. Every terrible detail.

She wasn't going to die again.

Then why did air seem so far away? Why did Lincoln's hand seem so distant? Was she falling? Was she sinking?

Nikki gasped for air as they bobbed back above the waves, her vision slowly coming back into focus and feeling gradually returning to her body, realizing how tightly Lincoln was gripping her.

Lincoln hadn't let go of her.

Just like he promised back at the Outown's villa.

None of her friends had let go. In fact, they just seemed to burn brighter.

Nikki looked over her shoulder to see the waves crashing over the docks. She took a deep breath and steadied herself as she turned to glare at the upcoming waves.

Felicity let out a gasp. "It's here," she breathed.

Nikki's lips parted as she turned in horror, her eyes widening as an enormous earthy head rose out of the storming waves. It shook, sending chunks of earth flying. The eyes were nothing but pitted orbs. The head was an enormous skull, clad in mud, bone showing through. Moss blanketed the enormous creature, plants tangled atop of it.

On the crown of the skull were stone antlers that curved up into an arc, but hardly touching as it reared its head back. Its roar was nothing like an animal. It almost rang out like thousands of bells, but as if the bells were screaming. It was beautiful, but made Nikki's eyes prick with tears and made her want to run. Get away at any cost.

The sound was torture.

It sounded like grief. The cries of her younger siblings. The echoes of her younger self behind a locked door.

"Craig!" Felicity cried out.

The creature came crashing down into the water, sending the sub rolling over with a new wave.

"There!" Tabitha yelled.

Craig was enormous. He could've been an entire island. Nikki couldn't process all of him in once glance, and as he swam closer, Nikki took in a deep breath.

The creature might as well have been its own coast line, but all she could focus on was the glowing eyes of Sergia standing atop the head in the stone circle.

Kathryn wasn't there, but the sleeping figure of Nathaniel was in Sergia's arms.

"Nathaniel!" Lincoln cried out, tugging against the glowing line, but Matteo and Nikki pulled him back.

Silas stood sheepishly to the side, clutching his arm, and a few other Exerticus stood opposite him.

"I didn't think you'd live this long," one of the Exerticus scoffed.

Sergia stepped forward, looking far down at them. "Centuries ago, the First Council stood at the very Stone circle we stand on to curse a Soul. It's ironic. You're only children. I would prefer not to slaughter you."

"You say that as you hold a literal baby captive!" Lincoln shouted at the top of his lungs to her. "Let him go!"

"And it will stay that way," Sergia said, her voice thundering over the waves. "This is your last chance, Members, or I regret to inform you that your city will drown due to the creature's might."

"The creature doesn't want to do this!" Felicity shouted. "You're torturing it to do your bidding!"

"What the Lady of the Universe sees fit, I see fit."

"Where is she anyway?" Lincoln shouted. "Too cowardly to show her face? She'd rather just torture children's minds?"

Even in its glowing majesty, Nikki could see the fury in Lincoln's expression. He believed he was the reason Nathaniel had been taken.

But in reality, all of this had been Kathryn.

Kathryn had killed Nikki, just to torture her for two weeks straight with her horrifying memories of Kathryn's own pain.

Just so Nikki knew how she felt. A cruel, pointless mockery.

Nikki wanted to be angry, but part of her understood. She understood Kathryn's anger.

And it terrified her.

"None of your banter changes anything. Give the remaining Council Members' blood, or the city drowns."

"We don't even have all of the Members!" Tabitha pleaded.

"Sergia!" Nikki cried, hoping that the name would strike

something.

Sergia simply flinched.

"If you do this, you risk damaging the Void! You risk damaging this whole world!"

"Well, you aren't exactly willing to help her break her curse," Sergia scoffed. She took a deep breath. "I see how it is."

"No!" Felicity screamed.

Sergia turned to Silas. "Instruct the creature, young Idicous."

Her voice was surprisingly gentle toward him as Silas pulled himself forward beside Sergia.

Nikki could hear the voices of the other Members around her go quiet. She knew they wanted to scream, but much like herself, she couldn't.

"Whatever you do," Cole said, in a shaky voice. "Stand your ground. We're not going down without a fight."

Even if this fight was against an enormous sea monster? It was suicide, but Nikki couldn't live with herself if she didn't try.

All she could do was watch as Silas knelt before Sergia.

They'd failed.

Silas bowed. "As she wishes."

And then he kicked Sergia's feet from under her.

Nikki's jaw dropped in horror as he took the split second to tear Nathaniel from her arms, waking him from his peaceful slumber, before jumping off the Leviathan's head and into the crashing waves below.

"Get the Idicous prince back!" an Exerticus shouted.

"Nathaniel!"

Nikki didn't even stop to think about the crashing waves or drowning. She broke the line, not hesitating before diving into the waves.

Avalon began to glow under the waves. The green light revealed Silas not too far away, clutching onto Nathaniel. Nikki moved toward them. She pulled out her shield, prepared to bash Silas in the face, just like he had to leave the scar across her face, but she stopped herself.

Silas let Nathaniel go before swimming up for air.

Nathaniel's face lit up, floating in place until Nikki clicked Fidelis back in place, swimming to him.

As soon as she touched the child, a bubble of air formed

around her head.

She could hear the shallow echoes of Nathaniel's laugh as he clung to her. "Linc!"

Wrong person, but she still hugged the tiny child back, not daring to look down.

"Nat, we need to get to Linc, okay?" she said, hoping the baby could hear. "Linc is up!"

She pointed upward, hoping the baby would get the message.

But before Nathaniel could seem to process it, a shock-wave exploding under the water, which sent Nikki and Nathaniel tumbling. The bubble popped, water going up Nikki's mother and nose. She held onto Nathaniel.

Her lungs began to scream.

The world around her was dark. The waves wouldn't stop tossing and turning.

The Leviathan was coming, and Nikki would drown underneath it.

Suddenly, her head surfaced above water. She gasped for air, trying to stay afloat while clinging to Nathaniel. She caught sight of something bobbing in the water. She couldn't even scream for help before she was pulled back under.

Nikki refused to die like this.

She refused to let Kathryn make a fool of her.

She grabbed Fidelis and sunk it into the floating piece, pulling herself up by the metal strap, onto the floating metal wing or what looked to be the remains of a transport ship wing.

She pulled herself on top, holding Nathaniel.

She looked to the child at her hip as he stared with his big green eyes toward the monster crashing into the ocean.

There was no sign of the Council.

"Linc?" Nathaniel whimpered, turning back to Nikki. "Linc okay? Bad lady want Linc."

She looked at him, swallowing hard. "We're going to get Linc."

She turned to look back at the docks, the waves now obscuring the shoreline. The warehouses still stuck out of the water.

They didn't have the Stone, and they didn't have the power to stop the Exerticus.

All Nikki had was a shield and a supernatural toddler.

"Nat!" Nikki said, forcing excitement into her voice. "I know where Linc is!"

Nathaniel turned to her, his eyes widening.

She pointed to the warehouses. "There! Linc!"

"LINC!"

The waves rose, and Nikki's heart sank, her mind flashing back to tumbling below the water, lost and helpless. But instead of being pulled under, their metal plank was pushed forward, remaining above the water as Nathaniel looked intensely toward the warehouse and they rode the waves toward it.

Nathaniel kept muttering Lincoln's name as they went, and Nikki clung to Fidelis, trying to not to think too hard about how insane the situation was. They surfaced on the dock, and Nikki's feet met the ground. She pulled Fidelis out, clipping it to her back, picking Nathaniel up.

The water was up to her ankles.

"Uh! Nik! Look!" Nathaniel tugged on Nikki's shirt, pointing behind her. Nikki turned, her heart skipping a beat at seeing an enormous wave rolling quickly toward them.

"We gotta go!" she shouted, running through the water with all her might. She reached the ladder up the side of the warehouse, struggling to pull herself up with one arm. She rose higher and higher, Nathaniel giggling excitedly.

She rose to the top of the building, the wind beating up against them. She could feel the crystal shards of the Aguarious Stone in her pocket. She rushed to the edge of the warehouse, struggling to fish them out, trying to not look at the incoming wave.

There was no way this would work, but she had no other choice.

There had to be a reason Kathryn wanted to keep Nathaniel so badly.

She held out the shards in her hand. They zapped her skin. Nikki cried out, jerking back, the shards slipping out and falling over the edge of the warehouse.

"No!"

Hot tears pricked at her eyes as she watched them sink into the water. What had she done?

"Linc," Nathaniel muttered, lifting his eyes, reaching his

arms out toward the waves.

Nikki looked at him curiously, trying not to let her tears overcome her. The burning grew stronger inside of her. What was it? What was it for the feeling inside her? It felt like it was caged inside her, fighting to escape free. It was unbridled. It was dangerous. And it burned.

"Linc," was all Nathaniel would say.

Nikki got to her feet, forcing herself not to tremble as she held Nathaniel up, his arms outstretched toward the enormous creature charging toward them.

She closed her eyes, preparing herself.

This was it.

Ma, please help us.

And then Nathaniel giggled. Nikki cracked an eye open. Craig had paused, tilting its enormous earthy head at the little boy.

Nikki's eyes widened, and she stepped back as the blue shards of the Aguarious Stone began to rise out of the water around them.

Nathaniel talked in his gibberish, the creature watching him intently. The waves began to calm. Craig crouched closer.

Nikki froze, its enormous shadow towering them.

Nathaniel cooed, the Aguarious Stone growing brighter. "It okay," Nathaniel whispered. "Go home."

And then the creature bowed its head, sending waves up around them, the Aguarious shards beginning to spin faster around them before they exploded apart. The creature sank below the surface, and the waves crashed down. Nikki threw herself to the ground, covering Nathaniel as the water pounded down above them.

Even after the water subsided, Nikki lay on the ground, trying to breathe, closing her eyes.

The air was still. The wind didn't rage. The rain didn't fall. She could only hear the soft crash of the waves. Her entire body was sore, feeling bruised.

A tiny, cold hand touched her face.

She dared to open her eyes to see Nathaniel sitting beside her, his head tilted as he looked at her.

"Nik," he whispered, poking her mouth. She pushed away his little hand gently while sitting up.

She couldn't believe the sight of the ocean. There was no Dome blocking the view of the water that spread out for miles and miles, as far as the eye could see.

Below, the dock was still flooded, but behind them, Liberty remained untouched.

Nikki jerked up. The Council.

Anyone? She begged mentally, picking Nathaniel up. *Are you all okay? PLEASE SOMEONE?*

No, no, no.

She scanned the murky, flooded dock, rushing to climb down the ladder, landing to the ground with a splash and screaming her friends' names.

"Lawrence! Lincoln!"

She ran, her lungs already on fire from the saltwater. She had a sharp pain in her ribs, but she ignored it, jumping over floating debris.

"Matteo! Mercy! Felicity!"

Why was it so quiet? Was it over? Or was another attack just waiting right around the corner?

"Tabitha! Cole! Anyone!"

Was all of this even worth it if she lost them? They were the world to her. She needed them.

"Nikki?"

"Linc!" Nathaniel cried.

Nikki stopped in her tracks, turning to see Lincoln standing in the water, only a few feet away from the submarine, which was still half submerged underwater.

"Lincoln!" she shouted with Nathaniel, rushing through the water to him. She threw herself at him, burying her face in his neck, crying with relief. Nathaniel clung to Lincoln, repeating his name over and over.

"Nik. Nat. Oh my gosh." Lincoln was out of breath, holding them both tightly.

She finally managed to pull away, Nathaniel wriggling out of her arms and into Lincoln's. Lincoln hugged the little boy, tears slipping down his cheeks. "I'm never letting you go ever again," he choked, kissing Nathaniel's wet curls.

"I fight bad guy, Linc!"

"Look at you! Sentences now!"

The other Council Members tumbled out of the sub, and Nikki rushed to them. She didn't know who started it, but the next moment she knew, she was wrapped in everyone's arms as they clung together like their lives depended on it. She never wanted to let go. She wanted to stay like this forever.

They all slowly moved out of the hug, everyone seeming out of breath and as tired as the next.

"How did you do it?" Cole finally managed to say in a ragged whisper.

"It was Nathaniel," Nikki said, quietly looking at the child happily playing with Lincoln's hoodie strings. "I think that's why Kathryn wanted him so badly. The Leviathan...or Craig, is an Aguarious-created creature. Just like how Fire Wolf is a Ywondie creature, which means he obeys Lawrence."

No one said a word as they stared at Nathaniel.

"Silas saved him," Felicity finally broke the silence with a gasp. "Silas."

"So far, it seems like Silas isn't totally against us," Ray shrugged. "At least when he's not under Kathryn's control...we have a common enemy."

"I can't believe she didn't have guts enough to show her face," Matteo said, crossing his arms.

He spoke for all of them.

"Do you think she's afraid of us?" Matteo asked, looking around hopefully.

"Or maybe she just doesn't think we're enough of a threat," Lincoln muttered.

Nikki tightened her fists.

"Whatever it is, we don't have a lot of time to waste," Cole said. "We need to go to Liberty, get injuries accounted for, and get this mess cleaned up."

No one argued as they followed Cole. They were all too tired to. A good sort of tired.

At least a temporary assurance that they'd won.

But Nikki couldn't help but look back at the crashing waves.

The strange feeling still hadn't left.

Kathryn would show her face.

And Nikki would make sure Kathryn knew she was a threat.

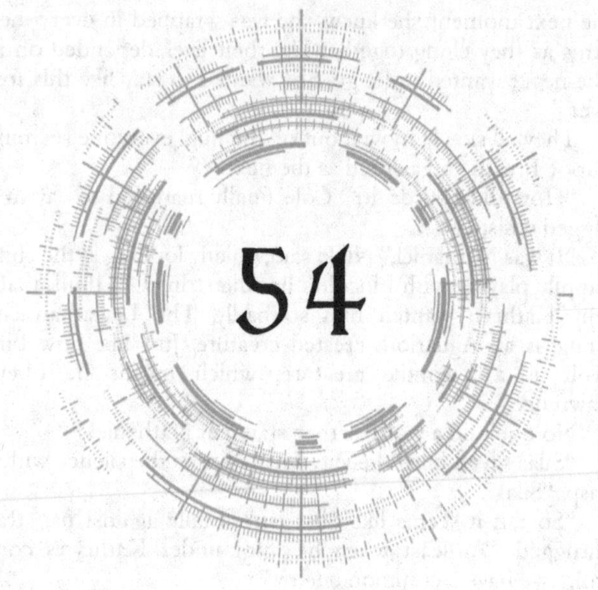

54

NIKKI ONCE AGAIN stood in front of the enormous mirror in Felicity's parlor, hearing the echoes of voices below and the soft strain of music that followed faintly.

Two days didn't feel like enough time.

Two days, and the elites of Liberty had already come to terms. All they knew was they were safe, and much to their awkward reluctance, it was somehow due to the group of teenagers with a supernatural connection they couldn't begin to understand.

"Ah Nikki, you look— you look amazing!"

Nikki jumped at Felicity's voice, spinning around to see her friend. It took her a moment to process Felicity's long curled hair, half-up in an intricate bun and pinned in place with silver ornaments.

Her green dress hugged around her shoulders, revealing light scars across her chest. The sleeves hung around her elbows, and the outer skirt draped over her chair and onto the ground, her inner dress more tightly fit to her. She sat straight, a certain power in her beauty as she looked at Nikki.

A confidence.

"You think so?" Nikki said, looking down at herself before turning back to the mirror.

Felicity moved over to her, tugging Nikki down to her level to adjust the Stone around her neck. The bright green stood out against the simple black dress that fit Nikki's frame snugly, the skirt going down to her knees, with solid straps around her shoulders. Her feet were covered by simple slip-ons, nothing like the green heels Felicity wore.

Felicity tucked a curl behind Nikki's ear, brushing her bangs out of her face. "I know so."

Nikki turned to face herself again in the mirror. She'd never seen her hair treated to its natural curls. And she had to admit that she liked it.

She almost even liked the scar that marred the right side of her face.

She looked so fragile.

Felicity took Nikki's hand. "Look, I know the last few weeks have been hard on you, but tonight is a night to relax."

That was easy for Felicity to say. She was on good terms with her parents. Mercy was finally getting along with the other Members, even cracking a few jokes on Ray's height and Lawrence's goggles along the way.

Nikki should've felt happy. Everything could go back to the way it was.

But the burning, unnamed feeling festered inside her.

"Everyone will be watching," Nikki said quietly. "They think we're heroes."

Felicity was quiet a moment. "Is there anything you think we did...wrong?"

Nikki jumped. "I mean. No. You are a hero. I meant...I don't know." She sighed, fiddling with the Stone. "Maybe I do just need to relax."

Felicity gave her hand a small squeeze and a gentle smile. "I'm thinking that too. Come on, I think you might like this."

Nikki smiled back, taking a deep breath. "Alright."

She let Felicity take her hand and lead her out of the room. She already knew from Renee that they were scheduled to meet with the other Members before descending into the party together.

That was the part Nikki was most terrified of.

But she trusted Felicity to guide her as they moved on the elevator up to the next level.

They approached the doors. Nikki tensed as they swung opened.

"Oh my gosh, it's like a fashion show!"

Immediately, she felt like she could breathe as Ray toppled over a sofa, his gelled-back hair already messed up and his jacket missing.

Despite that, she'd never seen Ray look so formal thanks to his vest and button-up black shirt.

In fact, she'd never seen any of her friends look so formal. It took her a moment to process it all, seeing all the boys in their own variations of a suit. Lawrence had managed to convince someone to give him a longer jacket that echoed his trench coat. She almost didn't recognize him with his curls matted down.

Matteo had also managed to get a bright green button-up, his sleeves rolled back for a rare occasion.

Lincoln looked entirely uncomfortable in his suit, his usually wild hair trimmed for the occasion. Even little Nathaniel, who sat in on the sofa beside them, was all done up in a tiny tuxedo.

Nikki could've studied Mercy and Tabitha all day. Tabitha's dress was simple like hers, a red flowy satin dress with two slits down the sides, and pockets that she was already making use of. She was wearing heels confidently, with her deadly anklet, a gift from Cole, proudly on display.

Mercy's dress had a navy blue mesh train draping off her arms, decorated in silver embroidery of stars and constellations. The skirt swooped down to her feet, custom made for her height and dimensions, fitting her perfectly. Her hair was down, little braids pulled up with crystal clips, and gold-accented eyeliner similar to her marks. A glove covered her injured hand.

She waved nervously to Nikki.

Nikki couldn't help but smile. "You look amazing!"

"So do you!" Mercy said, giving her a shaky smile back.

Felicity rolled over to hug Mercy, and most likely to give her the same pep talk as Nikki. Nikki took no hesitation to run over to Nathaniel and give him a hug.

Nathaniel cried out with delight.

"I see how it is. You chose him over me," Lincoln sighed dramatically. "Don't worry, I get it. He's very cute in his little suit."

Nikki set Nathaniel back down, rolling her eyes at Lincoln. "You look good in your little suit too."

Lincoln blushed. "Well, thank you. You don't look too bad yourself."

"So they let her keep the curls, but not me?" Lawrence said, butting in between them. "And people say we look nothing alike."

"You don't," Matteo said.

Lawrence ignored him. "That's how my mother wore her hair," he said, his face gentle in the rare occasion.

Nikki's aunt she didn't remember, and yet, it made her grow warm at the compliment. There was a distance in Lawrence's eyes but a small smile on his lips. Her only remaining family stood right in front of her, living and breathing.

She took Lawrence's hand, warm due to his Ywondie nature, tracing her finger over the faint scorch marks on his palms. "She would've been proud of you," she said softly.

Lawrence was quiet a moment.

"She would've been proud of you too, Nik," he said, his voice so quiet she almost missed it.

The door banged open.

Nikki spun around, bracing herself before she registered Veronica barreling into the room, nearly tripping on her purple train. "They're in here!" she cried back over her shoulder.

Who was she talking to?

Who was she bringing in?

Guests? MEDIA writers?

"Well, aren't you kids all dressed up," Officer Miriam Outown said, tucking away a loose hair and settling her hands on her hips.

Nikki's heart leaped, her mind going a million miles a minute as the Defenders stepped through the door.

The room exploded from its shock all at once, but no one was as frantic as Felicity, who didn't even hesitate as she cried, "Armstance Giles!"

Nikki didn't even recognize the Officer. It was rare she saw him without his Defender uniform and in a suit, his tie tight in his collar.

But that wasn't the most shocking. He looked so much younger…so much more like a terrified nineteen-year-old kid with his hair cropped short.

"You finally got rid of that stupid mullet!" Felicity raced toward Giles, nearly knocking him off his feet.

Giles didn't even seem to hear her as he scooped her off her feet into a hug, spinning her around.

Felicity held onto him tightly, beginning to cry. "I thought you were going to die, you idiot. I thought you were dead."

"Bentsworth, Bentsworth, it's okay," Giles said, setting her back down and holding onto her shoulders. "I'm alive. Everything's fine. We won. It's okay. Don't cry."

"You won?" Nikki's heart skipped a beat as she spun to Miriam and Jack, who were now talking to Cole and the others excitedly.

"Yes! Dean dropped her charges," Miriam said, talking quickly. "About darn time. It's stupid that she had a threat against Giles in the first place."

"So Nikki is no longer wanted?" Lincoln said.

Nikki's heart flipped.

"She dropped those charges as well," Miriam said with a nod.

Relief flooded over her. Nikki felt like she could breathe again. She didn't have to wear that face distorter anymore. Did that mean Aalto wouldn't come back?

Was she truly safe again?

Why had Dean dropped them so quickly?

"Do we get to know what super illegal secrets Giles knows yet?" Ray asked impatiently, peering back to Giles, who was totally engrossed in conversation with Felicity.

"Sadly, no," Miriam sighed. "Even we don't fully know. Only Taryn was allowed."

That's who was missing.

"Where is Taryn?" Nikki asked.

"She said she'd be back later. She had to handle some things with Dean," Miriam said, before lowering her voice with a mischievous smile. "And I also think she just wanted to avoid a party."

"And we all know Miriam just can't say no to a good

party," Jack scoffed.

"Jack, this is a Bentsworth gala!" Miriam said, exasperated. "How could I possibly say no to that? Do you know who caters these events?"

"Food?" at least three of the boys said in unison.

"What kind of food?" Tabitha said, shoving through them.

Miriam smiled. "I guess we'll just have to find out, shall we?"

"I'm in!" Tabitha said, hooking her arm with Cole's. "Trust me, the Bentsworths have taste."

"So I take this to mean you're ready?" Miriam asked, scanning the room. "I mean, of course, once Giles and Rusty are done over there."

"Hilarious, Outown," Giles said, returning to his grumpy self, getting to his feet and dusting himself off.

"Well then, that settles it. Felicity's Renee Kitts friend wanted us to meet her on the first floor, by the west wing exit."

Felicity nodded, seeming to have no problem taking the lead, patting her face dry on her way out the door.

Nikki hesitated. There was no going back after this.

"You scared?" she heard Mercy whisper.

Nikki looked to see Mercy also petrified beside her. Nikki gave a shallow laugh. "A little."

"You'd think after facing literal sea monsters, this would be nothing," Mercy said.

And yet, Nikki would rather be doing just that.

"Should we go?" Nikki said, turning to Mercy with a smile. "Together?"

Mercy's eyes flickered with surprise, and Nikki was prepared for her to step back. But instead, Mercy smiled. "Together. I like the sound of that."

The two ran to catch up with the rest of the Members. They all crammed into an elevator, taking in the silence. Nikki drew in a deep breath.

Would the world understand?

They only knew them as the kids who helped take down the Oquelite in Imperial. Cole's reputation had been slandered, Nikki's true identity was a security threat, and Ray was an Oquelite that the world feared.

If they only knew the true threats.

"You look worried, Nikki," Lawrence whispered beside her. "You okay?"

Nikki looked up to her older cousin. "It's just— Up until now, it's only been us. And now we're being presented to the world…like this."

"Who said anything would change?" Lawrence said, raising a brow. "It is still just us. Whatever they're going to think is irrelevant."

He had a point.

She took a deep breath. This was her family, and no one could take that away from her.

The doors to the elevator opened. Nikki could hear the music more clearly now along with the rolls of conversation, and light seeped out from under the huge twin doors to the courtyard.

Renee Kitts rushed to arrange them.

Nikki grabbed Lawrence's hand, relieved when he held it back. Mercy stood beside her, casting her a nervous glance. They shared a nod.

Nikki held her breath.

The crowd outside went quiet.

She could hear the echoes of an introduction. The group of youth with knowledge of the supernatural threats. The teenagers who stopped the flood.

The doors flew open and light spilled in.

"Presenting the Phoenix Council."

Everything went into slow motion. Lights hovered in the air, over a hundred glittering guests' eyes were glued on them, an uproar of applause and plenty of suspicious eyes as the music picked back up to the pace of Nikki's heart as they descended the stairs. Not once did she let go of Lawrence.

She could feel herself loosening, her chest letting her breathe as she stood a little straighter.

They were led to their seats. Nikki quickly sat down, happily taking a glass of water offered to her. The festivities returned slowly to normal. Nikki stayed seated, watching as the women's dresses spun and the people laughed and moved on a hard floor a few feet away.

Dancing.

It was beautiful.

Ray and Matteo had raided the buffet table, coming back with their exploits and unloading them to the table. Some Nikki had never seen before, including a strange spiky fruit with a yellow inside that Ray dared to try. He claimed it was amazing, but no one else was willing to take a chance.

Out of the corner of her eye, Nikki caught sight of a familiar yellow. She moved a plate of pie out of the way, her heart leaping to see the familiar fruit. She picked up the lemon, rubbing her thumb over its waxy skin.

Just like her lemon trees back in North Cordell. She smiled.

"Uh. Lemon?" Nikki looked down, seeing Nathaniel tugging on her skirt. She looked around before crouching onto the ground.

"Yes. You're right. It's a lemon," she explained to the little boy, who watched with fascinated eyes.

He held out his hands, and she placed the fruit in it, scooping him up into her arms. Nathaniel attempted to put the lemon in his mouth but removed it with disdain, looking at Nikki with betrayal. She couldn't help but laugh. "You just have to give it a chance."

The music took a lively turn.

"We need to dance," Tabitha said suddenly, setting down her glass of water and getting to her feet.

"I'd rather stay put," Lawrence grumbled. "Too many people."

"Matteo, grab your grumpy friend. The Council is not going to be boring tonight."

Lawrence's eyebrows shot up, choking on his own argument as Matteo happily obeyed Tabitha in pulling Lawrence to his feet. "Hey! I-I can't dance!" Lawrence said, struggling to slip off his coat before being dragged away.

"We can teach you!"

Tabitha pulled Cole into it as well, though he seemed far more willing. The music reminded Nikki of the night they'd all been together on the shore of the lake at the Outown's villa.

Matteo tried to show a fumbling Lawrence a few simple steps. Lawrence, an expert of instinct in a fight, couldn't seem to grasp the concept of dance.

Mercy leaned against Nikki's chair. "Cole never really opened up about his talent for dancing," she said with a snort.

Nikki looked to Cole and Tabitha, who seemed to be in their own world, ignoring the others around them, moving perfectly to the beat and even making conversation throughout, both of them unable to wipe smiles from their faces.

The music spun faster, and so did Cole and Tabitha, neither seeming to break a sweat as Cole spun her.

Nikki glanced back to Lawrence and Matteo. Lawrence had stepped on Matteo's foot.

The song rose to its climax. Nikki felt like she should hold her breath, and Tabitha spun again before the music came to a triumphant close. Tabitha's spin came to a stop, Cole grabbing her hand and waist, dipping her.

The air hung for moment as the two looked at each other before Cole pulled her back to her feet.

The floor was too full for people to have watched them, except for Mercy and Nikki, who exchanged stunned glances.

Lawrence and Matteo stumbled back to the table.

"Never again," Lawrence attempted to grumble as he failed to hide his laughter.

Tabitha and Cole returned hand in hand, Tabitha stealing a quick kiss before rushing back to grab a glass of water.

It wasn't even a minute before she had dragged Cole back into it.

This time, the rest of the Council got more ideas. Ray took Mercy's hands, suggesting the fantastic idea they dance terribly on purpose, which she surprisingly agreed to.

Lawrence got out of any more dancing by taking Nathaniel from Nikki and naming himself babysitter. Nathaniel was surprisingly okay with that, beginning to doze off in Lawrence's arms. Matteo recruited Lincoln in his dancing antics, which was beyond entertaining to watch as Lincoln tried to follow Matteo's steps, his brows furrowed as if he was trying to figure out one of his inventions.

Giles convinced Felicity to dance, though she'd originally argued that her dancing days were beyond her. Giles wouldn't have it, insisting that he would carry her if need be.

Nikki turned down Lincoln's offer to join them.

She much preferred to watch. It made her feel warm inside, bringing a smile to her face seeing them look so alive. Even though Lawrence eventually fell asleep in his seat with Nathaniel on his lap, seeing him at peace was enough for her.

Nikki got to her feet, stretching her arms.

She needed fresh air.

The gardens behind the Manor were massive, and there was a lit path down through the grasses. Nikki followed it, the music becoming a hum in the distance as she went. The path led her to a bridge over a small running river.

She took a deep breath.

She hadn't had much time to think in the past few days. She almost felt like there hadn't been enough time to breathe.

The echoes of the memories in the warehouses threatened her, but she refused to let them triumph.

She'd watched her mother die, and her mind liked to remind her of the fact. Her mind had also shown her horrifying images of blank walls and needles, and harsh voices, and blood on walls.

She closed her eyes, trying to focus on the good things she could remember.

Her mother's smile.

Her father's comforting arms.

The giggling of her baby sister.

Even the memories of her little brother curiously grabbing her hair.

It reminded her of Nathaniel.

She opened her eyes, looking back to the glowing event in the distance, and she couldn't help but give a weary smile.

"Hey Nik! What are you doing all the way out here?"

Nikki spun, seeing Lincoln running down the path. His hair had fallen out of order, both his vest and jacket missing. He wiped the sweat from his forehead as he collapsed against the railing beside her, out of breath. "That was quite the workout."

She laughed. "Maybe Taryn should change the training regimen."

"I don't think I'd be able to survive that," Lincoln laughed with her. He finally caught his breath, stretching. "How're you feeling, Nik?"

"Alright," she said. The word felt good to say.

Everything did feel alright. For a moment, the strange feeling subsided.

"How about you?"

"A little tired, not going to lie," Lincoln said with a smile. "But good, pretty good."

The two stood in silence, watching the dancing lights from a distance.

"You want to dance?" Lincoln said suddenly.

Nikki blinked. "Here?"

Lincoln shrugged, offering a hand. "Why not?"

She smiled, taking it. "I don't know what I'm doing," she warned.

Lincoln smiled back, placing a cautious hand on her hip. "It's okay. Neither do I."

She placed her hands on his shoulders as he instructed her with the steps. It was a simple square, and it fit the rhythm of the distant music.

With Lincoln's arms around her, she felt safe. Nothing could hurt her. Kathryn could do her worst, but as long as she could still have these quiet moments, Nikki would be happy.

The music came to a close. Lincoln let go of her, giving a small dramatic bow.

"Thank you for that," she said.

"Anytime."

There was a moment of silence, and Nikki savored it.

She wanted it to go on forever.

She never wanted to hear her last name shouted through the night air.

"Miss Aguirre!"

Nikki jerked around, bracing herself as two unfamiliar Defenders approached.

Lincoln threw himself in front of her. "What do you want with her?"

The burning feeling quickly returned.

"The Sergeant requested the Aguirre alone," the Officer said, his face hardening as he met Nikki's eyes. "The Commander only gives her an hour."

55

ONLY TWENTY MINUTES ago, the world had been perfect.

And now Nikki was racing down the streets of Liberty, not caring who got shoved out of her way. She'd only had enough time to change back into more suitable clothes for running through the streets, ruining her curls to tie it up, before tearing out of the Bentsworth Manor and down the streets.

What did they mean, the Sergeant only had an hour?

An hour to talk?

An hour before she went back to North Cordell?

Nikki refused to consider the other option. She wouldn't. She couldn't. She was just supposed to be finishing up the deal with Dean!

Not when tonight was supposed to be the night everything was okay. She could hear the confused whispering around her. She leaped over a slow-moving bot, dashing across the street, an auto screeching to a stop.

Her mother was lying on the ground, blood gushing from the bullet wound, the culprit slain only a few feet down the hall. Her eyes looked so tired as she touched Nik's face.

No!

She shook her head, nearly tripping on her own feet as she raced up the sidewalk. She saw the Defender building in the distance, at the end of the street.

She couldn't be late. She didn't know what she'd do with herself if she was late.

She ran faster. She burst through the doors, two guards immediately jumping up to grab her. She fought against them.

"I need to see her!" Nikki shouted. "Is she okay? Where is Taryn?"

The secretary leaped to his feet. "Who are you?"

"My name is Nikki Aguirre," Nikki said, out of breath, kicking one of the Officers hard in the knee. "And I need to see Sergeant Jessica Taryn Hunter."

The feeling burned through her veins, spreading through her entire body.

The secretary rose to his feet, his face going pale. "So you're real—"

"There's no time for questions!" Nikki begged. "Where is she?"

"I'm not sure now is a good time. You're a bit late, and I don't think the Commander was aware you were so young—"

Nikki broke free from the guards, rushing to the desk and slamming her hands down on it. Her blood boiled, her face hardening. "WHERE IS SHE?"

The secretary stumbled back. "I-if you insist," he said, stumbling his way out from behind the desk. He ushered the guards to follow him, though they kept a healthy distance from Nikki.

The secretary tapped a button on his watch, leading her through a hallway. "I'm not sure you really want to be here, Aguirre."

"I need to see her. What's going on?" Nikki rushed to meet their pace. Miriam had said Taryn was just finalizing the negotiations with Commander Cadissa Dean.

Why was the secretary so tense?

"Don't get your hopes up. It might be better if you miss this."

"I don't want to miss this," Nikki said. "I need to see her."

The secretary eyed her suspiciously, before letting out a deep breath. "As you insist."

They led Nikki down the twisting halls. The clock ticked in the back of Nikki's mind. They were running out of time. What was this hour? What happened when it was up?

She had to see Taryn.

They went down a flight of stairs, the lights becoming dimmer as they descended. Nikki's stomach began to churn. They approached a door. The secretary pressed an ID against it, the door glowing.

"Reason for entering?" a robotic voice echoed.

The secretary glanced over his shoulder to Nikki before turning back to the door. "Sergeant Hunter requested an Aguirre."

There was a moment of silence.

Every second that passed, the more Nikki wanted to go tear down the door herself.

Finally, the door clicked, and the secretary opened it. There was a shiny white hallway and a giant glass window looking into a padded room with a chair in the middle, straps on the arms and legs.

Two people stood inside, completely covered in white uniforms, full face masks and all. One was wiping down the chair, and the other checking a syringe.

The secretary let out a sigh of relief, turning to usher Nikki out. "Well, it looks like you missed it. We better be going now—"

"Nikki?"

Taryn's tired voice. "Taryn?" Nikki cried out, pushing past the secretary and stopping dead in her tracks as she met Taryn's eyes.

Her blood went cold.

Taryn's arms were held harshly behind her back, her posture bent and pained. She wasn't wearing her uniform, only an undershirt and leggings, her feet bare. She was stained in blood, cuts littering her arms, and a gash in her lip.

Her eyes looked at Nikki's. They were blue. Just like they'd been when Reyna had told Nikki the stories of the unstoppable Jess.

Those blue eyes were full of tears.

"Taryn!" Nikki cried out again, running to her.

The guards quickly dropped Taryn to the floor, rushing to stop her. They grabbed her arms, but Nikki fought furiously. Taryn had trained her better than this. "Run, Taryn! Run!"

But Taryn just sat, her hands pressed against the floor, trying to breathe.

Nikki sent a fist to one of the guard's faces, squeezing through. She dropped to her knees, helping Taryn sit up.

The guards started toward them again, but another voice stepped in. "Stop. Leave them be."

Nikki recognized the voice from public broadcasts. The voice of Commander Cadissa Dean. Her pristine white hair looked more unnatural in person, her face perfectly sharp and condescending.

This was the woman who'd ordered Nikki to be killed in the womb seventeen years ago.

But she was giving Nikki a moment with Taryn, and she was forever grateful.

"T-Taryn, what's going on?" Nikki said, tears beginning to burn at her eyes. "Miriam just said you were negotiating."

Taryn smiled weakly at Nikki. "This was the negotiation."

"What was the negotiation?" Nikki said, tears beginning to fall. "What was it?"

"Instead of arresting you, Hunter volunteered herself in your place," Dean said, her voice cold.

Her place.

"What do you mean?"

"There are many crimes to answer for," Dean said, her face unfeeling and unmoving, but Nikki could see the smallest hint of a smile on her lips.

It slowly dawned on her.

"I'm the full-blooded Ewyon! If anyone deserves to die, it's me!" Nikki couldn't breathe before a sob wretched her. "Taryn, no! Please don't go! Please!"

Taryn's strong arms wrapped around her. Nikki sobbed into her shoulder, the smell of Taryn's blood making her sick. She didn't want to let go.

This wasn't fair.

Taryn didn't deserve this. Dean *wanted* this.

"You can't go," Nikki choked. "You promised you'd stay."

"N-Nikki." Taryn's voice was fragile. "Please understand."

Nikki didn't want to understand. Everything hurt. She couldn't let go. She wouldn't let go of Taryn. She would die with her if that's what if took.

"Take me instead of her," Nikki begged, looking up to Dean, still holding onto Taryn with her life, tears streaming down her face. "She doesn't deserve this."

Dean wasn't even looking at her, her face unchanging.

"Nikki. Nikki, listen to me," Taryn commanded.

Nikki looked back to Taryn. Taryn was crying too now. She cupped Nikki's face with her hands with a weak smile. "Let me do this," she said weakly. "Let me protect you."

Nikki felt so weak. So helpless as she just cried, pressing her hand against Taryn's. "I don't want you to go," she begged. "Taryn, we need you. We need Jessica."

Taryn bit her lip, struggling to breathe. "Nikki, I don't want to leave you," she choked. "I love you all so much."

"I-I love you too."

"I want you to promise me you're going to stay strong for me, okay?" Taryn said, forcing a pained smile as tears streamed down her face. "Keep being the Nikki that sees the best in the world?"

Nikki could only weakly nod, sinking into Taryn's chest as the Sergeant hugged her.

As Jessica hugged her.

The door opened. "Time's up. We don't have all night," a gruff voice barked.

Nikki wanted to scream, but Taryn shook her head, tucking away her bangs with a shaky hand, pressing something hard into Nikki's hand.

Neither could manage a word as Taryn was forced to her feet and dragged through the door and into the room, the door locked behind them.

Nikki couldn't stop. She leaped to her feet. A guard grabbed her. Nikki felt too tired to break away, screaming and fighting anyway against the hold. She screamed Jessica's name over and over.

Jessica kept her eyes closed the entire time as they set her down in the chair.

It felt like cruel mockery as they locked her in.

They knew she wouldn't try and escape.

Jessica was doing this for them.

"No!" Nikki screamed as the assistant took up the syringe. Nikki couldn't look. She couldn't say she'd watched another mother die in front of her.

She couldn't.

The next moments felt like the longest of her life as she was trapped in the arms of a gruff Defender, sobbing and trying to breathe.

Trying to not let the voices echo when Dean announced, "The final Curatrix Member is gone."

The final Curatrix Member was murdered.

Nikki made the mistake of opening her eyes.

She couldn't believe Jessica was dead.

Nikki was dropped to the ground, and she held back the wave of nausea that ripped through her.

She can't be dead. She can't be dead.

"It's time to go, Aguirre," the secretary said, clearing his throat.

"Don't call me that." Nikki looked up at him, breathless.

The secretary stumbled back, crying out for security. Nikki found the strength to push herself up. She couldn't feel anything.

The world was slow around her. Echoes and screams and bright lights....

She found the word to describe the burning now that reigned in her mind. That burned every bone in her body. A feeling that she had never felt so weak to. So helpless, and so powerful.

Rage.

The Unanswered Questions

Book Five

Coming Soon

GLOSSARY

(A GUIDE TO ALL THE CONFUSING STUFF BY TABITHA A. DELOROUS HERSELF)

THE JOINED WORLD

95 REGIONS OF EARTH, ALL JOINED UNDER ONE GOVERNMENT AFTER THE EARTHSHAKER

THE EARTHSHAKER – APOCALYPTIC WAR 340 YEARS AGO, WHICH SENT HUMANITY INTO REBUILDING EARTH

THE DEFENDING DEPARTMENT – THE "DEPARTMENT" OF LAW ENFORCEMENT TO KEEP EACH REGION IN ORDER

    COMMANDER – IN CHARGE OF ENTIRE DEPARTMENT

      NOTE: EXECUTIVE CADISSA DEAN IS ACTING COMMANDER AFTER THE DEATH OF JAMES R. KORDIN

    EXECUTIVE – ASSISTANT TO THE COMMANDER

    GENERALS – IN CHARGE OF MULTIPLE REGIONS

    AGENTS – SPECIAL TASK FORCE UNDER GENERALS

    SERGEANTS – IN CHARGE OF A REGION

    OFFICERS – UNDER SERGEANT'S COMMANDS

    THE CURATRIX TEAM – WELL KNOWN TEAM OF DEFENDERS, MURDERED OVER A DECADE AGO. MADE IMPORTANT CONTRIBUTIONS TO THE DEPARTMENT

      MEMBERS: AGENT REYNA WENTS AGUIRRE, AGENT LYELL AGUIRRE, SERGEANT JESSICA HUNTER, OFFICER AARON OUTOWN

COMMON TECH

SCROLL – UNRAVELING DEVICE THAT CONNECTS TO NET AND CAN PROJECT HOLOGRAM

TELE – GLASS DEVICE THAT FUNCTIONS AS A SMALL SCROLL AND COMM

COMM – GOVERNMENT ISSUED COMMUNICATION DEVICE

BUDS – EAR BUDS THAT READ TEXT TO ITS USER

IMPORTANT PLACES

DEFENDING DEPARTMENT HEADQUARTERS – LOCATED IN THE GLASS TOWER IN IMPERIAL, HEAD OF OPERATIONS

THE MARKET – HIDDEN SYSTEM IN THE REGIONS, AND HOME TO IT'S OWN SOCIETY, AND CULTURE. VERY OPPOSED TO DEFENDERS.

THE LABYRINTH – OQUELITE UNDERGROUND LIARS. LOCATED IN MULTIPLE REGIONS.

THE (EVER GROWING) WOODS – THE WOODS COMING FROM THE VOID AND BRINGING THINGS BACK FROM THE PAST. RAPIDLY GROWING THROUGHOUT THE WORLD.

THE INN 2.0 – THE ALL IMPORTANT HOME BASE OF OPERATIONS. (INN 1.0 BURNED DOWN...)

THE IMPURE

OVERALL NAME FOR THE SUPERNATURAL BEINGS AND HAPPENINGS OF EARTH

ILLIAH/ESSENCE — THE "SECOND BLOODSTREAM" CONTAINING THE SUPERNATURAL ASPECTS OF HUMANITY

THE IMPURE RACES— THE SEVEN "TYPES" OF ESSENCE, WHICH ADAPTED TO A CERTAIN WORLDLY ELEMENT

- **EWYON** — ILLUSION, APPEARANCE
- **AVIDUOUS**— EARTH, STRENGTH, CREATURES
- **OQUELITE** — ESSENCE ITSELF?? (UNKNOWN)
- **YWONDIE** — FIRE
- **AGUARIOUS** — OCEANS, WATER
- **SUBLINIGHT** — EMOTION, FEELING
- **WINGOR** — SKY, WEATHER

HUMANIC — TECHNICALLY "PURE" AS THEY HOLD NO SUPERNATURAL ASPECTS IN THEIR ESSENCE, EVEN IF FULL-BLOOD

MYTHICS— SUPERNATURAL CREATURES, CREATED BY IMPURE

SHIFTERS — MYTHIC CREATURES THAT CAN SHIFT BETWEEN A HUMAN FORM AND ANIMAL

- **LYNTOX**— SHIFTS TO MAMMALS
- **REPITOX** — SHIFTS TO REPTILES

THE COUNCIL
LEGENDARY GROUP OF 12 MEMBERS CHOSEN BY 'FATE'.

MEMBERS
(EACH MEMBERS REPRESENTS AN IMPORTANT ASPECT OF THE WORLD)

EWYON (POWER OF ILLUSION) ✓ nikki
??? SUBLINIGHT (POWER OF EMOTION)
AVIDUOUS (EARTH, NATURE) ✓ lincoln
??? OQUELITE (THE SUPERNATURAL?)
YWONDIE (FIRE.) ✓ lawrence
AGUARIOUS (WATER, THE OCEANS) ✓ nathaniel
WINGOR (SKY, WEATHER) ✓ matteo
HUMANIC (...HUMANS) ✓ tabitha

ILLUMINATE HOLDER — HOLDER OF THE ILLUMINATE BLADE; REPRESENTATION OF LIGHT ✓ cole

SHADOW HOLDER — HOLDER OF THE SHADOW BLADE; REPRESENTATION OF DARK ✓ ray

KEYPER — "KEY" TO THE COUNCIL. UNITES THE MEMBER'S POWER ✓ mercy

GUARDIAN — REPRESENTATIVE OF THE MYTHIC ✓ felicity

✓ = FOUND

ACKNOWLEDGEMENTS

walks onto stage
dodges tomatoes being thrown at my head
runs away as Nikki chases me off the stage

Sorry, not sorry about that ending.

It feels like a giant weight has been lifted from my shoulders. This story is finally out in the world, and if you're reading this, it means we both have completed FOUR installments of this series together.

Book Four is so near and dear to my heart. The Council has become some of my closest friends. They've helped me through high school and now into this treacherous journey known as college.

First and foremost, I must thank Jesus Christ, the person who puts up with my antics every day, all day, every day, and the reason I'm here today, standing on my two feet. Thank you, Lord, for keeping me upright.

Thank you to my parents, who have allowed me to chase after crazy dreams and take crazy risks. Thank you for being the stable sanity I need when my stories have me going 100 miles a minute.

Sorry, Mom, there are no birds OR fire on this cover either. One day.

Thank you to my siblings (Dominic, Grace, Audrey, and Isaac), who always argue about who gets to be in the acknowledgments. So ha! I mentioned you all! So you can't argue!

Thank you to Millie Florence, my best friend and all-time partner in crime. Thank you for being the one person I can call for hours upon hours without realizing how much time has passed. Thank you for your brutal honesty and your good hugs. You have truly changed the way I've looked at life. Little LDF would be floored to know we're friends.

Actually, thank you to Millie's whole family, who let me crash their couch and eat their food. And to Millie's dad, who drove 2.5 hours to pick me up from the airport once.

Thank you to my roommate, Mary. You had no idea what storm you had coming when you accepted being roommates with an extroverted, hyperactive author, and yet, you've become one of my biggest supporters and closest friends. There's no one I'd rather be wake up to reciting murder mystery facts.

Thank you to Ariana Tosado for introducing me to *Legally Blonde*, attacking me (with pillows) in my own home, and making me realize how lucky I am not to have a biological older sister.

Thank you to Lorelei R. Jensen for being the best coffee date a writer could ask for. We're never productive when we work together, but you're the highlight of my visits home, and I love ranting about Keefe Sencen with you.

Of course, to the author's mom, Brigitte Cromey, who gives great hugs and great advice. You're my favorite motherly goblin, and thank you for the fruit snacks you sent to me in college.

Thank you to my numerous author friends I wish I could give all essays to: Susan L. Markloff, Naomi Kenyon, McKenna Rowell, Paris Kaufman, Larissa Gault, Hannah Lindsey, MT Zimny, Rachel Scheller, Julie Mozart, EK Seaver, Tuesday Simon (she gets a special shoutout for saving me when I got stranded in Denver), Sara Francis, Mel TorreFranca, and probably many more!

Thank you to all my college friends!! I wish I could name you all and all you've done for me, but I might run out of room. Thank you for keeping me company and keeping me alive.

Thank you to Professor Megan Eccles for keeping my fire for writing alive even when it was starting to flicker out during one of my lowest points.

Thank you to my betas, whose comments and suggestions truly made this book come to life: Samantha Crago, MT Zimny, Rachel Scheller, Tatyanah Hall, MC Pending, Leigh Crescent, and Lydia.

Thank you to the Kickstarter backers for helping out this broke college student and being the sole reason this book ever got to readers' hands: Hannah Gaudette, Tuesday Simon, Hannah Lindsey, K.H Salustro, Sophia Chamblee, Paris Kaufman, Alicia Hill, Maggie, Eve Griego, Melissa Ball, Liz Sum, Anne Marie Wells, Millie Florence, Debra Rogers, Ariana Tosado, Kayla T, Sarah Baran, Sera Amoroso, Elsa Singer, Sara Francis, Rachel Scheller, Cecilia Blackwell, Jennifer Syer, Laurel Burgess, Luca Hoang, Audrey, Zosia Kudla, and Alexandra Corrsin.

Thank you to those who made this book possible with the contribution of their talents: Jade Lew (for not only being a show-stopping artist but becoming a dear friend in the process), Michaela Bush, and Rachel Scheller (for editing this book to perfection!), Benita J. Thompson (for making people "wow!" every time they flip open the book and see the EPIC formatting), and Susan L. Markloff (for designing the cover! Thank you for saving the day and making it look as amazing as the rest!)

And thank you to my co-workers at Chick-fil-A during my gap year for showing me how much I love pickles.

And to that Door Dasher, Brandon, who always talked to me on shift. You were cool. Hope you're doing well, buddy.

Photo credit: Jozef Raiche

Lauren D. Fulter is an young American fiction author, after publishing her first book at the age of sixteen. After learning the word 'author' at age five, she's been captivated by the art of storytelling, and the little people roaming her mind. Though she longs for the cold, she lives in the desert with her large family, spending her days drawing, dabbling in fictional dimensions, and attempting to make something edible.